THE ROSEMARY TREE

ELIZABETH GOUDGE

THE
ROSEMARY
TREE

COWARD-McCANN, INC.

NEW YORK

FOR

MARJORIE

The Old Knight

His golden locks time hath to silver turned;
O time too swift, O swiftness never ceasing!
His youth 'gainst time and age hath ever spurned,
But spurned in vain; youth waneth by increasing:
Beauty, strength, youth, are flowers but fading seen;
Duty, faith, love, are roots, and ever green.
His helmet now shall make a hive for bees;
And, lovers' sonnets turned to holy psalms,
A man-at-arms must now serve on his knees,
And feed on prayers, which are age's alms:
But though from court to cottage he depart,
His saint is sure of his unspotted heart.
And when he saddest sits in homely cell,
He'll teach his swains this carol for a song:
"Blest be the hearts that wish my sovereign well,
Curst be the souls that think her any wrong."
Goddess, allow this aged man his right,
To be your beadsman now, that was your knight.

GEORGE PEELE

THE ROSEMARY TREE

1

HARRIET at her window watched the gulls with delight. It meant bad weather at sea when they came up-river, and she had known when she woke this morning in the waiting stillness, and had seen the misted sky, that the only spell of fine weather was going to break in a gale; and she did not enjoy the March winds in this draughty, bone-searching house whose cold and damp had already crippled her. But she enjoyed the gulls, and would enjoy them more when she had found the right pair of spectacles. She had been reading her Bible when she first heard that strange, exciting cry, and her reading spectacles were no good for distance. She wasted a few precious moments finding her distant ones on the table beside her, knocking over the teacup on her breakfast tray as she did so, for her hands were knotted with arthritis, slow and fumbling. Daphne might have sharp words to say later about the dregs in the teacup staining the traycloth, and for a moment she flinched from the thought of them, but when she got the gulls into focus she forgot Daphne. She had never been able to remember other things when the gulls came inland.

Over the river they were weaving their patterns against the background of fields that lifted to the beech woods on the sky-line, and the grey sky above. There were only pale colors in the world today. Yesterday, in the sunshine, the fields that had already fallen under the harrow for spring ploughing had shone like ridged crimson satin and the pastures had been emerald green. The hawthorns and nut trees in the spinneys, and the beech woods beyond, had been beautiful with the colors of the swelling buds. But today the colors were hidden and imprisoned, even as the sun was imprisoned. "For when there's a grey wall between one and another who's to say which is prisoner and which is free?" thought Harriet. "When the heart aches one for the other there's little to choose between them."

Her thoughts had been obsessed by prisons and prisoners these last few days. Since she had had to lead this shut-in invalid life she had found illness involved suffering almost as much from the tyranny of painful thoughts as from physical pain. Outside this lovely valley where she lived the world was a dreadful place and first one misery would possess her mind and then another. Crimes against children would take hold of her one day, and on another she would be grieving for the blind or mad. She lacked the physical strength to thrust tormenting thought from her even if she had wanted to, but she did not want to. The fortunate, she thought, and she counted herself fortunate, should not insulate themselves in their good fortune. If they could do nothing else they could pray, and she prayed as she was able, grieving over the childishness of her prayer but trying to make it real to herself by letting the travail of her mind bring forth one concrete fact at a time to pray about; one child in danger, some particular man in darkness, some particular prisoner facing the world again with fear and shame; God knew who they were even if she did not. That prisoner had been with her for three days and nights now, and the greyness of this day had made him more real to her than ever. Yet she liked these grey days. They had their own beauty. When the sun was out the world was a young knight riding out with armor flashing and pennon flying, but on a day like this it was an old beadsman turned to his prayers, wrapped in a dun cloak of stillness and silence.

And the grey days made the perfect setting for the brilliance and freedom of the gulls. Her eyes followed their flight, the long sweeping curves, the slow beat of the great wings, and then

14

a more gentle rise and fall as though the still air had unseen waves whose rhythm rocked them. There was a great spaciousness about their movements. Both the sea and the sky were theirs. They were content now in this valley between the hills because their wings could carry them where they would whenever they wished. Birds were more satisfactory symbols of the heavenly spirits, Harriet thought, than any of those sentimental angels that one saw in the children's picture books. There was nothing so swift and free as a bird. Yet crippled though she was she felt nothing but joy in watching them. She had always known how to wait.

The clock on her mantelpiece chimed the half-hour and her joy was lost in sudden anxiety. Half-past eight and no sign of John bringing the car round. The children would be late for school again and would be scolded, and Margary would miss the beginning of the arithmetic class and be more wretchedly bogged down than ever in the miseries of subtraction. Pat and Winkle would be all right because Pat's scornfulness and Winkle's placidity usually insulated them against scoldings, but their all-rightness was apt by contrast to make Margary the more aware of her chronic state of misfortune and that was bad for her. Harriet listened anxiously, then relaxed as the familiar sounds of backfiring came from the battered garage by the lilac bush. The poor old car bounced out and forward, two wheels on the flower bed, and bumped into the scraper by the front door.

John drove as badly as a man can and once he had got the car as far as the house Daphne allowed him no further part in getting the children to school. Unless prevented by unavoidable crisis she drove them there herself and fetched them again in the afternoon. The nearest school that she considered worthy of her children was at Silverbridge, a small country town three miles down the river, and that meant twelve miles driving daily and a greater expenditure of time and strength and gasoline than she could afford. Harriet sighed over Daphne's pride, that would not even consider the village school, her unpunctuality and extravagance, and then smiled delightedly as Daphne herself came out of the front door below her window in her shabby, beautifully cut tweeds, ran down the steps, and got into the car. At this distance she looked the lovely girl she had been, not the worn, impatient woman she had become; more lithe and gay than her small daughters, hurrying after her with their unbecoming grey felt uniform hats askew, dropping schoolbooks on the steps as they ran and then stooping to pick them up so that their stiff grey skirts, now too short, stuck out vertically and showed their underclothes. Yet the posterior view of all three was engaging in this position, Winkle's being particularly so. "But those skirts must be let down," thought Harriet, regarding Winkle's pink knickers, and the fat legs that bulged from beneath them. "It's hardly respectable; not with Daphne never seeming to get them into knickers that match their skirts."

To her horror, and self-scorn, Harriet found that she had tears in her eyes. Until a couple of years ago, when the arthritis had to a certain extent crippled her hands, she had done all the vicarage sewing. Four years ago she had been able to stand long enough to do the washing and ironing as well. Seven years ago she had done nearly all the work of the house, and been able to hide the difficulty with which she did it with complete success. Ten years ago, when Daphne had married her cousin John Wentworth and she had come to be their housekeeper at the vicarage, she had felt only a few aches and twinges to which she paid no attention and had believed herself capable of another fifteen years' hard work. She had been sixty-five then and had felt fifty. Now she was seventy-five and felt ninety. Though the years of steadily increasing pain had seemed long as she endured them, in retrospect they seemed to have passed quickly. She had become imprisoned in this uselessness almost overnight, it seemed, and now she must bear it as best she could. She told herself she could have put up with it better if John and Daphne had done as she had begged them and sent her to some institution, but they wouldn't do that. She had been nanny to John

16

and his stepbrothers in the old manor house up on the hill a mile away, and his bleak childhood had been redeemed from disaster by her love. He said he could not face life without her. They all said they could not do without her. In the paradoxical nature of things if she could have believed them she would have been a much happier woman, but not the woman whom they could not do without.

2

The car moved down the steep, moss-grown drive and disappeared from sight in the lane that wound through the village and then along by the river to Silverbridge. John stood waving to the children until he could no longer see them, and then with his hands in his pockets and his pipe drooping from the side of his mouth he gazed dejectedly at the view, his long thin figure sagging a little. He hated to see them going off to that apparently most desirable school where he had a feeling that Pat and Margary were not happy, though they had not told him so, and Winkle perhaps would not be when she was older. It was a small and most select school, for young children only, and rather celebrated in the neighborhood because it had been run by the same charming old lady for many years, but he was not at all sure it was a good school. Daphne said it was and with no evidence to the contrary it was only his instinct that contradicted her. The children would have been happy at the village school taught by good old Miss Baker, or at the Silverbridge convent school that was equally disliked by Daphne because such a mixture of children went there, but where they were stank in his nostrils. Yes, stank. He repeated the ugly word forcibly in his mind, and then, with that uncertainty and self-distrust that followed immediately upon all his decisions, he retracted it. After all, what did he know about it? He'd only been to the place two or three times. Daphne, who went every day, said it was all right. She should know. Obviously, mothers were more knowledgeable about little girls than fathers could hope to be. Especially when the father was a man such as himself; a negligible failure.

He took his pipe from his mouth and stared at the empty bowl. Sundays excepted he had given up smoking for economy's sake, for Pat was to go to boarding school in the autumn and he suspected that she had first-class brains. He wanted to save every penny he could to give her her chance later on. But in moments of perplexity he sometimes found solace in sucking his empty pipe. That is, when he knew he was alone. He was alone now, and in that fact too there was solace.

He straightened himself and became aware of the gulls, and instantly delight leaped up in him, a flame of pure joy that burned against the habitual sadness of his thoughts much as the brilliant white of the gulls' wings shone against the sunless landscape. Seen from this distance the flight of the gulls was perfection of beauty, and his joy that leaped to meet it was equally perfect. Meeting, the two were one and his joy was taken from him, the pain of its loss as sharp as the joy had been. It had been that way with him all his life, at sight or sound of beauty. The joy, and then the total loss. The beauty that robbed him was, he supposed, always stronger than he, for he was a weak man. Strong men perhaps could retain the gift and give the beauty to the world again in verse or music; and from that too some other fellow would with his joy snatch beauty. What a divine traffic! Yet he did not regret his total loss. It was his own particular mode of giving.

Aware of a sense of companionship so delicate that it was no intrusion upon his loneliness he looked round and up and saw Harriet's smiling face at the window. He had not said good morning to her yet. He laughed, leapt up the steps to the front door and went quickly, with a shambling but boyish stride, through the cold echoing hall, up the dark staircase and across the large, draughty landing to her room. In his eagerness he hardly stopped to wonder, as he normally did whenever he entered his home, why the builders of Victorian vicarages had so concentrated upon darkness, draughts and unwanted space. Harriet's face had been like the whiteness of the gulls against the somber fields; the darkness and cold had become a mere background. He tapped lightly on her door and went in.

"How are you, Harriet?" he asked a little anxiously. "How's the beastly pain? Did you sleep well?"

"What a man you are for asking unnecessary questions," said Harriet with annoyance. "Can't you see I'm as flourishing as a spoilt old woman can be? Sit down and eat a bit of toast and marmalade. It's likely you read your letters at breakfast and forgot your food."

He laughed, sat down opposite her and helped himself to a piece of toast to please her. She smiled at him, sorry for her irritation. The one thing that tried her patience was family fuss about her state of health. Commiseration, monotonous daily enquiries, anxiety, drove her quite distracted. Of course she had pain, and of course it kept her awake, but what of it? Did they expect old age to be a bed of roses? John was the most trying because he loved her most; during her bad times he went about looking more miserable than she herself ever felt even at her worst. Daphne's concern tried Harriet less because it was partly for herself; the worse Harriet was the more she had to do for her. But they both made her feel herself a burden when they fussed and worried... She pulled herself up... How wicked to think of burdens on this still and peaceful morning, with the gulls here. They were no burden to the air that supported them, nor the air to the fields to which it brought the sunshine and the rain. There should be no thought of burdens in the mysterious interweaving of one life with another. It must be that the weakness in oneself which one thought pressed most heavily upon others to their harm was in reality a blessing to them, while on the occasions when one thought oneself doing great good, one was as likely as not doing great harm; if self-congratulation were present, sure to be doing harm.

19

She smiled at John, who so far as she knew had never congratulated himself upon anything whatever, and wondered to what extent his lifelong sense of failure was his greatest asset. She could not know. No one could know, least of all John. All she could know was the love it had called out in her from the day she had arrived at Belmaray Manor, and found the little boy of three years old sobbing in a dark corner of the nursery in a welter of spilt water, broken glass and wilting yellow petals. He had been struggling after a floral decoration of dandelions in his toothglass to welcome the new nanny, but had dropped it. Looking at him now she marvelled how little he had changed in forty-one years. He was stooped and careworn, his sandy hair greying and receding at the temples, his mouth always a little open from chronic catarrh, his face overweighted by his beak of a nose, but his eager impulsive movements, ending generally in disaster and combining so oddly with the Wentworth charm and distinction, his smile and anxious clear blue eyes, were exactly the same as when she had first known him.

He too was thinking how little she had changed. Her dark eyes had never lost their brightness or her small determined face its clear contours. She had always been a sallow, plain little woman, her charm lying in her birdlike quickness, her vitality and humor; and the wrinkling of her skin and the whitening of her hair had changed her very little.

"The gulls are here, Harriet," he said. "That means a storm before night."

"I knew there was a change coming when I woke this morning," said Harriet. "And not only in the weather."

"Change for us all?" asked John. "How do you know these things, Harriet?"

"I couldn't rightly say," said Harriet. "But don't you feel it yourself? The pause. The shuttle goes backwards and forwards, much the same year after year, and then the pause, like a new color being threaded in for a new pattern."

"Dull old sticks like myself don't feel these things," said

John. "Though I've often thought the gulls have news to tell of a pattern somewhere, when they weave in and out like that."

They smiled at each other, remembering the nursery days when they had watched the gulls together from the manor house garden. Then they had looked down on them from a height, and seen the river winding like a ribbon through the valley, and the village so far below it looked a toy village. Sometimes a solitary gull had swept away from the others and folded its great wings on the top of the church tower, and that had always thrilled John. In those days he had insisted on calling the gulls doves, and held to his own way even when the older boys laughed at him. They had always laughed at him, and knocked him about a good deal, for he had been a weakling and they strong, but in spite of that he had always been tenacious of his own ideas. Harriet had read psalms to the children and "O that I had wings like a dove!" had been one of his favorites. Even in those days the church tower, as well as the gull upon it, had been important to him. He had spent a good deal of time in the small paved court where the sundial was, looking down upon it, and watching the birds flying in and out of the nests they had made for themselves in its nooks and crannies. "The sparrow hath found her an house, and the swallow a nest," had been another of his favorites, for his Franciscan love of birds had been born early in him. He had not known then that the weather-beaten, sturdy old tower was one of the oldest in England but even to look at it had always given him a sense of rest and refuge... As it did today, though from the vicarage garden it could not be seen once the buds had come crowding thickly upon the beeches by the gate.

"What are you going to do today?" asked Harriet with a touch of bracing sharpness. She was always keeping him up to it, and so was Daphne, for his conviction that whatever he did he'd be sure to make a mess of it had a tendency to make him shrink from action. Not that he was lazy. The inertia of physical weakness was a thing he fought daily and at lonely tasks he would work untiringly. He could hurt no one's feelings, drop no bricks, praying for them or digging potatoes for them. It was personal contacts that terrified him and a parson's life seemed full of them. His conviction that he was a very bad priest and should never have been one he kept to himself, for it was too late now and useless remorse should not be inflicted on others; but like the worst kind of wound it bled inwardly.

"Wash up the breakfast things to save Daphne's time," he said. "She's extra busy today with the Mother's Union to tea and the church flowers to do. Cut the flowers she wants and take them to the church for her. Chop the wood. Mend Winkle's tricycle. Talk to you. Go on writing Sunday's sermons."

"They say old Bob Hewitt is poorly," suggested Harriet with twinkling eyes.

"The old curmudgeon," said John.

"That don't prevent him being poorly," said Harriet.

"He hates busybodies pushing in on him," said John.

"He's cantankerous," agreed Harriet. "And there won't be any except that daft cousin of his as'll trouble to climb up to the lodge and maybe get the door shut in his face for his pains. But old Bob likes to see a Wentworth. And he likes a drop of brandy."

John grinned, stretching himself comfortably in his chair. "Where'll I get the brandy?" he asked.

"In the wardrobe, behind my dressing-gown," said Harriet. "You can take a look if you don't believe me. If you don't get up out of that chair you won't get nothing done this day."

John walked to the wardrobe, looked behind her dressing-gown and whistled incredulously.

"I've had it by me for some while," said Harriet placidly. "Two years to be exact. My nephew Harry brought it to me. I like to feel I've something by me should I be took bad. There's that little flask of your father's we used to take on picnics in my top drawer. You can fill that for Bob."

22

"This is the first time you've suggested I should encourage the parishioners in secret drinking," said John. But he did as she told him, subduing the revulsion that the smell of brandy invariably gave him. He always did as Harriet told him. She had a shrewd knowledge of human nature and an almost uncanny instinct for knowing just the thing to say, the thing to do, that would open a door and not close it.

"Bob's no drunkard," said Harriet. "Too near. But he likes comfort if another pays for it, I used to notice in the old days, and when a man's taken against religion he'll maybe change his mind if it brings him a bit of what he fancies."

"Worldly wisdom, Harriet," said John, slipping the flask in his pocket.

"I've no other," said Harriet briefly, but she gave him a delightful smile as he picked up her tray. It was a smile he had known well since his boyhood. Harriet had never praised a child in words, but with that particular smile she both recognized merit and rewarded it. He had the other sort of wisdom, her smile told him now. He did not believe her but her smile was the balm it had always been.

"Anything I can do before I go?" he asked.

"You can turn the radio on," said Harriet. "And when Mrs. Wilmot comes tell her to put that traycloth to soak before she comes up to me. I've spilt tea on it." Their eyes met involuntarily, for both of them dreaded an annoyed Daphne, but loyalty did not allow the glance to be long enough for mutual sympathy.

John carried the tray down the dark stairs and across the hall to the kitchen. It was a dreary stone-flagged place where an aroma of mice fought daily with a smell of cabbage and fish. However much Daphne opened the window she could never quite get rid of the smells, for the damp of the kitchen imprisoned them. The walls were stained with the damp, for the kitchen got no sun, the house had no damp-proofing and there was an old disused well under the kitchen floor. It had been im-

23

proved as much as possible, with a modern cooking stove and electric light, and Daphne had bright copper pots and pans on the mantelpiece and pots of scarlet geraniums on the window sill, yet it remained a dreary cave, a symbol somehow of the whole house that was too large, too dark, too damp ever to make a comfortable home. And he and Daphne were not as happy as they should have been, though they loved each other and their children. It couldn't be altogether the fault of the house and he refused to admit any fault in Daphne. It must be his fault. He had made a failure of marriage, as of everything else. A feeling of hopelessness welled up in him and he put the tray down at an angle, so that the sugar basin rolled off it and was smashed on the floor.

The crash restored him and for very shame he battened down the depression that had caused it. If he could not measure up to the big demands life made upon him, if he were a poor priest, an unsatisfactory husband and father, he might at least endeavor to be competent as a hewer of wood and drawer of water. He took off his coat, rolled up his shirtsleeves, lifted up to Almighty God the magnitude of his failure and the triviality of his task, and applied himself to the latter. The hot water warmed his cold hands and the pile of cleansed china grew satisfactorily on the draining board. There was a pleasure in getting things clean. Small beauties slid one by one into his consciousness, quietly and unobtrusively like growing light. The sinuous curves of Orlando the marmalade cat, washing himself on the window sill, the comfortable sound of ash settling in the stove, a thrush singing somewhere, the scent of Daphne's geraniums, the gold of the crocuses that were growing round the trunk of the apple tree outside the kitchen window... What in the name of wonder had happened to the apple tree? He knew its fantastic beauty of old, and he thought by heart, but he had never seen it quite like this. He went on with the washing up deftly and surely, for the rhythm of the work had taken charge, but quite unconsciously, and joy leaped up in him again, joy even greater than when he had seen the gulls.

The apple tree was a personality, older than the house, tall and twisted and encrusted with lichen, its widely spread roots clutching the earth with the splayed feet of a giant, its trunk knobbly with knot holes, its branches flung crazily skyward like the arms of a madman praying. In spite of its fantastic skeleton it was always beautiful. In April the new green leaves were sharp and delicate, prickly-pointed with silver, a mist of pale color that became slowly studded with crimson points of fire, and then suddenly submerged by a foam of pink blossom. Then as the petals paled and drifted away in flakes of moony white the leaves reappeared, darker now, expanding into exquisite spears of glossy green, unusually thin, a shape peculiar to that apple tree alone. The apples came early, a multitude of them, round and small and deep red, with a skin so shiny that it reflected the light in sparkling points of brilliance all over the tree. Their flesh had a pink flush in the white. They were bitter to eat, but Daphne made them into a clear rosy jelly that lasted the children all the winter through. The birds loved the tree. Nuthatches and creepers, a yaffingale and a greater spotted woodpecker, attacked the trunk for grubs; tits and chaffinches brought color to the bare branches. In the spring they nested in the tree and at all seasons the thrush sang in the top branches. The snow, when it came, lodged in the intricate tracery of the twigs so that the tree seemed weighted with a midwinter burgeoning of blossom. But though the leaves had not come yet John had never seen it quite so amazingly lovely as today. The whole tree was blazing with light, sparkling yet so gentle that it did not blind the eyes. Its clean, clear silveriness washed into the dark smelly old kitchen like a wave of sea water washing into a cave, in and out again, cleansing it. Yet the light had never left the tree and was composed of the myriad minute globes of water with which the mist had spangled every twig. The sun had come out for a moment and been born, a microcosm of itself, in the heart of each globe.

"My God," ejaculated John. It was not a profane exclamation but an acknowledgement of a miracle and a revelation.

3

"Comin' in dirty," said Mrs. Wilmot, referring to the weather. John turned round and met her pitying glance as she unbuttoned her coat. His extraordinarily sweet smile flashed out in welcome. He had, he knew, been gazing at the apple tree with his mouth more than usually open, like a small boy contemplating fireworks, but he was unabashed. He knew that his parishioners considered him to be a little "tootlish," not quite so mentally on the spot as they were themselves, but he was so chronically aware himself of his total inadequacy that the awareness of others did not worry him. Indeed he was glad of it for it prevented them from placing him upon some pedestal removed from the humdrum happenings of their daily lives. He might be a complete failure but at least he was down in the dust with the other failures.

Turning his back on the apple tree he propped himself against the sink for the preliminary gossip before the morning's work without which Mrs. Wilmot did not function. It was to her as oil to a machine and she could not get started without it. Daphne, with a multitude of tasks of her own waiting for attention, was always trying to escape, but John agreed with Mrs. Wilmot that it was ridiculous to make such a fetish of housework as Daphne did. What did a little dust more or less matter? The communing of one soul with another was really more important even if it were only on the subject of mice.

He thought to himself now that it did not much matter, in itself, what one did. It was chiefly as the vehicle of love or the symbol of prayer that action was important. Or did he only think that because in action he was himself generally such a bungler?

26

Perhaps, if he faced the truth, he would find that one of the reasons why he spent so much time in prayer was because the results of prayer were unknown and one could indulge in the sin of wishful thinking. For it most certainly was sin for a man to sit back picturing the pleasing results of his prayer. Unless prayer was bread cast upon the waters in blind faith, without hope or desire for knowledge or reward, then it was nothing more than a selfish and dangerous indulgence of fantasy. It is difficult, he thought, for a human being to face the fact that he is really quite superfluous. He is always trying to find a loophole somewhere.

"... and so it's scarcely the boy's fault, really," said Mrs. Wilmot, buttoning her smock. "Not with the nut working loose. 'E did feel the wheel wobble like, but as I says to 'is father, you can't expect an old 'ead on young shoulders. Of course it's a loss, I know, all that milk, but boys is boys, and as I says to Mr. Linkwort, boys don't put two and two together and act according, as an older person do. You 'ad your milk?"

"Mrs. Wilmot, I do beg your pardon, but I'm afraid I was wool gathering," said John apologetically. "Which was the nut that worked loose?"

Daphne, when she lost the thread, just made what she hoped were appropriate noises, but John, though he did most things badly, always did them to the best of his ability. Deeply ashamed he braced himself more firmly against the sink and tried to rivet his attention upon Mrs. Wilmot's narrative. One of these days someone would be telling him something really important and a soul would be lost because he had missed the first half. Besides, how could he know that this narrative of Mrs. Wilmot's was not important? It might, for all he knew, have a great bearing upon all their lives. Though it is true that for the power of God all things are superfluous it is also true that for the mercy of God nothing is. Every sparrow. Every hair. Every soul. Every nut.

"... and then, of course, 'e 'ad to swerve or 'e'd 'ave run the poor chap down," said Mrs. Wilmot, opening the back door and looking outside. "And that must 'ave jolted the nut, like. No,

27

the milk ain't there. Short they're bound to be this morning. But 'e'll bring a drop by lunch time, never fear. 'E's a good boy. As I ses to 'is father, 'e may be careless-like but 'e's a good boy. But there'll be none for elevenses. Well, we must be thankful there wasn't no serious accident. Only the milk. Dreadful thing, drink. I will say for Ted 'e don't drink. Nor the boy. 'E's a good boy, Bert is. Staggered right across the road, 'e did. Where'd 'e get it, so early in the morning? Serve 'im right if 'e *'ad* been run over. But it sobered 'im up, poor chap. Tried to 'elp get the spare wheel on, 'e did, till 'e come over queer. The boy couldn't stop, and 'im late already. Just by Pizzle bridge, it was. Well, sir, I'll be going up to Harriet. I'll see 'er comfortable and then 'tis me flues."

John put away the clean crockery and carried the broken sugar basin out to the bin, where he hid it from Daphne's sight beneath a couple of empty tins, and then, ashamed of such deception, fished it out again and placed it where it would be sure to catch her eye when she next went to the bin. Then he went into the garden to cut the flowers for the church vases but on his way to the daffodils was deflected by the sight of a dead hedge sparrow lying on the lawn. Shame upon Orlando. Well fed though he was he did occasionally forget himself and kill from wanton cruelty. A stab of pain went through John as he bent and picked up the small body, still warm. . . . Not a sparrow falls to the ground . . . The little bird wore a sober livery and in the company of a bullfinch or a yaffingale one would not have looked at him twice, yet lying there in his palm he seemed to John incomparably beautiful. The back and wing feathers were of different shades of brown, tender, warm colors, the throat and soft breast a silvery slate color. The bill was slender and exquisitely curved and the little legs glowed bright orange. A short while ago the eyes had been as bright as the drops of water on the apple tree but now they were filmed. He would not again utter his thin pretty little song, and the children would not this year find his nest of moss and roots with the eggs of pure bright

28

blue. John had what Daphne considered a ridiculous, inordinate love of the creatures. When he came to himself he was out in the lane, the small corpse still in his hand.

His idea, he believed, had been to carry it right out of the garden, so that Winkle should not find it and grieve; for Winkle felt like her father about the creatures. He glanced round for somewhere to put it, and then his eye was caught by the lovely loops of the river, winding away down the valley. Through a break in the trees that bordered the lane he could see it clearly, and Pizzle bridge, the boundary of his parish upon the west, spanning the water with its beautiful triple arches. Now what had Mrs. Wilmot been saying about Pizzle bridge? Some narrative about a drunken man whose staggerings had caused young Bert to have an accident with the milk van. Probably Bert's fault, for he never looked where he was going. His mother considered him a good boy but John did not. A thoughtless heartless young limb who had once kept a lark in a cage. Almost John's first action upon becoming vicar of Belmaray had been to lose his temper and liberate that lark. Just like Bert to leave the drunk who had tried to help him with the wheel to "come over queer" without assistance.

John stood still in the middle of the lane and fought one of the familiar dreaded battles that came upon him almost daily. The sweat came out on his forehead and his fingers clenched upon the dead bird. He was too ashamed of these paltry battles to speak of them. Since his boyhood he had been plagued by ridiculous obsessions, inhibitions, childish fears and torments of all sorts, but in maturity he had been able to keep them firmly battened down; it was only since the war that they had thrust themselves out again in new forms but with all their old strength. But this particular obsession, the dread of a drunken man, was not much altered since his childhood, when he had been shut in the nursery out of his father's way. Yet it had been altered. Its present edge of intensity had been given to it by some appalling months during the war when he had fought his father's demon in himself. How it had happened that he had come out victorious he had no idea. He had no idea, either, how he came out upon the other side of these ridiculous contemptible struggles. It was rather like a particularly painful sojourn at the dentist. You endured, apparently for an eternity, and then it was over, but not due to any action of your own.

It was over and he was walking down the lane towards the road beside the river. The trees had been thickened by the crowding buds and he did not see the car flash along the road, cross the bottom of the lane and go on to the church where Daphne was expecting to find her daffodils. When he reached the road he did not look back, as he usually did, to catch a glimpse of the church tower rising above the trees. He turned to the right and went resolutely loping on beside the river, still holding the dead bird.

2

MICHAEL leaned his arms on the parapet of the bridge, watching the gulls. The attack of dizziness had passed. He was all right as long as he kept still. He merely felt a bit lightheaded, and the sensation was pleasant rather than otherwise for it was a dreamy lightheadedness that softened the edges of things. Past and future no longer pressed sharply upon him and the dream of the moment was shot through with incredible beauty. It flowed in to him through sight and sound and even touch, filling him with such an airy lightness that he seemed floating even while the rough stone of the grand old bridge held him up so strongly. He felt like a small child swinging on his father's hand, in delicious danger and delicious safety at the same time.

Below him the river was pearl grey, faintly flecked with the light of a clouded day. He was glad there was no sun to sparkle too brightly on the water. He liked it like this. It wound away through the lovely valley very quietly, making no sound except where its eddies chuckled about the piers of the bridge. Upon either side of the valley the fields lifted to the beech woods and their color did not seem so dim to him as it had to Harriet, for he had not seen them yesterday. For him the green was a laughing green and the color of the ploughed fields a song. But the laughter and song were distant. What was near was the voice of the water about the piers of the bridge and the sweep of the gulls' wings all about him. They were not uttering their strange cries now. Those that were over the river were dipping and wheeling and soaring silently, those in the fields were facing all one way into the wind and gliding along as though the ridges of the ploughed land were the waves of an inland sea. Against the deep crimson of the turned earth their wings gleamed white as unsoiled snow, but when he looked up at those that were about him he could see the grey feathers among the white, that same exquisite mother-of-pearl grey of the slipping water, and the greenish tinge of the hooked beaks. And their flight! The freedom that was in those great sweeping curves. The freedom of the water flowing unchecked to the sea. The freedom of the lifting fields and the beech woods, and the great hills that swelled against the sky. The ecstasy of this freedom was such music in his blood that his whole body pulsed with intense joy. It was the beat of this joy in freedom that kept him swinging in light even when the stone of the parapet gripped his right hand that was laid upon it.

The throbbing increased and became an almost monotonous beat like that of a footfall. It thrummed in his head, too, and behind his eyes, and hammered in his chest. He could no longer hear the water, only the ugly hammering in his ears and the monotonous steps coming down the passage to take him away. The light in which he had swung was thinning to darkness. He clutched at the hand that had held his but it was not there. He turned, groping for it, and the ground slid away like ice beneath his feet. He would have fallen had he not found the hand again. Or rather it found him, gripping his arm.

"Hold on!" said a startled voice. "Steady, now. This way, and you can sit down."

He was sitting down, on a wooden bench by the bridge, his back against the hard stone.

"Take a pull at this disgusting liquid," said the voice again. "It won't do you any harm for I doubt if you're drunk."

Michael took a gulp at the flask for politeness' sake and then pushed it gently away. "Certainly not," he said. Then he smiled. "At least I wasn't, but I am now. That's very good brandy." For even the small dose he had had, on a completely empty stomach, had sent the world reeling round him again. But he was aware that he was under scrutiny and was not surprised when the voice said, "When was your last meal?"

"Breakfast," said Michael.

"Liar," said the voice equably. "Stay where you are. I won't be a moment."

Michael stayed where he was. Coming down the road he had noticed a gate and a cart track leading to a farm, and he guessed that the owner of the voice had gone there. He had seen a board by the gate announcing "Bed and Breakfast" and had gazed longingly at the breakfast bit of the notice. But a bed for the night at Silverbridge, and the razor and toothbrush he had bought there, had taken the last of his cash. There was nothing in his pocket now but a half-penny and two farthings. What a crazy fool he had been. The fumes of the brandy slowly cleared from his mind, and sitting down now withdrawn within himself behind the shutters of his closed eyes, the beauty that had so exalted him shut out, the fool that he had been yesterday was very much with him. He had completely lost control of himself yesterday. Damn fool. Cowardly fool. Just because he had seen a gleam of recognition in the eyes of a man he had known he must bolt as senselessly as a terrified rabbit driven out of the last of the standing corn. He'd been momentarily happy yesterday, leaning on the parapet of that other bridge, with the roar of the indifferent city behind his back, the blank grey sky over his head and the river below. The huge blank indifference of the city, the sky and the river had been balm to him. No one had known or cared. He had swung round to enjoy the indifference of the city, and had been leaning comfortably with his back against the parapet, when he had met the eyes of the man he had known and seen that flash of recognition.

It was then that he had lost his nerve. He had gone straight to the station, without even going back to his flat, and caught the west-country express. He could not take up work again in

33

London and meet the contempt of men and women he had known. A brave man would have faced it. He couldn't; at least not yet. So he'd run away. Taken a ticket for that place in the far southwest whose name had stuck in his mind since he'd seen it in some months' old newspaper he'd got hold of years ago in the war . . . Silverbridge . . . Fighting in Africa it had been incredible to read about angling at Silverbridge. It had been much the same as reading about harping in heaven. He'd never forgotten the name and he'd always meant to go there.

And now here he was; but forgetting to pick up his wallet again when he'd put it down to buy his ticket, and arriving at Silverbridge with only the loose change he had in his pocket had landed him in a tiresome, if temporary, mess, and now the virtue had gone out of Silverbridge. When he had arrived there in the sunset light it had seemed a paradise, hungry though he was, but when he had got up in the morning, even hungrier, it was just a little country town like any other. Yet he had had the curiosity to ask where it was they held the angling competitions, and when the river road had been pointed out to him he had followed it aimlessly, until his attack of dizziness had nearly upset the milk van. Then upon the bridge had come that strange, almost anguished experience of incomparable beauty. That had been paradise, for a moment or two. But what now? Where did he go from here? Any grain of common sense that he might have had in the past was now entirely lost. He was the greatest fool who ever lived.

"Bread and cold bacon and coffee. My own breakfast was a bit sketchy. We'll share it, shall we? You don't see a dead bird anywhere about, do you?"

Michael drank some coffee from the mug into which his host had poured it from a brown earthenware jug, devoured a thick bacon sandwich like a famished dog, and then enquired, "What did you say? I don't think I quite understood."

"No matter," said the vague and gentle voice. "I was carrying a dead bird but I seem to have mislaid it."

A bit cracked, thought Michael, and reached for another sandwich. Yet sufficiently intelligent to have produced a thoroughly
good breakfast. And probably not as crackers as he was himself.

"Did you want it?" he asked politely. "Might I have some
more coffee?"

"Help yourself," said John. "There it is, on the bridge. I must
have dropped it when I caught hold of you. Excuse me a
moment."

He mounted the arc of the bridge, stooped and picked something up. He brought it back and showed it sadly to Michael.

"A hedge sparrow," said Michael. "The dun-colored birds are
the most beautiful, don't you think? I'd rather have that little
chap than a goldfinch any day."

John picked a dock leaf, laid the bird gently upon it and then
launched the small boat upon the river. Borne by the current it
floated slowly away towards the sea.

"The Lady of Shalott," said Michael, a little breathless with
suppressed laughter.

"I think it was the cock," said John with extreme gravity.
"Though there's so little difference in the plumage that it's
difficult to tell."

"I know," said Michael weakly. "It was the boat that made
me think of that tuneful lady. 'The broad stream bore her far
away, the Lady of Shalott.'" He suppressed the last of his
laughter. It was unkind to laugh at these amiable lunatics, and
this one, when he had stooped from his great spindly height
to launch the hedge sparrow upon its journey, had looked
exactly like Michael's idea of Don Quixote, "the luminary and
mirror of all knight-errantry," and for that gentle and melancholy knight Michael had always had the greatest affection.
Indeed, he was almost his favorite character in literature... And
he had been created by a man in prison... The thought of the
great Cervantes, "the maimed perfection," and of his sufferings
so triumphantly endured, was one of the things that had helped
to keep him sane many times, he imagined. He was young

enough to believe that men go mad, that men die, more easily than in fact they do. He put the point where endurance is no longer possible at a reasonable distance along the way, not at that distant point where John could have told him that it does in fact exist.

"It would be such a pity if a child saw it," explained John. "Children grieve over these things."

"There you're wrong," said Michael bitterly. "Children are heartless little beasts. Compassion is a late development. And rare. Most of the kindness one meets is bogus."

John turned round, his lean face alight with amusement. "You're young still," he said. When John was amused his smile was like wintry sunshine. His cadaverous boniness was suddenly transformed with brilliant promise and one almost expected to see him blossom into spring upon the instant. Michael was taken aback by the promise.

"Not your kindness," he said with quick humility. "I believe I've eaten the last sandwich. We were to have shared this meal, but we don't seem to have done so." He peered into the coffee jug. "Only dregs there. And you paid for it. That, I imagine, is typical."

"Of what?" asked John.

"Of the kind of man you are. Of the kind of man I am."

"It's early days to pass judgment on each other," said John. "Though in any case I think that's an unprofitable employment. Human character is so full of surprises. Even those one knows best continually surprise one." He paused. "And in the things one does sometimes, the thoughts one has, one surprises oneself most of all. Invariably unpleasantly."

"There you're right," said Michael, shortly, grimly and desperately.

John sat down beside him, absent-mindedly pulled out his empty pipe and sucked at it. He was remembering what Harriet had said this morning. "A new color being threaded in for a new pattern." He gazed straight in front of him but he did not

36

see the gulls riding the wine-dark sea of the ploughed lands, the sight that was once more absorbing Michael; he saw instead, as clearly as though he looked upon a painted portrait, the face of the man beside him. He had always had this queer visual gift. He could take in, with a few quick glances, every detail of a face, and then see it again as though memory were a lantern that projected the picture upon the purity of his compassion. He would not so have explained it to himself. His love for men, existing side by side with his self-distrustful shrinking from them when they were not actually confronting him, and his compassion for them that had been bled white and stretched taut with use, were remarkable but had not been remarked by himself.

Though he could not trust his own judgment he nevertheless knew men, and the face he was looking at both interested and touched him. It was the face of a fairly young man, though not so young as his bitterness had at first led him to expect. But not yet forty. It was a brittle-looking, charming face, thin and dark, with a certain childishness about it that was contradicted by the wariness of the eyes and the weather-beaten appearance of the skin. It was a weak face, obstinately and rather angrily set in repose but with a delightful puckish humor breaking through when he laughed or spoke. His dark hair, closely cropped, stood vitally and unbecomingly on end like the fur of an infuriated short-haired cat. Indeed in his lithe wiriness, wariness and hungryness he reminded John of a stray black tom-cat spitting sparks at a would-be rescuer. Not that there was any sign of spitting at the moment, but any attempt at rescuing would undoubtedly produce it. The man wore good, well-cut clothes but he was the untidy type. Wrinkled socks and a tie askew were obviously a part of his temperament. But a good shave and clean hands were a part of his temperament too, and those with clean hands and expensive clothes in a prosperous country are seldom hungry.

"What is the matter? And what do I do?" wondered John in an appalling state of worry. It was perpetually his duty as a

37

priest to do something about somebody and his prayers for guidance were seldom answered in any way that was apparent to him. He prayed now, frantically, and remained as worried as before. And he liked this man, not only with his habitual love of mankind but with an intense personal sympathy as well. He was not adult any more than he was himself. Most probably the child in him had not been able to meet the challenge with which life confronts a man. He might spit defiance with an angry attempt at courage, with deliberate deception he might swagger along with an apparent crust of toughness upon the surface of his weakness, but any sudden test would shatter the crust. In the depths of his failure he would know an exceedingly bitter shame. John almost sweated in sympathy. It was merely the good fortune of circumstance, he thought, that none of his own failures had let him down into degradation... But for the grace of God... That was a consideration that always made it impossible to get up and go away, even if he were justified in doing so, which at the moment he was not. One had to do something, no matter how futile. One had to stick like a bur, and as irritatingly. It was the other chap who had to do the pulling off, when he could no longer stand the irritation.

"Now what do we do?" he asked, and his blue eyes, as he turned them on Michael, were full of bewilderment.

Michael laughed and a most invigorating sense of strength came to him. This chap seemed even more incompetent than he was himself. Any appeal for help always touched and steeled him as nothing else did. It was so rare.

"I go on my way and you go on yours," he suggested. "That is, you go on to Silverbridge and I go to wherever this road's going to."

"I wasn't going to Silverbridge," said John, "I was coming to find you. And if you were going to where this road leads to, it's Belmaray, and we'll go there together."

He sighed with relief as he unfolded himself and stood up.

So far, so good. The next ten minutes of their existences were now mapped out for them.

"Nothing to worry about for ten minutes," he said. "Fifteen, if we go slowly."

"Should we make it twenty and return the mugs and jug to the farm?" suggested Michael.

John looked at him with admiration. "I should have forgotten them," he said.

"You stay here," said Michael. "I'll take them."

John did as he was told. The initiative had passed now to the younger man and he rejoiced in nothing so much as in obedience. But when Michael came back he was once more sucking at his empty pipe because he had just remembered that he had not told Mrs. Wilmot to wash the traycloth.

"Are you temporarily out of tobacco or do you prefer it that way?" asked Michael, as they strolled companionably along the road.

"Except on Sundays I don't smoke now," said John. "It's not necessary. But my pipe has got a bit of a habit with me. I pull at it without thinking what I'm doing." He put it away. "And it's not necessary."

"In this damnable world smoking is most necessary," said Michael, and offered a silver cigarette case with one cigarette in it.

John stopped dead in horror, about to protest, for the cigarette cried aloud to him that it had been kept for a particularly bad moment. Then he took it, and felt at once in his own spirit the balm he had given to the spirit of the other. In terms of sacrifice the meal was now more than paid for.

"What did you mean, that you were coming to look for me?" asked Michael as they strolled on again. "How did you know I was draped over the bridge?"

"The milk van," said John. "We've not had our milk yet."

"I'm sorry," said Michael. "And I was reported drunk? Have you a particular affection for drunkards?"

39

"Not at all," said John. "But I'm the vicar, you know."

"I didn't know," said Michael. "Of Belmaray? Is it a large parish? If it is, and there are many drunks, and your sense of duty is what it appears to be, your time must be much occupied."

John was delighted to see the man was enjoying himself, pulling his leg. His impish humor was now entirely in the ascendant, and he looked young as he laughed. But why was he drifting along the roads of the world in this hungry, well-dressed and peculiar fashion? "I find it hard to preserve an attitude of Christian charity towards those who ask questions," he said.

"Not being a Christian I don't have to," said Michael.

"What is your attitude towards the inquisitive?" asked John anxiously.

"I knock them down," said Michael.

"You have a fine imagination," stated John gently.

"Why is that so obvious?" asked Michael.

"A deduction from your tendency to exaggeration," said John. "You will like Belmaray for it has its exaggerations also. The name comes from the French—*belle marée*—the river is tidal there and very lovely. Beyond the village it widens and runs down to the sea between banks of rhododendrons and azaleas that my great-uncle planted. They are flame color, rose and gold. They look wonderful from the manor above. He spent a fortune on them. He's been dead for thirty years but the village still remembers him and calls him the 'mad squire'."

Michael cocked an interested eye in John's direction. "Are you lord of the manor as well as the parson?" he asked. "I know I'm asking questions but I've already ascertained that your only reaction to them is Christian charity."

"Technically," said John. "For many reasons it is not possible for me to live there. My great-aunt lives there."

"Is she as mad as your great-uncle?" asked Michael.

John considered the question seriously, striving for a truthful answer. "I think most people would consider her to be unusual," he said at last. "I don't. I did not consider my great-uncle mad;

40

only a little peculiar at times. I think the fact of the matter is that we are rather an odd family but we seem quite normal to each other."

Michael was chuckling now and his eyes were twinkling. Talking to this Mad Hatter of a parson (upon further acquaintance he seemed to Michael a perfect blend of the Mad Hatter and Don Quixote) was the first entertaining thing that had happened to him in years. First that experience of beauty upon the bridge, then a good meal, and now this comic relief. Where exactly was this lost valley, ringed about with these high hills? It was not in any world that he knew. In what country did a river of mother-of-pearl slip to the sea between banks flaming with rhododendrons, while up above them an old woman with great rubies in her ears lived with her peacocks and spiders in the splendid dust of a ruined house, and walked the tangled paths of a mad garden full of roses that had known no pruning knife in a hundred years? In no country of concrete experience, only in some country that his soul had known. If John had the gift of recreating before his mind's eye a face he had seen in a few quick glances, Michael out of chance phrases and flashes of beauty had always in old days been able to build for himself his country of escape. "Rest and ease, a convenient place, pleasant fields and groves, murmuring springs, and a sweet repose of mind." Cervantes had known the same country, and had doubtless retained the power to create it even in the midst of misery, so great were his own interior riches. But Michael's imagination had always been dependent upon exterior bounty, and cut off from that he had been cut off from his country too.

"Flame color, rose and gold," he said. "No white ones? Not the yunnanense?"

"Just where the river turns there is a stream that comes down from the hills and makes a small waterfall," said John, "and there is a white rhododendron growing beside it, but I never knew its name. Are you a gardener? Forgive me! That's one of

41

my opening gambits with newcomers to the parish. One must say something. It was only a rhetorical question."

"So it can be answered," said Michael. "I know how to prune roses to an outward facing bud and I know wistaria grows eastward to greet the rising sun. I know potatoes are planted on Good Friday and if I'm not quite sure which way up to plant a bulb I'm not above taking advice." He looked mockingly at John. "Could you recommend me to your great-aunt as a gardener? What fun to prune her roses for her and grow daffodils to fill the *jardinières* in her crimson salon. Has she *jardinières* and a salon? I feel that she has, even if only ghosts frequent it. Forgive me, it was only a joke. Why, what's the matter?"

"Daffodils," said John miserably. "I've forgotten them. I was to have picked daffodils for my wife. Did a car pass you on the road when I was at the farm?"

"I didn't notice it," said Michael. "But then I was not in a very noticing frame of mind."

"She may have stayed to do some shopping in Silverbridge," said John. "Perhaps I've time yet."

They were nearly at the vicarage gate and he strode along so fast that Michael decided that the pleasure of his company, though great, was not worth the effort entailed in keeping up with him. "Good-bye," he said firmly. John halted at once and swung round. "Good-bye. Thank you for an excellent breakfast." He held out his hand but John did not take it. The distress upon his face struck Michael first as comic and then as profoundly moving. The man looked as Pharaoh might have looked watching the death of his son, his grief carved upon the high nobility of his acquiline face and biting inward, so that the lines of the face sharpened and the hollows deepened. And all because he must say good-bye to a strange vagabond whom he could not invite to his house for fear of his wife, and whose condition he could not discuss because the vagabond resented questions. Michael formed a swift mental picture of John's wife; older than he was with greying hair skewered back in a bun, shrewish, houseproud, and insistent that her husband's quixotic charity should function out of doors only. Of the mental suffering of a truly charitable man he had no conception, for he had little experience of true charity, but he perceived it to be in circumstances such as the present extremely great and all the more moving because of the human weakness that marred it. For the man had not courage enough to say, "Come in and spend the day with me," and take the consequences with his wife. Michael was so moved that he doubled back upon the path of his escape and returned to the place where he had been when he fled from recognition. He would not deceive this man. Even though cowardice had halted Don Quixote's hospitality he must know whom it was he had wanted to ask into his house.

"My name is Michael Stone," he said, pronouncing the words with almost a touch of insolence, so great was his shrinking. "Michael Stone. You don't know it, of course," he added with bravado, and then meeting John's puzzled eyes he nearly choked on a sudden gust of nervous laughter, for both insolence and bravado had been quite unnecessary. Michael Stone had never been heard of in this lost valley. Or else he had been forgotten already. Or else he had never been so important in any valley as he had hitherto liked to believe. "I won't leave Belmaray without seeing you again," he said with sudden gentle humility, looking at his shoes. "I give you my word. And don't worry. My luck's going to turn."

He raised his hand and swung away up the lane and round the corner by the forge and the elder tree. John turned in at the vicarage gate reassured. Michael Stone would keep his word. Then he broke into a loping run and five minutes later was picking daffodils with the headlong haste of remorse.

Powerless to stop him Harriet watched from her window, as earlier she had watched Daphne picking with the haste of anger, and had been powerless to stop her either. To Daphne she had longed to cry, "Give him time to remember," and to John she wanted to say, "Give her time to forget." But she could not get the window open. They never gave each other time. The nervous irritation of the one and the nervous anxiety of the other, meeting head on, were the source of all their clashes; and of their indigestion too. "Nerves," thought Harriet, "we never had them when I was young. Tinned food and aeroplanes. Strawberries at Christmas and travelling faster than sound. Flying in the face of Providence don't give the stomach a chance. Dear God, why can't they laugh at each other? There's a yaffingale laughing." She folded her hands under her rug. "Dear God, why can't they let that laughing bird teach them a bit of sense?"

2

Annoyance never impaired Daphne's artistic skill. With her whole being flaming with resentment at John's forgetfulness, the boredom of the country, too large a house, too little money, too much work in house and parish, too little strength, she could yet arrange daffodils and pussy palm in stiff vases as no other woman could arrange them; beautifully, delicately, something of her own beauty seeming to fuse with theirs, her conscious life mingling with their unconscious being, so that it seemed that they took of her willed striving towards perfection and made it their own, and gave her in exchange something of their own serene obedience to the law of their being... Gradually, as she worked, her resentment died away and acquiescence took its place. It was quiet in the church and she heard a yaffingale laughing.

She had always had this gift of correspondence with natural beauty, especially with flowers. It was not the same thing as John's gift of sympathy with the creatures and with humanity, that caused him so much pain, for in her correspondence there was only pleasure. Her pain always came from inside herself, from her resentment of the contrariness and frustration of life, while his came most often from outside himself, growing inevitably from his compassion. It was a simplification of the

44

difference between them to say that to the selfish comfort comes from the external things, while to the selfless consolation comes interiorly, but that was the way Daphne put it to herself. She reverenced her husband even when he drove her wild.

She finished arranging her flowers, slipped into the vicarage pew and sat down, her hands in her lap. It was always to her own seat that she gravitated when she found herself alone in the church. She had no love for the thing, for it had been especially designed to produce a maddening ache in the small of the back, and all the draughts in the church, and there were many, met about her ankles, but it was hers, the cranny in the rock that was her appointed place, and unconsciously she clung to it.

"The cranny in the rock," she said to herself. In her thoughts of the church where she had so unwillingly worshipped week by week for ten years imagination had hitherto played little part, for they had been irritated and practical thoughts concerned chiefly with draughts and crumpled surplices, but now as the dimness of the church weighed upon her eyelids, and her weary body relaxed against the hard wood, pictures of the church rose in her memory, and it was each time as a rock that it rose.

She was in the manor house garden, on the day John had brought her to see Great-Aunt Maria after they had got engaged, standing in the paved court by the rosemary bush, and she looked down and saw the church below her with its square Norman tower, its buttresses and walls foreshortened by the height upon which she stood. It looked a rock down there in the valley, with the sea of leaves washing about it. In the dilapidated house behind her there might be an old woman who did not like her and with whom she would never get on, resentful as she was of what she considered Aunt Maria's selfishness in letting John maintain her in the manor house, but what were the animosities and resentments of women compared with the permanence of the rock down below? No more than blown spume.

She was in their boat on the river, paddling the children home from a picnic, in those days when Harriet had still been able to

45

do much of the work of the house and there had been time for picnics, and saw the church towering up above the trees in their spring green, beyond the golden kingcups that enamelled the banks of the Belle Marée. It was not foreshortened now, a rock washed by the sea, for she was looking at it from below, but one of those "hills whose heads touch heaven." Such cliffs are full of hiding places. "The high hills are a refuge for the wild goats: and so are the stony rocks for the conies." She was as restless as any mountain creature, beating herself against the bars of her mistaken marriage and her lost valley. But neither could the rock go free. It must remain immovable if the wild creatures were always to find it there, as she must stay where she was for her children's sake; her little girls whom she had not much wanted. She did not like girls, or women either for that matter. She was a man's woman, and had longed with desperation for a son.

She was struggling towards the church on a winter's evening, ankle deep in one of those rare snowfalls of the sheltered valley, tired out after all the Christmas parish parties and rebellious that she must leave her warm fireside in such weather just because it was Sunday evening and she was the parson's wife. Why should parson's wives always be expected to be in church upon every conceivable occasion? A butcher's wife was not expected to haunt the butcher's shop, or an auctioneer's wife to sit beneath her husband's rostrum listening to his eloquence with bated breath. "And it's not as though my religion ever brought me any joy," she thought. "Since I married John I've tried to believe what he believes and that's all there is to it." If any of her prayers had ever been answered, if Aunt Maria could have had the decency to tell John to sell the manor house so that they need not be so wretchedly poor, or if she had had a son, it might have been different. But how could one rejoice in a God of granite who paid not the slightest attention to what one said? Granite. The church was built of granite, heavy, cold, dead stuff. Absorbed in herself she turned the corner unexpectedly and there it was, black and massive against the snow but pouring out warm glowing color from the gashes in its great walls. The snow was rosy where the glow touched it and gold seemed to spill down the stone. She had a swift impression of fire in the rock and was scared for a moment or two. Even when she quickened her steps with grateful thoughts of light and warmth the remembrance of fire did not quite leave her and at the back of her mind she remained uneasy.

And here she was inside the rock, lodged in her own particular cranny within the permanence, the shelter, the strength and fire. Rock of Ages. The only thing she liked about that sentimental old hymn, to which John was so tiresomely attached, was the story of how it had been written. She liked to think of that man creeping into the cleft of the rock in the Somersetshire valley and taking shelter there from the storm, sitting hunched up inside (she had seen it and it was such an uncomfortable cranny, as uncomfortable as this of hers) while the rhythm of the storm beat out the verses in his mind. She thought the verses doggerel, but she could never sing them without hearing the roll of thunder and feeling a thrill of fear.

> While I draw this fleeting breath,
> When my eyelids close in death,
> When I soar through tracts unknown,
> See Thee on Thy Judgment Throne;
> Rock of ages, cleft for me—

What was the time? Her watch had stopped... There was that laughing yaffingale again... Bother the time. For once in a way she was feeling peaceful, and happy, she who was always so depressed and restless. Seeds blow into crannies in the rock, dead-looking brown things hardly larger than grains of dust, and then unbelievably flower into snapdragon and valerian. It was miraculous how such gay things could grow in the rock. And if she stayed here much longer it would be miraculous if there was any lunch. She got up quickly and turned, seeing before her a blaze of red and gold, the flowers that grow from seeds in the rock, and just coming through the doorway was John with his arms full of daffodils.

She looked so gay that he thought suddenly of the sparkling apple tree. Fresh from some experience that had been happy her joy shone about her still as though she was enclosed in one of those spheres of light that had hung upon the tree. The moment was ripe for one of their clashes, but it did not come. She was seeing him as part of a rock that glowed with warmth and color and he was seeing her made one with the miracle of the tree... And he had brought the daffodils too late... The incident seemed to them not annoying but humorous and they burst out laughing. Behind John, out in the churchyard, there was a flash of scarlet and green as the merry yaffingale flew laughing by.

3

THEIR laughter reached their second daughter Margary
and eased her wretchedness. She did not know that they
laughed, but even separated from them she was never unaffected
by their moods and actions. She was one of those children who
cannot detach themselves from their parents and the shelter of
their home. Had she been a fledgling sparrow it would have
taken the united efforts of both parents to heave her over the
side of the nest. Had she been a kitten she would always have
been down at the bottom of the prickly pile, with the rest on top.
Daphne, equally despairing over her and irritated by her, could
not imagine how she would ever survive boarding school, how
she would ever be launched in a career of her own. She would
stay at home always, Daphne feared, perpetually underfoot,
and when her parents died she would develop into one of those
old maids who sit forlornly in draughty cottages, surrounded by
mementos of the past, and talk incessantly about the old home.
Daphne disliked old maids and felt that to be the mother of
one would be the final humiliation of her life of humiliations.

John felt differently, for Margary was his favorite child. He
was not irritated by her incompetence, her lack of beauty or her
present terror of all that existed beyond her home, for in her he
saw again the child he had once been himself. And he did not
fear eventual loneliness for her, for he knew the preciousness
of the single state... The cell, and the sunlight moving on the
bare wall... He had chosen it once, knowing it the life for him,

49

and then had come the ending of Daphne's engagement to some young rotter whom he had never met, and her despair, the despair of the girl whom he had loved all her life, and to serve her he had shut the door of the cell behind him with himself outside. He had lost his cell yet, paradoxically, it existed now somewhere within him. He believed that in dying he might leave it to Margary as other men leave their daughter a material house. When she was old she would go in and find peace. He did not fear for her old age, though he did worry over the stretch of time that lay between, for she had his temperament and he knew the burden that it was to bear. His whole being was one great apology to her.

He did not know about her private joys, though he supposed she had them, as he had. He did not know how his own awareness of beauty, his intense joy in it for a moment or two, and then his willing loss of joy, was in Margary an awareness of delight in others. She knew when people were happy, whether they laughed or not. Indeed at eight years old she knew already that laughter was not always a sign of happiness. Sometimes when people were completely quiet there came to her that wonderful sense of well being, and her taut nerves relaxed in peace. But there was the other side of the picture. When others were wretched, even though hiddenly so, she was strung up and anguished. A child still, she knew nothing of herself. She did not understand the reason for the deep alternations of mood that afflicted her, and could not know yet how acceptance of the change from well-being to its opposite, offered for those who suffered, could serve them. That supreme usefulness to which her awareness of the needs of others would eventually lead her was a long way in the future, and before she found the bare cell there would be the desert of ineffectiveness to cross, for she was one whose fear and reserve would make it hard for her to have the normal happy traffic with her fellow human beings.

But now, three miles away, a man and woman laughed within the shelter of a grey rock, and though a minute before her throat had been tight with the tears she could not shed, now her burden was eased and such a sense of joyous well-being came to her body that her shoulders straightened and she lifted her bent head. Her eyes, blue and lovely, the only beauty she had, looked bravely up at Miss Giles. It was not so much because she had been scathingly scolded for errors in arithmetic that she had been so wretched as because of the ugly misery in the mind of the woman in front of her. It had created a miasma of hopelessness in the classroom. The others had not felt it so much because they hated Miss Giles and got a kick out of their hatred. Margary did not hate. She never would. She was like the mother in Herbert Trench's dreadful poem whose heart had gone on loving the son who had cut it out of her body. But now the hopelessness was gone, sucked up by distant laughter like unhealthy vapors by the sun, and she looked up at her tormentor and smiled.

Miss Giles was checked in mid torrent, for this was the first time that this thin, meek child, whom she so delighted to punish for her own wretchedness, had stood up to her; not in the obvious way that Pat stood up to her, with cheekiness and rebellion, but in a way that was new to her. The tranquility in the child's eyes was something that she did not recognize because she knew nothing of it, but it withstood her. She could not go on. She turned to Winkle, who was solacing her anger at Margary being scolded, and her own boredom with lessons she could not understand, by trying to lick ink off her ruler, and was about to tell her sharply to bring her the ruler, that she might apply it to Winkle's fat palm, but found she could not. As well as tranquility some power of immense delight came through the child Margary, from a far distance, and withstood her. She was not conscious of the power for she had forfeited her right to any awareness of the amazing joy behind the curtain of material things, she had even forgotten that there had once been a time when she had sometimes caught her breath with awe because the curtain had rippled as though with laughter, but there was a half memory of a forgotten memory and she could not go on tormenting these children.

"Next please," she said, and put the question that had baffled eight-year-old Margary to nine-year-old Pat.

Pat answered it accurately, quickly and contemptuously, her contempt being not for Margary's ignorance but for Miss Giles's bad temper. Pat had a cool and critical mind. Admittedly Miss Giles was having a difficult time this morning because Miss O'Hara, who taught the little ones, had gone to have a tooth out and she was having to teach the whole school together, but that was no reason for getting in a filthy temper. And what good did it do? You couldn't teach kids anything by saying beastly things to them and whacking them. What had Margary and Winkle learned at this stinking school? Nothing. She, Pat, had only picked up a rich and varied vocabulary which she dared not use unedited at home, and a knowledge of the nasty ways of nasty women which made her feel ashamed when she remembered them in her mother's presence. What she knew in the academic sense, and she knew a good deal, she had picked up from studying her school books at home. She wished Father would take Margary and Winkle away from Oaklands. The fire of questions having passed beyond her she looked out of the window and wrinkled her fine brows in perplexity. She wished she could tell Father about Miss Giles. It was all right for her, for she was leaving, but she was worried about Margary left without her protection. She had tried to tell Mother once that they didn't like school, but Daphne had replied impatiently that of course they didn't, no one liked school, but one had to go there all the same. And Oaklands was the only private school within reasonable distance. It was expensive, and Father had all he could do to pay the school bills, and Pat ought to be grateful. She didn't want to go to the village school, surely?

"Yes," Pat had replied cheekily, with a flash of her dark eyes, and Daphne had hastily left the kitchen, where this conversation had taken place, lest they have one of their rows. She and Pat were far too much alike and struck sparks from each other. Father, of course, thought Pat, would listen carefully if she told him about Miss Giles, and remove them instantly from Oaklands. But that would be telling tales. Pat had fine, if extremely eccentric, blood in her veins, loyalty and courage. She could not tell tales. She also had strong nerves, a sturdy body and a stout heart, and though she knew Margary suffered at school she did not know how much she suffered. For Margary never complained. She also had a high, if different, brand of courage.

Pat sighed, removed her gaze from the window, withdrew a sticky striped sweet from the paper bag in her pocket, and popped it into her left cheek. She sucked blissfully for a moment or two and then suffered a pang of apprehension. "Golly, it's peppermint," she thought. The aroma might possibly betray her but even had the peppermint not stuck very firmly to a back tooth she would have scorned to take it out. Only cowards went back on things. People of spunk continued in the chosen course. Besides, she was generally equal to Miss Giles after the wretched woman had been getting her knife into poor old Margary because anger quickened her wits. But she took up her pencil and bent her head over the sum she was supposed to be doing, breathing very carefully downwards. She knew a good deal for her age but she was unaware as yet that hot air always rises.

Margary, stealing a glance at her, thought how beautiful she looked, serious and absorbed like that. She was nearly as beautiful as Mother, only not quite because Mother's hair was long and wavy and Pat's was short and straight. But if it was straight it was dark and silky, not sandy and dull like Margary's, and fell away from the fringe on her forehead in lovely half moon curves on either side of her thin brown face. Pat's thinness was not angular like Margary's but lithe and strong, and under the satin smooth skin her cheeks had a warm flush. She had fine dark eyebrows, a short straight nose, full rosy lips and a strong cleft chin. Mother did not have that chin, and it was perhaps a blemish, but Margary liked it because it was comic, and gave Pat's face the look that Puck had in Father's illustrated Shakespeare. Pat was always laughing, always equal to things, and Margary adored her.

"Who is sucking a peppermint?" demanded Miss Giles suddenly.

There was no answer, and Pat breathed heavily downwards. Miss Giles located the direction.

"Patricia!" she ejaculated. "Come here at once."

Pat leapt to her feet, placed finger and thumb inside her mouth, dragged the offender from the back tooth and held it triumphantly aloft.

"Ninepence a quarter at Jackson's, Miss Giles," she said. "I can highly recommend them. Will you have one?"

Miss Giles, now perambulating the room to look at the children's sums, put a hand against the wall to steady herself. Her head was worse than usual today; in fact she felt, as always, desperately ill. Her chronic nervous dyspepsia was driving her nearly mad. Only indigestion, people said. Little did they know! Day after day, night after night, never a moment of ease, and sleep, when it came briefly, nightmare ridden. She had been to doctor after doctor but none of them had been interested because nervous dyspepsia was not interesting and neither was she. No one nowadays ever looked at her twice. Yet she had a good brain and in her youth she had had a fine contralto voice and a deep love of music, and given a good training she could have done something worth while. But everything had been done for the boys, because they were boys, and nothing for her. And now look at the boys, wasters both of them, and all her father's money lost in paying their debts. She had been left to sink or swim, marry or die. And she had died. For what had her life been but death? One wretched job after another, and everyone hating her because she had acne that no treatment, however expensive, could get rid of, and a dyspeptic temper as maddening as her pain. The money she had spent on medicines! If she could have had, now, the money she had spent on treatments that did no good, and if her father at his death had been able to leave her a mere tenth of all that had been flung in the sink of the boys' debts, then she could have bought that cottage on a village green that she had longed for all her life and had peace now she was turned fifty; and would not have had to teach these wretched children, in this third-rate little school. Yes, this was a bad school. What were the parents of these children thinking of to send them to such a place? They didn't know, of course. It was a pleasant looking house. Mrs. Belling appeared the saintliest of old dears. Mary O'Hara had a face like an advertisement for tooth powder and a name like a glamorous film star, and as for herself she did her best to keep out of the way when parents came... That detestable, conceited child Patricia Wentworth had come right up to her and was holding out a paper bag of horrible looking sweets, melted by the warmth of the child's body and sticking together in a soggy mess. Faintness and nausea swept over Miss Giles but through it she was dimly aware of the wicked merriment in Pat's eyes and the titter of the class.

"Patricia, go to Mrs. Belling," she said.

For a child like Pat it was no punishment, Mrs. Belling being what she was, but it was all she could think of in this moment of weakness. Pat always seemed on the warpath when she was most unwell; and also, she was inclined to think, after that little fool Margary had been scolded. Pat was clever.

"Thank you, Miss Giles," said Pat, and vanished from the room with a delightful swirl of her tunic skirt. Only Pat could have made a skimpy inadequate skirt swirl like that. She had the gift of imparting her own vivacity even to the things she used and the clothes she wore. The moment she had gone the titter stopped and the class was silent with apprehension. Without Pat here they were all afraid of Miss Giles.

All except Winkle who was merely angry and bored. Lessons were fun with Miss O'Hara but she could not understand these grown-up lessons. Nor did she want to. What was the use of arithmetic? It seemed to have no purpose except to make people lose their tempers. She hated it here and decided she had had enough. Up went her hand.

"Please may I be excused?"

Miss Giles gave impatient permission but was not deceived by the face of dewy innocence raised to hers. Winkle, too, in her different way, was clever. She arose and stumped off. Dreadful despair, all the worse because it was such a swing of the pendulum from her previous joy, fell upon Margary. Without her two warm brave sisters she was alone indeed, and all the powers of evil were arrayed against her.

2

In the passage Winkle bypassed the lavatory and went into the broom cupboard next door. There was a housemaid's box on the floor and she sat down upon it with much satisfaction. She had a naturally cheerful disposition and could be happy anywhere, but in school hours she was happiest inside the weeping willow on Mrs. Belling's lawn or inside the broom cupboard. It was the peace and privacy that she liked in these retreats. No one bothered her and she could escape to her country without fear of being seized and dragged back again before she had even had time to knock on the door. Sitting with her fat hands folded in her lap she looked with affection at the whitewashed wall opposite her, and wished the sun would move upon it in the way she liked. But it was a grey day today. She turned towards the small square high window and saw it framing the branch of a plum tree with its blossom white against the grey sky. A ringdove alighted on the branch and swung there. She sighed with contentment and her eyes did not leave the flowering branch and the blue-grey wonder of the bird.

"Please," she said softly, "could I go there now?"

She had a moment of anxiety, wondering if she would be able to go. When she had been very small she had never wondered, the mere flash of a bird's wing, a snowflake looking in at the

56

window or the scent of a flower had been enough to send her back. Lying in her cot, rolling about on a rug on the lawn, sitting in her high chair eating her bread and milk, she had gone back with ease to that other place. And she had not exactly gone back, she had been lifted back by the small lovely sights and sounds and scents as though it were easier for her to be there than here. But now she was five years old it was easier to be here than there. She could not go back without first secluding herself in some hiding place such as the apple tree at home, the rosemary tree in the manor house garden or the willow tree here, without climbing the steps to the door with the least suspicion of an effort, and that little pang of anxiety lest today she might not be able to make the effort. And always at the back of her mind nowadays there was the fear that the day might come when not only would she be unable to make the effort, but that she would not want to go back. Even now, at home, she did not find herself wanting to go back very often, because it was nice at home. It was here at school that the longing to go back came upon her so overwhelmingly, though not so overwhelmingly as it used to do. Perhaps one day she would have forgotten that she ever had gone back. Nothing would remain of her returns to the other place but a vague longing.

But that time was a long way off yet, and meanwhile with relief and unspeakable joy she found herself making the effort and climbing the steps. They were silvery steps and might have been made of light, and they led to the low small door in the rock that had a knocker on it, just like the knocker on the door of the doll's house where Hunca Munca and Tom Thumb had such adventures in the *Tale of Two Bad Mice*. When Winkle knocked with the knocker the door was opened from the inside. A year ago the door had opened at once but now she sometimes had to wait a little, and just occasionally felt worried lest this time it should not open. A year ago she had been small enough to pass through the door without bending her head, but now she had to stoop. If she got much bigger even stooping would not get her through for it was an exceedingly small door.

She knocked, waited a moment, the door opened and she stepped through into the branch of swaying blossom. Beside her was the dove and they swung there together in the still grey peace.

"Coo *coo*, coo-coo," said the dove. Winkle never knew quite what it would be that cradled her. It might be golden praise or the blue of purity or scarlet courage, or just light, or just darkness. It depended on the day and the time. They were all good, but the light was very good because it enabled her to see right to the horizons of the country where the mountains were. The darkness was best of all even though she saw nothing and did nothing in it, because it loved her.

Nowadays she always enjoyed the nearest things first because they were the most familiar, bearing some likeness to the things she had left behind. As she passed on things became more glorious and less familiar. Once, she half remembered, it had been the other way. The things that bore some likeness to the things of this world had been less familiar than what was beyond, and she had passed through them very quickly in her haste to get home.

Yet though there was a likeness in the silvery whiteness of the flowers about her to the blossoms on Mrs. Belling's plum tree, that bloomed before the apple tree at home had even stuck out its first green spikes of leaves, they were different here from there. They were beautiful there but here they were not just beautiful but beauty. They were so light that they were a foam of whiteness like moonbeams about her, and yet she could lie back on them, and they held her so gently that she felt nothing but the gentleness and yet so strongly that she had never felt so safe. The whiteness was not just something that was clean for the moment, like a newly washed pinafore that trembled for itself, but something that sparkled with a purity that was fearless because it was for ever. The gentleness was not only gentleness but an absence of all violence for always. The strength was not just strength but no possibility of weakness or failure. Everything here was like that. It was two things, and the second thing was always something that made the first thing immortal with its own immortality.

With invisible sweet airs rocking the fragrance and the light that held her Winkle gazed at the miracle of a plum blossom that swung above her. It seemed to her the same size as she was and so she could see its perfection in a way that she could not do in the world on the other side of the door. But perhaps it was not quite true to say it was the same size as she was, because size did not exist here. It was simply that here she and a flower and a dove were on a complete equality. She could not, here, have trodden on a plum blossom and crushed it. The dove beside her could not have pecked her and hurt her. That sort of thing did not happen here. But the remembrance that she had once trodden on a flower made Winkle look at the blossom with a humble adoration that was the same as being on her knees. Indeed she thought she was kneeling as she looked at the flower face to face. The six white petals were like the sails of a small ship, exactly the size for a child to sail away in upon the sea of peace. They were exquisitely shaped, beautifully shadowed, and veined with light, and a fragrance drifted from them that was the scent of the grey peace. The group of long silvery stamens tipped with gold, rising from the delicate green heart of the flower, were like an angel's crown. She could look deep into the heart, down into a green cavern of refreshment. It was like drinking cold water when you are thirsty. Beyond the flowers light shone through the silk curtains of the green leaves, and beyond them was depth beyond depth of peace. It held Winkle, and held the dove too as she leaned back against its warm breast.

She turned her head so that her cheek was against its feathers. She knew it would not fly away. Here, nothing you loved ever flew away. She could stay here for a hundred years if she liked, nestled up against this dove. One didn't talk about years here, any more than one talked about size, because there wasn't any time, but the language of the world into which she had been born five years ago was beginning to be a part of her now, and was becoming the language of her thought. Once it had not been so. Once she had known a far more wonderful language than the earthly one, but she had forgotten it now, and heard only vague echoes of it in the song of the birds and the sound of the wind blowing. Out in the world she grieved sometimes because she had forgotten it, and could not talk about the things that that language only could express; but perhaps no one would have listened to her if she had because there she was only a child. Here there was no question of being one age or another, young or old, and she had had great wisdom here once, and she believed she had it still, only the more worldly wisdom she acquired there the less she seemed able to remember this country's wisdom. There, she was sorry about that too sometimes, but here she knew it did not matter. When her life out there was over she would come back here again, like a tired bird returning full circle to its nest. All that she seemed to lose she would find again; only she would be even richer than she had been because she would bring back with her the gathered treasure of her flight to add to the treasure of this heavenly country. But she wouldn't keep it, for one kept nothing here. One gave it, as the flowers were giving their scent and the dove her warm breast. There was equality here. To give everything was, in this place, the meaning of equality.

She looked down at the dove's soft feathers and stroked them. When she looked closely at them she saw that they were not grey at all but iridescent with color. It seemed you could not have peace without the other colors too, the praise and joy and courage and all the other lovely tints. They all went to the making of it, and so it was lovelier even than they were. And the light was better still. And the darkness best of all.

"Dear night," she whispered, and shut her eyes and wriggled closer to the dove. The dove's eyes too, she knew, were hooded now, and the petals of the flower were closed. The three of them were equal as the darkness held them. But presently the dove would wake and stir, and she would wake too, and the petals would open and make themselves a boat for her, and she would sail away over the grey sea to the far horizons where the mountains were. She had never been to the mountains but she had always known that she would go. Perhaps it would be today. Soon. Now.

"Winkle!"

The dove's feathers were ruffled and she was not at ease. The flowers were sighing about her, stirred by an alien wind. Their fragrance seemed dying.

"Winkle!"

There were waves on the grey sea, and they were carrying her to a place where she did not want to be.

"Winkle! Come out at once!"

She was in prison, sitting on a hard seat in a small white-washed cell. She looked up and saw a small square of window, and a flowering branch against the grey sky. A bird was there among the flowers but as she looked it spread its wings and flew away. She was so desolate that she felt she could not bear it.

"Winkle, you are a very naughty little girl! Winkle!"

Winkle's desolation vanished and she smiled. The words were cross but the voice had the music of her lost country. It was the loveliest voice in the world, with a lilt in it like the taste of honey. Winkle adored honey and she adored the owner of that voice. She literally fell off the housemaid's box in her haste, picked herself up and bundled across to the door where she was picked up in two plump arms and held against the softness of the angora jumper that clothed the warm breast of a very angry girl. But the anger was not directed against Winkle, of which fact Winkle was well aware as she burrowed in. Miss O'Hara was so soft and warm that she might have been the dove, had it not been for the agitation of her very un-dovelike fury.

"No I won't, Miss Giles," stormed Mary O'Hara, her cheeks

like poppies, for she had a shocking temper. "Winkle is in my form and if she has been naughty it is my business to punish her, not yours."

"She was in my form when the incident occurred," said Miss Giles coldly. She was in a fury too, but a cold fury. The more volcanic Mary became the more glacial and cruelly cutting became Miss Giles. They affected each other like that, and the way they affected each other did nothing to increase the peace of Oaklands.

"Put that child down. You look ridiculous, clutching her as though she were a baby. Put her down. Winkle, come with me."

Winkle clung like a bur.

"I will punish her, Miss Giles," promised Mary hotly. "She's a very naughty little girl." But her cheek was warm against Winkle's and her curly red hair was delightfully tickly.

Miss Giles advanced a step, her thin hand outstretched. Mary knew the feel of Miss Giles's hand, cold and clammy from ill health and to her vivid imagination somehow evil. She would not have it on the child. She swung away with revulsion, set Winkle on her feet and ran, Winkle's hand in hers. They reached the shelter of Mary's own little classroom, where she taught the babies, and went in, and Miss Giles heard the key click in the lock as Mary turned it. Their feet had been light as summer rain pattering on leaves as they ran along the passage, and all the light of the grey day had seemed to gather about Mary's red head and Winkle's golden one. Gurgles of suppressed merriment had seemed to sparkle, like ripples on water. When they had gone the passage seemed like night. Miss Giles, turning shakily away into her darkness, found that she was crying. Unlike Winkle, she was not aware of any particular beneficence in darkness.

3

As she was not teaching until the next period Mary O'Hara's classroom was empty of everything except fresh air, daffodils and violets, and six little ink-stained desks. Instinctively, ever since she had come to this school she hated, Mary had fought its queer combined atmosphere of luxurious fugginess and bitter darkness with fresh air, bright colors and cleanliness. Mrs. Belling's drawing room, facing south, had pink brocade curtains, nearly always a large fire burning, dead flowers in the vases (except when parents were expected) and the windows closed. It was never clean because Annie, Mrs. Belling's maid, had been with her a great many years and suffered now from that chronic indolence that afflicts those who have been in long service with an indifferent and careless mistress. Miss Giles's class room looked north and had walls distempered just the wrong shade of buff. The curtains, dragged back from the hard light of the windows as angrily and tightly as Miss Giles's grey hair from her ravaged face, were a slimy green, that green which is not worthy to be called green at all so much is it the antithesis of freshness. The room was scrupulously clean, for Miss Giles knew how to put the fear of God into Annie, but bare, cold and quite hopeless. In the matter of cleanliness in her room Mary steered a halfway course by letting Annie give it her idea of a cleaning and then cleaning it again when Annie was out of the way, and as Mrs. Belling did not care what anybody did, provided they let her alone, she had distempered the walls sunshine yellow and hung flowered curtains at the eastward-facing windows. She had a little money of her own, and it enabled her to put up such flags of battle in her fight against the opposing forces in this place.

Mary was a born fighter and it was because there was a battle raging here that she stayed, glorying in the fight, every red curl on end with the zest of it, her vitality tingling even to her finger tips whenever she was aware of an inch gained here or there, a slackening of the onslaught of evil. Though that, she thought during wakeful nights, was a melodramatic and ridiculous way of putting it. For what, after all, was wrong here? Mrs. Belling was old, lazy and self-indulgent, and Miss Giles was sick and embittered. That, so far as she knew, was all. Only the laziness of the one and the bitterness of the other seemed somehow a focus for more than themselves. Murkiness seemed gathered to them as bats and spiders are drawn to the unclean and forgotten corners, and it was this murkiness that was a threat to the children. Mary adored children, and when a battle was for them there was more zest in it than ever.

"Though what do I think I am?" she would ask herself during these same wakeful nights. "A rallying point for the hosts of heaven, or what? Mary O'Hara, you are clean crazy." But discouragement was not for long and she remained where she was, clean and fresh in her clean fresh room, teaching the children to speak the truth, keeping her temper with difficulty, passionate in sympathy with the truly afflicted, intolerant of malingerers, loyal to superiors she hated and only twenty years old. Like Miss Giles she had not been trained for anything. She had just run wild in Ireland till her parents died and her aunt Mrs. Belling, her father's sister, had invited her to come and teach at her little school. Without knowing Mrs. Belling, who had left Ireland as a girl and had never returned to it, she had come for the fun of it, for the experience, and was finding it a different sort of fun and experience from anything she had expected.

Sitting in her chair, Winkle standing before her, she held the child lightly between her hands and looked at her. Of the six small girls whom she taught in this room Winkle was her favorite. She was a bunchy little creature, with bright dark eyes and a turned up nose that had earned her the nickname of Winkle, after Mrs. Tiggy Winkle of immortal fame. Her dark eyes were arresting in contrast with her shining straight gold hair, confined by an Alice-in-Wonderland snood. Her forehead was broad and peaceful, and oddly mature above her rosy chubby cheeks. She was nearly always merry and could extract the maximum of amusement out of anything, as Mary could herself. She was brave and tolerant, and the one child in the school who was neither frightened nor repelled by Miss Giles, but merely bored. Yet Mary suffered a pang of fear as she remembered that quite soon now Winkle would leave the east room and its daffodils for the north room and its slimy green curtains. For the first time she questioned her own loyalty. Ought she to let Winkle go to that room? Ought she to bring some definite accusation against Miss Giles? But that would be hateful. Would it be more hateful than letting children suffer?

"You have a new sweater on," said Winkle.

Mary was thankful to have her attention deflected and for a moment or two she and Winkle were both lost in admiration of her sweater. She had knitted it herself, in blue wool the color of her Irish eyes, and it went beautifully with her brown tweed skirt and newly washed curly red hair. Mary's dual purpose both as regarding sweater and shampoo had been the sustaining of her courage in a trying situation and the fascination of the dentist. Results had satisfied her. She had seated herself in the chair without a tremor and had had her tooth most tenderly extracted by a young man with a heightened color and a kindling eye, and had known that only professional etiquette, and the condition of her mouth, had prevented her from being asked out to lunch on the spot. Mary liked men only a little less than she liked children and took an entirely healthy delight in the reciprocity of the liking. Untrained though she was she had no anxieties about her future.

"A beautiful blue sweater," said Winkle. "There wasn't a blue window today in the cupboard. It was a grey window."

Mary suddenly remembered why they were here. "Winkle," she said, "you are a very naughty girl. You mustn't play games in the broom cupboard during lesson time."

"I wasn't playing games," said Winkle. "I went out through the window to the country."

"What country?" asked Mary.

"*The* country," said Winkle. "*You* know." She did not mention her country to grown-ups as a rule because she was not sure that they did know, and one didn't like to have one's realities dismissed as idle tales. But Mary was different. Mary was one of those people who made you feel that what you knew they knew too, only better, and where you had been they had been too, only further. Winkle suspected that her father was that kind of person, only she did not know her father very well yet, he seemed a bit high up and remote. But Mary was lower down and more accessible.

"One goes back there," she said, jogging Mary's memory.

Mary wrinkled her forehead, trying to remember. The shadow of a memory touched her, filling her with sadness, because she could not quite remember; the same sadness that came sometimes with the scent of violets on a cold spring evening, with birds' voices, with the sound of rain on a roof in a summer dawn, with a thousand little things that touched you and stabbed you and were gone. A great symphony or a flaming sunset might fill you with intolerable longing, but it was the longing for something to come and had triumph in it. But this sadness was the ache for something that seemed lost.

> The source . . .
> The voice of the hidden waterfall
> And the children in the apple tree.

It seemed to her strange and wonderful that Winkle could find a blue window in this place that always felt to her so profoundly unclean.

"I expect you go back more often at home, Winkle," she said.

"No, I go back more often here," said Winkle.

Mary smiled. Why, yes, of course. The frontiers would move closer in a place like this. One was apt to forget that an increase of power upon the one side meant a corresponding increase of power upon the other. What waves of light there must be washing against all the dirty walls of all dark strongholds, what power, gentle, inexorable and undefeatable, an ocean of power and patience. If it was hard to abide its time it should not be hard to trust its power, and Mary's heart sang within her.

A bell rang.

"That's drill," said Winkle, and pulled Mary to the door, for she loved drill. Mary took drill, out of doors by the willow tree when it was fine. The whole school loved drill. They went down the passage together and met Miss Giles coming out of her class room with the rest of the school. Mary noticed that Margary Wentworth was looking as no child should look, and that Miss Giles was looking even worse, but she had no time to do more than wonder briefly what the one had done to the other before Miss Giles was upon her.

"You have punished Henrietta, Miss O'Hara?" Miss Giles disapproved of nicknames. She was the only person at Oaklands who called Winkle Henrietta.

Mary's very white skin flushed scarlet with mounting anger and shame. Miss Giles had no right to question her in front of the children, yet on the other hand she had told Miss Giles that she would punish Winkle, and she should have at least explained to the child that the other country must be journeyed to in playtime only. The apportioning of different activities to appropriate moments was one of the disciplines of life, and she was not teaching it to Winkle. It must be hard even for the holiest and most disciplined of nuns to leave off praying when the dinner bell rang, and harder still to start praying again after dinner when they didn't feel that way, but Winkle must learn. And she herself must learn not to commit herself impulsively to a course of action which it might not be advisable afterwards to carry out. She was always doing that. The Irish did.

"Winkle," she said desperately. "Go to Mrs. Belling."

"Miss drill?" whispered Winkle, stricken.

"Yes," whispered Mary, still more stricken. Trying to be fair to Miss Giles she was not now being fair to Winkle. Life was dreadfully difficult. Her hand tightened lovingly and remorsefully on Winkle's, and then withdrew itself. Winkle sighed, turned and went slowly away. She looked a desolate little object, trailing down the passage towards that hateful room of Mrs. Belling's, and unaccustomed tears came into Mary's eyes. "Fool," she said to herself. "It's the tooth. The world seems so abominably wicked when a tooth is still in and so dreadfully pathetic when a tooth's just out. I expect the only really balanced people are the people with dentures."

"Now come along, children," she said, and with the tears glittering on her fabulously long eyelashes she reached blindly for Margary's cold hand and holding it closely and warmly headed the procession to the garden door.

Miss Giles, left alone, felt bitterly frustrated. Margary had been wrested from her and Henrietta punished quite inadequately. Yet she could not complain. Margary had to be drilled at this hour, and Mrs. Belling had been the only punishment she herself had been able to think of for Patricia on the spur of the moment. The oldest and youngest of the Wentworth children were difficult to punish. Margary, thank heaven, was easier. She went slowly to her room. She must take a couple of aspirins and then lie down, for her head was worse than ever.

4

PAT was still in the drawing room for Mrs. Belling had asked her to hold her wool for her, and as Mrs. Belling wound very slowly indeed, and had a great deal of wool to wind, they were still at it. Lazy though Mrs. Belling was, she did knit. It was practically the only thing she did do, besides eating and sleeping, and reading a chapter of her Bible every day. And surprisingly, for she was an entirely selfish woman, she knitted for the poor. Like the daily chapter it had been part of the original pose and was now as much a part of Mrs. Belling as her soft white hands and china blue eyes. Mrs. Belling was a very sweet woman and had been a very beautiful one. She had no idea at all that seventy years and the addition of a great deal of weight to her originally slim figure had robbed her of her beauty, and her conviction that she was still lovely enabled her to retain the airs and graces, the self assurance of a consciously lovely woman, and had its effect on those who were with her. They tended to see her as she saw herself and to be as captivated by her as she was captivated by herself. That is, for a short time. To see more of Mrs. Belling was to be less attracted to her. To see a great deal of her was not to be attracted at all. But there were few people who actively disliked her. They merely thought her negligible.

Fifty years ago she had married the Silverbridge solicitor, a dashing young man with a fine house by the river and apparently considerable wealth. She had been one of a large family, the daughter of a hard-working Irish doctor. She had known hardship in her youth and had hated it. Then at eighteen she had come to England as a nursery governess and had been segregated on the top floor of a country house with her small charges, and had hated that. She was not fond of teaching, and knowing herself to be far more beautiful than any of the women who enjoyed themselves and their jewels on the floors below she had resented her seclusion with bitterness. But she had had her wits about her in those days, and had known how to make good use of a chance meeting with Edward Belling when he came to the house to supervise some alteration to a will. He was able to give her what she wanted and in return she graced his fine house with her beauty, charmed his guests, wore the expensive dresses he gave her with great elegance, and made herself agreeable to him personally with no diminution of her smiling sweetness for four prosperous years. Then he died, leaving her the house by the river and all his debts. Stricken and lovely in her widows' weeds she was for a short while utterly prostrated by her anger, for her sense of property was very strong. Death had removed her husband and now poverty seemed likely to remove her home. She wept with rage in private and appeared in public most movingly pallid and red-eyed. So pathetic was she that all her husband's friends rallied round her and the debts were paid. She pulled herself together and wondered what to do for the best. She had no intention of leaving her charming house, in which she had made herself extremely comfortable. She did not want to marry again, for she had found even an indulgent husband exacting in his demands upon her time and attention, and a less indulgent one would be more so. Also she had had one child, born dead, and she did not want to repeat a process which she had found disagreeable.

In this dilemma it occurred to her to stay where she was and open a school for the little girls of the élite of Silverbridge. It was true that she disliked teaching, and indeed exertion of any kind, but if she could make a success of her venture she would be able to employ teachers and gradually delegate to them the tasks she disliked herself. Everything worked according to plan. She and her husband had always been regular church-goers at eleven o'clock matins, because it had been her husband's correct belief that a solicitor praying into his top hat Sunday by Sunday, with a beautiful and devout wife by his side in white kid gloves, was a sight to inspire trust in prospective clients, and so it had been her good fortune to awaken trust as well as pity and admiration in the breasts of Silverbridge churchgoers. They gave their little daughters to her care without a shadow of hesi-tation and her school grew and flourished. Able business men, parents of her pupils, touched by her lonely plight, invested her earnings for her with great skill and she became very comfort-ably off. Oaklands acquired an enviable reputation in Silver-bridge and after forty-five years, even though it was declining now both in numbers and prosperity, it still retained it, as the scent of a rose still clings to it after the petals have begun to fall. Parents knew it was old-fashioned but Mrs. Belling was so charming, with her white hair and blue eyes, that they did not doubt that her influence upon the children was everything that could be wished. And she only took small girls. Boarding school later would correct any deficiencies in educational methods. The atmosphere at Oaklands must be excellent. How could it be otherwise with that sweet old lady at the head?

But the scent of a dying rose becomes at last tinged with the smell of decay and so had the atmosphere of Oaklands, emanat-ing as it did from the extraordinarily strong personality of Mrs. Belling. For beneath her sweetness and gentleness she had always been strong, in her youth determined in appropriation, and now in her age just as determined in relinquishment. It was not easy to realize that strength could exist enclosed in such fatness and flabbiness, such laziness and self indulgence, and hardly anyone did realize it; apart from a few of the children, and their unconscious knowledge showed itself only as a curious shrinking from Mrs. Belling's sweetness. Even Mary, intuitive as she was, at present regarded her aunt as less dangerous to the children's well-being than Miss Giles with her cruel tongue.

Mrs. Belling's present state of torpor had not crept upon her unawares but had been deliberately willed by herself. This condition in which she merely sat and everything she wanted came to her without any effort on her part was what she had always wanted. Comfort had always been her god and to achieve union with what she wanted she had in her earlier days been willing to work hard, heartily though she loathed work. Now it was no longer necessary. Opposite the armchair where she sat was a cabinet and on top of it a porcelain figure of the Chinese god of plenty, brought back from the East long ago by her sailor father-in-law. He sat cross-legged, obese and horrible, his flowered robe dropped to expose his bare stomach with its rolls of fat, his half-moon of a face with its slits of eyes smiling at her with unholy glee. She did not know whom the figure was supposed to represent, and had never bothered to find out, but to her he represented that which she possessed, and sitting in her comfortable chair, beside her warm fire, she sometimes smiled back at him by the hour. She had never known the emotion of love, but the sense of pleasurable possession of a source of satisfactory supply which she mistook for love she felt in his presence almost as strongly as she had once felt it in her husband's. She gloried in her god with its own unholy glee and from her laughter the rot had spread. In her warm musty-smelling bedroom, so thickly carpeted and curtained, snuggled down in her feather bed beneath her pink eiderdown, she was visited by no fears in the dark hours, for in spite of the daily chapter, in spite of her past churchgoing activities in white kid gloves and her present ones in grey suede, she remained entirely unaware that this world has frontiers.

"Thank you, dear," she said sweetly to Pat as they finished a skein and rested after their frightful exertions. "Have another chocolate, darling, and give another to Baba."

Pat gave one to the little Pekinese and took another herself, because any chocolate is better than none, but she did not really like Mrs. Belling's chocolates. They never had hard insides and Pat liked confectionery with a good crunch to it or alternatively with good staying power. Mrs. Belling's sweets were scented and squashy like herself. Pat found that she finished one of them quickly, and then wanted another, even though she was feeling slightly sick from the first. Mrs. Belling never seemed to feel sick, and she had eaten five chocolates to Pat's three during the last twenty minutes.

"Just one more skein, dear," said Mrs. Belling.

Pat straightened herself, feeling very odd. It was partly the heat of the room, she thought. Mrs. Belling had as big a fire as though it were the middle of winter, and the windows were closed. Pat was not herself one of the children who shrank from Mrs. Belling, she just thought she was a silly old thing, but she did dislike Mrs. Belling's room. She had her mother's love of the beautiful and she did not like the pink brocade curtains; they were too pink, and not clean either, and neither were the chair covers. The patches of wallpaper that could be seen between the anemic water colors in chipped gilt frames that crowded the walls were faded and dirty, and Pat felt quite sure that behind the pictures there were cobwebs. The flowers in the vases were dead as usual and Baba on the hearthrug was much too fat. Pat had a sudden wave of nostalgia for the cold austerity of the vicarage and her mother's lofty drawing room with its sea green curtains. Going home, only a few hours away, seemed suddenly to be at the other end of time.

"I *do* feel odd," she thought.

But mercifully her attention was distracted by a knock on the door, and Winkle came in. Winkle so disliked Mrs. Belling that it took all the will power she possessed to shut the door behind her and advance to her chair. Her dislike dated from the day when she had been with Mrs. Belling in the drawing room and Baba had brought in a live mole from the garden and tormented it upon the carpet, and Mrs. Belling had laughed.

73

"What have you done dear?" said Mrs. Belling languidly. She had no desire for an answer, and Winkle gave her none. All her pupils understood that her question was rhetorical and that she would have been very much annoyed if they had answered her. The way her staff sent her naughty children to deal with might have been a nuisance to Mrs. Belling, but by not dealing with them she avoided the nuisance. She did not object to the children in themselves for her hidden strength of will had always made her able to command their obedience.

"Brush and comb Baba, darling," she commanded.

Winkle brushed and combed Baba with reluctance, for she always thought of him as a part of Mrs. Belling. In his obesity, his laziness, his indifference to the suffering of moles, he was so very like her that it was a natural mistake to make. But today, possessed as she was of the extra awareness that was always hers when she had been back to the other country, he seemed under her hands to detach himself from Mrs. Belling. Not that he moved. He lay quite still, not complaining at all when the brush bumped him on the nose and the comb got tangled in his fur, just panting patiently in the heat of the fire and looking up affectionately at Winkle out of his great goggle eyes. They would have been beautiful eyes, Winkle realized suddenly, if they had been set back in his head in a proper manner, for they were as dark and soft as those of Walsingham, Great-Aunt Maria's dog. And it was not his fault if they goggled. And perhaps it was not his fault about the mole. Orlando was the same with birds. Cats and dogs were made that way and she hated what they did but not them. Perhaps he would not have been such a long time over the mole if Mrs. Belling had not been enjoying what he did. And if he was fat and lazy perhaps that was because Mrs. Belling let him have all the chocolates he wanted and did not take him for walks. He was like her because he had to be. Dogs were always at the mercy of the sort of people their owners were. Baba would not have been like this if mother had had him.

74

Winkle sat back on her heels and looked at him with attention. He was pale golden brown with a white waistcoat, and the golden brown part of him was the color of an acorn and the waistcoat was as soft as the inside of a chestnut case. But there was not the gloss on his coat that there should have been and his plume of a tail was ragged. Winkle stroked one of his ears gently and then pulled her hand away because it was so hot. Her arm tingled to the elbow with quick awareness of something wrong there, but she lacked courage to lift up the flap and look. Mother would have looked. Mother would have known what was wrong. Mrs. Belling seemed not even to know there was anything wrong.

Winkle turned round on the floor and looked at Mrs. Belling, absorbed in winding her wool. People said she had a sweet face and certainly it was white and plump, but Winkle thought that if she pushed her finger into it there would be a permanent dent, like in dough. It was dead-looking like dough, and a very faint dead sort of smell came from her dress, that had stains on the front half hidden by the pretty scarf Mrs. Belling wore round her neck, and from her curly white hair that somehow did not look as white as it ought to have looked. Mrs. Belling used plenty of violet scent, but it did not quite disguise the other, and though in Miss O'Hara's room Winkle had thought the smell of violets the loveliest in the world it seemed horrible here because fresh violets were not what Mrs. Belling really smelled of. It was a sham smell. And Mrs. Belling's way of loving Baba was a sham way. And shams were—Winkle did not quite know what they were and did not want to know, because the smell of them was enough for her, but suddenly the heat of the room overpowered her and she wanted to scream. She grabbed Baba and raced to the French window that opened into the garden. But it was firmly closed and with the dog in her arms she could not get it unlatched. She began to tug at it and to sob, making queer breathless sounds that were more like some small animal behind bars than a little girl trying to get out of a French

75

window. Pat ran after them, opened it, set the two of them free and closed it again.

"Was poor little Winkle going to be sick?" enquired Mrs. Belling placidly.

"Yes," said Pat, going back and picking up the wool.

"But she has taken Baba!" exclaimed Mrs. Belling, suddenly aware of this fact.

"Only out into the garden," said Pat.

"Pat, fetch Baba back to me at once," said Mrs. Belling. She showed no agitation, for it was always too much trouble to be agitated, but she had never at any time allowed any personal possessions to be removed from her against her will, except only that one removal of her husband by death; and when she thought of that she still, after all these years, boiled with resentment deep within her sham serenity. But Winkle was not death and Baba must return at once.

"At once. Do as I tell you, Pat."

She did not raise her soft voice but the sweetness had gone out of it. Pat had not realized before how entirely they all obeyed Mrs. Belling, but she realized it now. It was as though an iron hand had picked her up and put her by the French window. She opened it and ran across the lawn towards the willow tree, where the drilling class had come to an abrupt end and Miss O'Hara and the children were gathered around Winkle, sobbing with Baba in her arms.

"What is it?" Mary was asking. "What is it, Winkle?"

"She shan't have him," sobbed Winkle. "Mother's going to have him."

"Who shan't have him?" asked Mary. She had never seen the placid Winkle in such a state. The sobs were now developing into angry roars, and it was as alarming as though the gentle willow tree had suddenly spouted flames.

"Mrs. Belling," roared Winkle. "She shan't have Baba."

Pat arrived upon the scene with two long leaps. "Winkle, let go," she ordered. "Baba is Mrs. Belling's, not yours. She wants him back. Give him to me at once."

"I won't," yelled Winkle. "I'm taking him home."

"Miss O'Hara, tell her to give him to me," said Pat. "Mrs. Belling sent me to fetch him."

"Winkle, give Baba to Pat," commanded Mary, but without her usual crisp authority, for she hated commanding a child in a situation she did not understand.

"No," yelled Winkle. "His ears are hot."

Baba panted and struggled, for though he liked Winkle the grip of her arms was asphyxiating and he wanted to get down. With a final heave he freed himself and rolled over and over luxuriously on the cool grass. Mary bent over him, looked in his ears and gave an exclamation of anger. Then she picked him up and ran to the French window, burst in upon Mrs. Belling and shut it behind her. Winkle, she realized upon looking round, had bolted roaring into the willow tree and the class was entirely disintegrated. She opened the window for a moment to call out, "Pat, drill them," and then addressed herself to Mrs. Belling.

"Aunt Rose, Baba has eczema in his ears. He's got it very badly."

"It is not as a veterinarian that I engaged you, Mary," said Mrs. Belling with extreme sweetness.

"Look, he's got it everywhere. Aunt Rose, didn't you know?"

"No, darling, I didn't," said Mrs. Belling with increasing sweetness.

"But didn't you see him scratching and shaking his head?"

"Put that dog down before the fire," said Mrs. Belling.

"You did see him, and you didn't bother to look," flashed Mary. "I must take him to the vet. There is just time before lunch."

"No, dear," said Mrs. Belling. "I will send for the vet myself if I think it necessary. While you remain with me you will attend to the duties for which I pay you. Put Baba down and go back to your class."

77

Mary did as she was told. Aunt Rose was absolutely right, of course, for she should not have left her class. She had lost both her temper and her head. But as she slowly crossed the lawn she realized she was returning to her duty not because it was her duty but because she could not help herself. For the first time she felt frightened by her aunt's compelling power, and as she disposed her class for drill again she felt too shaken to make any comment either upon the silence that had succeeded the roars within the willow tree or upon the fact that Margary too had now disappeared.

2

Neither child was at dinner but Mrs. Belling was unaware of the fact because she did not attend school dinner. Special food had to be cooked for a digestion that might have been delicate if not nourished on soufflé and it was nicer for her to eat it in private. Miss Giles did not know either for by this time she had such an appalling migraine that she was unaware of anything but the necessity of controlling her pain sufficiently to do her duty, in this case the dealing round of mutton stew and boiled potatoes that she could scarcely see, so blinding was the migraine. Mary made no comment upon the absence of Margary and Winkle, nor did the children. They just applied themselves sorrowfully to mutton stew.

Annie cooked so badly that it might almost be said that she had a genius for abominable cookery. Her stews were full of fat and as anything she served was always lukewarm, part of the fat quickly congealed on top of the stew. Miss Giles never removed the lid of fat and dived beneath it but apportioned it out fairly between everybody; even to herself on non-migraine days, for she never shirked. Not that it would have done much good if it had been removed, because somehow that fat seemed to go right down to the bottom of the stew and to saturate the vegetables and gristly meat. The boiled potatoes were grey and soapy looking. Upon the side table corn-flour moulds as hard as tombstones awaited them for a second course, together with dishes of stewed prunes of an inconceivable toughness. It was odd about Annie's cooking. She must have been a good cook once, because she had come to Oaklands when Mrs. Belling was a bride and had cooked for her dinner parties, and she could still make delicious things for Mrs. Belling's private meals... The stews and moulds were all Aunt Rose's fault, Mary thought suddenly. Such was her power that if she had wanted the school to have decent meals, the school would have had them.

The atmosphere of the dining room was unusual today. Usually the little girls ate scourged on by the lash of Miss Giles's tongue, but today it was obvious that the yellow faced woman at the head of the table would not know what they did. They would be able to hide bits of fat under their knives and forks and get away with it. But at the other end of the table was Mary O'Hara with her flaming red hair and her blue eyes flashing fire at them. She said nothing, only applied herself to her own nauseating plateful with apparent zest, but even the smallest child understood. They would be mean skunks if they took advantage of Miss Giles's inability to see what they were doing to do what she wouldn't approve of. They hated her but they knew she was game. They ate silently and desperately, and Pat, who had the kind of gallantry that in a man might have won her the Victoria Cross, asked for a second helping. Annie, removing the plates, was surprised at the almost scoured appearance of each one of them. Mary relaxed and smiled. Each child might have worn the white disc of her plate as a halo, she thought. Then the tombstones and prunes arrived, and her eyes and the rebracing of her shoulders nerved them afresh for the final effort. For some it was even more difficult than the first course, the tombstones were so very hard and so very sticky. The swallows were audible, especially from the boarders, six little Anglo-Indian children who lived always at Oaklands and had to face up to Annie's cooking at breakfast and supper as well as dinner.

Miss Giles held to the arms of the chair and her knuckles were white.

"She's brave," thought Mary. "No other woman would have come down to dinner at all. But she knows I have no sense of discipline. She has, both for herself and the children. And of duty. But she's a cruel woman and more to blame than Aunt Rose for all that is wrong in this place." Yet though Mary was at the moment quite sure she was right she was aware that nothing was wrong in this room just now, there was nothing here to frighten her like the strength that had moved her body and her will in Mrs. Belling's room. And as for the little girls, they had been angels. As they got to their feet to say grace she decided that on the whole, though it had been unusually horrible, it had been a good dinner and a quite resounding victory for the forces of light.

Miss Giles said grace in a clear voice that had most surprisingly a sudden timbre of beauty in it, but Mary realized it was the last thing even she could do and took it upon herself to give commands for the afternoon.

"Miss Giles has a headache and so I'm taking English Literature for all of you this afternoon," she said. "Pat, take them to have their rest in the hall and then come to me in my room when I ring the bell. Pat, lead out."

Pat led out and Miss Giles abruptly disappeared. While the children lay flat on their backs in the hall, to assist the processes of digestion, Mary had ten minutes in which to deal with the two little girls under the willow tree. She raced up the back stairs to her bedroom and took from her drawer a tin of biscuits and a box of chocolates, then remembering Miss Giles's admirable sense of discipline she put back the box of chocolates; for really they were very naughty little girls and when she had fed them she must scold them. Then she went to the larder and fetched two mugs of milk and with them and the biscuits on a tray went out to the willow tree.

It was a fresh, fair world under the weeping willow. The arching branches touched the grass all the way round so that one was enclosed in a dome of beauty, and the light of the grey day shining through the golden-green new leaves was the light of another world. It seemed to Mary to be a many colored light, silver and green and gold, with the mauve and blue of the crocuses and scillas in the grass caught up into it. Words of great poetry shone in her mind.

> Life, like a dome of many-colored glass,
> Stains the white radiance of Eternity.

But here the dome sheltered a microcosm of existence, a world small as a drop of sun-shot water swinging high upon a tree, so fragile that it might disappear at any moment, but lifted up so high on the tree that it was as near the white radiance as a world could be. Mary felt as though Oaklands was no more than a point of darkness in shadows far below.

> Heaven's light for ever shines, Earth's shadows fly.

The words drifted like feathers from the wings of the bird that sang in the tree, down and down. She could not remember any more, but that was enough to comfort the poor woman down below. "In heaven their angels do always behold..." Each child in his own world of memory swinging on the highest branches of the tree, seeing still a faint shadow of what his angels see, trying to get back to the light that is so near. Each man, each woman, in his own world of lonely experience swinging upon the gaunt lower branches, seeing nothing, remembering nothing, yet possessing the light in apparent darkness and returning to it as surely as the drops of water are drawn in vapor towards the sun. If it were possible to escape from lonely experience for a moment and stand back from the tree one would see the myriad bright worlds sparkling upon it. But only the greatest could do that. For all but the greatest their own experience was a prison house until the ending of the days. But one could know how bright was the light that carried all souls back to the light when for a moment one entered the world of a child. And how clearly one could hear the bird singing!

"This morning it was a dove," said Winkle. "This afternoon it's a thrush."

"A stormcock," said Margary gently. "There's a storm coming, Harriet said."

Mary looked up and there he was just above her. Through a break in the new leaves she could see him, as through a window. She had never been so near to him before and she caught her breath as she met his fierce bright eye and saw the light rippling down his magnificent speckled breast. He lifted the strong greyish wings and she saw them lined with white, the outside tail feathers tipped with snow. He sang a stave of his song and she thought of a crimson banner unfurling. He was courage itself; a spirit singing.

"Dove, stormcock, lark or linnet, nightingale or swan," she thought. "The Seraph has so many feathers in his wings."

"Winkle and I are here together," said Margary, as though this was delightful but somehow surprising.

"And I am here," said Mary.

The fact that it was the three of them, and not one in the loneliness of uncommunicable experience, was something so strange and wonderful that it made Mary's heart beat with that same thrilling delight that was hers when she heard great music. "I may not hear this again. This may not happen again. This is given to me. To me, a sinner."

She set the tray on the grass, between a clump of crocuses and a clump of scillas, and sat down. Around her the long graceful branches of the weeping willow, the Salix Babylonica, whispered and swayed, for a small fresh breeze had come into the garden. "By the waters of Babylon we sat down and wept, when we remembered thee, O Zion." But in this remembering there was no sorrow, and overhead the stormcock was singing one of the songs of Zion at the top of his voice. She was glad to see that she had put a traycloth on the tray and had chosen pretty mugs for the milk, little old pink and blue mugs with gold handles, and that her biscuit tin had flowers on the lid, for only a dainty feast was suitable to this fresh green place. But she was glad she had decided against the chocolates, for somehow they were not suitable.

> For he on honeydew hath fed,
> And drunk the milk of paradise.

Crisp, sweet ginger biscuits were not out of place, but not chocolates that reminded one of Aunt Rose... Aunt Rose... She seemed so far away that it was almost as though she had no existence. Yet Miss Giles in the shadows seemed not far.

She looked at the children's faces, smiling at her as they reached for their mugs of milk. Margary, whom she had last seen white and fear-stricken, had color in her cheeks now and her eyes shone. What astonishingly beautiful eyes she had, not sparkling when she was happy, like Winkle's, but full of tranquil light. Winkle's face, puce with rage a short time ago, had now resumed its normal rosiness and it was obvious that if Winkle had ever had a care she had forgotten it. Care, for Winkle, was as far off as was Aunt Rose from Mary and fear from Margary. Such things had no existence here. And neither had time. The children ate their biscuits and drank their milk, and the stormcock sang, and Mary thought, "I will remember about this rainbow place. When my own particular experience seems dark and hard I'll remember that it's really a shining thing holding like a flower to the branches of the tree, and that I travel in it, like Cinderella in her coach, to the ending of the days. And up above me in the tree the Seraph sings, and sometimes he sings peace for us and sometimes courage, praise, truth, love, death, but he is always the same Seraph. Who is he? On

83

Mount Alverno Saint Francis saw a great crucified Seraph above him, filling the heavens. I'll remember."

"How nice it is, missing English Literature," said Winkle, who was not an intellectual child.

Her remark brought them all floating down to earth and Mary jumped to her feet. "Of all the useless schools!" she thought. "The whole staff incapacitated by laziness, headache or phantasmagoria, and no one left to teach the children but the sparrows under the eaves."

Yet as she put the mugs on the tray, and pulled Winkle ruthlessly to her feet, she knew it had not been phantasmagoria; but having regard to the failings of herself and her colleagues she thought there was a good deal to be said for the sparrows. They did at least persevere in passing those remarks to which it appeared to be their vocation to give utterance.

"Must we go in?" asked Margary.

"Yes," said Mary. "We are only given times like these so that we can go back again. Come along." And she parted the trailing branches of the willow and led the way out.

"I don't like lessons very much," whispered Margary, and looking at her as they crossed the lawn Mary saw that the color had gone from her cheeks and the tranquil light from her eyes, and her heart swelled with rage. That woman!

"*I'm* taking English Literature this afternoon," she said fiercely. Then she looked at her watch and for a moment stood still in horror. "No, I'm not," she said. "At least not for long. In another ten minutes it will be time for you to go home." It had seemed only a moment of time under the willow tree, but it had been a great many moments.

At the garden door they were met by Pat, reproachful but self-satisfied and quite mistress of the occasion.

"We have started English Literature," she said. "I am teaching them."

"Thank you, Pat," said Mary weakly. "What are you teaching them?"

84

"I am telling them the story of Cinderella," said Pat.

"You couldn't tell them a better story," said Mary. "Go on with it. I have just time to run up and see how Miss Giles is feeling before the period ends."

4

She went into the kitchen to make tea for Miss Giles. There was just one thing to be said for Annie, and that was that she always seemed to have a kettle near the boil. "Not that one fancies even a cup of tea out of this kitchen," thought Mary, regarding with revulsion the grease in the sink and the pile of unwashed saucepans on the dirty floor. "Cleanliness is next to godliness is an old wives' saying but there's a lot in it. It wouldn't surprise me if one slid down the road to hell all the quicker if it's slimy with grease; kitchen grease and the grease of an un-washed skin." Averting her eyes from the saucepans she saw Annie slumped in the kitchen armchair, asleep with her mouth open while she waited for the arrival of the woman who helped her with the washing-up. With her down-at-heel shoes, her un-corseted figure and her personal uncleanliness she was not a pretty sight, and while the kettle came to the boil Mary averted her eyes again and looked out of the window at the gooseberry bushes. Their sturdiness and prickliness were reassuring. One could not slide anywhere on gooseberry bushes. She began to think about Annie again. "When she came to Aunt Rose she must have been young and pretty and clean, and now she is as horrid as the kitchen. Has this happened to her and the kitchen because she has lived with Aunt Rose for so long? Could it happen to me?" The kettle came to the boil and she was glad to have her thoughts deflected to Giles and her tea.

John, so ashamed of the contemptible small battles in which his weakness daily involved him, would have been encouraged if he could have seen the strong-minded Mary brought to a standstill in the passage leading to Miss Giles's room, with the

85

tea tray on the window sill and her hands over her face, while she fought her detestable, detested, uncharitable loathing of sickness in unattractive people in no way related to her. "You hateful woman, aren't you a doctor's daughter?" she admonished herself. "You loathsome reptile, do you call yourself a Christian? Do you or don't you? Yes, but she is so horrid when she's ill. I can't go in. Besides, I'm sure she doesn't want me. I'm sure she dislikes me as much as I dislike her. And why should I be kind to her when she is so cruel to the children? Why cannot Margary's parents see that the child is being hurt by somebody or something? Why are parents always such fools? The tea is getting cold. No, it isn't, for I've put a cosy over the pot. I'm sure she doesn't want me. What's that? You say I saw her down in the shadows when I was so happy swinging up above her in that shining world? Did I? I'd forgotten. I expect I only imagined it. I hate her. I hate sick people, unless they are people I love, and even then I am not so keen on them when they are ill as when they are well. I can't go in and it's not a bit of good you telling me I can. And who are you, anyway? Yes, I know she seemed near when I was under the willow tree. You needn't keep reminding me. Mary O'Hara, once and for all, are you carrying this tray into that room or are you not? I hate her. Very well then, hate her, but carry that tray into that room or damn your soul in hell for ever. Please, may I come in?"

There was no answer to her knock and she went in. After the heat of Annie's kitchen the chilliness of Miss Giles's room came upon her with the shock of a cold shower; and she was reproached by its extreme tidiness. If she had gone to bed with a shocking headache she would have kicked her shoes anywhere, dropped her skirt on the floor and flung herself on the pillows with complete abandon. But Miss Giles had folded her skirt on a chair, placed her shoes side by side and covered herself with a carefully darned grey woollen shawl. She had partly drawn her curtains and her room was dim; though in any case the one small window only looked out upon the wall of the next-door house. She lay with her face to the wall and made no sign of recognition as Mary came up to her and put the tray on her bedside table.

"Giles, I've brought you some tea."

"I don't want it," said Miss Giles rudely.

"It will do you good," said Mary. "Take two aspirins with it. My father says aspirins do much more good if you take them with a cup of tea."

"Nothing does me any good," snapped Miss Giles. "Why can't you let me alone? Did I ask you to come fussing here? Take the tray away."

With her cheeks scarlet Mary sat down on the bed, her temper as flaming as her hair. "What was the good of sending me in here?" she demanded silently of whoever it was. "Just look at us. We'll murder each other in a minute or two, and then where shall we be? But I'm darned if I'll be driven away by her vile temper. Here I sit till she takes those two aspirins."

She sat, looking round the room. It was so bare, so utterly unlike her own. No pretty things on the dressing table. Not even a powder bowl. Didn't she ever powder her nose? No photographs. Hadn't Giles got any family? Hadn't she any friends even? Didn't anybody ever give her anything, a pretty dressing jacket or nightdress case or something? Just the old grey darned shawl over her. But how spotless the room was. "You couldn't say that of mine," thought Mary, her anger beginning to evaporate. "I don't go in for all this spit and polish. Of the two of us she is less likely to end up a slut like Annie than I am. She's disciplined and I'm not. I could be a slut. Yes, I could. I could be cruel too. I am. Look at me sitting here in a temper trying to force the poor wretch to drink tea she doesn't want. Mary, Mother of God, have mercy upon all women, for all women are beasts underneath excepting only you."

She got off the bed and picked up the tray. "I'm sorry," she said gently. "I'm going away and leaving you in peace. But I'm sorry."

Gasping with the pain the movement gave her Miss Giles turned over and opened her eyes. In the changed voice there was some compulsion that she was not able to disobey. It was Mary's voice yet it had in it a depth of compassion far beyond this Mary's capacity.

"I will do as you say," she murmured, and did not know to whom she spoke.

Astonished, Mary put the tray down again, poured out a cup of tea, took two aspirins from the bottle beside the bed and helped Miss Giles to hold the cup while she drank and swallowed them. Even with the cosy the tea was by this time lukewarm and Miss Giles had a moment of panic lest she be sick. "Don't let me be sick," she prayed. She had not prayed for years and to whom was she praying now? She had lost her faith long ago. And what a ridiculous prayer. She shut her eyes, fighting down the nausea. Then she opened them again and found Mary was once more sitting on her bed. In the dim room she could not see the girl's face very well but she could see her hair, touched by a beam of light that shone through the chink in the curtains. It looked like curling red-gold feathers. Before Mary had come, when the pain had been at its worst, she had had a queer delusion that a few bright feathers had come floating down upon her bed. After that she had slept for a few minutes. What was this gold-crested creature sitting so patiently on her bed, a cock, or what? "Patience fills His crisp combs." Ridiculous the way poets were always using the birds as types of different aspects of divinity. If they were so silly as to believe in divinity at least you would think they would express their idiocy under more fitting symbols than doves and swans and cocks and what not.

"I believe I'm going to sleep," she murmured.

"That's the aspirins working," said Mary. "I'll go now."

"Thank you for the tea," said Miss Giles, raising herself a little. She was not an attractive sight as she turned her face towards Mary, with scarlet blotches on her sallow skin and her straight grey hair in wisps about her face, but her bitter down-

88

turned mouth had a suspicion of a smile about it and Mary smiled broadly back. Miss Giles's ugliness, and the rather aggressive health of Mary's hearty smile, were veiled by the dimness of the room, so that neither felt repulsed. Instead each felt that strange movement of the spirit that can come when two strangers meet and know they are no longer strangers. Mary picked up the tray and went quickly out of the room and down the stairs. She could hear the church clock striking three as she went down; time for the day girls to put on their things and go home. But there seemed in the striking of the hour more than the ending of the school period. "I've always adored the clock striking," she thought. "I never knew why. And I never knew why some people always pray when the clock strikes. I do now. It's one hour nearer the ending of the days. How incredible it seems that the Seraph should bother with such horrid women as Giles and me."

5

There was a happy chirping in the cloakroom as the children put on their walking shoes. Mary, standing at the door, thought they might have been sparrows, so loud was the chirping and so fulfilled with satisfaction. Perhaps the purpose of sparrows, as of children let out of school, was just to remark loudly and with repetition that in spite of any appearance to the contrary everything is quite all right. If the repetition seemed a little monotonous at times that was one's own fault; in a world where thrushes sing and willow trees are golden in the spring, boredom should have been included among the seven deadly sins.

Pat, Margary and Winkle were the last to leave because Winkle had lost the rear end of a marzipan rabbit, which she thought must have been whisked out of her pocket with her handkerchief (in which she kept it) when last she blew her nose, and it took a long time to run it to earth beneath the radiator in the passage. And as Annie never dusted under the radiator a little more time was lost while Winkle picked a dead

89

spider off the rabbit preparatory to eating it; for it would be best to eat it now, she explained, for fear she should lose it again. "How patient Mrs. Wentworth is today," thought Mary, for usually Daphne came in to fetch the children if she suspected they were dawdling. Mary admired Daphne immensely, and plump and rather obviously pretty as she was herself she envied her her height and grace and beautiful worn face, and the distinction with which she wore her shabby clothes, but she did not think she was a patient woman. It was surprising that she had not come in. But when they came out into the Oaklands drive it was not Daphne who was in the car but John.

"Father! Father!" shouted the three little girls in delight.

"Mummy couldn't leave the Mother's Union tea," explained John.

He opened the door of the car and got out, and Mary, who had not seen him before, watched in delight as his ramshackle length of limb emerged from the ramshackle contraption of a machine that was the vicarage car. Daphne's beauty tended to obliterate the charm of the vicarage car, one saw her and not it, but John and the car were all of a piece, the one the perfect setting for the other. And though neither was an object of beauty they both seemed all of a piece with the gleam of the river behind them and the tall elms beyond, with the willow tree and the song of the thrush and Mary's gay heart and love of life.

This sense of kinship with particular things and people was not new to Mary. As one lived in a place certain things about one, the branches of a tree seen through one's window, certain aspects of the light, a church tower in the distance perhaps, or an old horse browsing in a green field, moved forward from the rest of one's surroundings and became the furniture of one's own private world. One could not part from that particular tree, that old horse, without a sense of personal loss; and from memory they would never be lost. And so with certain people. In a moment of time a woman perhaps known before, perhaps not known, would step forward from the millions of the world, part the branches of the tree and come right in. Or the old horse one day would have a man upon its back, a long angular fellow in dented armor, with a pasteboard visor covering his comical face, and he would not ride away. And so it was fitting that those elms beyond the gleam of water, that Mary could see from her window and would not forget until she died, should now form the boundary of her world as Don Quixote came riding into it.

In a hatless age John clung to a battered felt hat that he had had for a decade because his bald head felt the draughts that blew in through all the gaping cracks in his car. But never, even after years of practice, could he get out of the car without knocking it over his nose. He removed it, saw Mary, and bowed. "He is like a very tall scarecrow," thought Mary, "not at all the knight errant I would have chosen, but one does not choose them, they are sent. He has Margary's eyes. He is a better father than most."

Mary, like all good schoolmistresses, and she was a good schoolmistress in spite of many derelictions of duty, had formed a poor opinion of all parents and this was for her high praise.

"How do you do?" she said severely, for she was always severe with parents. "I am Mary O'Hara, Winkle's form mistress." Then her severity abruptly vanished and she chuckled. "There *are* only two forms," she said, "Miss Giles has the other, and Margary and Pat."

"I have not yet had the pleasure of meeting either of you," said John, standing hat in hand before her and speaking with a humble courtesy that delighted Mary. She was a red-hot radical, and gloried in plebeian birth, but she handed it to these aristocrats. They had something. They might be as poor as church mice, or as comic as Don Quixote, but you knew them by the air of assurance with which they wore their rags, or paradoxically by the almost deprecating courtesy that was the outward sign of an inward grieving that they had been born one of the few and not one of the many whom they loved. There was a third species of the breed, those with wealth but no love, who wore their splendid manners with the same slightly contemptuous arrogance as they wore their splendid clothes, but though her very hair crisped with anger at the sight of them Mary tried to withhold her judgment. She believed the arrogance to be unconscious and she had been told that they died well.

"You have met Mrs. Belling?" asked Mary, and discovered slightly to her surprise that she really wanted to know.

"Yes," said John gently but briefly.

Mary looked at him attentively, for he was the first parent she had talked to who had not commented upon Mrs. Belling's sweetness. "I am her niece," she said, and found that the honest admission cost her something.

"You are not at all like her," said John with the same noncommittal gentleness.

Mary stood looking at the elm trees, and found that Margary and Winkle were one on each side of her and that she was holding their hands rather tightly. Pat had left them and was already inside the car. That was as it should be, for Pat had nearly finished with Oaklands and this did not concern her. She pressed the children's hands warmly for a minute, and then released them, unconsciously holding hers at her sides in closed balls of fists, and standing straight as a spindle, which had always been her habit as a little girl when facing something unpleasant. John saw the attitude and smiled.

"Run and get in the car, kids," he said, and Margary and Winkle did as they were told. "Something wrong?" he asked.

"It's Miss Giles," Mary said breathlessly. "She's not good for Margary."

"In what way?" asked John. The question came out very sharply, and looking at him Mary hastily looked away again, for his blue eyes were probing her with a steely penetration which was as uncomfortable as it was unexpected. She must fix her own eyes on the serene elm trees, or she could never do it.

"She's a cruel woman," she said breathlessly. "She's cruel to Margary, and to others among the children too, but chiefly to Margary. You see, Margary's vulnerable."

"Have you an explanation?" snapped John. His voice had become both hard and hoarse and Mary realized that where his children were concerned he was as vulnerable as Margary.

"She's a sick woman," said Mary. "She suffers a great deal."

"From what disease?" demanded John.

"None," said Mary. "Just dreadful headaches and so on. You know what I mean?"

"Yes," said John grimly. "And she retaliates?"

"Retaliates?" asked Mary, puzzled.

"No one helps her. In such circumstances it is natural to have a grudge against the callousness of the whole human race, and to revenge it upon such as are vulnerable. It's unconscious revenge probably. You and Miss Giles are friends?"

Mary fancied sarcasm in his tone and flushed scarlet. Did he think she was one of those detestable women who delight in running down other women in the presence of a man? Well, it didn't matter what he thought, but sudden anger made her take her eyes from the elms and face him squarely. "Yes. Until ten minutes ago I thought I hated her, but ten minutes ago we became friends." Looking at him she saw he was not sarcastic. She had been a fool to think he could be, for sarcasm doesn't grow on the same stalk as humility. He had really wanted to know. "That sounds odd, I expect, but you know how it happens. Someone you have known perhaps for years, perhaps for minutes, steps forward from the background and is suddenly inside with you."

"Inside what?" demanded John.

"Inside your own little world that you carry with you," said Mary, and looked at him with an almost despairing pleading. Didn't he know he also had stepped inside? "Surely you know what I mean?"

"Yes," said John, and now there was the warmth of amusement in his voice. "You like to be well understood, don't you? And you like to have as many people as possible right inside. Yes, I do know what you mean. It's bad luck that the moment Miss Giles becomes your friends you have to do your best to get her dismissed. I'm sorry."

Mary suddenly discovered that she was crying. She despised tears and was mad with herself. "Damn," she said, feeling savagely for her handkerchief. John took her arm for a moment and turned round, so that she turned too, with her back to the house. The windows looked blank but Oaklands struck him as the sort of place where people peeped from behind curtains. He took his hand from her arm and they strolled together towards the gate and the car. "You did perfectly right," he said. "Loyalty is difficult, isn't it? Loyalties so often conflict. But the children always come first." He paused at the gate and was suddenly uncertain and deeply troubled. "I wish I had your gift of quick decision. Those who have it don't realize what a blessed gift it is. I have no idea, now, what to do about it. Do you believe in prayer?"

"Of course," flashed Mary. "I'm a Roman Catholic," she added belligerently.

"And I'm not," said John, smiling at her vehemence. "But a mutual belief in prayer is almost the greatest bond between two human beings. Don't you think so?"

Mary laughed. "If you are asking me to pray that you may do the right thing over this, well, I will," she conceded graciously.

"Thank you," said John humbly. "And will you come over and see us at Belmaray? It's a pretty place."

"I'm Labor," Mary told him, her head back, the tears still wet on her face.

"And my wife and I are Conservative, and so you won't come and see us," said John sadly. "What a pity."

"Yes, I'll come," said Mary. "I was only warning you."

"Thank you," said John, opening the door of the car. "Sorry

94

to keep you waiting, you three. Good-bye, Miss O'Hara. If you'll give us warning of your coming we'll hang out a red flag in welcome."

He bowed and put on his hat, knocking it off again while inserting his length into the car. He replaced it and peered anxiously at the switchboard, pressing the self-starter as though it was likely to explode a bomb beyond the elm trees. The engine stalled. "I don't drive very well," he said to Mary. "That's why I'm so seldom allowed to fetch the children. Good-bye." He lifted his hat to Mary and pressed the self-starter once more. The car struggled valiantly but remained where it was.

"Poor Rozinante!" giggled Mary. "Did you take the brake off?"

"Rozinante?" queried John in a puzzled tone, and his hat remained in his hand while he searched around in his mind for the origin of the familiar name.

Mary flushed again, for her thought had turned into speech without her knowledge. But she did not evade the issue. "Your car looked so thin and bony, like Don Quixote's horse," she explained. "But being so leftist I like your car. Nothing plutocratic about it."

"Nor about Don Quixote either," said John, and laughed delightedly. "And I hope you will remember that while deploring my politics. And you're quite right. The brake is still on."

He took the brake off, replaced his hat once more that he might lift it to Mary again, pressed the self-starter once more, and they were off.

"I believe that's a very good man," thought Mary, watching Rozinante zigzagging down the road. "Or rather two good men, the mad knight and the man who rapped out those questions like a consulting physician with no time to waste. No, it's not that there are two men but that vulnerability always makes a garment for itself; a jester's cap and bells or a Franciscan's peasant tunic or—something."

She turned round towards the house and saw a slight move-

95

ment of one of the curtains of an upstairs window. "That'll be Annie," she thought resignedly. "Now there'll be trouble." She went slowly towards the house and entered it with distaste and reluctance. It was a horrid house.

5

"WELL, why not?" thought Michael, sitting on a gate at the top of old Mr. Witteringham's orchard. Mr. Witteringham was the landlord of the Wheatsheaf and had just provided him with a gorgeous high tea, sausage and mash, rhubarb pie, strong tea, strawberry jam and new bread, and having an excellent digestion he now had that feeling of happy repletion which encourages optimism. "It's a mad idea but they are all mad here. No harm in trying it on. Why should I ever go back? I'll feed the peacocks and prune the roses until I die."

It was not only good food that had made Michael so optimistic but also Mr. Witteringham's astounding faith in human nature. In a village where the landlord of the local fed you on the fat of the land simply on trust one's outlook on the future became similarly trustful. Michael was unaware that old Mr. Witteringham had in his youth been the Wentworth's gamekeeper and knew expensive clothes when he saw them; likewise the value of a gold watch and signet ring. It was obvious to Mr. Witteringham that the young gent's severance from the source of financial supply, though apparently complete just now, need not be permanent. Even if they had run dry for the moment these young gents nearly always possessed some paternal or avuncular spring at the source. And if not in this case, well, the young man had been seen by Mrs. Witteringham (who saw and heard everything that was done or said in the village, whether present in the corporeal body or not) in intimate conversation with the vicar, and the vicar could be relied on to let no one suffer if he could help it; not even for their own misdeeds; proper tootlish he was.

Meanwhile Michael, saved from hunger by the cut of his coat and John's reputation for benevolence, sat on the gate and surveyed the scene. The Wheatsheaf was at the highest point of the village, and the orchard sloped steeply above it. Below him the old unpruned apple trees were still without blossom, but here and there a plum tree or a cherry tree was a froth of white. In the rough grass under the trees were drifts of wild daffodils, and primroses and white violets were growing under the hedge by the gate. Below the orchard were the tall chimneys and tiled roof of the Wheatsheaf, and to the right the village street with its whitewashed cob cottages wound down the hill to the river and the church. All the cottage gardens had their daffodils and early polyanthus and in the water meadows the kingcups were a sheet of gold. The smoke from the cottage chimneys rose gently, wreathed itself into strange shapes and then was lost in the grey of the sky.

It was a quiet, sleepy day and Michael had slept hardly at all the night before. He nodded, jerked himself awake, and then climbing off the gate sat down in the orchard grass with his back against it. Through a break in the trees he could see the splendid old church porch and the tower rising above it. "That porch might be the gateway of a fortress," he thought sleepily, "with the keep above. It might be the gate of Tintagel from which they rode out to find the grail."

Malory had been his favorite author when he was a boy. His eyelids felt heavy as lead. He shut them and was in that strange borderland country between sleeping and waking. He drifted there for what seemed a long while and then, so he thought, was suddenly awake. A trumpet had sounded. He was alert, attentive, and then spellbound by what he saw. A gaunt old man on a bony white horse had come riding out from the gateway. He rode bareheaded, his hair and pointed beard and the white ruff above the gleam of his breastplate catching the light, so that he and his old horse seemed made of silver. He rode away among the trees and another horseman came after him, and another, and then a young man with the lovelocks of a cavalier, riding gallantly, a scarlet sash worn over one shoulder and across his cuirass. He too rode away and those who followed him seemed shadowy figures to Michael, though he knew they were knights bound upon the same journey as the rest. They passed quickly and as they crossed the road their horses' feet made no sound on the metal surface. Last of all an old monk came out on foot, a twisted old man with a fine fierce face, and shut the door behind him.

With the bang of the door Michael was instantly fully awake, amused yet a little shaken by the startling vividness of the dream. He had always been the victim of absurdly vivid dreams. "Smoke takes strange shapes," he told himself. "It was the smoke started the dream, and remembering Malory. But that grand church is no illusion. And if instead of sitting dreaming here like the lunatic you are you were to get up and walk up that lane, and round that green hill with lambs stuck all over it, that heraldic hill with mutton argent on a field vert, you would find the manor house and the old lady with the rubies in her ears. Come on now, step on it. You have always had what it takes and now you can try out your charms on the old dame. You meant it as a joke? You did then but you don't now. Unscrupulous? Well, so you are. Don't you remember what the judge told you? My God, I will never forget it till I die."

It was the incentive he needed and he was on his feet in a flash, as though a snake had bitten him, and through the other orchard gate that opened on the lane. He strode up it for a minute or two without seeing it, overwhelmed by one of those visitations of misery and fear that often came to him. Beyond his encircling wall of personal experience was such an immensity of darkness, and his wall had always had many cracks. "Look at this place," he told himself. "Look at the wall, not the cracks. Just now it's a good wall. Look at it."

He was in a narrow stony lane with steep banks on either side and a stream running down one side of it beneath the coolness and shade of arching ferns. The banks were clothed with periwinkle, which country people call joy-of-the-ground. The leaves were deep green, so smooth that even on this grey day they reflected the light as though from polished mirrors. The flowers were a pure blue, as cool as the arching green ferns and the sound of the tinkling water. Michael stopped, for the impetus of his shame had spent itself. He stood still and remembered something; what he would have done had he still been a child.

He would have made himself very small and crept under the ferns. They would have arched above him as mightily as the sky, enclosing him so securely in their green world that for a moment or two he would have known the meaning of security. He had been one of those children who can make themselves Tom Thumbs at will. "I'd forgotten that I'd ever done that sort of thing," he thought. "Was that a linnet singing?"

He walked on slowly, trying to recapture memories of childhood's escapes to the smaller worlds. To the world down among the grass stems, where the forests are almost impenetrable and the dragons wear scaly armor. To the world inside a foxglove flower, where you swing at the end of a golden rope and lick at a suspended ball of honey with the tip of your tongue. And then the returns to—somewhere—to which the smaller worlds have each their door. He had forgotten those too until this moment, and now he remembered nothing but that there had been something—the immensity—only in those earliest days it had held no fear.

He kicked angrily at a stone in the path. What was the good of fumbling back after the magical experiences of childhood? They had vanished. What was with him now was the misery of going exhausted to bed and lying awake dreading the years ahead, or waking from nightmare with the first cock-crow and feeling the darkness lying on him with appalling weight, or with the second cock-crow and knowing he could never undo what he had done. Then the fear could be sickening. "Ye know not when the master of the house cometh, at even, or at midnight or at the cock-crowing or in the morning." From what recesses of his memory had that quotation come? The master. What a name to give to those visitations of the darkness. Yet not unsuitable because for most men in these days fear was the master of life.

"Come on," he said to himself, "this isn't these days. This may be escape from these days into a second childhood. Come on round this hill and find the peacocks and the old lady." Yet as he rounded the hill he vaguely remembered a poem he had read somewhere about a man who tried to remove himself from these days by escape to an enchanted island, and when he had got there had found it hell. But he would not find Belmaray hell, for Don Quixote and Mr. Witteringham were not the kind of men one met in hell, and neither was this round green hill with the sheep upon it the landscape of hell.

Far up above him a lark was filling the sky with praise.

2

He rounded the hill and saw the manor house in front of him at the bottom of a sloping field. He climbed upon the gate of the field and sat and stared. It was a timber framed house, small for a manor house but quite perfect, built in the shape of an E, with tall chimneys, and facing south across the river. The steep roof, irregular and stained with red-gold lichen, had dormer windows in it. The big porch which formed the central part of the E, and most of the front of the house, appeared to be covered with wistaria. Behind the house cob walls protected by penthouses of thatch enclosed the kitchen garden and orchard and in front of the house yews surrounded a garden that seemed to slope in terraces towards the river. From where he sat Michael could not see the garden behind the yew hedges, or see how its formal loveliness lost itself in the azaleas and rhododendrons down below, nor how upon the east side the garden looked down upon the church tower, and the churchyard with its drifts of daffodils. He could only guess at these things from where he sat, and he jumped off the gate and strode across the field. The lark was still singing over his head.

As he came nearer Michael became increasingly aware of dilapidation. His conjecture that the roses had not been pruned for a hundred years was going to prove correct. The yew hedges had not been cut for a long time either. They looked like green waves with tossing spray. And three of the manor house windows, that looked westward over the field he was crossing, had lost small diamond panes of glass and been stuffed not with dirty rags, in the old-time fashion of cottage poverty, but with rolled up kid gloves. Upon this west side of the house the field came right up to the wall and he could not only get a good view of the gloves but also see into a lower room. It was a small library entirely lined with books. Michael gave an exclamation of pleasure. They'd have Cervantes there. They'd have Chaucer and Malory, Trollope and Jane, and all the writers in whom he delighted because they wrote of a world in which men did not live on the edge of a volcano, counting out the last minutes before the flames; their laughter while they did it set one's teeth on edge and drove one to do rotten things. "Don't make excuses," Michael said to himself. "You did rotten things because you're a rotten chap."

He swung away from the window and walked on beside the yew hedge that bordered the garden on the west, and was so overgrown and impenetrable that he could see nothing either through it or over it, but he imagined there would be a gate soon. He found it under an arch of yew, a low gate half overgrown with honeysuckle as though it were never opened. Not

wanting to disturb the honeysuckle he did not unlatch it but climbed over.

He surveyed the garden with amazement and delight. There appeared to be no one about and he could stare as he pleased. It had once been laid out in formal parterres of grass and flower beds, and stone paved paths with steps leading terrace by terrace down the slope to the river, and with a queer flicker of imaginative retrospection he saw it as once it had been. He saw the small trim green lawns and beds of mignonette and heliotrope and sops-in-wine, the rose garden with its standard rose trees, like Tenniel's illustrations in *Alice in Wonderland*, the hedges of sweetbriar bordering the paved court and the sundial. For a moment, through the song of the lark, he could hear the bees humming in the mignonette, and smell the flowers and the scent of the new mown grass drawn up by the heat of a summer sun.

The vision passed and he saw a grey day and such ruin that his delight turned to sadness. Yet still there was the scent of flowers, for as he moved forward he found clumps of small purple violets running riot over the edges of the weed-filled flower beds and the mossgrown paths, and there were drifts and pools of daffodils and narcissus in the wild rough grass. The sweetbriar hedges and the standard roses had flung out wild sprays of branches in all directions but they were glowing with new leaves. The plants in the border were not quite buried. The green tide of the weeds and grass had not killed the lupins or peonies, and strong spires of madonna lilies had pushed up, reaching for air and light. There would still be summer sun and scent here in three months' time and the bees would find plenty to do. A garden, once given life, struggles to maintain its life, and there were signs that someone still cared for it. A small stone gazebo looking south down to the river had been kept in repair and in front of it the paved court surrounding the sundial had been swept. The sundial itself had had the moss scraped from the inscription carved upon two sides of the pedestal.

Michael bent down to make out the faint lettering, but after he had read a word or two he found they were two couplets from an Elizabethan poem he knew almost by heart.

> Beauty, strength, youth, are flowers but fading seen;
> Duty, faith, love, are roots, and ever green.
>
> . . . .
>
> Goddess, allow this aged man his right,
> To be your beadsman now that was your knight.

This memorial of another man's faithfulness reproached him, who had not himself been faithful in love, and he left the sundial and walked to the edge of the little court, leaning on the low wall and looking down upon the old church in its trees below. A gull was sitting on one of the battlements of the tower; seen from this distance it might have been a dove. To the right, behind the beech trees, he could see the chimneys of the ugly red brick vicarage. What was Don Quixote doing at this moment, the knight who should have been up here, lord of this garden? Who was the other knight, his ancestor perhaps, whose faithfulness was kept in remembrance on that sundial? Who were these Wentworths? It was a delightful Elizabethan name. He remembered Maistress Margary Wentworth.

> With Marjerain gentle,
> The flower of goodly head.
> Embroider'd the mantle
> Is of your maidenhead.

A rosemary tree grew just on the other side of the old wall where he stood. It had grown to such a size that it was a small tree, not a bush, with a knotted trunk, and big enough to make a hiding place for a child. He picked a few silvery leaves and rubbed them between his fingers. "Pray you, love, remember." Just over the wall there were lavender bushes too, and patches of lemon verbena that had maintained their hold, their roots

104

fast in the earth. "Duty, faith, love, are roots." He had failed in all three.

He walked to the south edge of the little court. Here a flight of worn steps, flanked by broken marble urns, led down to a terrace of grass and from this terrace the steps lost themselves in the slope of a meadow leading down to the river. This field, and the opposite one on the other side, were planted with rhododendrons and azaleas, and so were the river banks upon either side until the river was lost to sight beyond the spur of a hill, and Michael could see only in imagination the silver loops of the Belle Marée winding away through the green hills to the sea. Upon the other side of the river the rhododendrons climbed the steep field until they reached the edge of a larch wood. In another two months the larches would wear their heavenly green above a flaming mass of rose and saffron, crimson and gold. And just there, where the river was lost to sight, would be the waterfall, and the white rhododendron.

Somewhere behind him upon one of the flagged paths he heard the pattering of feet, a strange pattering that sounded like a very old lady walking in pattens. There was a swishing sound too, as though long silken skirts fell from step to step. Michael, his back turned, stood still. She was coming. His heart was beating as ridiculously hard as though he were a lover waiting for his sovereign, his lovely goddess. And he knew most certainly that the coming of this old lady did matter to him as much as all that, perhaps more, for by letting him stay or sending him away she had it in her power to save or damn him. So he believed, and though his power of self-dramatization had led him into disaster time and again it had at other times given him a sure instinct for the moment when he should play the hero for his own advancement. He stood for a moment, visualizing her, the swishing silk dress the same deep ruby as her jewels, her small hand holding it up in front above the pattens, the dark waves of it caressing the stones behind, her peacocks one on each side.

He turned slowly, gracefully, dramatically, ready to bow, and found himself confronting a large white pig. The shock was so great that he bowed to the pig. "Michael Stone, you are the most unutterable ass," he said to himself and bowed again, this time with exaggeration. Then he bowed the third time with real admiration, for it was the most remarkable pig. To his town-bred ignorance a pig was a dirty repulsive brute, and this rosy porcine beauty was a revelation to him of what a pig can be.

"Don't let Josephine go down those steps," called a husky voice.

Recovering from his shock he was aware that the swishing sound continued, and taking his fascinated eyes from the pig he looked up and saw the most peculiar old woman swishing away at the nettles behind the rosemary tree with a stick. "The slope is steep down to the river," she continued. "Remember the Gadarene swine?"

"I often do," Michael called back. "I'm full of devils. Have you a large herd?"

"No," said the old woman. "A small one. But they are not to receive your devils, young man. Far too valuable. I show them. That is why I am exercising Josephine. Keep your devils to yourself if you please. These nettles have got a real hold here. Who are you, by the way? Have you a message?"

"Yes," said Michael desperately. "I'd come and deliver it only Josephine seems anxious to go down these steps."

"Stay where you are," commanded the old woman. "Keep your eye on her and I'll come. Though really you could shout it. There's nobody here but the sundial and it keeps its secrets."

She climbed over the low wall with ease, though Michael perceived her to be of a great age. She stamped her feet on the stones of the terrace, to get the earth off them, and came towards him. She wore a peat brown tweed coat and skirt, pulled out of shape and faded by work and weather, with the skirt reaching only just below her knees, thick brown worsted stockings and a pair of clumping lace-up boots of the type which

106

Michael up to now had seen only in pictures. A battered felt hat was placed well forward over her forehead and skewered into position above the knot of grey hair at the back of her head with a large hat pin that protruded several inches each way. The figure and the headgear, though not the face, reminded him instantly of Tenniel's Red Queen. Her small clawlike hands were grimed with dirt. Yet she herself was delightfully fresh and trim and as she came close to him he could see she wore a blouse of priceless lace, freshly laundered, and that her thick grey hair was carefully brushed and coiled. Her figure was tiny and her little face deeply wrinkled and gipsy-brown, her black eyes keen and sparkling under beautiful arched brows, the sucked in puckered mouth above the nutcracker chin matching it in iron determination. Michael knew that once she had had great beauty; vital and compelling and very sure of itself. Even now the vitality and assurance compelled him. He had meant to practice his charms upon this old lady, but instead he found himself being hooked and landed by her own.

"Well now, young man, what is it?" she asked, but though the husky voice was sharp she seemed in no hurry. She did not belong to a generation that had ever hurried. Her tasks might be herculean but she had all the time there was for whoever came. She took a gold cigarette case from her pocket, offered him one and took one herself. As he lit hers and then his own she watched him not narrowly but with a benevolence that was at the same time both keen and gracious. He realized that she had been in her day the mistress of many servants and the hostess of many guests. It had been her life to extract service and give pleasure with equal competence. Adversity might have made an oddity of her now, as something or other or many things had made an oddity of Don Quixote, but her air of kindly command was still that of the great lady and she wore it, as he wore his air of distinction, with unconscious and disarming grace. As from Don Quixote's manner Michael had been aware of the man's love of souls so in this old lady he was aware of a dedication to social duty that was selfless in its single-mindedness. To her any guest would be sacrosanct.

"Sit down," she said, motioning with her cigarette towards the steps. "If we sit on them Josephine can't go down them. Also I have reached the age when I'd sooner sit than stand. And you yourself, if I may say so, have been so long standing around in my garden that I wonder you have not sat down before. But you're young. Now where's that pig?"

"She's gone into the gazebo," said Michael.

"She can stay there," said the old lady. "She's had her exercise."

"Do you exercise all the pigs?" asked Michael weakly.

"At present," she said. "Bob Hewitt, my man, is sick, and the boy who comes up from the village is not much good. Do you like pigs?"

"My acquaintance with them has never been intimate," said Michael.

"Nothing but pork and a receptacle for devils, you think. There you are wrong. A pig, young man, when properly treated and rightly understood, is one of the most intelligent and lovable of God's creatures."

She was leaning back against one of the urns beside the steps, regarding him shrewdly and kindly, but he could see how tired she looked.

"Mistress Wentworth, I won't keep you," he said humbly and gently. "I have no message. I was simply trespassing."

"Why do you call me Mistress Wentworth?" she asked.

"It should be Mistress Margary Wentworth."

She knew what he was quoting and smiled. "I'm not married," she said. "And I am Maria, not Margary. My great-great-niece is Margary. And why were you trespassing?"

"I was going to ask you to take me on as your gardener," said Michael baldly, stating a fact and exerting no charm.

"Do you know anything about gardening?"

"Very little."

"Then why should I want you for my gardener?"

"I was not thinking about it from your point of view," said Michael.

"And how were you thinking about it from your own?" she asked. "Did you by any chance think this would be a good place to get rid of those devils you spoke of?"

"That's exactly what I did think," said Michael.

"My dear boy, devils are not so easy to get rid of as you seem to imagine."

"I realize that," said Michael.

"How long have you been in Belmaray?" she asked.

"Since this morning."

"Have you met my great-nephew the vicar?"

"Yes."

"Did he suggest that I might take you on as my gardener?"

"No," said Michael. "The suggestion was mine. He thought I was joking. And so I was then. But now, well, I'm not joking." He paused and forced himself on. "Though I don't know much about gardening I could learn," he finished desperately.

"You might, of course, be good with the pigs," she said, considering him. "Are you staying anywhere?"

"I had high tea at the Wheatsheaf."

"You left your luggage there?"

"I haven't any luggage except what's in my pocket, just a tooth brush and so on that I bought yesterday in Silverbridge. I spent last night in Silverbridge."

"And where did you spend the night before that?"

"In prison. I caught the afternoon train from Paddington and left everything I possessed in London."

"Did you possess much?"

"No, not much. A flat and so on. And something in my bank balance. It accumulates while you're in prison."

"So I've heard. But how very odd to leave London without any tooth brush."

"Leaving was a very sudden decision."

109

"So I should imagine. How much of this have you told my great-nephew?"

"None of it. He found me hungry on Pizzle bridge, fetched me breakfast from the farm, and then we walked down the road and talked about your rhododendrons. I like rhododendrons and I said in joke that I'd like to be your gardener."

"Then you can't know much about rhododendrons. When you've planted a rhododendron in the right soil you've planted it in the right soil, and that's all there is to it. With pigs, now, it's different. The proper care of a pedigree pig is a life's work for an intelligent man. Where's Josephine?"

"Still in the gazebo."

"What's your name?"

"Michael Stone," said Michael, gazing down the field with a face as still and hard as his own name.

"Never heard of you," said Miss Wentworth. "And I would be obliged if you would take another cigarette and stop gazing into the middle distance like that tiresome young man Orestes."

"It was not murder I was in for," Michael assured her. "Though I was in for a very serious offence."

"There are worse things than murder," said Miss Wentworth placidly. "And all those Agamemnons were better dead. Do you want the whole of Belmaray to know you're just out?"

"No I don't," said Michael.

"Then why did you tell me you'd been in? Don't you know all old maids tittle-tattle?"

"You don't," said Michael. "You are like the sundial."

"This is a most peculiar affair," said Miss Wentworth.

"I wouldn't know if I were awake or asleep," said Michael.

Miss Wentworth looked at him shrewdly. "You'd be better asleep," she said. "A good deal to make up by the looks of you. And that's a nasty cough you have. But I've a good deal to do before I can get your sheets aired. My pig man is sick, as I told you, and Jane Prescott only comes in the mornings."

She got up more nimbly than he did, and his mingled shame

and reluctance made him stumble awkwardly as he came up the steps and held out his hand. "Good-bye, Miss Wentworth," he said. "I won't say I didn't mean it, because I did. I did come here meaning to impose myself on you in some capacity or other. I thought I'd try it on. I don't know what I expected to happen. Not what has happened. I didn't know I had enough decency left in me to feel so profoundly ashamed."

"Shame is a good thing," said the old lady, taking his hand. "When it's your own, that is. To shame another is one of the worst of crimes."

He had a good hand, well shaped, broad and long, while hers was frail, light and dry as an autumn leaf, yet his shook so much in hers that she tightened her grip. "Even that can be forgiven," she said. "Shame can be offered for shame. No, I am not saying good-bye. I am holding you where you are. I shall find an able-bodied young man exceedingly useful, however ignorant." Feeling his hand once more steady she dropped it abruptly. "Josephine!"

Obedient as a dog Josephine appeared from the gazebo and trotted towards them, and Miss Wentworth handed Michael the stick. "Now take her up to the house. Don't strike her. Touch her gently on the right flank if you want her to go to the left, and the other way on. Let me see if you have the makings of a pig man in you."

"Now, angels and ministers of light," murmured Michael desperately below his breath, "if it be that you exist at all in contraposition to the terrestrial furies, be with me now and grant my hand and eye and resolution that perfect co-ordination which shall project this pig—in through the front door?" he asked Miss Wentworth in interpolation.

"Through the front door and out of the garden door," said Miss Wentworth, following serenely after.

"Through the front door," whispered Michael. "Amen."

Josephine went sedately along the flagged paths, obedient to every light touch of the stick. Coming after her, observing her noble proportions from behind, Michael perceived that she was indeed a magnificent animal with a skin like pale pink satin. "I expect I wash her," he thought. "Lux?"

Following at the tail of the procession, where he could not see her, Miss Wentworth said gruffly, "I should apologize too. I was brought up never to mention money in conversation, never to mention health and never to ask questions. I asked at least twenty. I ask your pardon and I will never put another question to you except this final one—do you like your coffee black or white?"

"Black," said Michael.

"Good," said Miss Wentworth. "I never trust a man who takes his coffee white."

Michael, who had known many trustworthy men who did, had no wish to argue the point. It was enough for him to know that she trusted him.

"Do you really mean through the front door?" he asked.

"I always mean what I say," said Miss Wentworth. "Let us get that clear before we make a start. It's a short cut and when you get to my age you save your steps."

Led by Josephine, who was now heading for home, they came up the last flight of steps to the mossgrown court in front of the house. A carriage drive, overgrown upon each side by the tall untrimmed flowering laurels that edged it, approached the court from the east, winding uphill from the village, and a balustrade separated it from the garden. There were urns on the balustrade and moon-shaped beds in the court, but they were full of nothing but weeds. "They'll be full of something better very soon," vowed Michael, and he felt a little dizzy with sudden visions of geraniums, scarlet, white and salmon pink, sturdy and strong and smelling like heaven in the hot sun.

"You like geraniums?" he enquired.

"Cannot abide 'em," said Miss Wentworth, and then paused. "Plant 'em where you like," she added abruptly, with a keen glance at him. "I mean that."

It would help, she thought. When he'd made a clean breast of it he must go back where he belonged and take up again the burden of his circumstances. "A body hast thou prepared me." It did not only mean a body. It meant character and what came of it, gifts, health or the lack of it, one's position in the soil, in the shade or the sun, bearing fragrant flowers or scentless. But you didn't come back to it easily when you'd been plunged down into that germinal suffering where men are locked in equality like roots in the soil. After being cramped in the dark you needed to stretch yourself, do something different, do perhaps what you wanted to do, even if it was planting geraniums in unsuitable soil... Nothing had even grown in those urns... Then a sense of direction was restored to you again.

The front door of grey weathered oak was closed and while Josephine sat patiently on the rusty wire mat they looked up for a moment at the house. It stood so high that it got the full force of the Atlantic gales from the southwest, and was scarred and battered. The subsidence of the soil through the centuries had given to its walls in places a perilous tilt and buttresses of old weathered brick shored it up here and there, while its steep strong old roof pressed down upon it with determined firmness. It was rather like Miss Wentworth, a combination of fragility and indomitable strength. Like her it looked worth knowing. Like her it had weathered many storms and was serene in its old age. The E shape of the house gave one a sense of being gathered in and it was not in keeping with either of them that the front door should be shut.

"I left the garden one open," explained Miss Wentworth, "and even when there is no wind there is a draught."

She turned the handle and preceded by Josephine they went into the old porch, as large as a room with its recessed windows with seats in them. The inner door was open and a wide flagged passage led through the depth of the house to the open door into the kitchen garden. Josephine trotted purposefully down and Michael followed after.

"Come back when you have shut her in her sty in the orchard," Miss Wentworth called after him. "You will probably find me upstairs in the linen closet."

The linen closet, thought Michael as he tramped down the passage, his feet and Josephine's trotters ringing on the stone flags. Was there a stillroom? He was aware of panelled walls on each side of him hung with portraits. He caught the gleam of a white ruff above Elizabethan armor. He especially noticed one of a woman with curls on her forehead whose pale face seemed vaguely familiar. There were pearls twisted in her hair and she had a sprig of rosemary fastened in her grey silk dress. He noticed too a young man with a long melancholy face, wearing a cuirass crossed by a scarlet sash. Then he came to the further door and stepped out into what was to his modern mind the impossibility of the kitchen garden.

3

His parents might have been familiar with such old gardens but he had never seen one. It was completely enclosed by the house, and the high cob walls that sheltered it upon the three sides, and it held warmth within it as a house does, as though it were itself a living thing. The other garden had had no frontier, it had enlarged itself to meet the fields and the river and to look to wide horizons, but this garden was warm and luxuriant within prescribed lines and its solidity had a most comfortable and comforting beauty. Nothing could get in here, thought Michael. The furies might visit the outer garden but they would not get in here. The place was so stuffed with potential food that there was simply no room for them.

The walls were covered with old fruit trees, peaches, plums, apricots, nectarines and pears. Beyond the kitchen garden he could see the tops of the apple trees in the orchard, still with their winter beauty of old bare branches twisted into strange shapes that seemed to have language in them, some rune or other written against the parchment sky, full of wisdom if one had the wisdom to read it. "But what the dickens does she do with all the fruit?" wondered Michael. There was more of it in the kitchen garden; two old mulberry trees held up with chains, an ancient quince and two medlars that he gazed at uncomprehendingly, never having seen such things, strawberry beds, raspberry canes, gooseberry and currant bushes.

Entirely forgetting all about Josephine he began walking round the garden and found the vegetables, a jungle of cabbages, broccoli and spinach, and neat inner spaces in the jungle where his ignorance supposed that seeds were coming up. There were traces of a herb garden in one place, perhaps one of the Elizabethan knot gardens, where the herbs were grown in the shape of fantastic knots. They would all have grown here once, marjoram, rue, sage, cumin, thyme, hyssop, marigold, balm, camomile, basil and all the rest of them. He had known all the good old names once but he had forgotten them with other good things. There were several of them here still, and the air was rich and heavy with their scent. Mossgrown paths, edged with miniature box hedges about a foot high, wandered in and out through the jungle and as a crowning glory there was a large magnolia tree facing the sun in the angle of the wall. Though there were weeds everywhere the kitchen garden was not neglected like the flower garden in front of the house. Michael felt no sadness here, only a profound astonishment that Bob Hewitt, if it were he who labored here, should be only sick and not dead. And what did they do with it all? he wondered again. And where the dickens was Josephine?

He found her waiting before a small door in the orchard wall and when he opened the door she preceded him with alacrity through it. The orchard too was enclosed upon three sides by cob walls, the fourth side being walled in by the back of the stables and the wall of the stableyard. Part of the stable wall had been taken down to make an entrance to the pigsties. Josephine hurried along there through the drifts of daffodils in the orchard grass, scattering the hens who bobbed among them, but when Michael opened the half-door to let her go in he saw that the word sty was an insult, and shutting the door again he leaned his elbows on it and gazed in admiration. Apartment would have been a better word than sty, such devotion had obviously gone to the preparation of accommodation for the goddesses who dwelt within. The walls were well scrubbed and the cobbles were covered with clean fresh straw upon which the other three matrons were taking their ease. They looked at Michael with the utmost benignity. Their eyes, if small, were bright and they had long wise faces that made him think of sibyls. The rosettes of their snouts had beauty if one thought about it; they might have been made of pink velvet. They were so clean that the smell of them was entirely pleasant and wholesome. "Ladies," he said, "my thoughts have done you great wrong for many years. My profound apologies."

A further door in the wall led through into the stableyard, where the door of a great coach house swung open on broken hinges and the cobbles were needing a wash. He looked through the door and saw loose boxes festooned with cobwebs, a dilapidated old governess cart and a lady's rusty bicycle. It was almost as sad as the front garden. He went out through a big archway surmounted by a shield, of which he could see only the reverse side, and found himself in the same drive that he had noticed sweeping round the front of the house. It wound away downhill towards the village through a tall beech wood echoing with bird song. Later in the year there would be a sheet of bluebells under the trees.

Standing in the drive Michael saw down below him a queer little round grey lodge. It had a circular sloping roof like a hat with a chimney at the apex to take it off by. He saw a tall lean stooping figure toiling up the steep road below it and drew back towards the archway, for it was Don Quixote. He was full of shame, for how was he to explain the way in which the joke had become a reality? There was no explaining it for the thing had

116

just happened. Nevertheless he must have some sort of explanation ready. What should he say? But there was no need to say anything for the moment, for Don Quixote swerved aside and went into the lodge.

He turned and looked up at the device on the shield over the archway. At the top was a beehive shaped like a helmet and below it a broken sword. Round the bottom of the shield were the words, *Dona nobis pacem*, give us peace.

He went back the way he had come, through the stableyard into the orchard and from there into the vegetable garden. Under one of the mulberry bushes he stood still. It was intensely quiet and with the sky so overcast twilight seemed not far away. It was growing cold with already a hint of coming rain, and the scent of violets came to him from somewhere. It was that moment of a spring evening when the birds sing with such a piercing sweetness that the hour is charmed. The swift flight of the spring is halted and though one listens for only ten minutes of pure peace it might be ten years. The cold sweet spring, thought Michael, the cold sweet spring. *Dona nobis pacem.*

A window in the house opened and a gruff voice called, "Is there a broccoli down there?"

"A gross of them," Michael called back.

"Bring me one. Do you like them with cheese?"

Michael, stooping to cut one with his pocket knife, called back, "If that's a thing trustworthy men like, yes."

In a few strides he was under the window and looking up at her. She had taken off her hideous hat and in the dim light her face had almost a look of youth. Mistress Wentworth. For a moment he wished with all his heart that she was young. Then he did not. Where would her deftness have been then, her wisdom and compassion? Like honey to the discarded helmet these things come to their full glory only when the pride of life is past.

She smiled at him. "I did not need that reassurance," she said.

6

*A*T THE door of the lodge John lifted his hand to knock and then dropped it again. Bob wouldn't want him. What could he say to the old man that would be of the least use? What could he say to any of his parishioners to which they would ever pay the slightest attention? Other priests, coming unknown to their parishes, could wear anonymity as a cloak of office that was not without impressiveness if they did not stay too long, but he could not do that. The older among his parishioners had known him in his weak and miserable childhood, his ineffectual boyhood and manhood. They knew all about the Wentworths and had told what they knew to their children. No one would ever listen to him here. But then, being what he was, he would never be listened to anywhere, and here he was at least in his own place, and he had proved himself to be one of those whose physical life decays if uprooted from familiar soil. Here he could at least keep some sort of hold upon the very poor health which was all he had ever attained to, and not fall sick as he did whenever he went to strange places. He was at least less of a nuisance here than anywhere else, and here he could pray better than in other places.

He looked up and round at the familiar wood, with its great aspiring beech trees. "For whom do we pray?" he asked them. The great titles of the old love poem so bound up with the story of this place came to him. Saint. Sovereign. Goddess. For him, no woman, in spite of his love for Daphne, but the soul.

For the soul both he and this place aspired. Any soul. Every soul. All souls. The soul of the man encountered on the road this morning. The soul of that woman who tormented his child in that abominable school. The soul of old Bob in there. Yes, old Bob. In there was a soul, his lady, his love. By knocking at the door, going in, making a fool of himself and coming out again, he prayed for that soul. As he knocked his heart was beating faster than usual, but not so much with the habitual dread of making a fool of himself as with amazement and wonder at God's use of fools.

From inside came a low growl. John opened the door cautiously and stuck his foot inside, but there was no need for the precaution. Old Bob was obviously not well enough even to shut the door in a visitor's face and his diffidence vanished in concern. He forgot himself and entered almost precipitately. The stuffy little room inside was very dark. The lodge was extremely picturesque outside but the creepers hanging over the small diamond-paned windows kept out most of the light. Air was kept out by the fact that old Bob never opened the windows, such as they were, from year's end to year's end. He would have died of asphyxia had it not been that he always kept a fire burning to combat the damp of the rotting boards and mildewed walls of his abode. The one living room was the shape of a half circle and behind it was the half circle of the kitchen. Above were two bedrooms. There was a well in the garden behind but no running water and no drains.

In this little house Bob had been born and lived for seventy-five years. His father, who had been coachman at the manor, had lived here for thirty years, his three children had been born here, and his wife and two of the children had died here. Bob, the youngest, had been only twenty-five when his father died and he had taken his place as coachman. He had married, but his wife had died in childbirth, and the child soon after, and he had not married again. He had been coachman until horses went out and cars came in, but his surly temper had never taken kindly to any form of change and he could not stomach cars. And so the family had driven their own car and he had become butler at the manor; a rather uncouth butler, but the Wentworths had always had a keener eye for character than for veneer, and unconventional themselves, outward conformity had meant little to them. Then the family fortunes had declined and he had become butler-cum-gardener. They had declined still further and he had taken over the pigs and the poultry. And now, help from the village hardly counting, he alone gave to Maria Wentworth the loyalty of a long line of devoted servants to a long line of devoted masters and mistresses.

Their attitude to each other was peculiar, and difficult of comprehension to those who were not of their generation. With far too much to do and far too little pay for the doing of it Bob was prepared to serve Miss Wentworth until he dropped. It never occurred to him to do anything else. Now that his health had failed and he was old he could have retired to an old people's home, but when John had once suggested this course old Bob had only been able to master his fury by remembering that the poor daft vicar was when all was said and done a Wentworth, lord of the manor by rights though not in the direct line. He would have died for a Wentworth as a matter of course and as casually as he cleaned out the pigsties. Yet he had no conscious appreciation of Miss Wentworth as a woman and he was abominably rude to her at times. Though she was to him his saint, sovereign, goddess, he did not know it. All he knew was that she was a Wentworth of Belmaray Manor and he was a Hewitt of the lodge.

Miss Wentworth on her side would never have thought of dismissing old Bob no matter how rude or incompetent he might be. Had he taken to drink or stealing it would have made no difference. He had been a little boy at the lodge when she had been a girl at the manor and she had never known life without him. Had it been necessary she would have given her life for him as casually as he would have given his for her, yet it never occurred to her that her pigs were better housed than the man who looked after them, and that she ought to do something about the unhealthy little lodge in which he lived, and suffered the tortures of acute rheumatism. It never occurred to her that a few of the premature deaths in that lodge might have been caused by unhealthy living conditions, and that Bob himself might move with less pain if he lived in a modern lodge nearer the road where the sun would have reached him, or alternatively in one of the many unused rooms at the manor. She had the softest of hearts but to her Bob and the lodge were unseparable, and the lodge and the beech wood inseparable. Everything had its allotted place in Belmaray, like jewels in a crown, and to move anything from where it had always been would have seemed to her an act of sacrilege, had she thought of it.

John, however, did think of it, but Bob's language when he once suggested removal to the manor had been such that from then on he had kept his thoughts to himself. Old Bob in his lodge was like a snail in its shell. Dug out of it he would probably now be more ill than he was in it, as was John himself when separated from Belmaray.

"You there, Bob?" he asked unnecessarily, feeling his way past the circular table with its plush table cover, and the family photograph album and Bible upon it, to the bamboo stand with the aspidistra that stood near the window and further assisted the geraniums on the window sill and the creepers outside to make the room nearly as dark as night. He knew the pitfalls now, as a ship sailing familiar seas knows the submerged reefs, but he was so clumsy in his embarrassment that he caught his foot in the bamboo stand and nearly fell headlong, and in saving himself he knocked against the horsehair armchair where the old man sat, jarring him badly.

"Careful now, Vicar, you clumsy—!" Bob Hewitt bit off the word without speaking it. He had always been able to do that, even in the years before John became a parson. For the poor dolt was a Wentworth. Now, as then, he expressed his feelings in a low growl like distant thunder, and jerked with his pipe towards the armchair opposite.

"I'm sorry, Bob," said John apologetically. "It's dark in here, coming from outside." He lowered himself carefully to the slippery armchair. It was the most uncomfortable chair in the world and he could not imagine how Bob, in the grip of the screws, could endure to sit in a similar one hour upon hour. Yet he had been sitting there all day, perfectly still, while the pain waxed and waned, and would continue to sit there until a cousin came up from the village to help him to his bed. "So I can sit here too," thought John. "I can at least do that." And he stretched out his long legs before him, laid his arms along the arms of the chair, sat back as far as he could, and held on firmly. He was feeling as always madly restless and fidgety, and sharp needles of horsehair pierced through his trousers to his legs, and into his protruding wrists, and tormented him, but he managed to make no movement. In the shadowed room each man sat as though immovable in his dark clothes, in his dark chair, and looked as though carved out of rock. They sat silently for a few moments and each to the other seemed to gather stature, to become a focus of power and dignity, but while John's mind speculated upon the reason with that same conscious strain with which he was imposing stillness upon his body, old Bob accepted the phenomenon as unquestioningly as his body accepted the tyranny of pain. Bob's mind and body were still with that primeval stillness which the countryman shares with patient tethered beasts, with water gripped by frost and flowers heavy and sodden with rain. Circumstance held him still, and he merely sat and awaited his release.

"Is it the screws?" asked John at last.

"Screws and me stomach," said Bob. And removing his pipe he embarked upon the history of his illness from the first moment of its onset a couple of days ago, when it took him in the back like a pronged fork while he was mixing the pig wash, until this very moment when it was as though someone were twisting his knees round and round in their sockets. His narrative was clear, detailed, almost dramatic in parts, spoken with none of the growling discourtesy of his reception of his visitor but carefully and almost sweetly and without a trace of self pity. When it was finished he replaced his pipe and had no more to say, inviting neither pity nor comment, withdrawn once more into the silent dignity of his inviolable rock. This was typical of old Bob. When his privacy was invaded he was like a snarling animal surprised in its lair, but once adjusted to the interruption the instinct of the animal gave way to the splendid natural instinct of the countryman who realized its rightness and its right. It is the difference between beasts and men that the first desert each other in pain and the second go in to each other and bear each other company. Bob's instinct knew this, and so he put the facts of the case before the one who had come in to him, that he might bear him company with understanding. But that was all he did. He made no appeal. Patience was the basic fact in his pain. His narrative was like a flower sprung up out of that rock but soon withered, while the rock remained.

John thought how through all the ages the patience of the poor had been the foundation stone of all life; no food without it, no fire on the hearth, no roads to travel, no houses to live in. Art might spring from other suffering, from the suffering of such men as had been in his family, such as he might have been himself had not the vein of gold died out in the dying breed, but that lay lightly like the soil upon the rock and took its value from the deep primeval pain. It was significant that the attitude of men like Bob to men such as he might have been was protective rather than reverential, while his to them was compounded of reverence. He wished he was the man he might have been had he lived a few centuries earlier, he wished he were the Rupert Wentworth who had painted the self portrait of the young man in armor, and of his queen Henrietta Maria, so that he could have left a portrait of old Bob upon the walls of the manor. Such light as there was fell full upon the old man's face and he could see it clearly, his eyes being accustomed now to the dimness of the room. It was an entirely medieval face and should have been framed in steel, or in a bowman's cap. It was a flat face, of a yellowish stone color, and deeply furrowed. The eyes were small and deeply sunk under a penthouse of bushy grey eyebrows. When Bob was well they were extremely sharp, shrewd and observant, but now they were dull and bewildered, for it was in his eyes that Bob showed he suffered. The great trap of a mouth was set grimly and the jaw was alarming in its square-cut strength, but there was no sullenness in the face and in the lines round the eyes there was humor. Bob had not shaved for a couple of days and the grey stubble of his beard was like lichen on the stone of his face. To those who did not know him it was a matter for astonishment when he smiled, showing great square teeth with gaps between them, for the smile was as full of charm and innocence as that of a child. Bob was innocent. He had been born of good stock and had had neither time nor inclination for vice, and his work had kept him in close contact with ways of life where the standards of excellence had been high.

The Wentworths had for generations been austere, gentle and sensitive. There had been artists among them, and a few saints, but no gross sinners, no bullies and no cheats. When called upon they had fought with gallantry and dash, champions of lost causes but not really the stuff of which soldiers are made, and always thankful to come home again. They had always been an intensely clannish family, clinging to what was familiar, shrinking from strange places and strange faces, and with inbreeding physical and nervous weakness had grown upon them, so that now their power and endurance had weakened. No earlier Wentworth would have drunk himself to death when he lost his wife as John's father had done, or allowed such a small affair as the South African War to shadow the rest of his life as John's great-uncle had done, or had his nerves shattered and almost the last remnants of his self confidence destroyed as had been the case with John himself in the last of the world wars. Yet even in their decadence these men had retained to the full the Wentworth chivalry, gentleness and austerity, and with this family old Bob had spent his life; with them and the things they loved, their gardens and orchards, dogs and horses. He had never even wanted to do a gross or ignoble thing, and his childish innocence, like light on the rock, had the charm of a new spring, something entirely fresh and individual garlanding what had remained immovable through countless winters. If I could only paint him, thought John, or immortalize him in a poem, or serve him in some way. But he won't be served. I can't even remove the screws, only keep him company when he would probably rather be by himself. Would he? Does he recognize I'm keeping him company in the first sort of prayer men ever learned? What does he feel about it?

Old Bob felt nothing about it, he was merely glad the vicar was there and noted that he seemed to be a larger and more powerful man sitting down than standing up. Sitting with his back to the window as John was doing Bob could not see his face, but he could see the fine shape of the head and the width of the shoulders, and when John turned his head for a moment he could see his dark profile with the beak of a nose and the receding chin, and thought oddly of an eagle; and anything less like an eagle than the vicar he could not imagine.

"They shall mount up with wings as eagles," he remarked unexpectedly. "Is that a text, Vicar?"

"Yes," said John. "The eagle is a symbol of strength, the sort of strength we shall have when the ending of the days has come."

The ending of the days. What a futile thing to say, he thought, for what could the phrase mean to Bob? Tough old countrymen such as Bob accepted death when it came as they accepted the vagaries of the weather, with resignation and as a matter of course, but they did not long for it as weaklings like himself did. Nor had they any realization of the process of

125

purgation leading through the long days, the aeons of the days, to eventual freedom, a falling away of the weakness and the sin, the pain and the inhibition and the whole appalling bondage of sinful mortality. If they thought sometimes of another world the thought touched them lightly and was gone again, it did not ravish and madden them together as they struggled to see the coasts of it through their tears and longed for it through the walls of a breaking heart that would not break and let them go. Bob and his like were wise in their generation, and much braver than he and his like whose perpetual straining forward had in it an element of escapism of which he was ashamed.

Bob sighed and the sigh caused him to belch slightly. "Pardon," he said with a grave and sad dignity. It was a matter for regret that he should belch in front of a Wentworth, but a belch is one of the inflictions of infirmity which are not always under a man's control, and so he felt more of resignation than shame in the matter.

"What a fool I am!" ejaculated John. "I'm entirely forgetting what I came for," and he dived into his pocket and produced Harriet's little flask of brandy, putting it on the table beside Bob. "Nothing like it for indigestion, Bob, and you won't be able to get down to the Wheatsheaf for your usual tot."

A spark of their usual shrewd brightness came into the old man's eyes. "That'll set me up fine," he said. "Thankee Master John—sir—Vicar." He was so touched that the various titles by which he had addressed John through the years fell from him in some confusion. "Vicar," he added finally, remembering that was the way things were now. This was an ecclesiastical gift and he took it with a deep respect. He felt there was something to be said for religion and had seldom felt more attracted by it. John felt the moment to be auspicious and knelt down and repeated the collect he always said with ailing parishioners before he left them, the prayer composed by that sick and crippled Pope who was carried everywhere in a litter.

"O God, who knowest us to be set in the midst of so many and great dangers, that by reason of the frailty of our nature we cannot always stand upright; Grant to us such strength and protection, as may support us in all dangers, and carry us through all temptations; through Jesus Christ our Lord."

"Amen," said old Bob with absence of mind but unusual enthusiasm, and his gnarled old hand closed more tightly round the flask.

2

John got himself clumsily out of the room, catching his foot in the rag rug this time, and out of the dark little house into the cool spring evening.

"Now I'm here I must go and see Aunt Maria," he thought. "If I don't she might be hurt if she hears I was at the lodge. But I must hurry or I'll be late for supper, and that will hurt Daphne."

He toiled up the steep drive through the beeches as quickly as he could, but just opposite the archway with the escutcheon of his family he stopped, suddenly remembering that the man he had met on the road this morning had drunk most of the brandy. Fool! Ass! Bungling ass! Criminal fool! Shame seized him, abysmal bitterness and shame. He had little sense of proportion and all his failings ranked as crimes in his eyes. He turned and ran down the hill again, but before he reached old Bob's door he stopped, halted miserably and uncertainly and then turned back up the hill once more. For what was the good? How could he explain what had happened? It was such a mixed up story. The fool that he was could never get it disentangled. If he tried he would probably only hurt the poor old chap still further, better let it be. What a bad priest he was. Priests needed wisdom and tact and he had neither. Such bungling as his could lose a soul. The unspeakably precious soul. He should never have been a priest. He pulled his hair shirt about him and toiled on wretchedly up the hill. He should never have been a priest. Only God knew how many souls were lost because he was one. Only God knew.

Inside the lodge Bob was enjoying the best laugh he had had in weeks. Proper tootlish the vicar was. Left it about careless like, and someone had taken a nip. Just like Master John. His mind slipped suddenly back into the past and a happy old memory came to him. He stopped laughing and smiled with infinite tenderness. Yes, just like that, just the same. He remembered it as though it were yesterday.

It had been Bob's birthday and John, seven or eight years old at the time, had saved up his pocket money and bought him a packet of cigarettes. But on his way through the kitchen garden to the stableyard to present them he had remembered that he had forgotten to give his kitten her milk, and had put the cigarettes under the rhubarb while he ran back to Tibby. A half-witted garden boy had been weeding in the garden at the time, and when a couple of hours later he suddenly remembered the cigarettes, fetched the packet and presented it to Bob, all had been filched but two. Poor little chap, how he had cried! Tootlish even then. But Bob had laughed and tweaked his hair and vowed that what was left was—what had been his phrase?—"worth more to me from you, Master John, than a box of cigars at five quid a box from the King of England himself." That had comforted the little chap but he had not been able to laugh about it. Too tender-hearted. Always had been. Always the same.

The memory passed and he drank off what was left of the brandy, laughing again. "Done me a power of good," he chuckled, looking at the empty flask. "That's Master John all over. He don't change. Always the same."

He became silent, thinking back over the years once more. "Always the same." The countryman has no higher praise to bestow. "He'll see me out, thank God," thought old Bob, and comforting himself with that thought and the warmth of the brandy he presently fell asleep.

Coming in the dusk round to the front of the house John was surprised to see candlelight shining from the windows of the room Miss Wentworth still called "the dining parlor." She usually had her supper very early and the dining parlor was not used as late as this unless she had visitors. John turned hastily away, for he hated visitors, either his own or other people's. He was aware of inconsistency in loving souls and hating visitors, but the fact was that try as he might he found it hard to realize that the well-clothed body of a visitor was inhabited by an immortal soul. He just could not reconcile the two. His definition of a visitor was narrow. No one lacking this world's goods was a visitor. No one sick, or in any trouble or perplexity, was a visitor, nor anyone below a certain social level. Nothing male was a visitor, nothing holy or humble or unattractive, nothing very old and nothing very young. In fact what it boiled down to was that he was terrified of all well-born, well-dressed, prosperous, good-looking, self assured females between the ages of twenty and seventy-five. Flying from such a lady, or unable to fly and standing desperately at bay, he made an act of faith that she had a soul and committed the same and his plight into the hands of his Maker, recalling (if calamity befell him in his own home) 1 Peter Chapter IV Verse 7. "Use hospitality one to another without grudging." Though he did not really grudge hospitality to such ladies, it was just that he was not clever with a teacup and he never could think what to say to them. What *did* such females talk about? Whatever it was the subject seemed inexhaustible for they never stopped at all, except when he stood before them with his teacup rattling in its saucer, when after a few feeble trickles the fountain seemed to dry up at the source.

"And yet you're a Wentworth," Aunt Maria had said once, in his undergraduate days, when this particular inhibition had just made itself most distressingly apparent. "Our family have always had such easy manners. Your poor father could be charming even in his cups, indeed in the earlier days more charming in them than out, and your lovely mother had manners to match her pretty face. What's the matter with you?"

"Sobriety and my face," John had replied gloomily. And there had been truth in his reply. Soberness went right through to the marrow of him and the sparkle of easy enjoyment was something he had never known, and as the one blot on the beauty of a good-looking family his beak-nosed face had always confronted him from every mirror with a pained reproach.

"Now who's there with Aunt Maria?" he wondered, escaping back again round the corner of the house. "Lady Robinson? Mrs. Anstruther? That frightful woman with the eyelashes?" Miss Wentworth did not often have visitors in these days of family decay but there were still those who had known her in her younger days, and those who came to see her out of motives of curiosity, or to cultivate a name that was still a "county" name. And whatever their motives in coming (and she always knew their motives) she received them as she had always received all who came, with that keen and gracious benevolence that put all she had and was at their disposal. Remembering her manners as a hostess John halted, and holding to the drainpipe that traversed the height of the house at this point fought out one of his ludicrous battles, harder than usual today because he had been so shaken by his failure with old Bob.

"It's my house, whose honor she upholds. It would have fallen into ruin long ago but for her, and the way the world is going we shan't have it much longer. Yet it's still my house and she entertains in it for me. It's my guest in there. 'Use hospitality without grudging.' The house has never grudged." He was a figure of fun, holding to the drainpipe; but his mind was suddenly alight with the remembrance of the lavishness of this house through the centuries. From Belmaray blood and treasure had drained away for the king. The poor had always been fed here, fugitives sheltered, the sorrowful comforted and prisoners courteously entertained. Unconsciously he lifted his hand from the drainpipe, a modern accretion, and laid it against the old wall as a man might lay his hand against his horse's flank. In this sort of house hospitality meant more than in some places. Hospitality, here, was as sacramental as his going to old Bob. Prayer, that he had always thought of as oblation, was also hospitality. You offered your being for another and you also took another into your being. And with a house like this one's being was scarcely separable from the being of one's house, and so he must go in and see who was there.

"And all this nonsense," he thought, as he once more made his way towards the front door, "because I am so very much alarmed by that Mrs. Whats-her-name with the eyelashes. Daphne says she has them sewn on, but is such a thing possible? It must be most painful. It's wonderful how courageous women are in the pursuit of beauty. One should admire them for it. I wish I could. The wind is getting up and I'm going to sneeze. Now what is that knot in my handkerchief for? Was it to order the coke? Well, I didn't."

A gust of wind buffeted him and its freshness put new life into him. As he walked along the terrace and in through the porch to the passage his step rang so firmly on the stone flags that Miss Wentworth, used to his shambling hesitating mode of progress, did not recognize it. For a moment she listened, startled, visited by the odd conviction that it was some sailor or soldier host of this house home from war; Francis, the builder of the house, who had chosen the device of helmet and broken sword as an act of homage to his queen Elizabeth, home from the Armada, Rupert Wentworth home from Naseby or her brother Richard back from South Africa. Then she heard John's familiar explosive sneeze (his catarrh must be bad today) and smiled at herself. "I'm too much alone," she thought. "I keep the dead too much with me in the wrong way, as they used to be and not as they are. I can no longer serve them as they used to be, only as they are." She smiled at the young man opposite her. It was her belief that one could serve the dead as they are only in emulation of their essential greatness. That lived in another world and by God's grace could still live in this if one willed it so, for one had the seed of it in oneself. Their life must be the richer if one could bring the seed to harvest. Richard had been if possible even more hospitable than she was herself. His guests had always been the objects of his reverence. She could see him now, his huge grey head bent, listening with absorbed attention to the vapid remarks of some very dull young man who was their guest. Michael's remarks were not vapid but would she have accepted him in quite this headlong fashion if she had not seen him first standing by Francis Wentworth's sundial that Richard had loved so much?

The door opened and John came in and her reaction to the fact of him was what it always was, mingled affection, pity and exasperation, exasperation predominating. He was a Wentworth, and a good man as nearly all the Wentworths had been, his childhood had been pitiable and she had not done all she might at the time to make it less so, and for that she reproached herself now, but it tried her sorely that such a poor weak creature should be the only man left to them, and should have no sons... Though for that she blamed Daphne, who had made only three efforts and then desisted for reasons of finance. Finance! In her young day a little thing like finance never deterred a woman from carrying out the duties of her state... Now she must stop thinking about Daphne, an irritating subject, and attend to the matter in hand.

"Michael, I think you've already met my great-nephew," she said. "John, Mr. Stone is paying me a visit."

Michael flushed and got to his feet. In old days he could have carried it off; now, in this house, he could not. "Mr. Wentworth," he said, "when I talked to you this morning about wanting to come here it was only the joke you took it to be. Please believe me. Then, later, I thought I'd try it on. I don't really quite know what happened, but anyway I'm staying here for a bit and I mean to make myself useful. If you've summed me up as no good you're quite right, but while I am here I am to be trusted. Please believe that."

All his natural ease had deserted him and he stammered over the spate of words in a ridiculous fashion. John, completely taken aback, merely stood and gaped, his mouth open. They looked like a couple of embarrassed schoolboys and Miss Wentworth had no patience with either of them. "Now sit down, both of you," she said in annoyance, "and eat this broccoli gratin before it gets cold. John, take a plate for yourself and one for the dog off the dresser, and a knife and fork out of that drawer. Michael has fetched a bottle of white wine from the cellar for us to drink with our meal. I know you don't like it but it is a very long time since I have entertained a guest in the house and I am enjoying the occasion. You can have some of that revolting orangeade. I opened it four months ago when the children came. Michael, where did you put Walsingham's food?"

John came out of his bewilderment and was once more the man whose step had rung out so firmly in the flagged passage. He smiled at Michael and the smile transformed his woeful countenance almost into the roundness of delight which Michael remembered from a childhood's picture of the moon.

Hey diddle diddle,
The cat and the fiddle,
The cow jumped over the moon.
The little dog laughed to see such sport
And the dish ran away with the spoon.

How he had loved that moon, not itself enjoying the pleasure of motion but so delighted by the movement of others. John's face had rounded out in just the same way and shone with his pleasure. Michael smiled back. He had not realized before how poignant can be the pleasure of a host.

"That unfortunate dog," prompted Miss Wentworth. Walsingham thumped his tail appealingly and both men sprang to their allotted tasks. Michael severed an appropriate portion from the large glutinous mass of offal which he had brought from the larder on a Wedgwood dish, and John took down a couple of Crown Derby plates of crimson and gold from the dresser for himself and Walsingham. A priceless collection of plates was displayed on the old dresser of black oak and Walsingham was fed off a different one each day, to keep them all washed and clean. John remembered, as he took down his own plate, that Daphne suspected that Aunt Maria did not always remember to wash Walsingham's plate, and that it was replaced on the dresser cleaned and polished merely by the moisture and friction of Walsingham's tongue. But he felt no revulsion, for his love of the creatures was entirely Franciscan.

Walsingham fed, the three of them sat down together and Miss Wentworth, who for some reason or other had replaced her hat, helped the broccoli gratin out of a Staffordshire dish while John poured the wine from the cobwebbed old bottle into exquisite goblets of amber-colored glass. There were daffodils in a Spode mug. There was a large brown loaf on the table in a pewter dish, biscuits in a posset pot of Bristol Delft, apples in a bowl of white jade and a strong brew of black coffee in a Lowestoft jug.

In spite of the high tea at the Wheatsheaf Michael found he was hungry again. For a long time now he had not had enough food. Not that there had been a shortage of it but it had been so revolting that he had not been able to get it down. Those ghastly suppers of dark sticky cocoa, like sickly mud, and the great slabs of doughy bread and margarine on the tin plate; and then when they had given it to you the re-locking of the cell door, and the long night before you when you couldn't read and the man in the next cell began to shout and curse. He lifted his glass to taste the wine but his hand was shaking so much that he put it down. He must not, his first meal here, spill anything. He waited a moment and tried again. His host and hostess were talking quietly to each other and were apparently oblivious of him, but he knew their lack of notice was in reality a most delicate cour-

134

tesy. At exactly the right moment Miss Wentworth turned to him and began to tell him about Josephine's last litter, and John refilled his glass, his gentle smile entirely masking his conviction that alcohol of any sort had the most nauseating smell of anything in the world except onions and silage. Should he have refilled Michael's glass? The instinct of a host had been irrepressible.

"Anyone would think I was a piece of Bristol Delft myself," thought Michael, "the way they and the house and the dog behave to me. They must be all mad together. But this is perfection, like one of those little worlds that I used to escape to. Was there ever before a room like this, or a meal like this, or a dog like that, or such an oddly assorted trio as we three? It's all entirely crazy and entirely fitting and the best thing that ever happened to me."

He was able to take it all in now; the low room, raftered and panelled, the windows, curtained in faded and torn red damask, closed against the rising storm, the fire of logs burning in the wide hearth. The table, like the dresser, was polished black oak, and the old silver candlesticks gleamed upon it. There was no electric light but the six blue-hearted, crocus-colored candle flames gave to the panelled walls a lustre no other light could have given them. The high-backed chairs had tapestry seats embroidered with hunting scenes in faded colors. The Persian rug on the floor had holes in it, and where there were hollows in the stone flags underneath they had been padded with newspapers.

Walsingham, his meal finished, was digesting it before the hearth. He was a spaniel. He was an aristocrat and was still handsome, though his rusty back was so broad and flat that one might have used it for a table. His black head was domed and full of wisdom, his ears long and pendulous upon each side of the long grave face, which had a pencil of white running down from between the white eyebrows to the tip of the nose. His chest was covered with curly white fur that was yellowing with age. He lay with his long forepaws extended and his chin laid upon them. His eyes, fixed on John, were dark wells of sadness, but Michael thought it was a reflected sadness that mirrored unconsciously the mind of his master and the age of the house. Walsingham himself, replete and warm, was content.

When all things in a microcosm of a world are entirely fitting each holds within it some reflection of the rest. The light of the candles shone in the darkness of the panelling, the daffodils looked down at their own beauty mirrored below them on the polished table, the shadows of the flames on the hearth moved among the rafters and the tranquility that was now in Michael's heart was not his own. He was aware of its source and lifted his glass to Miss Wentworth. He wished he could lift his glass to every lovely thing about him for each, he felt, was somehow in him at this moment, and he in them. This then was what one meant when one described any coming together as fitting. It meant the union of things and people in a harmony like that of music; take away one note and the symphony was no longer a perfect thing. In this particular place, at this particular moment, the removal of even the mustard pot would have seemed to him a disaster.

The meal progressed in contented peacefulness, spiced with laughter. There are many ways of being a good hostess and Miss Wentworth's way was that of the enlargement of her orbit. She did not so much referee her guests as describe her own charmed circle round them and little could come within the radius of her circle without becoming what the French call *en rapport*. And few people could be so dull as not to sparkle with some reflection of her own delightful humor. Safe from mockery or misunderstanding within the circle one was surprised to find oneself possessed of so much wit. "She is a great woman," thought Michael, "the greatest I have known."

They finished their meal and turned their chairs round to the fire. The two older people found the younger man easy to talk to, for he appeared to have nourished himself upon the books of their youth through the turmoils of his own, which touched them oddly, as though they had themselves ministered to his needs. He told them about his particular war, in Crete and Africa, frankly and easily. They talked, and Walsingham stretched himself, and slept and snored again, until John said suddenly, "Aunt Maria, did I telephone to Daphne?"

"Not that I know of," said Miss Wentworth. "Why?"

"To tell her I am here."

"Was she expecting you at home for supper?"

"I rather think she was," said John slowly. "I rather think she had something special for supper, and I forgot."

"Then you'd better go home at once," said Miss Wentworth soberly.

It was over. The charmed circle vanished and though the door was still shut and the windows closed the wind seemed in the room. John got up and kissed his great-aunt, patted Walsingham and smiled at Michael, and his eyes as well as Walsingham's were full of the sadness of his knowledge of himself. He went to the door followed by Walsingham, opened it, went out and closed it gently again in the dog's woeful countenance. "No, Walsingham." They heard him go out of the front door and run round the corner of the house in the rising wind. Walsingham flopped across the threshold of the door and laid his chin on his paws again with a deep sigh.

"We'll take these things to the kitchen and Jane will wash up in the morning," said Miss Wentworth. "I like to go to bed early."

"So do I," said Michael. "With a good book."

"There are plenty in the library," she said.

"I know," said Michael. "I saw them through the window."

"Choose what you like," she said. "And sleep well. There's a gale getting up. You don't mind a storm at night?"

"Of course not," lied Michael.

They were in the old raftered kitchen now, the wind was booming in the chimney and Miss Wentworth's tranquility seemed momentarily to have deserted her. "So temporary," she murmured, and Michael knew she was not thinking of the storm of nature. Did Don Quixote and his Dulcinea del Toboso have storms? Yet Don Quixote must love Dulcinea, for he had rushed off to her apparently entirely forgetting that he was leaving his great-aunt alone with an unknown vagabond who might possibly murder her in the night. But Miss Wentworth was talking again as she stacked the plates, though more to herself than him.

"Sometimes I wonder if the inherited weaknesses for which we are not responsible do not cause more trouble to ourselves and others than the sins for which we *are* responsible," she said sadly.

Michael, filling her hot water bottle as though he had been doing it every day of his life for ten years, flinched but longed to comfort her. "Trouble, perhaps, but not injury," he said slowly. "I mean, you may cause others a spot of bother by your weaknesses, perhaps, but coping with you may possibly increase their strength and sympathy. But if you sin deliberately, even if it seems only against yourself—well—you won't be the only one to suffer. You may even be the one who suffers least."

She was with him again and not with John. "Choose an amusing book," she commanded. "Concentrate upon it and then sleep well."

7

MICHAEL chose *The Pickwick Papers* and half an hour later was in bed with it, but time went by and though he held the book open he could not concentrate upon it. And the cough that had been with him since an attack of bronchitis in the winter was bothering him. He put the book down and looked about him. "If I've hated my life up till now it has at least been varied," he thought. "The places I've slept in, for instance; the rooms, dormitories, bunks, wards, dugouts, trains, cells, and now this. It's like Mother's and my room when we lived with Grandmother. Mother had a double bed like this, and I slept beside it in my cot. And there was a basin and jug with storks on them too. She used to tell me stories about those storks. We called them Jemima and Jim. Is there by any chance one of those china dressing-table sets patterned with pink roses, with a queer thing with antlers sticking up? Mother used to give me her rings to put on the antlers."

He rolled over on his elbow and looked at the old mahogany chest of drawers that did duty for a dressing-table. There was a china set there but patterned with forget-me-nots, not roses. But there was an antlered thing and unknowingly he had hung his wristwatch on it. He lay back and looked round the room again. The storks on the old washstand set were brown, and Jemima and Jim had been red, but otherwise they might have been identical. The bunches of faded pink moss roses on the wall-paper must have been there for a number of years, and the heavy old furniture for perhaps a century. The solidity of the furniture gave him a feeling of safety, the sort of safety he vaguely remembered from that brief time in his childhood when he and his mother had gone to live with his grandmother after his father had died. It had been such a short time, and its ending had seen the beginning of all his sins and fears. He did not remember his father but in this room he remembered his mother with a new vividness. In the early mornings he had crept out of his cot into her bed and she had told him about Jemima and Jim. His mother had been killed in a street accident when he was eight years old but he had not forgotten her... Nothing had gone right with him since he had seen her killed.

He turned restlessly and looked towards the blackness of the dormer window. He had pulled back the old chintz curtains but the wind, blowing from the southwest and now bringing the rain with it, was so strong that he had had to shut the window to keep the rain out, though he was a fanatical lover of fresh air. One of the recurrent nightmares, after his mother had died, had been that she was outside in the darkness, the wind and the rain, and no one would let her in. There would be crowds of people in the warm lighted room, as there had been a crowd of people about her when she had died, but they would not let her in. He would see her white bleeding face pressed against the streaming window, the pitiable mouth and eyes begging him to let her in, but he would not be able to move hand or foot, and he would wake up screaming. It had been a waking nightmare too. On stormy nights, whenever he was warm and sheltered inside it would seem that she was outside, and he grew to hate storms and darkness with a morbid numinous dread. His grandmother, who had believed in nothing but four square meals a day and as much comfort as possible, had made a bungling attempt to tell him some fairy tale of harps in heaven, but she did not tell tales well, as his mother had done, and it had carried no sort of conviction. The nightmares had been far more real, for some years the most real thing in his life, until with the loss of his belief that the numinous had its roots in anything more solid than superstition they too were lost; or rather transmuted, for it was chiefly as a writer of tales of fear and horror that he had made his reputation. But he had retained his loathing of storms. At the first rush of wind, the first spatter of raindrops hurled against the window, there would come that tremor along the nerves, the feeling of cold, as though a bucket of snow water had been emptied over him. Even tonight, in spite of this feeling of safety, his nerves were too taut for him to be able to read. He was so ashamed of his ridiculous childish fear that he always fought it with the same savage contempt, the same stiffness of nerves and muscles, with which he had fought his fear of injury in battle. Mercifully, being so short-lived and trivial an ordeal, it could not bring him to the scene of humiliation.

Another fear had dogged him always, the fear of poverty, and passing now in thought through the gamut of his fears he remembered the day of its inception. He had been ten when his grandmother had died but even now he could never smell boiled cod without revulsion, because the dining room had smelled of cod on the day when he and Mr. Davidson the lawyer had sat one on each side of the table with the inkstained cover, and he had stared at the inkstains while Mr. Davidson explained that his mother and grandmother had not been clever about money and so now there was nothing left for him. The kindness of friends would provide for his schooldays, and food and shelter in the holidays, but after that he must fend for himself. He must work very hard at school, and be very clever and do very well, for he would only have himself to depend on when he left it. Mr. Davidson had meant well but he had explained himself badly, and he had made that which awaited Michael seem like a black pool of horror into which he was to be tipped headlong in only eight years' time. Michael had gazed at the largest inkstain while Mr. Davidson talked and it had got larger and blacker as he gazed. It was destitution into which he would fall when his schooldays ended. For he knew very well that he could neither work hard nor be very clever. He was at a day school at present and the other boys laughed at him because he stuttered and was not good at either work or games; not good at anything at all except telling himself stories behind the toolshed in which he was revenged upon his tormentors by sticking pins into all their tenderest parts. They were horrid stories, and had taken the place of the escapes into foxglove bells and down among the grasses with which he had consoled himself for his grandmother's scoldings before he went to school. With a thin brown finger he had traced an imaginary line round the big inkblot, and then round two smaller stains which were the twin horrors of his schooldays and his holidays. He had been able to find no relief anywhere except in the thought of the tool shed. He had slipped off his chair and gone there.

The two smaller blots had grown less unendurable as time went on, for as he had grown older he had grown tougher. He had grown out of his stammer, and developed good looks, vivacity and charm, and a brilliance of imagination that had tricked all but the most discerning into thinking that he was a good deal cleverer than he actually was. But he did not trick himself and the fear of poverty had been with him all his life and had brought him to the ultimate disaster.

The old house shuddered beneath a more violent blast of wind, recalling him to the room where he was. He could not remember that he had been afraid of storms while his mother had lived, but then her imagination had always made such fun out of them for his entertainment. Had she been here now, and he a small boy in bed beside her, she would have said that this room, with its small window and sloping whitewashed ceiling, was his cabin, the captain's cabin on an Elizabethan galleon, driving across stormy seas to Eldorado; in perfect safety, of course, because her stories, unlike those which he himself wrote later, were always happy. Any ship of whose voyage she had control would be sure to let down its anchor at last in a safe and quiet harbor... A voyage of which she had control... A safe and quiet harbor... "Good lord, is it possible that I'm feeling sleepy?" he wondered. "I haven't had a decent night for weeks."

He blew out the candles. The window was now an oblong of light in the darkness and through a break in the scudding clouds he could see a star. The brief spring storm had passed its peak and his taut nerves relaxed. He got up and opened the window. Back in bed he lay thinking bemusedly of the china ornament with the antlers and of Jemima and Jim. "I'm thirty-eight and I'm not even adult yet," he thought, "not even after that filthy war and what happened to Bill Harris, and that girl and the way I treated her, and then the other business and prison." But there was less shame in the thought than usual. It was good to be able to remember Jemima and Jim. Had he been adult he might have forgotten them, and forgotten about his escapes into the little worlds. Perhaps even the memory of his mother might have become a little dim, and as things were with him it was vivid.

He was drifting into a dream. The ship rocked, but delightfully, for she had control of the voyage. "Why, you're not outside any more," he said to her, and fell asleep.

2

In her own room down the passage Miss Wentworth was sitting up in her big old curtained bed, an ancient pink flannel bedjacket round her shoulders, adding up lists of figures with the help of her account book and passbook. Her face in the candlelight looked haggard and old. She was badly in debt. Even with the allowance that John gave her she was in a very bad way. The little she made over her pigs, and selling her fruit and vegetables, were only drops in a bucket that had many holes in it. She put the books on her bedside table, blew out the candles and lay down, but not to sleep. She lay facing the window, watching for the moon and stars that shone out occasionally now that the rain had stopped, and when they gave their faint light she looked round at the dim outline of the furniture. She had slept in this room since she was sixteen years old and now she was eighty-two. She was wedded to the house and could not leave it. Things were undoubtedly in a bad way but she would contrive somehow, as she had always contrived. She would write to Entwistle, her lawyer, who was also good at contriving. They had been in very tight places before but they had always managed, by selling land or jewels, or by selling out investments. It was as unthinkable that she should leave Belmaray as it had in the past been unthinkable that she should leave Richard. The two of them had been and were the passion of her life.

Yet lying in her bed and looking back over the years, just as Michael had been doing, she realized more sharply than she had ever done that the exclusiveness of her caring had been a sin in her. If in the beginning she had loved John's father, Charles, he might not have married his second wife Judith and both he and John would have been spared much misery. Looking back on one's life at the end of it the perspective was changed and one saw things differently. At the beginning she had prided herself upon the fact that longing to be alone with Richard she had nevertheless faithfully done her duty by Charles and his boy; now she saw that to have kept all her love for Richard had been no virtue. Richard and Belmaray being a part of her, loving them had merely been loving herself. To have loved the other two would have been true love; they had needed love just as badly as she could have given it to them if it had occurred to her to ask for the grace of God. But she had been too self-confident in those days to realize her own bitter need and poverty, and perhaps too proud to cast herself in her lovelessness upon God's mercy if she had. "Duty, faith, love." For metrical reasons the poet had put love last but she was sure that in his heart he had had the humility to know better. Her own past pride she regarded now as the worst sin of her life. Too late, her heart ached over Charles. The only real love he had known had been given him by his first wife Anne, and she had died on the second anniversary of their wedding day.

Reliving it all again she realized that Charles had always seemed a little remote from her; perhaps because his father Philip had been so remote. They had been a family of four boys and three girls. Philip had been the eldest and she the youngest, with twenty years between them. Her mother had died while she was still a baby and Philip had left home when she was only four. In the various scourges of illness that so cruelly swept Victorian schoolrooms and nurseries two boys and two girls had died and she and Richard had been left alone with their father, a morose unloving man, unlike any Wentworth before or since. He had taken little notice of them and they had only had each other; but that had seemed to them no misfortune, for the ten years between them had been no hindrance to the delightfulness and fullness of their love. Even as a schoolboy of fifteen, home from Eton, Richard had found the five-year-old Maria the best company in the world. She had been small and dainty, vivacious, quick-witted and extremely practical. He had been tall and fair, good-looking with his fine large head and breadth of shoulder, scholarly, sensitive and inclined to melancholy. He had been a fine host, a connoisseur of old books and old wines, a lover of gardens and all beautiful things. His years at Oxford had been brilliant and he had read for the bar, but his lack of self-confidence had not made him a good barrister and he had been glad to come home and take over the management of the estate from his eccentric father, and help Maria entertain the guests whom he delighted to gather about him. He and Maria had been the perfect complement the one of the other and entirely satisfied with her company, he had never wanted to marry. Maria refused all her own offers of marriage that she might stay with him at Belmaray.

Philip, married and with his regiment in India, had hardly come into their lives at all. When he and his wife died of fever Richard and Maria had heard of their deaths as of the deaths of strangers, and when the ten-year-old Charles was brought home from India to live at Belmaray he seemed the child of strangers, and something of an embarrassment to his young aunt.

For by this time Maria's life-long struggle to keep the manor, the estate and her family with their heads above water had begun. Her father had grown steadily more odd and now he was very odd indeed. He had never thought much of the human race and now he thought nothing of it. He eschewed all human company but retained a passion for his horses and his dogs. In their company he lived in the fields, on the racecourse and in the gun room; but increasingly upon the racecourse, even though there were far too many people there. When he was at home his meals were served to him in the gun room and he never spoke except to complain of the cooking. Richard was now squire in all but name and Maria his lady. As mistress of Belmaray she had a vast amount to do for Richard was not very competent in the management of the estate and she had to advise him. Nor did he enjoy coping with the financial problems created by their father's racing debts and his own expensive tastes and she had to help him there too. And though he was so delightful a host he was also an absent-minded one, inclined to forget whom he had asked to stay, and for how long, and to invite more people to dinner than the table would hold, and there too her tact and charm and gift of practical contrivance were very necessary to him. And at all times he wanted her entire love.

And so the addition of a small boy to her other burdens was not very welcome and she was thankful when she could pack him off to boarding school.

She was twenty-three when the Boer War broke out. At first it seemed to make little difference to them but as soon as things went badly all the quixotic chivalry of Richard's nature flamed up into the conviction that he must go. As captain of the local militia, a post he held because the Wentworths had always held it, this was possible but not necessary and Maria pleaded against it. She was young but she had good sense and intuition and she had a shrewd idea of the sort of effect that war would have upon his nerves and temperament. She argued that the Wentworths had seldom been fighting men; Philip had been the only professional soldier in two generations. They were not the type. It was not likely that Richard would find himself a great deal of use when he got there. But even while she argued she knew it was no good. Though the Wentworths were not the type for war they were the type for knight-errantry and they had always gone to the rescue when things went badly. And Richard went, returning eighteen months later blinded and nervously shattered by an experience that had been too much for him, yet capable on the unexpected night of his return to Belmaray of walking along the terrace to the front door with a quick firm step, and opening the door with a cheery shout to her before he tripped over the mat and collapsed sobbing on the bench inside the porch. That spurt of gallantry and the quick collapse afterwards had been typical of all the remaining years of his life at Belmaray, twenty-three years of recurrent melancholia, alternate periods of courage and despair throughout which he never lost his charm, his love of humankind, of books that had to be read to him and beauty that must always reach him now at second-hand.

Maria poured herself out in devotion to him. It made little difference to her that in one of those early years her father had a stroke and thereafter lay a useless hulk of a man, for she had scarcely ever seen him. His racing career was now at an end but the money still drained away. There were his nurses, and Richard's schemes for the beautifying of Belmaray grew more and more expensive. Though he would never see them he planted the banks of the river with masses of rhododendrons and azaleas, and he bought rare roses and shrubs for the garden. He would sit in the gazebo that Rupert had built for love of Queen Henrietta Maria, beside the sundial that Francis Wentworth had put up for love of Queen Elizabeth, and think out more and more garments of beauty in which to deck Belmaray and delight Maria and their guests. He would imagine beds of flaming tulips, rivers of daffodils flowing down the terraces, a froth of white narcissi waving in the spring wind, and then order hundreds of bulbs from Holland. And then there would have to be extra gardeners to keep the beauty just as he visualized it. Maria did all that he wanted, that being the reason for her existence. And she loved to see Belmaray so beautiful and their guests so happy and refreshed. If Richard endured at times almost intolerable mental suffering, and she with him and for him, it was the ground from which much beauty sprang.

Through these years she continued to do her duty by Charles, growing up, coming and going to public school and university, getting engaged to his pretty cousin Anne Wentworth. She was glad about Anne because of the transformation that she wrought in Charles. He had been a delicate boy, inclined to melancholy and self-distrust, but Anne transformed him. Beloved at last he blossomed into good looks, rather effeminate looks but undoubtedly good and even distinguished, with liveliness to match. There was joy at Belmaray over their engagement, and it cast only a small shadow upon Maria's happiness when in the midst of the rejoicing her father suddenly died. For years some mercy had seen to it that there was a blind spot in her mind and she could not understand the commiserating looks that she surprised on the faces of servants and old friends. Why? Her father had always been such a stranger to his children that they could scarcely be expected to grieve, and for him his death was a happy release. Throughout the days preceding the funeral, through the funeral itself, she remained entirely obtuse and it was not until they were assembled for the reading of the will that she understood. The estate was entailed and Charles, not Richard, was now squire of Belmaray.

The old Maria of eighty-two, lying in her bed, was reliving that day as though it were present with her, for she knew it now for a turning point in her life. It had been then that she had known, for the first time in her own experience, the meaning of the phrase "conviction of sin."

Charles, not Richard. As the will was read she gave no sign, only straightened herself in her chair and looked at Richard. It was one of his good times and he was with them, sitting with his great grey head bent forward, his hand behind his ear because he was growing a little deaf. He was only forty then but he was aging very quickly. His face remained impassive and Maria thought he had not understood, but when the lawyer had left them he got up, made his way unerringly to where Charles was sitting, laid his hands on his shoulder and said in his steady, deep, musical voice, "God bless you, boy. May you and Anne reign happily. I am your humble and obedient servant." Then a pitiful confusion fell upon him and turning to face what he thought was Maria's chair, but was in reality the piano, he said, "Maria, are you there? We must go. From court to cottage. You understand, Maria. From court to cottage."

But Charles, with effeminate tears in his eyes, flung his arm round his uncle's shoulders and told him he must stay; Belmaray would not be Belmaray without him and Aunt Maria. They must never leave it. He and Anne wanted them. He became incoherent and letting go of Richard he hugged Maria, who disliked effeminacy and thought a man in tears (excepting only Richard upon that one occasion when they had been flayed out of him on the night of his return) as contemptible a sight as a man in drink. But now the contempt that she felt was not for him but for herself. All these years he had come and gone at Belmaray bearing his burden of unrequited love for her and for Richard, and engrossed in each other they had neither recognized nor accepted the treasure that he had for them.

She looked up at him. "God forgive me, Charles," she said. "I take everything you have to give from this day on."

He looked puzzled, for he still thought of love exclusively in terms of giving and not of taking, but her tone was so warm that he returned her smile with delight. He had never bothered as to whether he understood things or not. All he had ever wanted was to be loved and be happy.

He was amazingly happy in his marriage and in the birth of John, and so was Richard, whose delight in Anne and her baby gave him the longest period of respite that he had known. The two years of Charles's marriage were so perfect an idyll that from beginning to end Maria watched it with a sort of dread. Somehow the Wentworths had never quite had the knack of making entirely happy marriages and this one seemed too good to be true. She was not surprised when the news of Anne's accident and death was brought to her. This world would not be this world if such a wonder of perfection could last. But she got up from the garden chair where she had been sitting blanched and shaking. She knew very well that it was not only Charles's life that was darkened. Belmaray itself, the place, the family, the whole entity that she adored, had turned now to face the shadows because she had not loved.

She did her best, but it was too late. Her idea of her duty to Charles had not included the attempt to train him in any sort of mental or moral toughness, and so now neither his will nor his reason could help him. Only his emotions were strong and his grief defeated him utterly. Maria tried to rouse him to attempt some sort of valiance but though he had always loved her he had never been able to give her his confidence, because she had not wanted it, and it was too late for her to win it now.

He began drinking and fearing the effect of this on Richard, Maria persuaded him to go abroad for a while. He went to France with a friend of his, to Spain and then to Italy, and about eighteen months after Anne's death came back to Belmaray married to Judith. She was eight years older than he, a widow with two young sons of four and six years. Maria had not seen them together for more than ten minutes before she knew that Charles had married Judith because he had been too weak to oppose her wishes, and she had married him for social position. Her vitality and dominance, her worldliness and high spirits, were like a whirling stream that rushed him along stunned and half-conscious. For a few months he imagined that he was happy, then he took to drinking again. If Wentworth marriages had never been entirely happy they had never until now been disastrous. This one was. The wretchedness of the man and woman with each other seemed to poison the whole life of Belmaray. Richard's attacks of melancholia became more frequent, but he would not leave Belmaray, even to avoid Judith's noisy house parties. The more it was desecrated the more he clung to it. The first World War broke out but Charles was by this time too ill to fight and except that it made housekeeping more difficult Maria hardly noticed it. She became almost too weary to notice anything except Richard. Her whole being was gathered up and absorbed in the struggle to protect and cherish him. She knew vaguely that the fragile little John, so cruelly tormented by his stepbrothers, should not have been at Belmaray at all but she was too tired to think what to do about him, and comforted herself by remembering that he had Harriet to cherish him. He was Harriet's business, as Richard was hers.

Towards the end of the war Judith left Charles for another man, taking her boys with her, and a year later Charles died. Slowly a little renewal of happiness came to Belmaray. John, squire at eight years old, could occasionally be heard laughing in the garden. Maria recovered her old energy. Richard thought out more schemes for the garden and for the last few years of his life was almost a happy man.

He died in the summer of 1924. Returning from church early one Sunday morning he went to the gazebo to wait until breakfast was ready. There he fell asleep in the sun and passed from sleep to death in tranquility and peace.

The evening before his death he and Maria had been sitting together in the gazebo. Reliving that evening again Maria could remember every word they had said to each other, as though they had been talking together only yesterday. It was rhododendron time and she had been telling him how wonderful the valley looked in the afterglow, with the golden river winding through the banks of flaming color. Splendid as had been the love between them, that lifelong love of a brother and a sister that at its greatest can be almost deeper than that of husband and wife, they had never spoken to each other very intimately either of their love or of Richard's afflictions. Their generation had never felt the need of having their exact spiritual, emotional, nervous and physical state, as conceived by themselves, thoroughly understood by those about them. Richard in addition had been naturally reticent. He had endured as best he could and said as little as possible about it. She had helped him to endure as best she could and asked as few questions as possible. As for their love, it had grown with their growth and was to them both as the ground beneath their feet. Whatever else was missing that was always there and for that very reason called for no comment. But that evening he had spoken simply and naturally of the last twelve years.

"I should like you to know that they have not been as hard for me as you probably think," he said. "To be at times imprisoned in melancholy, to be at all times imprisoned in blindness, yes, it's bad, but all imprisonment has its compensations. Now what was the name of the woman who wrote with such simplicity of the enclosure of God's love?"

"Dame Julian of Norwich," said Maria. "I don't approve of these people who shut themselves up but I read her aloud because you wanted me to. And I like the things she says. 'Here is our clothing, that for love wrappeth us, and windeth us, halseth us and all becloseth us for tender love, that He may never leave us.'"

"Yes," said Richard. "Her imprisonment was worse than mine. Walled up for life in an anchor hold. Yet those men and women of the so-called dark ages chose it. Enclosed to feed on prayer. Have you ever thought what they must have gone through? There must have been times in the early days when they were afraid they would go mad. Then they passed in. You remember what she said about going in? 'I saw the soul so large, as it were an endless world, and as it were a blissful kingdom...

And when it cometh above all creatures in to itself, yet may it not abide in the beholding of itself, but all the beholding is blissfully set in God, that is the Maker dwelling therein, for in man's soul is his very dwelling.' I said to myself, I didn't want this anchor hold. Like the old knight, it's a case of 'must.' But I choose it, I said to myself. Ridiculous though it sounds when the thing had happened already, it was a hard choice. Yet when I'd made it—" He paused.

"You passed in?" asked Maria.

"Hardly that," he said. "The time has been short and I had had no training before enclosure. But I do know there is a threshold. Forgive me for talking about myself but I wanted you to know that."

Maria said nothing but gazed at the glowing beauty spread out below them, that he had created but never seen. "Belmaray is much more beautiful because of your blindness," she said. "Now I understand you better. In there you saw much beauty and as best you could you had to pass it on to the world outside enclosure."

"I never forgot you in there," he said. "In there I was your beadsman still."

"I'm glad you remembered me," said Maria. "I'm not much of a woman but I might have been a worse one had you not been enclosed."

As they walked towards the house he said, "Memory. No one knows how powerful it is." He paused, picked a sprig from the tree beside him and gave it to her. " 'There's rosemary, that's for remembrance; pray you, love, remember.' "

They went indoors after that, and to bed, and she did not see him alive again. At first it was hard to go on living, but she still had Belmaray, and John, to whom she must learn to give more than faith and duty. The heavenly, natural, effortless devotion that had been hers for Richard was not a thing that could be achieved by herself, but she could love him in the sense of centering her thought and work upon him with the utmost affection of which she was capable, meanwhile longing and praying that the other might be given to her. It might, or it might not. It was not in her hands.

It was not given. John always had exasperated her, and always did, but she loved him and served him. With no sense of doing her duty, but with gladness, she sold land and farms to keep him at Winchester, and precious family heirlooms to send him to Oxford. She cut down the staff at the manor to the bare minimum to send him to a theological college, even though of this latter course she strongly disapproved. She was a churchwoman but no Wentworth before John had ever been a priest and she disliked the idea of the squire of Belmaray in a dog collar. And how did he suppose he could combine the double duties, she asked him? John said he wanted to work in the slums while she continued to look after Belmaray. She was a better squire than he could ever be and she was happiest by herself. This was true and she did not deny it. She liked being by herself at Belmaray and meeting Richard's stooping figure at every turn.

So John overworked himself in the slums, and she at Belmaray, until the war broke out and he became a naval chaplain. She fought this decision of his as she had fought Richard's decision to go to South Africa, for she knew these Wentworth men and what war did to them, but John was as obstinate as Richard had been and had his way. His ship was torpedoed and he was in a hospital for nerve cases for a year. What he suffered there she did not know, for he would not let her go and see him, but seeing him when he came out again she was able to guess. But she thanked God that it was not as bad with him as it had been with Richard, and she also thanked God for sending to the old vicar of Belmaray at this juncture a quick and merciful demise in his garage, cranking up his car, a thing which with his weak heart he had been forbidden to do.

John was given the living but he would not live at the manor. He said he must live at the vicarage, closer to his people, and he wanted to have Harriet as his housekeeper, for she was not happy housekeeping for her nephew Harry at his pub. Also he had just got engaged to his cousin Daphne Gilliard, and he did hope Aunt Maria would be pleased.

Maria was far from pleased. She had not seen Daphne for years but she remembered her as a naughty girl, impudent and self-willed. They had not got on at all. And all that she had later heard of Daphne had not improved her opinion of her. She had gone on the stage, a thing no member of Maria's family had hitherto done. In the war she had become engaged to some rather fast young man who had left her in a particularly heartless manner, so Maria had been told, and now she had become engaged to John on the rebound. What would such a girl make of the remoteness of Belmaray, and of the enclosed life she would have to lead within the valley? When John brought Daphne to see her Maria could see that she did not love him, while John was as much in love as a man of his type could be. Maria in great distress of mind foresaw a marriage as unhappy as had been that of John's father to Judith.

She was not very sure how it had worked out; not very happy, she thought, but better than she had expected. At least Daphne had stuck to the job and had never wanted to come and live at the manor and force Maria to take second place; as she had had to do with Judith. "I dislike playing second fiddle," she confessed to herself, lying in her bed and watching the shimmer of the stars through the drifting clouds. "I am not yet a humble woman."

In old age, she thought, how it all falls away. Your good opinion of yourself, all the virtues you had thought you had, your beauty, your wealth. But she still had Belmaray. The old house had held her from her birth and she was resolved it should hold her to the end.

Though the wind was still blowing she suddenly felt sleepy, as though the house were a cradle that rocked her as it swung in the wind. Disconnected thoughts drifted through her mind. "That young man down the passage. What has he done? Not my affair. How attached God is to bushes as a means of revealing Himself. Moses's bush. Brother Lawrence's. Now why a bush? The rosemary tree by the sundial is choked with weeds. Michael is probably capable of that much. How John loved running off to the river when he was a child. I remember once I found him sitting cross-legged under the white rhododendron, looking like the infant Buddha with his eyes in slits and smiling fatuously. What a peculiar-looking little boy he was, so yellow." She drifted towards sleep and thought that white feathers were falling on her face, softly as snow, and that a swan was singing. The music was familiar but just as she was trying to remember where she had heard it she fell asleep.

8

THE morning dawned calm and lovely. From her bed Harriet could see the hills beyond the river, the woods and the sky. Like all those who spend much of their life in one room she had come to have an almost personal love for her window. She slept with her curtains drawn back and whenever she woke in the night she looked towards it instantly with eager wonder as to what it had to show her; clouds like galleons crossing the face of the moon, gems of stars set in a pall of blue velvet, Aurora like a golden lamp blazing above the brown rim of a dawn sky. Once she had woken up in the dawn she did not often go to sleep again; for her window faced east and she could not bear to miss a moment of the sun's rising. She loved to see the distant woods, grey and colorless while Aurora still blazed, dressing themselves in color as the starlight faded. She liked to see the nearer trees catching the light on their plumed crests, and the cattle standing knee deep in the white swathes of mist. Above all, she loved the dawn skies with their alternations of bright beauty, flaming so quickly to the penultimate splendor, then passing from glory to glory until the colors were lost in the splendor of the full day. Her eyes could never seem to catch the moment of change; in the span of a breath one glory had passed and another was passing and she could not halt the moments as they came; and perhaps only Harriet Martin was awake in Belmaray to tell of what had been.

Yet how could she tell? That was what bothered her. She

would say to Daphne, "It was a lovely dawn this morning, red and pink and all sorts," and Daphne would answer, "Was it, Harriet? Could you manage pork for lunch or would you rather have an egg?" And she would say, "Egg, please, dearie," and think how lopsided are the gifts of God. Now why give a woman eyes to see and no words to tell of it? Well, they had to see for themselves, that was what it was, and they all slept too heavy. "He was in the world . . . and the world knew Him not." The way God squandered Himself had always hurt her; and annoyed her too. The sky full of wings and only the shepherds awake. That golden voice speaking and only a few fishermen there to hear; and perhaps some of the words He spoke carried away on the wind or lost in the sound of the waves lapping against the side of the boat. A thousand blossoms shimmering over the orchard, each a world of wonder all to itself, and then the whole thing blown away on a southwest gale as though the delicate little worlds were of no value at all. Well, of all the spendthrifts, she would think and then pull herself up. It was not for her to criticize the ways of Almighty God; if He liked to go to all that trouble over the snowflakes, millions and millions of them, their intricate patterns too small to be seen by human eyes, and melting as soon as made, that was His affair and not hers. All she could do about it was to catch in her window, and save from entire waste, as much of the squandered beauty as she could.

The birds' voices woke her that morning, and she lay listening to them while she watched the changing sky. What did the voices mean? The longer she lived the more deeply aware did she become of profundities of meaning in everything about her. To grow old was to become less aware of the normal aspect of things, which hitherto you had taken for granted as all that there was, and to sink more deeply into the darkness of their meaning. As she watched and listened the bright clouds and the birds' voices became as a growing darkness. She fought against it for a moment, not wanting to waste the color and the sound, then yielded, for the darkness was a better thing than either.

She was roused by a volley of sneezes and John bringing her an early morning cup of tea. Winter and summer alike he entered her room, scrupulously shaved and meticulously dressed at six-thirty, carrying her tea. He might have all the trouble in the world keeping his mind to the point, controlling his nerves and emotions, but at least he had now got his early morning routine running on rails. He leapt from bed as soon as his alarm clock rang five-forty-five, stifling it promptly lest Daphne in the next room should be disturbed, stumbled in a state of trembling misery to the bathroom and took a cold bath, to the accompaniment of the Sursum Corda which he intoned with groanings and croakings like those of a frog in a marsh. His bath over his misery hardened to a hard and resolute depression and he dressed and shaved in silence, as for the scaffold. It was useless to pray while he shaved for if he did he cut himself. That done he made Harriet's cup of tea but did not have one himself, considering it contrary to discipline. But he made her cup of tea extremely well, exactly as she liked it, for at this time of day he was so focused upon the ideal of perfection that he could scarcely go wrong. There were no distractions yet, there had been no headlong failure to plunge him into despair. He did not take much notice of Harriet when he took in her tea, unless she were unwell and needing care, but kept his greetings and enquiries until later. He merely satisfied himself that all was well with her, wrapped her shawl round her, delivered the tea and went out again, for he kept silence before breakfast. Drinking her cup of tea, the best she had in the day, Harriet heard him going downstairs, opening the front door and walking quickly down the drive towards the church. Now, she knew, his early depression would lift a little, and by the time he got to church it would have lifted altogether. From seven to eight he prayed and meditated in the church, on Wednesday and saints' days remaining to celebrate Holy Communion for the few faithful;

old Mrs. Johnson, old Bartomy the sexton, and on saints' days (under extreme protest) Daphne. Though he had never told her so Harriet knew these early morning hours in the church seemed to him not only the happiest in his life but life itself. They were like the short periods of ease in the existence of a man who is chronically sick. He stayed himself upon the thought that they would come again.

When she had finished her tea Harriet lay back against her pillows and tasted the flavor of the day. She always had a shrewd idea as to what sort of day it was going to be at the vicarage, and adjusted herself beforehand to storms or peace. Yesterday had been on the whole a good day. After what had seemed a dangerous start with the daffodils John and Daphne had come back from church in harmony with each other, and the children had come back from school older and wiser than when they had gone, but in the last event happy. They had gone to bed happy but Daphne and John had not. Daphne, who could be a wonderful cook when she had the heart, had in her joy at the morning's harmony prepared a very special supper and told John not to be late for it. He had not come back to supper at all. Daphne never protested when she was hurt, she was merely proudly silent. The silence in which she and John had come upstairs last night, the coldness of her good-night, had lain on Harriet's heart like a heavy weight until she slept. And she had felt exasperated with both of them. Why could not John take more pains to remember? With his catarrh he used his handkerchief often enough and a knot in one corner of it would have told him what he ought to be doing. Why could not Daphne be more tolerant of his forgetfulness? He had been that way from a boy and Daphne who had known him as a boy should surely have learned to laugh at it by this time. But it takes a happy marriage to make light of small things and they were not happy. Harriet knew that John had gone off to church this morning sick at heart, and sure, as always, that it was all his fault. Daphne, she suspected, could have uncovered the root of their unhappiness had she tried, but she didn't; roots can be ugly things. "One of these days," thought Harriet with mounting exasperation, "I'll make her." Then she controlled her exasperation and put the thought from her. She did not believe in forcing anything, in having things out; things came out by themselves, with patience and good will. She comforted herself with the sight of the trees against the shining sky, for undoubtedly it was going to be a difficult day. Saturday was usually happy, for the children did not go to school, but today she was sure was going to be difficult. "And I'll not be able to do a thing for any of them," she thought. "I'm just a useless hulk of an old woman who can't even die." Well, there it was. There was nothing she could do about it except bear the burden that she was with what patience she could.

2

His pen in his hand, ink all over his fingers, John looked down at his sermons in despair. He was no preacher. The very glory of what he wanted to say seemed to get in the way of his saying it. Try as he might he could not write down what he knew. He was like a man trying to catch the moonlight on the water with a fishing net. When he pulled the net into his boat there was nothing in it except two repulsive jelly fish and a bit of seaweed. Sometimes he thought that his greatest blessing, the gift of a faith that had never been shaken and was his food and drink and very life, was a hindrance in the writing of sermons. Had he ever had doubts, had he ever had to hold his faith at arm's length and argue about it, words might have come more easily. He wrestled with his two Sunday sermons the whole week long and would, he thought, have gone distracted but for the comfort of prayer, for the comfort of turning inward where no words were required. But he had to preach, and generally by about eleven-thirty on Saturday morning he reached the point where he knew there was no more he could do to make his sermons the worst ever written. At that point he put them away in his desk and knew peace until he had to mount the pulpit steps, falling over his cassock as he did so, and stumble through his pitiful dissection of his two jellyfish and his bit of seaweed.

But today he could not reach that point. His mind refused to produce the platitude for the peroration of the morning's sermon, or to tell him what was wrong with the grammar of the opening of the evening one. His mind was distracted by other worries, primarily the problem of that poor wretched woman and Margary. The chief worry was Margary, but there was Miss Giles too. It might be that her need of rescue was greater than Margary's. He couldn't think what to do about it. Fifty times if once he dragged his mind off Margary only to have it circling round his cowardice in not braving Daphne's displeasure and bringing Michael to the vicarage yesterday. It had turned out all right, for Aunt Maria had made good his deficiency, but that did not alter the fact of his deficiency. If he had done his duty he would not have had supper at the manor and would not have wounded Daphne so cruelly by his forgetfulness. The knot had been in his handkerchief all right, placed there when she told him there was something special for supper, but he had thought it was for the coke. "Which I haven't ordered even now," he thought, and hastily ordered it on a bit of sermon paper. Then leaving his untidy scribbled sermons on his desk he went to find Daphne, a more urgent problem at this moment even than Margary, for Daphne in one of her ice-age moods would cast a blight over the children's sacrosanct weekend, when they forgot Monday and were happy. Usually when he tried to make things better between himself and Daphne he only made them worse, but at least he had to try.

Daphne was ironing.

"Why on Saturday?" he asked her.

"I can't leave the whole lot till Monday," she snapped. "I washed out Harriet's messy traycloth and things, and the children's blouses, after supper last night when you were at the manor."

Her iron glided over the traycloth which he had forgotten to ask Mrs. Wilmot to wash and he felt as though it were burning his soul. "I'm sorry, Daphne."

"What for?" enquired Daphne coldly.

"For all my deficiencies, but chiefly because we cannot afford to send the washing to the laundry."

"Which we could do if you would bestir yourself," said Daphne. "Lack of means is a deficiency which you could make good if you liked to try."

"Daphne, not again!" cried John in anguish. This was the great bone of contention between them. As soon as John buried it, Daphne dug it up again. To turn Aunt Maria out of the manor and sell it would mean a great easing of their struggles, but John would not do it. Where Aunt Maria had been born and lived, there she must die if she so wished it. He would not turn her out. Daphne could never manage to look at the thing from Aunt Maria's point of view. She had never got on with her and now she disliked her intensely for her selfishness in clinging to the manor.

"She knows quite well she is bleeding us white," she said.

"No, she does not, Daphne," answered John gently. "I mean, she knows we are all in a bad state financially, but the idea of bettering things by selling the manor has never occurred to her. She and the manor are in this world as indivisible as soul and body. I am many sorts of a sinner but not a murderer."

"How you do dramatize things!" snapped Daphne.

"Be patient, darling," he pleaded. "She's eighty-two."

"And will live to a hundred-and-two," said Daphne. "I never saw a tougher old lady. Physically, that is. Mentally, of course, she's very odd. Mrs. Wilmot says she has now got the most extraordinary young man with her. He came to borrow five pounds and she invited him to stay. Is that true? You were there last night."

"Yes, Daphne, but he wouldn't have asked her for five pounds. He's a decent chap."

163

"How do you know?"

"I met him on the road yesterday morning by Pizzle bridge and we walked along together and talked a bit. I liked him."

"Who is he and where had he come from? Why did he go to the manor?"

"I don't know, darling."

"Don't keep calling me darling. You think you can stop a row from being a row by sticking darlings here and there, but you can't, so why try? Surely either he or Aunt Maria gave you some sort of explanation for his presence there? Is he a gentleman?"

"Yes, no," said John miserably. "I mean, yes. I don't think I quite understood his explanation of why he was there but he made me feel it was right that he should be. I thought he was a gentleman. I think he needs help."

"I don't doubt it," said Daphne.

"I don't mean financial help, I mean—"

"Spiritual? That'll mean he'll come to lunch a great deal. John, what are you doing? That's Margary's blouse you're rumpling to pieces. I have just ironed it ready for school on Monday."

"Daphne," said John desperately, "I don't want her to go to school on Monday."

"Why ever not?"

"I want her to have a week at home. She's looking fagged out."

"John, what absolute nonsense! She's perfectly fit. Has she been complaining to you?"

"Margary never complains," said John gently.

"Then why are you making this fuss? She's all behind her class now, little dunce that she is, and a week away in the middle of term will only make it harder for her when it comes to exams."

"I want Margary to have a week at home."

"But why? John, you are really the most maddening man who ever lived!"

He knew he was but he did not know how to explain about Miss Giles. Nor about the oneness of Aunt Maria and Belmaray. He could never manage to explain things to Daphne because they never looked at a thing in the same way. Her point of view was a straight line and his was a corkscrew. Hers judged everything, correctly and at once, from the standpoint of the material well-being of her family. His wavered backward and forward between body and soul, earth and heaven, the bank balance and the heavenly treasure, until his head went round. It was going round now. He could not remember what they were quarrelling about, though he believed it had begun with the ironing. He ducked under the ironing board, took the iron from her, put it on the stand and flung his arms round her.

"Daphne, we'll sell my stamps and send the whole blooming lot to the laundry always."

John had only one hobby, the continuation of the valuable collection of stamps that had been begun by his grandfather and carried on by his father. He loved the interest of his stamps, the beauty, the precision of the colored pictures so exactly arranged on the white page. Margary was getting to love them too and had her own collection made up from his duplicates. They would pore over them together, patient, methodical and studious. Whenever John examined his conscience on the subject of detachment he always spent a very worrying ten minutes over the stamps. Was he really detached from them? He found now to his horror that he did not want Daphne to accept his offer. To save her from fatigue he should have wanted to sell his stamps ten times over. He didn't. His shame was so great that the blood rushed into his face and his arms tightened round her in agonizing compunction.

She felt the sudden strength in his arms and her heart beat with exhilaration. He had never felt passion for her. The tender love he had felt for her as a little girl had become the chivalrous devotion of a subject for his queen, but it had never been passion. The Wentworth men did not love that way, and she, passionate herself, had looked for that in vain. Her first lover had set her on fire and then left her, yet when she had turned to John she had found no assuagement. She had thought ardor dead yet now it leapt in her again. She was in delicious confusion and fear, and it was not John who held her but another man. And then suddenly he was gone and she was being whirled away into an abyss of humiliation. She clung to something, some sort of rock, and was safe. It was John. She looked up at him, utterly confused. Not quite in control of herself she still held to her husband. It was as rock she had thought of him yesterday, she remembered, though anything less like rock than her poor weedy old John could not be imagined. She laughed a little, flushed and uncertain of herself.

"Not the stamps," she said. "Margary loves them and I don't mind ironing. I like it, really. It was just that I was in a shocking bad temper."

"Not now?" asked John.

"No, not now." She kissed him and pushed him gently away. She had got control of herself again and had no further use for him for the moment.

"Go back to your sermons and let me get on with the children's things. I'll iron that blouse again. Margary will want it for school on Monday."

He went, a little cast down by his dismissal. It was so often like that. Just when they seemed coming closer together she pushed him away. Yet back in his study he found that the required platitudes came quite easily. Things were right between them again and the children's weekend happiness was safe. Had he won the last argument, or Daphne? Daphne, of course, or things would not have been right between them. Margary so far was still going back to school on Monday.

166

3

"Elevenses!" called Pat's clear voice, and he got up obediently to join Daphne and the children in the kitchen. Mrs. Wilmot left early on Saturdays and they had their food there to save carrying it to the dining room. The kitchen was almost cheerful with the geraniums, Orlando purring loudly and the children gathered round the table. There was tea in a big brown teapot, milk for the children, and ginger biscuits on a blue plate. "Why are ginger biscuits such a heartening form of food?" John wondered. "It is difficult to see a plate of ginger biscuits and remain depressed."

"Has Harriet got hers?" he asked, hovering over his chair in the shape of a bent pin.

"I took it up," said Daphne with a touch of sharpness. John's habit of seizing any excuse for snooping upstairs to Harriet was apt to try her patience.

"You could fetch it down again after," said Pat cheekily.

John lowered himself into his chair and smiled at her indulgently. She was an impudent little baggage but she was angelic to look at and very like Daphne had been at her age, only Daphne had been a frail little creature, never happy with the uncle and aunt who had brought her up, her eyes sombre and her thin lips compressed upon her private woes. Pat, he thanked God, appeared to have no woes. Her lips were full and rosy, her face warmly flushed, her dark eyes sparkling with her joy in life.

"Father, you haven't heard a word," Pat reproached him. He had been vaguely aware of the music of her voice and Winkle's, in a duet upon the subject of Frederick, the toad who lived in the vegetable garden.

"I heard," he said. "Frederick has produced strings of jelly which will eventually turn into a family. He will now have to be called Frederica."

"Lots and lots of jellied babies!" squeaked Winkle, her chubby cheeks rosy with pleasure. The children did not wear their school clothes on Saturdays and she had a blue snood round her golden hair and wore a blue smock. Pat's smock was a red and white check.

"Freda, Fred, Florence, Fanny and Francesca," said John instantly. "Fiona, Flora, Fritz, Fry and Frumpy." There were times when he could leap out of his customary abstraction with startling suddenness and be thoroughly on the spot, and he was so now, leaning his arms on the table and consulting earnestly with an equally earnest Winkle. Their mutual earnestness about the creatures was their only likeness. The consultation finished he leaned back and smiled at Daphne, and she smiled back at him. All was well today with these two happy children. And Margary?

Because he loved her best John always looked at her last. Though she liked most animals she had a horror of the occult creatures, bats and owls, toads and spiders, snakes and even cats, and she was stirring her cup of warm sugary milk a little thoughtfully with one hand while with the other she counted up the number of toads who would presently be at large in the garden. Her head was bent and her straight sandy hair fell forward, shadowing her pale face. Her green smock had shrunk and lost color in the wash and clung about her sadly, like a cloak of drying seaweed about a stranded mermaid. She was, John thought suddenly, exactly like the little mermaid in Hans Andersen's story, " a singular child, very quiet and thoughtful." She never cried either. "Mermaids cannot weep, and therefore, when they are troubled, suffer infinitely more than human beings do."

"Don't count on your fingers, Margary," said Daphne sharply. For Margary it was a terrible reminder. On Monday there would be school again, school and arithmetic and Miss Giles. She looked up quickly, her face stricken, then braced her shoulders with habitual courage and smiled at Daphne. It was John's smile, apologetic and deprecating, and like his always annoyed Daphne, making her feel vaguely reproached when her intentions had been all for the best.

"I do it too," whispered John, slipping his hand under the table and moving his fingers on her lap to show her what he meant. It was perhaps disloyalty to Daphne but the others were talking again and only Margary could hear him. He was glad he had thought of that mermaid, who had followed the prince to the heights on bleeding feet. "All will I risk to win him—and an immortal soul." A rereading of Hans Andersen would help him to help Margary. She looked up and smiled at him and he was reassured, as always, by the serenity of her eyes.

"What are you doing this morning?" he asked her, for he knew she would not be engrossed with the toad like the others. "Could you sort some stamps for me? There's a whole boxfull to be looked through. Mrs. Johnson sent them for the choir boys."

She nodded her head, her eyes bright. "In your study? While you talk to Harriet?"

He laughed. For some reason or other she liked being alone in his study. He knew that she was as fond of being there alone as of being there with him. He was at a loss to account for either likeness.

"Yes," he said. "If you've finished your milk, come along with me and I'll show you what I want you to do."

He put a cushion in his writing chair, sat her upon it and pushed the chair into his desk. Then he gave her the box of stamps and explained how he wanted them sorted. She was quick to understand. He had always been puzzled that she was considered such a dunce at school because with him she was always the opposite. He understood now that her slowness there was the measure of her fear. He left her happily absorbed and went up to Harriet.

4

He had meant to chat briefly to Harriet upon trivial subjects and then get a bit of digging done before lunch, for he did his best to keep his worries from her, but sitting in the comfortable chair beside her, looking out over the sunlit garden, the trivial subjects failed to present themselves to his mind. He leaned forward anxiously, his hands on his knees, his long legs bent under him, making no use of the comfort of the comfortable chair, and racked his brains in vain. "We'll soon have the apple blossom out," he said at last.

"So we shall," said Harriet. "And now what's troubling you?"

"That damn school!" burst out John, and then stopped appalled. What language to use before Harriet!

"I always suspected it was a damn school," said Harriet placidly. "Now sit back, for goodness' sake, and get it off your chest so that we can have a bit of peace."

He hesitated, for he did not like to burden her with his worries, but his childhood's habit of turning to her in all perplexities was too strong. He leaned back, leaned forward again, and then leaned back finally and poured the whole thing out.

"That poor woman," said Harriet when he had finished. "But it's not her that's the trouble in that school."

"Mary O'Hara is a sensible girl and she thinks so."

"Sensible she may be," said Harriet, "but at that age they never know as much as they think they do. It's that Mrs. Belling. I've never liked her."

"You've never seen her, Harriet."

If Harriet had been a less fastidious woman the little sound she made might have been interpreted as a snort of contempt. "When you see the results what's the need for seeing? What sort of soil does it all grow out of? The language Pat uses! And the food that they have at that place. Shocking. And the kitchen filthy. Mrs. Wilmot's niece, Rita, washes up there and Mrs.

Wilmot's told me. It's a wonder the children aren't poisoned. And the teaching there cannot be good. Pat, she's sharp and she's taught herself, but Margary's learned nothing and yet she's bright enough."

"She's too frightened to learn, Harriet. Too terrified of Miss Giles's cruelty."

"And what sort of headmistress is it that keeps a cruel woman on her staff?"

"I expect she doesn't know, Harriet."

"And what sort of headmistress is it who doesn't know what's going on? That woman's no good. I can guess what she is. There's cruelty and bad language and dirt growing out of what she is. Let herself go, that's what she's done."

"But what are we to do, Harriet?"

"Have you consulted Daphne?"

"Not yet," said John.

"Then don't," said Harriet.

"But there's Margary, Harriet," said John. "Unless I tell Daphne about Miss Giles she'll never consent to keeping Margary away from school."

"And if you do tell her she'll go straight over to Silverbridge in one of her rages and get that poor woman dismissed."

"Wouldn't that be a good thing?" asked John.

"Not for Miss Giles," said Harriet.

"It's Margary I'm thinking about," said John.

But Harriet had not finished with Miss Giles. "She cannot be a bad woman," she said, "or that Mary O'Hara would not like her. She'd be a better headmistress than Mrs. Belling, I don't doubt. If she had a bit more scope, trust put in her, she'd maybe turn out well. Why don't you go and see her?"

"Go and see her? What on earth should I say when I got there?" demanded John in horror.

"How should I know?" asked Harriet. "You'd maybe find yourself saying something or other when you did get there." She paused. "Poor soul," she added briefly.

171

The soul. John sat suddenly upright in his chair, comically alert like a jack-in-the-box jumping up when the spring is pressed. Harriet smiled.

"I might go," he said.

"No harm in it," said Harriet.

There was a pause until he asked, "Harriet, why didn't you tell me, or tell Daphne, about the dirt?"

"And what could either of you have done if I had?" asked Harriet. "You can't take action on third-hand evidence. It's no good forcing things; one waits."

"I'm not going to wait before taking Margary away from Oaklands. I won't have her go back. She's a child who feels intensely. She never cries."

"Is it the non-criers who feel most?" asked Harriet.

"Yes, don't you remember Hans Andersen's little mermaid?"

"I never liked that story," said Harriet. "I don't hold with people trying to better themselves. We should all keep to where we belong. That mermaid should have stuck to the sea, tail and all. And Margary should stick to school till the end of term. You mustn't go pampering the child."

"She's endured enough, Harriet."

"That's for her to say," said Harriet. "Tell her you know about Miss Giles and give her her choice."

"What, now?"

"Yes, now."

John picked up Harriet's cup and saucer and went.

5

Margary sat in her father's writing chair and sorted stamps upon a sheet of white blotting paper. She knew enough about them to be able to sort the German from the French and the American from the Dominions without any hesitation. Miss Giles would have been astonished at her speed and accuracy.

Without the bewilderment of fear she knew exactly what she was doing and could bring her natural gift of concentration to bear upon it. Though she did not lift her eyes from her work, did not take her mind from it, was entirely what she called Here, she was aware in the part of her which went There that she was in her father's study, the room in the house which she liked best, partly because it was her father's and partly because its window looked out upon the walled garden behind the house, the garden that was secret and enclosed. Though it was the vegetable garden it had flowers in it too, and on fine days of spring and summer was warm and safe and scented. When she withdrew herself entirely, complete with all her powers, from Here to There, in bed at night or at break in school when she was too miserable to join the other children and went off by herself behind the woodshed with her mug of milk and her hunk of bread, it was always through the study that she passed to the peace and safety of the garden. The study window faced west and at evening when the sky was clear it was full of golden light, that seemed to wash in over the sill and bring the glory of the garden with it.

But at all times of day she was happy in the study, especially sitting at the desk where the letters were written. John's shabby old kneehole desk was in the center of the room, at right angles to the window. It had on it piles of notepaper and envelopes and unanswered letters weighted down with peculiar oddments; bits of stone John had picked up during walks, a carved bear from Berne, a glass paperweight with a picture of Margate inside which Harriet had given him as a little boy, and a bottle of ink.

John had a large correspondence. Men and women who had been boys and girls at Belmaray and had left the village would persist in writing to him. Men whom he had known in the war, at sea and in hospital, would persist in doing the same thing. All his old friends of school and college days liked to keep in touch. He could not think why they wrote to him when as friend, parish priest and chaplain he had been such a failure; and as fellow patient in the hospital for nerve cases such an appalling failure that he could scarcely bear to think now of the failure he had been. But they persisted in writing to him. Patiently, as best he could, he answered these letters, writing sometimes long into the night, covering many pages with his small neat hand-writing, pegging away at it until his neck ached and his fingers cramped, and then doggedly praying for the whole lot of them until he was too bemused with headache and sleep to know what he was doing. Then he would have to give up and go to bed.

Daphne had given up sharing a room with him soon after their marriage, for she couldn't stand being waked up in the small hours. She had no sympathy with all this correspondence but Margary thought it was wonderful to receive letters from all over the world, and that not only because of the foreign stamps brought into the house but because of the people. She argued it out that they must love her father or they wouldn't write so many letters, and because she loved her father too she liked them, though she'd never seen them, and had the odd feeling that they liked her, though perhaps they didn't even know that she existed. All this wealth of affection made a solid rock like a fortress, a place very like There.

Without lifting her eyes Margary was aware of the bright little fire of logs burning in the grate opposite her. Now that the spring had come John had given up his study fire that he always laid and lit himself. She knew that Daphne had got up extra early this morning to light it just once more as a surprise for him, so that the warmth should help him get his sermons by heart. Did he know? Margary wondered. He was odd about things like fires and food. He didn't always seem to know what he was eating or whether he was hot or cold. Margary didn't mind much about food herself but she adored a fire. This one had flames of orange and gold, saffron and rose pink, like the azaleas that Great-great-uncle Richard had planted.

On each side of the fireplace were two shabby comfortable armchairs, where parishioners sat when they came to talk to John, and in the corner of the room to the right was John's prayer desk with his crucifix hanging over it on a bare cream wall. Most of the rest of the wall space was covered with bookcases filled with books, and when the evening light fell on them the colors glowed. She looked up and found that John had come back. "Margary," he said, "come over here and tell me what I ought to do. I'm in a bit of a fix."

The faint color in her cheeks deepened so that she looked almost pretty. People never turned to her for help, as they did to Pat, because she wasn't good at things. This was the first time anyone had asked for her co-operation. She came and sat on the hearthrug at her father's feet. "Could I sit here?" she asked. "The fire is nice."

"The fire?" asked John in horror. "Good lord, there's a fire! Who lit it?"

"Mother," said Margary. "Before breakfast."

John was silent, and when she looked up at him she thought that he looked older than he had looked two minutes before. "I should never have married," he said, and though Margary knew he was not talking to her she replied, "Then you wouldn't have had Pat and Winkle—nor me." The tone in which she added herself as an afterthought, an unconsidered trifle, made him laugh and wince at the same time. He pulled her up to sit on his knees, as she had done when she was a baby, and as she had done as a baby she wriggled herself comfortable with her head on his shoulders.

"Margary," he said, "I'm in a fix about your Miss Giles."

"Miss Giles?" she gasped, and went rigid within the curve of his arm. "*Mine?*"

He tightened his grip. "Yes, yours. Your form mistress. I've

175

been told she loses her temper with some of the girls at the school, and frightens them and makes them unhappy."

"Who told you?" she whispered.

"One of the older girls. Not Pat. I met her in Silverbridge yesterday and she told me." Margary said nothing and he went on. "Now that won't do, because it's bad for girls to be frightened and unhappy. They can't pass exams that way. That must stop. The only thing for me to do, I think, don't you, is to tell Mrs. Belling and get her to send Miss Giles away?"

Margary swallowed, and managed to say, "I don't think many of them are frightened. They don't like it, but I think it's only me who really minds." The last words came out in a rush. He did not look at her and waited. "You can't have her sent away just for me."

"Why not?" asked John.

"Well, Father, you can't. Where would she go?"

"To another school."

"Pussy Harker—she's one of the boarders, the fat one—told me that Annie told her that she'd heard Mrs. Belling telling Miss O'Hara that she only kept Miss Giles out of charity. She had not passed exams when she was young and Mrs. Belling told Miss O'Hara that no other school would be likely to take her."

"Would you mind saying that again?" asked John. "I'm not sure that I took it all in."

Margary said it again, whispering it behind the veil of her hair, which had fallen forward over her flushed face.

"It's complicated," said John, "but I think I've got the gist of it. So she didn't pass exams. Who was unkind to her? Her parents, perhaps. Does she look to you like someone whose parents have been unkind to her?"

"I don't know what people look like when their parents have been unkind to them," said Margary. John was thankful to hear it. Perhaps his marriage was not so mistaken after all. "But I think she must be ill," went on Margary. "I went back to our form room once, when school was over, because I'd left my eraser behind, and Miss Giles had her head down on her desk and she was—she was—"

"Was what?" asked John.

A tremor went through Margary's body, for it still frightened her to think of that day. "Making sounds like I've never heard before," she said. "Hurt sounds, but not crying."

"I know," said John. "Your poor Miss Giles. It must have been colic. Unkind parents and an unkind body. Is no one kind to her?"

"Miss O'Hara is kind," said Margary.

"Not the girls?"

"But she's unkind to them so they can't be kind to her, can they?"

"Why not?"

Margary sat up and thought about this but the only answer she could find was, "But they don't feel kind."

"Why not?" asked John. "Have they all got colic?"

"What's colic?" asked Margary.

"A peculiarly painful form of indigestion," said John. "Now it's a very odd thing but certain illnesses give people certain very unpleasant feelings. Influenza makes them feel very ill-used, and measles makes them irritable, and indigestion makes them feel both ill-used and irritable to such an extent that they can't feel anything else. That's why I thought the whole school must have colic."

"I don't think so," said Margary.

"Then I'm at a loss to understand why they should be so unkind to Miss Giles."

"But they're not unkind, Father, they're just not kind."

"Then they must be unkind. You must be one thing or the other. Do the girls ever put flowers on Miss O'Hara's desk?"

Margary brightened. "Yes, often. Peggy Harris put anemones one week. Bought ones. She'd saved up her pocket money. She has a shilling a week. Her father has a bank."

"What a plutocrat," said John. "She gave anemones to Miss Giles too, of course?"

"No, she didn't," said Margary. "No one ever gives flowers to Miss Giles."

"Not even at this time of year, when they are out in the garden?"

"No."

"One can make up very pretty bunches, just with garden flowers," said John, and paused nervously as he came at last to the point. "Margary, I do not want you to be unhappy and frightened at school. Would you like to stay at home for the rest of this term and go to some other school next term?"

Margary looked up at him with incredulous joy. "Not go back on Monday?"

"No."

Her head went down again and there was silence. Never, except when he had asked Daphne to marry him, had he waited so anxiously for a woman's answer.

"I'll go back on Monday."

"Sure?"

"Sure."

"Mistress Margary Wentworth," he said with satisfaction.

> "With Margerain gentle,
> The flower of goodly head,
> Embroider'd the mantle
> Is of your maidenhead.

Now let's get on with the stamps."

Sitting side by side at his desk each knew that the other was happy. John was whistling under his breath, a thing Margary knew he only did when he was glad, and she had the light in her dark-blue eyes that he knew shone through from inward contentment.

"You know your violet frame?" she said shyly.

"I do," said John.

"Has it any violets in it?"

"A few," said John. "Tell me when you want them and I'll take the top off the frame for you."

"Thank you," said Margary. "There are plenty of primroses out in the lane."

9

O N Saturdays, after tea, Daphne always read to the children in the drawing room, and if he could John came and listened too. He came today, and sat in the armchair opposite his wife. Daphne was not one of those women who keep their drawing rooms for special occasions only; she loved hers and used it and enclosed in its beauty felt at rest and happy. For she had got this room as she wanted it. Nothing else in her life had worked out right but this room had. It had in part been John's wedding gift to her. Whenever she felt bitter towards her husband she remembered the Adam fireplace, the red lacquer Chinese cabinet and Queen Henrietta Maria's day bed, mirror and chairs.

When John had become engaged to Daphne he had tried to visualize her in the vicarage drawing room and failed entirely. Try as he might he had not been able to see his lady's delicate face against the background of the faded Morris wallpaper, purple pomegranates on a crimson background, or looking out of the windows between the crimson plush curtains with their bobble edging, which had been bequeathed to the vicarage by old Mr. Baker together with the black marble mantelpiece and the black marble clock like the British Museum. He had decided that she must not even see them, and at once gave orders for demolition. The Victorian mantelpiece and grate were wrenched from the wall, the paper was stripped off and the curtains taken down. This revealed a scene of desolation but a well-proportioned room full of sunlight, with two French windows opening on the garden. John then had an Adam fireplace removed from the spare room at the manor, for the first time in his life taking no notice of the feelings or the anger of Aunt Maria, and installed it in the vicarage drawing room. He had the walls and ceiling painted pearl color and delicate candle-brackets fitted round the walls. He had doubts of his own taste in the matter of furnishing but he trusted Rupert's, for Rupert Wentworth had been an artist and in love with Queen Henrietta Maria, and when she took refuge at the manor during the civil war he had attended to the furnishing of her sitting room himself. Not a great deal of her furniture was left now, but all there was John removed to the vicarage; the Queen's day bed and her chairs, and her oval French mirror surmounted with cupids. The red lacquer Chinese cabinet he had seen in a shop in Bond Street and bought instantly at an exorbitant price. It was a thing of such beauty that it did not look incongruous with the Queen's day bed. There he had stopped, leaving Daphne to do the rest.

She had done it with joy and pride, covering the floor with an oyster-grey carpet and hanging curtains of sea-green brocade at the windows. Venetian glass was on the mantelpiece and some Chinese color-prints of birds hung upon the walls. Daphne's treasures, some special pieces of china, carved jade figures, some old miniatures and a sandalwood box, were in the cabinet, and there were some bookshelves with her favorite books. There were always flowers in the room, cut flowers in the spring and summer and pots of chrysanthemums in the winter. Most people thought it was disgraceful that a country parson's wife should have such a room. John thought the room was entirely fitting and he could never come into it without hearing again Daphne's cry of joy when she had first seen it. The children loved it. Their mother was not quite the same mother in this as in the other rooms in the house. On the threshold of this room she seemed to shed her worries, to become younger and more beautiful, more loving and yet at the same time more remote and mysterious. They loved her here in rather the same way as they loved the room, as something beautiful apart from the stress and strain of everyday.

And the books that she read to them here were also something apart. The school stories beloved by Pat were banned in this room. She read them Hans Andersen and George Macdonald, *The Secret Garden* and *Puck of Pook's Hill*.

"The best thing in the family week," thought John, watching her as she read. "And today better than usual. Today best of all." He lay back in his chair and abandoned himself to the perfection of this gift.

Five o'clock and a fine March evening. The window was open and small scented violets grew just outside. A blackbird was singing and the sky was clear. The firelight glinted upon the satin-smooth heads of the children, dark-brown, red-gold and silver-gilt, and warmed Daphne's cheeks, giving back to her the youth she had lost. She wore a Chinese coat that John had given her years ago to match the cabinet. It had gold dragons on it and sleeves wide enough to carry one of the little sleeve dogs who years ago had been the fashion in Peking. John looked at her without any of his usual aching anxiety, his sense of inadequacy and failure, for her happiness at this moment was a part of the timelessness of this perfect hour. His love for her burned strong and joyous and the nimbus that it set about her held the children too where they sat on the hearthrug at her feet. Orlando was also there, just on the fringe of the light. His fur was like satin and his whiskers threads of silver. His white forepaws were tucked under him and he purred. John stretched out his long legs and was aware that he was without his customary headache. His catarrh was not bothering him and neither was his lumbago. He had no indigestion in spite of crumpets for tea. His body was so at ease that only the sight of his shoes reminded him that he had it.

" 'One evening, just as the sun was setting with unusual brilliancy,' " read Daphne, " 'a flock of large, beautiful birds rose from out of the brushwood; the Duckling had never seen anything so beautiful before; their plumage was of a dazzling white, and they had long slender necks. They were swans—' "

Though past failure and regret cannot obtrude into a perfect hour the memories that are a part of one's immortality can have their place in it. John was a boy again, sitting cross-legged under the white rhododendron bush by the river. It was in full flower and its blossoms were like snow. Yet when he put up his hands and pulled down two flowering branches one on each side of him like bent wings, the blossoms that touched his face were warm and scented in the sun. The bush was a living thing. He felt safe. He looked out and saw the green grass and the running river, and near at hand he heard the music of the waterfall where it fell from boulder to boulder under the ferns. And then he heard the voice singing. It was like no earthly music that he had ever heard, or ever would hear, though the loveliness of earth was in it. It was not a human voice, though it had something of the clear beauty of a boy's voice singing, neither was it a bird's voice, though it held the liquid note of a nightingale or thrush. He thought of the waterfall, of the running river and the wind in the trees, though it was not like any of these. He felt intense longing as he listened and yet triumph too, for the song was triumphant. The dazzling plumage of the bird was all about him . . . such light. . .

" 'They uttered a singular cry,' " read Daphne, " 'spread out their long, splendid wings, and flew away from these cold regions to warmer countries, across the open sea. They flew so high—' "

The telephone rang in the hall.

Daphne stopped short in her reading and pulling his legs in abruptly John suffered a sudden stab of pain in the lumbar muscles. Pat said, "Blast!" and Winkle most surprisingly burst into tears. Margary's hair was no longer red-gold but ginger, and the blackbird stopped singing. The perfect hour had ended almost before it had begun. Daphne's and John's eyes met and there passed between them a wordless message of fear; and the bell went on ringing.

"Now who's there?" asked Daphne with an effort. "John, why don't you go?"

"I'll go," said Pat, pirouetting to the door. "It's the grocer to say there's no chunky marmalade and will that other mucky stuff do."

"Pat's language!" mourned Daphne when she had gone. "Winkle, what *are* you crying about?"

"It was dark," sobbed Winkle, "and there was a nightingale singing. Now there isn't."

"It wasn't a nightingale," said Margary. "It was a blackbird."

"It wasn't," snapped Winkle. "It was a nightingale."

"You've never heard a nightingale, Winkle," said John gently. "They don't sing in these parts."

"Mine does," contradicted Winkle. "In the dark."

"You were asleep, Winkle," said Daphne.

"I wasn't," said Winkle crossly.

The swan sang in the light, thought John, and touched Winkle's cheek. "I believe you," he said.

Pat came back. "It's some man who's staying with Aunt Maria. She's got more rhubarb than she knows what to do with and would you like some, because if so he's bringing it down."

"So have I got more rhubarb than I know what to do with," said Daphne quickly. "Say thank you very much but I won't deprive Aunt Maria."

"I've said thank you very much and rung off," said Pat. "He's bringing it down."

"Pat! I've told you before you are not to ring off without bringing the message to me first. And you don't like rhubarb."

"I like men," said Pat simply.

John sighed. The idea that in the upbringing of Pat the worst was yet to come had occurred to him before. Then he brightened. "It's the chap I told you about, Daphne. I'd like you to meet him."

"I've not the least wish to meet him," said Daphne, almost as cross as Winkle. "We were just enjoying ourselves."

"Then let's go on enjoying ourselves until he comes," said John. "Let's finish *The Ugly Duckling*."

"You finish it," said Daphne, passing the book across. "I just don't feel like it any more."

She leaned back in her chair and John went on with the story. He read aloud well and though the perfection of the hour was shattered the perfection of the story did not fail to take hold of them again. At the end the children were laughing and talking so loudly that Michael, finding the vicarage bell out of order, could not make his knocking heard. During the last twenty-four hours such a measure of self-respect had been restored to him that instead of putting the basket of rhubarb down in the porch and going away again he opened the door and went into the hall. He saw the line of light showing under the drawing-room door and heard the children's voices, and a wave of nostalgia went over him; not for his own childhood, that had so soon become unhappy, but for the days when he had been a welcome guest at many homes. So often he had arrived unannounced like this, crossed the hall, turned the handle of the drawing-room door and walked in. Scarcely realizing what he was doing he did just that, only remembering as he opened the door the alarming mental picture he had already formed of John's wife; shrewish, middle-aged, with greying sandy hair screwed back in a bun. But it was too late to turn back now and he went in, shut the door behind him and presented himself.

His apologies were cut short by the beauty of the room and then by the beauty of the woman who first rose rather languidly to greet him and then stood extremely still, one hand at her throat, the other resting on the mantelpiece. The little silence lengthened painfully.

He had forgotten how tall and slender she was. The Chinese coat, a royal garment of gleaming gold and midnight blue, suited that little air of arrogance, of unapproachability, that she had always had. She wore it over a soft long black skirt and below the hem of the skirt were silken ankles and scarlet Chinese mules. She wore her long thick hair as she had always worn it, swept right back from her forehead and gathered into a knot at the nape of her neck. It was the rare kind of shining black hair that seems to have blue lights in it. He had seen her face so many times in his dreams; the dark eyes so full of light under the fine brows, the short straight nose, the lips that were a little too thin, a little lacking in generosity, the wide cheekbones and the rather hollowed cheeks. What detestable luck, what detestable damnable luck for both him and for her. Couldn't you ever do a thing and be done with it in this world? Could you never come to a new bit of road and not have the past running along behind the hedge on either side, mocking at you? ... Even in this lost valley...

She was coming towards him, her right hand held out, the charming noncommittal smile of the practiced hostess on her thin, vivid lips. She had always used a too-bright lipstick as though she had known her lips did not equal her eyes in warmth and beauty. She came nearer and he saw that the color in her cheeks was only from the warmth of the fire and that her skin had become roughened and lined, and there was grey in her hair. Only for a short moment of memory had she had her old astonishing beauty. He smiled and took her hand. John was murmuring an introduction and she was speaking clear words of welcome, and introducing her children. Her voice was the same. They had moved for long in the world, he and she, and had made a fine art of dissimulation. Nothing had betrayed her but that momentary stillness. Only he knew that the beads of sweat on his forehead had not been brought there by quick walking.

They sat down and talked for a while of trivial things, the burden of the conversation being sustained by Daphne and Michael. John leaned back in his chair and delighted in them both. So often, when he had met someone to whom he longed to be of use, Daphne did not share his longing, and in married life that tended to put a spanner in the works, but it was easy to see that Daphne had taken to Michael. He had seldom seen her so animated. Michael, too, was spilling charm in a remarkable manner; almost, if one wanted to be critical, too remarkable. He was more of a man of the world than John had realized yesterday. Older, too. Yet first impressions remained with John. Looking away a moment he could still see vividly that charming, young face that he had seen yesterday, the face of a boy who would not grow up, who might have been his son. His eyes came back to the man beside the fire and he felt again the intense sympathy that he had felt yesterday. Thank heaven Aunt Maria had invited Michael to stay. Thank heaven he had time before him. He found that in a pause in the talk Daphne had turned to him. She was looking at him, smiling at him, with great tenderness. She got up.

"John's reading to the children," she said to Michael. "Come and see the garden with me."

2

They walked across the lawn and stood together by the sweet-briar hedge, looking out across the valley, over the river to the hills beyond. On the lower slopes the woods were shrouded now in the faint blue of a rising mist, like woodsmoke, higher up they seemed in the golden light to show every gradation of soft color. The sky and the river were gold and it seemed to Michael that he stood knee-deep in gold. He had to go and the sorrow was so bitter that he stood in silence and could not say what he must say. Daphne waited, her body lightly and beautifully poised. Her face was expressionless and yet in the very lack of expression there was a hint of cruelty. She was not hating the man beside her, she was merely emptied of all human kindness.

Upstairs at her open window Harriet watched them. She had seen Michael come and had thought, "Now that's a nice upstanding young fellow. Must be the one who's staying at the manor."

Then as he came nearer she said to herself, "Older than I thought. He's seen too much. I'd rather be myself than him, for all his body gives him no trouble at all." And her quick sympathy had reached out to him as he took the front-door steps two at a time. And her delight too. It was grand to see a body like that, moving so smoothly and painlessly, with such delightful ease.

And now as she watched it was the beauty of the two bodies that at first enthralled her. Tall though he was he was only an inch or two taller than she. To her fancy they were like poplar trees and had the wind blown they would have swayed as gracefully, with the same silken murmur. But no; it was only the woman who wore silk. Yet the man should have worn it, for there seemed a shimmer of gold about him. Harriet looked more intently and her first delight changed to apprehension. She had never seen a man and woman who physically looked more fitted to stand together, and yet they were not in accord. The very fittingness of the outward picture gave cruel emphasis to a bitterness and emptiness that brought tears to her eyes and a constriction to her throat as she became aware of them. The endurance of much pain had brought her to the same sort of awareness of the happiness or unhappiness of others that Margary had already as her birthright. Margary had been born a beadsman, Harriet had received her sensitiveness as the alms of age that had refused to feed on self. If it were a doubtful blessing it was not the curse that absorption in self would have been. In the last resort there are only the two pains of redemption and damnation to choose from.

And there was nothing she could do. Though the man stood as it were rooted and held in light her intuition told her he was being swept away. It was as though she herself were being tumbled over and over in the dark current towards an end that horrified her. And though the royal-robed woman could have put out a hand and held him where he was she was incapable of that one small gesture of kindness. How many queens had made it. Just one small gesture of the hand and the life was spared.

"You silly old woman," said Harriet to herself. "It's likely the young man has come about the fire insurance." Nevertheless she fell to her prayers, for though she had too much humility to trust her intuitions she did not disregard them. There was never any harm in being on the safe side.

"Yet how am I to know, Lord?" she sighed deep inside herself. "Wretched I feel, downright wretched, and the sorrow is bitter-tasting, yet how am I to know it's not just my fancy that that's the way he feels? Yet there's sorrow in the world that's not my fancy... Men wandering the earth, homeless men... May God have pity.... Yet I needn't be asking You when the hairs on their heads are numbered. That's the queer thing about prayer, to my mind. There's men and women that shut themselves up and spend their whole lives telling You what You've known before they were born. Lord, have mercy, they say, and You the Everlasting Mercy from the beginning to the end. Prayer would seem plain silly if You hadn't said to do it. So I do it. Lord, have mercy. And what else can I do or say, a useless old woman like me? If I wasn't shut up here I'd be going down and giving Daphne a piece of my mind. You're like a painted picture when your pride's hurt, my girl. Like a hollow thing, empty of kindness. I'd rather have that taste of tears than this emptiness. It is hers? If not hers it's the poverty of many poor souls the world over. Lord, have mercy. He's nothing but a child. Lord, say it to her. It's a difficult way You go to work, I must say. Most times it's as though You must make use of every soul in the world but one to save that one, and yet there was a time when You used One to save every soul in the world. And that wasn't easy, either. Who's to know how difficult it was? But there's one thing I do know; and that's that when through whatever means You take a soul at last, Lord, she falls to You at a touch lighter than thistledown. I know, Lord, for I've felt it. And why You can't do it that way at the start I don't know. But I'll not understand the ways of Providence this side the grave.

189

And my prayers are a fair disgrace. Lord have mercy on me for I'm not an educated woman. Amen."

She leaned back in her chair, tired out. A wave of pain came over her, as always when she was tired, and she had to hold to the arms of her chair. She was lucky, she knew, that she could still use her hands to hold on with. So many people could not even do that. That wave passed and another came. Well, never mind, it was part of it, and maybe made up for her lack of education. Not knowing that she suffered Daphne and Michael talked in the garden.

"Daphne, I'm sorry," he said. "I'll go, of course."

"Of course," she answered. "And so you did not know John and I lived here?"

She hated herself for asking the question, but she had so hoped, when she married John only a year after he had left her, that he would see the notice of her marriage and be humiliated to see how little she had cared.

"No," he said. "I did not know you had married. I was in Africa. One did not often see the papers."

Even in Africa, she thought, he could have kept himself informed of her well-being through mutual friends, if he had wished. She took her revenge with charming politeness. "Are you as famous as ever?" she asked lightly. "I have no idea I'm afraid. I don't go to the theatre or read modern novels. I'm so busy with my home and the children."

He turned and looked at her so compellingly that she had to look at him, though she had not meant to flatter him with so much interest. Even his lips were white. Had she hurt him as much as all that? She was delighted if she had but, heavens, the vanity of men! She looked at him, trying to think of something else to say that would hurt his pride, but he forestalled her. "Daphne, do you really not know what I've been doing lately?"

"My apologies," she said. "I did not even know if you were alive or dead." She spoke as contemptuously as she could, and watched to see his face tauten still more at the flick of the lash.

190

Instead of that it softened and the color came back. He smiled a little and his whole body relaxed with relief. She realized with a pang that she had not hurt him. He was glad that she had refused all knowledge of him since they parted. It was she who was suffering from hurt pride, not he. That shook her, made her feel at a disadvantage. She did not know, now, what revenge to take.

He turned away from her and spoke with gentle humility. "I am so glad you live in this paradise of a place. I am so glad you have married this very great man."

She was astonished. Belmaray? John? It was not so that she had ever thought of either of them. He stuck his hands savagely in his pockets, as a small boy might do, and memory stabbed her. She had not forgotten a single one of his gestures. She still knew them by heart. He had always done that when he was deeply moved. Nervy, emotional creature that he was his hands would tremble and ashamed of it he would hide them. He had always lost his heart very suddenly to places and people. He did not want to leave Belmaray. He did not want to leave John. Nor would John want him to go. John, this morning, had said he liked him, had thought he needed help. Was that true? It might be, for John had a nose for souls in trouble like that of a pig for truffles. Her thoughts raced. To drive Michael from his paradise, to deprive him of John's friendship—that would be a revenge that would satisfy her. Her thoughts stopped with a jolt for one hand had come out of his pocket and, still trembling, held her arm. "I'm glad I came, though," he said. "I'm glad I know how safe you are. It's such a beastly, terrifying sort of world."

She looked round at him and the fear in his eyes shocked her. What a child he was. It was odd, she had not before thought of him as a child, though she was a little older than he. Did she think this because of the maternity that was now in her, or because of his faint but to her eyes unmistakable likeness to Pat? How it had shamed her when she had first noticed in John's child that fugitive likeness to the man she had not seen for two years. It had proved that say what they would the intense absorption of the mind can influence even the physical likeness of a child. For so long after he had left her he had haunted her like a ghost. She would see him running down the stairs in the twilight, hear his step on the gravel and his voice calling her. He was with her in her dreams and when she woke she would see his face as clearly as though he stood beside her bed. She had fought the obsession with shame and anger but it had not left her until after Pat's birth, and had left its mark on Pat, and because of it she could never love Pat as a mother should love her first-born. It was Winkle who was her best-beloved, Winkle who had roused all the motherhood in her and made it possible for her to be touched now by the child in this man beside her. She fought hard, her longing to hurt at war with her sudden pang of pity, and through intensity of feeling was suddenly aware of the golden light that was pouring over them. Its amazing beauty was like a voice speaking, a challenge like that of the flowers yesterday to her power of correspondence, and she could not react to it with the ugliness of refusal.

"Stay if you like," she said coldly. "It does not matter to me in the least what you do but I'd like you to stay for John's sake. He likes you."

"Likes me?" said Michael breathlessly. "He won't when he knows who I am! My God, he won't!"

"Why should he know who you are? For his sake I won't tell him."

"I told him I was Michael Stone. It didn't seem to ring any bell at the time, but later it will."

"I don't think so. Whenever I spoke of you to him it was always as Mike Davis—but I did not speak of you more than was necessary. He knew you were a writer but not the name under which you wrote. When in the old days he went to the theatre it was to see Shakespeare, not to see the horrible kind of macabre plays you used to write, and still do I expect, and he does not

192

read detective stories. I doubt if he's ever heard of Michael Stone. A lot of people haven't."

She was able again to put the flick of the lash into that, and was again aware not of his resentment but his profound relief. "You've changed, Michael," she said.

"Yes," he said. "Thank you, Daphne, I'd like to stay for a bit. If you're sure you don't mind?"

"Mind? Why should I mind? You don't suppose you mean a thing to me now, do you?"

"No, I don't," he said humbly, and did not remind her of the promptness with which she had agreed earlier that he must go.

"It's all so long ago and so entirely dead," she murmured.

"Yes," he agreed. He found he was still holding her arm, let go abruptly and went away. She walked slowly back to the drawing room.

"Stone hasn't gone, has he?" asked John surprised.

"Yes," she said, sitting down in her chair. Her legs would not hold her any longer and she felt as though her face was stiff and frozen.

"What a shame, Mother," said Pat. "Why did you let him go?"

"Aunt Maria wanted him. John, read another story. A short one. There's just time."

"*The Princess and the Pea*," said Winkle.

"That pea," thought Daphne. "It's just like Michael. However many layers of oblivion I spread over him he always comes through."

10

MARY O'HARA woke up on Monday morning in a shocking temper. Before she got her eyes open she knew she was in it. She also knew she had a slight headache and that ominous tickle at the back of the throat that presages the beginning of a cold in the head. Then came the realization that it was raining, that it was Monday morning, that her hot water bottle had leaked in the night and that she hated everybody. As a general rule her temper was of the fireworks variety, an affair of sparks and flashes that seemed a mere effervescence of her vitality and was enjoyed by all, but upon rare occasions she woke up in the morning possessed by an absolute demon... She could feel him muscling within her now... And yesterday she had spent most of her time in church, praying a great deal for poor old Giles, remembering that Don Quixote had urged her to it and was doing the same. Though probably, she had thought once or twice, not in the same manner, not so wordily; by bedtime she had been exhausted by the spate of her own words. And today she had intended to inaugurate a new epoch at Oaklands, an era of Christian charity which should gradually win each soul in the house to love first Mary O'Hara, and then that way of life of which throughout the whole of yesterday she had been such a shining example. She had intended to begin with old Giles, whose alarm clock was now shrilling in the next room.

"Damn that woman!" she ejaculated, and reaching for her bedroom slipper flung it at the partitioned wall. Mercifully it went wide of the mark, sending a vase of flowers on the dressing table crashing to the floor.

Mary got one eye open and looked at the stream of water trickling towards a wide crack in the floor. The drawing room was underneath. She closed the eye, smiled in unholy glee, and then in deliberate defiance of that conscientious shrilling next-door, rolled over and went to sleep again. But it was the hot fitful sleep of an incipient cold, and under it her conscience nagged at her and woke her up again. "Damn that water!" she groaned, and rolled out of bed. She flung her bath towel savagely into the center of the pool and stood shivering in her dainty green silk pyjamas, looking irritably about her. By the time she had gone to bed last night her virtue had been wearing a little thin and her room presented its usual morning-after-the-night-before appearance. Every drawer and cupboard was open, showing the confusion within. The clothes she had taken off were on the floor where her shoes should have been, and her shoes on the chair where her clothes should have been. The book she had been reading was also on the floor, and her dressing gown was nowhere to be seen.

For a moment she was aware of herself in her customary optimistic early morning manner, Mary O'Hara, young, pretty and charming, and made a half-turn towards the glass to greet this nymph and paragon. She was met with a scowl, and glowered back in return at the red-nosed, tousle-headed horror with the bleary eyes and half-open mouth. "How I hate you!" she said to it. "Hideous, revolting little prig!" On her demonic mornings her hatred of everybody always included herself, for even her rages had a wide generosity about them and left nothing without the pale. She poured cold water into her basin and washed herself with distaste but thoroughness. Untidy though she was over her belongings she was fastidious over her person and always herself rose immaculate above their welter. She did so now, but in the most severe of her tweed skirts and blouses, with her curly hair restrained by a sober brown velvet band and her make-up restricted to a dusting of powder on her already swollen nose. A chastened appearance was her armor in her warfare against the demon, and a sign to those about her to take shelter. The noise of the breakfast gong rolled through the house but she disregarded it while she banged her drawers shut, stripped her bed as one scalping the head of the enemy, and then fought herself to her knees to say her prayers; for on these mornings even her Maker fell under her disapprobation. If He had to make her at all why couldn't she have been made with smooth brown hair, dovelike eyes, a sweet temper and the ability to implement her beautiful intentions? "Holy Mary, Mother of God, pray for us sinners." Jumping up from her knees a little calmed she felt a ladder rip from knee to ankle in one of her nylon stockings and her calm was gone. With her teeth set she rummaged in a drawer for another pair and with one stocking off and one on looked up to see Annie standing in her bedroom door.

"Didn't you 'ear the gong?" asked Annie.

"Hear it? Of course I heard it!" flamed Mary. "You sound that gong as though it were the last trump. And what's it when we get there? Tepid tea and that revolting cereal gone limp and stale. Why can't you crisp it up in the oven? Why can't you wait until the kettle boils before you make the tea? I'd sell my soul to the devil that's in me for the hot coffee and sizzling bacon you've just taken to Aunt Rose."

She caught herself up. Disloyalty was not as a rule one of her failings, but when the demon was muscling for action she was like the princess in the fairy tale from whose mouth toads fell. The small part of her which remained outside the dominion of her temper stood aghast but inefficient as one after the other the reptiles showered forth.

Annie, when she could summon the energy, could also lose her temper. She came close to Mary. "And who are you, Miss, to be lecturing me on me duty? You don't see *me* carrying on with the children's fathers out in the drive where the whole of Silver-bridge can see me. As soon as you've finished your breakfast Mrs. Belling wants to see you."

"So you've been telling tales of me to my aunt, have you?" demanded Mary furiously. "What a slithy tove you are!"

The comparison was lost on Annie, who had not read *Through the Looking Glass;* but she recognized the tone of insult and came a few steps nearer, so that her greasy face was only a few inches from Mary's. Her lank hair had not been washed for a long time, and neither had her dress, and the sour smell of dried sweat so sickened Mary that she fell back a few paces, and caught sight of a torn petticoat trailing out of the drawer from which she had taken her stockings. She should have mended that petticoat weeks ago but she hadn't bothered. That was probably the way in which Annie's decay had started; tidy and clean in herself but with torn petticoats hanging out of drawers. Her temper fell from her suddenly and misery took its place. That was always the way when the demon let go for a moment. On these days she suffered from a see-saw of sin and its aftermath. Summoning every ounce of will power she possessed, and shuddering all over with distaste, she put her hands on Annie's shoulders and kissed her. "I'm sorry, Annie," she said, and turning quickly away stuffed the petticoat back in its place and shut the drawer. When she looked round again she saw to her dismay and astonishment that Annie was crying, sniffing and feeling with trembling dirty fingers for a non-existent handkerchief.

"Here's one, Annie," said Mary, diving into her pockets. "It's got an Irish shamrock on it and you can keep it afterwards for luck. Cheer up, Annie."

Annie grabbed the handkerchief and departed, sobbing uncontrollably. What was the matter with her that she should cry like that? Mary noticed for the first time how bowed her shoulders were. She was lazy now but throughout the years she must have carried many trays and buckets of coals, and scrubbed many floors, and she still did. Perhaps she was bone-weary as well as bone-lazy, and crying from sheer fatigue.

Mary sneezed and went downstairs, feeling her temper rising again as she heard the high squeaky voice of Pussy Harker demanding raspberry jam. She disliked children with squeaky voices. She hated raspberry jam made with turnips and chips of wood. She hated English breakfast anyway. It was the most uncivilized meal in the day, everyone herded together and slobbering cereal from bowls like pigs at a trough. It was symptomatic that the French, the only truly civilized people in Europe, partook of croissants and coffee only, and that in the privacy of their own rooms. The English were boors. She could find only one thing to be thankful for on a day like this; that there was not a single drop of English blood in her body. Upon both sides she was pure unadulterated Celt. She opened the dining room door and the faces of the boarders were lifted instantly towards her as flowers towards the sun, then dropped again to their plates as they beheld how darkly the sun was clouded. Miss Giles glanced at Mary and sighed. Her migraine had continued over the weekend and had left her limp and exhausted and O'Hara in a rage was not going to make a difficult day easier.

"Sorry I'm late," said Mary, accepting a plate of cereal with a martyrish air. "I knocked a vase over. My stocking laddered. One of those days." She sneezed.

"Have you a cold?" asked Miss Giles.

"Isn't that obvious?" snapped Mary. How yellow old Giles looked in the harsh morning light, revoltingly yellow and plain. Was it possible that only last Friday she had felt the first stirrings of friendship towards her? Was it possible that only yesterday she had been simmering with Christian charity like a kettle on the boil? One of the children giggled and she shot a look of hatred at her. Was it possible that only yesterday she had thought she loved children? She could have murdered the lot of the odious little beasts. Silence reigned. She had often thought how beautiful convent breakfasts must be, no word spoken and the nuns' minds busy with holy thoughts, but she realized now the horrid noisiness of a silent breakfast, with heavy breathings and champing jaws and the creakings of false teeth. Giles had false teeth, and Pussy as well as herself had a cold.

"Now I know why language was invented," she said suddenly to Miss Giles.

"Why?" asked Miss Giles.

"To disguise the noise people make when they eat."

Miss Giles flushed, conscious of the bad fit of her teeth, but her flush was as nothing to Mary's as she realized the ugliness and cruelty of her latest remark. Her eyes were suddenly piteous as they met those of Miss Giles, and Miss Giles smiled. What a child O'Hara was! On Friday, when she had brought her the tea and sat on her bed, she had believed herself conscious of a depth of compassion that had seemed far beyond the power of Mary's youth, and had afterwards marvelled at it. Even now, when Mary's childish behavior was proving it her fancy, she could not forget it, for it had been her first experience of compassion. Yet how could it have been her first when she had recognized it? We do not recognize the unknown. Nor does fancy produce it. O'Hara's gentleness that day had tapped something somewhere that she had once known. It was a crude way of putting it but she could find no other words. Yet she could have dispensed with the experience for it had left her with an ache of longing for which there was no possibility of satisfaction, and had if possible increased the hopelessness that always succeeded the worst of her migraines. She was fifty-five and as none of her infirmities was of the type that kills she might live for another twenty years. Another ten years of teaching, struggling on as best she could through pain and weakness, and then retirement on an old age pension, the only pension she was entitled to. Where would she go? How would she live? So many lonely old women ended it all in their lonely bed-sitting-rooms, but the coward's way was one she had never taken. Breakfast was over and she got up mechanically, said grace and stood by the door to watch the children file out. Mary, who should have gone upstairs to see Mrs. Belling, lingered.

"Giles, I'm in a frightful rage. "

"So I observe," said Miss Giles coldly.

"I shall be intolerable all day, so watch out. I'm sorry. I'm not disciplined, as you are."

It was the first time Miss Giles had ever received a compliment in this house, and she started, and then flushed. Discipline? It did not touch her thoughts. Mary looked at her curiously for this was the second time in ten minutes that she had made Giles blush. The poor old thing must be far more vulnerable than she had realized. "I suppose you hate the cinema?" she blurted out.

"I do rather," said Miss Giles. "It's my head."

"There's not much one can do in this one-horse place," said Mary. "To get away from school, I mean. But there's a good string orchestra coming to Otway next week. Did you know? We could take the bus and go. But you don't care about music, do you?"

"Yes," said Miss Giles briefly.

Again Mary looked at her curiously, for she had never known old Giles to go to a concert. "Then let's go together," she said lightly. "I'll get the tickets. It's a good programme. That's settled then."

She ran quickly up the stairs without looking back, leaving Miss Giles with her refusal no more advanced than an idiotically open mouth. She shut it and groped for the banisters. It was a long while since she had been to a recital. Years ago she had turned her back on music in the same sort of way that some people leave a house where they have suffered bereavement. As she went upstairs to tidy her room she was trying not to remember that night when Max Roundham had heard her sing and offered to train her for half the usual fees, and her father had refused . . . He would not spare a penny from the boys.

"Come in darling," said Mrs. Belling sweetly, and Mary entered jauntily. She was feeling jaunty, for she had vanquished the demon. Or, to be strictly accurate, at the very moment when she was informing Giles that he was present he had gone to sleep; like having your toothache vanish as you take the receiver off to ring up the dentist. It was out of the midst of the glow of virtue occasioned by his absence that she had been able to ask Giles to go to the concert with her. She felt extremely pleased with herself, and curling her tongue round into the empty place where the late tooth had been and now wasn't increased her pleasure.

"Sit down, sweetheart," said Mrs. Belling, and Mary sat, smiling a cocksure smile. Mrs. Belling was also smiling and her pretty blue eyes were fixed unblinkingly on Mary. It was one of her characteristics that she never seemed to blink. She was looking extremely comfortable, propped up against a quantity of soft but not over-clean pillows. A torn lace cap hid her white hair and she wore a quilted pink satin dressing jacket with egg stains down the front. She had not bothered to take off her rings last night and they gleamed on her pudgy fingers. Mary's smile became a little strained, but she held it. Mrs. Belling had no difficulty in holding hers. Baba was asleep on her soiled pink satin eiderdown and the eiderdown smelled of Baba. Mrs. Belling smelled of the scent she used and the cigarette she was smoking. The fire was alight (Mrs. Belling liked an old-fashioned coal fire in her bedroom) and the window was shut and the room was unbearably close and stuffy. Mrs. Belling's clothes were on the floor. "This is my bedroom, and me in bed forty-five years from now," thought Mary, and the cocksureness went from her smile; but she still held it, and still continued to look at her aunt. Mrs. Belling's smile became fatter and more smug until it seemed as though it were graven into the dough of her face. Her fixed regard became a blank blue stare. It struck Mary suddenly that the terrible emptiness of the stare was entirely evil. The sweat pricked out on her forehead but she maintained her strained smile and though she blinked once or twice she did not look away. To do so would have been to give ground. She was getting a bit dizzy with the heat of the room but she felt it was extremely important that she should not give ground. If only Aunt Rose would speak. Surely one always blinked when one spoke? Mrs. Belling flicked the ash off her cigarette into a dish on the breakfast tray beside her and spoke, but she did not blink, and even while her mouth moved the smile seemed somehow there.

"Mr. Wentworth is a very charming man, darling, isn't he?"

Mary swallowed. "I don't know that I should call him charming," she said. "Courteous and dignified, but not what one is accustomed to call charming."

"What is one accustomed to call charming?" asked Mrs. Belling.

"I hadn't exactly thought," said Mary uncertainly.

"No, darling, you don't think. You didn't think, perhaps, that it might give my school a bad name for you to be seen by the whole of Silverbridge standing in the drive with a man's arm round you, crying against his shoulder? And the man one of the parents, and a parson? Parsons are always the worst, of course."

Without this last remark the demon might have remained asleep. Mary might have forgiven Aunt Rose for listening to Annie's exaggerations but a libellous remark about Don Quixote was too much. She was on her feet in a rage before she knew what she was doing. "How dare you, Aunt Rose!" she stormed. "Yes, I was crying, and that's the only bit of truth in what you say. But, in any case, would it matter if this school were given a bad name? I mean—"

"Yes?" said Mrs. Belling sweetly, but something about her

eyes made Mary stammer over her next words. "I mean—I mean—fewer children would come here. Their parents would know that this is a horrid school."

She stopped, for in spite of her anger and the heat of the room she felt cold with fear. For the first time she could not look at her aunt. Her eyes fell and she gave ground. She hardly knew what she expected; almost that Aunt Rose would rise up in bed like the evil specter in that awful ghost story of M. R. James', and clothed in her sheets arch over her like a breaking wave; and she would be found later dead beneath the soiled linen, an expression of terror graven upon her dead face.

But Mrs. Belling did nothing of the sort. She merely lay back against her pillows and lit another cigarette. "How emotional you are, darling," she said. "And how childish. A horrid school? You frighten yourself with your imaginings. So very Irish. Poor little Mary. What frightened you? The owls? Why were you crying?"

"I think, for Miss Giles," said Mary uncertainly, and made herself look at her aunt again. Mrs. Belling was smiling slightly, and her eyes, now, were following the movement of her fingers as she lazily fondled one of Baba's ears. Now that she could no longer see that blue stare Mary felt that her moment of panic had been ridiculous. Nothing was less like a breaking wave than her aunt at this moment. Was it true that she imagined too much?

"And what is the matter with Anabel Giles?" asked Mrs. Belling. "Crossed in love?"

From a woman who in her day had been loved and desired that struck Mary as a cruel remark. She loathed the sarcasms of women at each other's expense. "Perhaps so, Aunt Rose," she said, squaring her shoulders. "But not for a man. There are lots of ways of being crossed in love."

"Really?" said Mrs. Belling. "I'm always delighted to learn."

Aware of the sarcasm Mary yet stood her ground. "One's in

love with life when one's young," she said. "One trusts it. I expect Giles did. And now look at her, after it's let her down."

"I look at her every day," said Mrs. Belling, "and see a woman in a most enviable position—easy work, a comfortable home and good food."

"You know nothing about our food, Aunt Rose," flashed Mary. "And you don't care. It's that that makes Oaklands such a vile house to live in—you don't care."

Mrs. Belling withdrew her hand from Baba. "What have you been putting on Baba's ear?" she asked.

"Some stuff the vet gave me."

"When did you take Baba to the vet?"

"On Saturday."

"Then you flatly disobeyed me."

"Yes," said Mary. "What else could I do with Baba in the state he was and you not caring? Aunt Rose, why do you have Baba, and pet him and pretend to love him when you don't care? What's the point of it?"

Mrs. Belling suddenly raised her eyes and for a brief moment of astonishment Mary saw fear in them, and then anger. Yes, actually, anger. Mary had not known it was possible for Aunt Rose to bother to be angry, but she was, and her cold, strong anger was of a sort that beat down Mary's hot little demon and made her afraid again. Yet, when she spoke, her aunt's voice was soft as ever.

"Mary, where is the ointment the vet gave you?"

"In my room."

"Then fetch it."

Moving like a sleepwalker Mary obeyed. She did not want to, but she was again dominated. She came back with the ointment and put it into her aunt's hand. Mrs. Belling leaned forward and tossed it over the foot of the bed into the fire. "Now go and make your bed," she said.

It had been a hateful scene. Trembling and ashamed, Mary went.

204

3

Mrs. Belling lay back on her pillows trembling not with shame but with the violence of her anger. She was angry not so much at Mary's abominable rudeness as at the fact of her own capitulation. Fear and anger, the two enemies, had come upon her by stealth and thrown her. As a girl she had had something of a temper but had subdued it with the immense strength of her will, realizing that cold, clear-headed calculation was a more valuable instrument for ambition. Once she had reached maturity nothing had made her angry except the inconvenience of her husband's death. In the same way she had dealt with fear; nothing was more inhibiting than fear, nothing more confusing to the judgment. Yet here she was, thrown into a panic by a silly girl's silly question. "What's the point of it?" For just a moment it had opened up an abyss of intolerable emptiness. Her comfort had appeared to her not as an achieved Lotus Land that would never know change but as a facade erected to hide that sharp brink beyond which there is nothingness. It was a strange but entirely true fact that until Mary had put her silly question she had never realized the fact of death in relation to herself. She had of course never wanted to, and never tried to, and having never loved she had never known the bitterness of death. Her husband's death had disturbed her only from the material point of view and she had missed him no more than she would have missed a tradesman who left the place and went elsewhere. But Mary's question had caused her to miss her own sense of security. It had abruptly left her. If after all there were no security then there was no achievement. The smooth succession of her comfortable days was only a stream carrying her to that sharp brink. She looked at the fat little dog on her bed. A lap-dog had seemed to her a necessary element in her comfort; an extra hot water bottle on a cold day, a sort of extenuation of herself upon whom to lavish the caresses

and indulgences of self-love, an aroma of devotion forever aris-
ing on the hearth. Now for the first time she saw what a repulsive object the little creature had become under this treatment
and with sudden energy she kicked him off the bed. He fell with
a yelp to the floor and lay there stunned with hurt astonishment,
then picked himself up and stood up against the bed to lick her
hand. In a spasm of exasperation she raised herself in bed and
slapped his head as hard as she could. One of her rings caught
the corner of his eye and he crept under the bed and hid there
whimpering.

Mrs. Belling lay back against her pillows, furious, exasperated and afraid. Not for years had she put forth so much energy.
She was panting and for the first time in her life she felt ill, not
just indisposed but deathly ill. Terror such as she had never
known, terror to which her past fear had been a mere nothing,
rose up before her like a black wave, crashed down and blotted
her out.

Yet presently she was lying in her bed as usual. She would
have said that she had gone down screaming, that the room had
fallen into ruins about her, but there was no one with her and
the room looked as before. Her sight seemed a little misted and
she could not see her clock, but she could hear the clink of
Annie washing up the breakfast things and realized that she had
been blotted out only a short while... Blotted out... The
phrase was full of horror for her. "Blot his name out of the
book of life." She did not know where she had heard the sentence but as it came sliding into her mind she felt sheeted with
cold. The iciness was creeping up from her feet and when it
reached her heart she would die. "I must have a hot bottle," she
mumbled. "Quick, quick, Annie, a hot bottle or I'll die." But
Annie was not there and when she tried to lift her right hand
to the bell she could not move it. She lay there for a full ten
minutes, breathing heavily, the sweat of her agony breaking
out on her forehead. Not physical agony, for she felt no pain,
but the agony of her realization. Then she tried again with her

left hand, found she had the use of it, reached across herself and rang the bell. Presently Annie, wiping red hands and arms on her greasy apron, was beside her. "Get me a hot bottle, Annie," she whispered thickly. "A hot bottle." The mist had cleared from her eyes now and she could guess what she looked like by Annie's face. How revolting Annie looked, with her mouth dropped open like that and her eyes popping out of her head.

"Why, ma'am, you do look poorly," ejaculated Annie. "Shall I get the doctor?"

"No. A bottle."

"Best get the doctor," pleaded Annie.

"No," repeated Mrs. Belling. "A bottle. Do as I say. Quickly."

Even now her will could compel and Annie ran. Mrs. Belling kept her eyes shut. She did not want the doctor. She did not want it put into words. It might pass. It might be nothing. It might be her imagination. If the hot bottle would only come. If she could only go to sleep. If she went to sleep she might wake up and find it had passed. But Annie must be quick with the bottle. Annie must be quick. Annie was quick, but even so she would not forget the misery of those moments until she felt the warmth of the bottle against her cold feet.

"Just tired," she mumbled to Annie. "A day in bed. Tell Miss—Miss—" She could not remember their names.

"Yes," said Annie. "Anything you'd fancy for lunch?"

"Let me alone," said Mrs. Belling, and reassured by the snappishness of her tone Annie tiptoed out of the room, leaving the door ajar.

"I'll never sleep," thought Mrs. Belling. "Never sleep. I'll never sleep." But surprisingly, mercifully, as the warmth stole up her body she began to feel a little sleepy. Between sleeping and waking she heard Baba whimpering under the bed and felt a momentary stirring of something like compunction. She swung on a dark tide but not overwhelmed yet because the compunction bore her up just once more. Suspended between one world and another she remembered dimly that there had been other times when some weakening of self-love had lifted her up like this to abide the questioning, the detested probing questioning. "Whom do men say that I am? Whom do men say that I am?" She had always refused even to consider an answer, struggled to get away from the intolerable claim made upon her, fought to get back to her ownership of herself. The questioning now was childishly simple, not the question which had been like the thundering of a great wave along a beach but a gentle question put to a child. "Won't you call the little dog out from under the bed? Won't you call the little dog out from under the bed?" Swinging in darkness on the dark tide she saw him quite clearly, shivering on the floor, a paw that had been hurt in his fall doubled under him, blood oozing from the corner of his eye where her ring had cut him, an obese unpleasant little dog who loved her and had tried to lick her hand. But it was too much trouble to drag herself out of sleep and call to him. Why should she? She was just getting warm and comfortable. Let him stay there. "No," she said.

The warm comfort of her feather bed seemed to rise up and lap itself about her and she slept. When she was deeply asleep, snoring heavily with her mouth open, Baba knew there was no more hope and he crept out from under the bed and dragged himself through the open door. Out on the landing he paused, his hurt paw lifted and trembling. The door of a cupboard across the landing was open and he limped towards it. He crept into the darkest corner and lay there, still trembling. He could not sleep.

4

Miss Giles, in her cold neat bedroom, stretched the quilt over the bed she had just finished making and glanced at her watch. They had no school matron at present (it was hard to get any staff to stay at Oaklands) and Mary, who should have super-

intended the bed-making of the boarders and then gone downstairs to receive the day girls, was still with Mrs. Belling. The
bed-making had superintended itself but she supposed she must
take Mary's place in the cloakroom, and then once more teach
the babies with her own children until Mrs. Belling had finished
with Mary. Every morning now she had to fight a desperate
reluctance to take up the burden of the day. The weight of her
despair was worst in the mornings. As the day went on it got a
bit easier, but at first it did not seem possible to face these children again. How she hated them! Especially that little whey-
faced Margary Wentworth whose defenselessness roused all the
cruelty in her. She was dimly aware that she was cruel but she
seemed as powerless to control the rush of sharp words to her
tongue as she was powerless to control the onset of pain in her
body. Both seemed to have their roots in her exhaustion, that
deep soul-exhaustion of which she was aware but did not understand. But she knew it was a vicious circle. The harder she fought
her pain and sin the more tired she was, and the more exhausted
she was the more ill and bad-tempered she became... She did
not believe it was possible for her to go downstairs and teach
this morning... The hall clock struck the hour and her sense of
duty and discipline asserted itself. She picked up a pile of exercise books from the table. Neat, efficient, upright, her thin sallow
face set in its bitter lines, she went downstairs.

Once again, her first lesson that morning was arithmetic. Of
the various subjects she taught arithmetic was the most agonizing
to her and her pupils. Yet in her own schooldays math had
been, after music, her favorite subject. Standing in the cloakroom she remembered she had even been rather brilliant at it.
The precision of it, the infinite variety within the framework of
eternal and lovely law, had roused her awe and delight in much
the same way as music had done, and the sight of the stars on a
clear night. There too, in the glory of the bright sky, the law
was inviolable... The music of the spheres. The dancing measure of words in great verse. The song of the birds, obedient to

209

the swing of the seasons and the dawning or waning of light. . .
In her youth she had never thought of the divine marriage of
order with infinite variety without longing to feel the pulse of
the dancing measure in her blood, aching to hear the unheard
music. "Not to the sensual ear, but, more endear'd. . ."

Crossing the hall to her classroom she was astonished to find
that she still remembered how she had once felt about these
things. She stopped in the hall and noticed how the mist of the
rain was thinning and the light breaking through. Outside the
hall window sprays of a rose tree hung low, heavy with the
rain, and each spray was strung with silver drops. What was
happening to her, that her eyes should be opened like this?
What was happening to the house, that its atmosphere should be
freshening about her? It was as though far off across a waste of
mud flats the bright tide had turned.

She opened the door of her classroom and went in. The rows
of detestable little girls were demurely yet rebelliously seated
behind their ugly inkstained desks. She felt, as always, their
hatred rising against her, forgot the bright tide and hated them
in return. She was aware again of that dull muffled feeling in
her head, the precursor of more headache, and of griping pain
below her breasts. Desolation seized her, and the sharp words
that she would use presently thrust through it like steel needles
in her mind. She walked erect to her desk and heard in anticipation, shrinking from it, the dull thud that the pile of exercise
books would make when she dropped them on the hard wood.

But she did not drop them. She stood holding them, gazing at
the bunch of flowers laid on her desk; stubby little snowdrops
with the earth still on them, wet primroses, wild white violets,
roots and all, some sprays of moss and a few beautiful great
purple violets, the whole bound about with a spray of ivy with
tiny deep-red leaves. It had been painstakingly arranged, yet
with a sweet wild grace that delighted her. She put the exercise
books down very gently and picked it up. She had forgotten
how lovely the scent of wet violets can be. The coolness of the

rain was on her hands... The cold, sweet spring... She lifted the bunch to her face, and was carried back forty-five years to the Cotswold village where she had gone to stay with her grandparents, a thin-faced town child whom no one had cared about. But she, in those days, had cared about the wild white violets and the moss.

She looked up and saw all the little girls watching, wondering how she would react to this unprecedented occasion; all but one staring at her with mockery, curiosity or dislike, but nothing else. The one was Margary Wentworth at the end of the row, who was gazing at her with an expression which at first she did not recognize, so long was it since anyone had looked at her in pure pleasure. It was thirty-five years since she had stood before a village audience and sung them the songs they loved in her untrained contralto voice that was lovelier than either she or they realized. They had looked up at her then as Margary was looking now, delighting in the music that was a bridge of light between them, yet greeting her across it. That was pure pleasure; two delighting together in the beauty that united them. She and Margary looked at each other and between them was the spring.

"Thank you, Margary," said Miss Giles. "Now who will fetch me a vase of water to keep them fresh?"

Every child in the room put up her hand. This was a grand arithmetic lesson. Five minutes of it gone already and another ten before the flowers were arranged.

"Henrietta," said Miss Giles. "You fetch it."

"Let *me*, Miss Giles," said Pat. "She'll spill the water."

"No, she won't," said Miss Giles. "Henrietta, ask Annie for a vase of water and carry it carefully."

She chose Winkle because a few moments ago the curiosity on the child's face had borne no likeness to the curiosity on the faces of the others. The rest had been wondering which of several possible reactions of her own they would have the pleasure of tearing to tatters during break, but Winkle had been merely wondering what expressions of pleasure would fall from Miss

Giles's lips when she saw the big violets from the frame. Miss Giles, still standing holding the little bunch, could visualize its gathering; the wild flowers gathered in the misty rain from garden and hedgerow, the big violets begged from the child's father as a final glory of decoration. She could see Margary bending over, her rubber boots squelching in the wet, her too-large mackintosh flapping round her like the tatters of a small scarecrow, wisps of straight hair struggling out from under her sou'wester. What a plain child she was. "And I was just such another," thought Miss Giles. She glanced at Margary with a shy smile, and wondered, "Did I have that expressive face?" For Margary's answering smile, equally shy, had illumined a face where all that she was feeling was most clearly written... Thankfulness that it had "come off," humble delight in the fact that she had given pleasure, an almost painful relief that there were to be no sarcasms at her expense. "And it's been my pleasure to torment this child," thought Miss Giles. "What have I become?" A new sort of pang wrung her, the first of its kind. It was as though a hand suddenly squeezed her heart, so that she was breathless. And she was supposed to be giving an arithmetic lesson.

"Isn't it March the twenty-first?" she asked her astonished class; for whatever reaction they had expected from Miss Giles it had not been this strange immobility, this complete absence of any action whatever. They gazed at her with awe, feeling to the full that medieval reverence for someone obviously touched in the head.

"Yes, Miss Giles," said Pat.

"The first day of spring?" asked Miss Giles uncertainly.

"Yes, Miss Giles," piped Pussy Harker.

"It scarcely seems a suitable day for arithmetic," said Miss Giles. "Shall I read to you instead?"

A breath of incredulous delight exhaled from the class, and Winkle returned with both hands gripped tightly around a small blue bowl full of water. Breathing stertorously, her tongue stuck out at the side of her mouth, her eyes fixed on the bowl, she advanced at a snail's pace. Enormous trust had been reposed in her. If she were to spill the water now she would never lift her head again. She could see the lower portion of Miss Giles's desk, like the foothills of a mountain, in front of her, and stopped almost in tears. If she were to lift the bowl up towards the summit the water would slop over and she would be undone. But Miss Giles bent over, her hands came down over Winkle's, grasped the bowl and lifted it up. Winkle breathed deeply, rubbed her numbed hands up and down her thighs and returned to her desk.

"Read us a *story*, Miss Giles?" gasped Pat.

"If you like," said Miss Giles. "Margary, fetch me something you would all enjoy from the bookcase in the dining room. Pussy, go with her."

How had Miss Giles known she would hate to go alone, wondered Margary? But with fat little Pussy with her it was joy to be sent to choose a book. "I'd not have liked to go alone, at her age," thought Miss Giles as the two little girls left the room. "Everyone looking at you as you cross the room; and you know you're gangling and awkward."

The bookcase in the dining room held a motley collection of tattered children's books, bought at odd times to keep the boarders quiet. Margary and Pussy squatted on their heels and surveyed them. "*The Pride of the Fourth Form*," suggested Pussy. "It's smashing."

"We don't want a school story on the first day of spring," said Margary.

"*The Princess and Curdie*," said Pussy with accommodating cheerfulness. She did not much care for that sort of soppy stuff herself but it was Margary who had won them this extraordinary deliverance and she deserved humoring.

"Too long," said Margary.

"Well, buck up," said Pussy. "What *do* you want?"

Margary was not quite sure, but she thought she would know

213

when she saw it. Her eyes ran over the titles, and she pulled out *The Secret Garden.*

"But that's just as long," complained Pussy.

"The part where she finds the garden is something by itself," said Margary. Back in the classroom again she said shyly to Miss Giles, "Please, could it be from the end of chapter eight for as long as we've time for?"

Miss Giles took the book. She remembered vaguely that this had been one of her childhood's favorites but she could not remember now what it had been about. Yet the moment she began to read it all came back to her, and she remembered why the child she had been had liked this book. It had been because Mary was a plain unattractive little girl whom no one had cared about particularly; and yet she had found the secret garden. With a sudden stab of longing Miss Giles thought she remembered a memory of something or other, then found that the memory had flashed and gone. But it had left her in a nostalgic mood. She told herself she would read aloud to the two little girls, Anabel and Margary, now for always linked together in her mind, as once she had sung to the village folk who had loved her singing. She would make music for them they would not forget. She sat down, opened the book and found the place.

Five minutes later Mary, running down the stairs in a great hurry, the ravages of a burst of angry tears in her bedroom only very clumsily repaired, stopped at the bottom in astonishment when she heard Miss Giles's voice. She had been about to retrieve Winkle and the rest of her babies for their singing lesson, but instead she sat down on the bottom stair and listened. The door was ajar and she could hear very clearly. Whatever did old Giles think she was doing, reading to the kids at this time of day? Had she gone crackers? Well, of course they all were in this place; it was the maddest, craziest school. And what in the world was she reading?

" '...she held back the swinging curtain of ivy and pushed back the door which opened slowly—slowly.' "

A broad smile illumined Mary's blotched and woebegone face. So *that* was what old Giles was reading. She moved along the stair and settled herself comfortably with her back against the wall.

" 'There were other trees in the garden, and one of the things which made the place look strangest and loveliest was that climbing roses had run all over them and swung down long tendrils which made light swaying curtains.' "

What an astonishingly lovely voice Giles had when she read aloud, deep and rather thrilling, a singer's voice.

" 'Everything was strange and silent and she seemed to be hundreds of miles away from everyone, but somehow she did not feel lonely at all.' "

Yet presently Mary would find Dickon, her young lover and take him to the secret garden.

Mary O'Hara lost the thread of the story and became instead lost in a mood as nostalgic as that of Miss Giles. "Shall I ever find him?" she wondered. "Five up to date, and I've liked them, but that's all. I liked that dentist—what's his name—Donald Woodcote—and he'll be asking me to go to a flick with him as soon as he's finished my stoppings. I saw it in his eye. Nice, but ordinary, and I've always wanted to marry a hero." She was about to sigh tragically but her eye was caught by a rose branch outside the window, with its curve of diamond drops, and she changed her mind. "Oh, the joy of the world," she thought abruptly. "Joy, even in a drop of rain on a green stem."

11

MARY'S joy was short-lived, for the rest of the morning went from bad to worse. Her cold increased and like all exceptionally healthy people she was apt to exaggerate minor ailments when they afflicted herself, though when they afflicted other people her optimism took a more hopeful view. "I'm sure I've got flu," she said to Miss Giles at break, over the tepid tea brought to them by a worried Annie. "It hurts to swallow."

"That's not to say you have flu," said Miss Giles with maddening calm, and not looking up from the *Daily Telegraph*. "Why not take your temperature? The thermometer is in the bathroom cupboard. It'll stop you fussing."

Mary flew from the room, lest she wring Giles's neck, and up the stairs to the bathroom, banging the door behind her. Fussing! And here she was with a temperature of a hundred and two keeping on her feet with the greatest difficulty just so as not to leave poor old Giles to do all the work alone. She inserted the thermometer under her tongue and sat down on the edge of the bath. "If I die will Donald Woodcote send a wreath?" she wondered. "Daffodils and tulips." She withdrew the thermometer. 98.4. She shook the thermometer furiously over the side of the bath, dropped it and smashed it. "Damn!" she said for about the sixth time that morning, gathered up the pieces and went downstairs again.

"A hundred and two?" asked Miss Giles, still not looking up from the *Daily Telegraph*.

"Sub-normal," snapped Mary.

"Bad luck," said Miss Giles.

"Heavens, I don't *want* to be ill!" ejaculated Mary.

"Don't you? I thought you did."

"I'm in such a rage. I just want to be what I'm not, that's all," said Mary.

"What would you like to be?" asked Miss Giles.

"Not a school marm. Those kids have been driving me so wild this morning that I've snapped the heads off the lot of them."

"Don't do that," said Miss Giles absently, her head still bent. "It's not their fault if you've caught a cold."

Mary gasped, holding to the edge of her chair with both hands lest she seize the tea-cosy and bring it down on Giles's head. *Giles* to tell her not to snap at the children! Giles! She sneezed explosively into her handkerchief.

Miss Giles looked up and met the accusing eyes above the handkerchief, then looked down again. "I know, O'Hara," she said. "It's not the children's fault that I'm not a happy woman. Yet I take it out of them. You're quite right. Yet, do you know, I've only just begun to realize it."

Mary's eyes became gentle. "One doesn't realize," she murmured.

"One doesn't want to," said Miss Giles. "Who wants to realize that human nature, not excepting one's own, is fundamentally cruel? Belsen, the torture chambers of Barcelona, all such things, they are putrescence pushing up from the general unhealthiness. We are all intolerably wicked."

"You've spent most of break staring at the *Daily Telegraph*," said Mary. "Are you reading it?"

"No," said Miss Giles.

"Then read it," said Mary. "You're in no state of health just now to stare at your own intolerable wickedness. You'd take a jaundiced view. Wait till you've had a tonic and a fortnight's holiday."

Miss Giles smiled. "It's your half-day, isn't it?"

"Yes. I'm going to get those tickets."

"Then get me a tonic at the same time, will you? And some for yourself too, I should think, with that cold. What do you usually take?"

"Anything that has one of those nice little booklets with pictures of before and after," said Mary. "It's the pictures that do me good. I'm very suggestible."

"That's the blessing of being a Celt," said Miss Giles. "I'm from the manufacturing midlands and I find faith hard. Break's over. Ring the bell, O'Hara."

The rest of the morning continued difficult, for resolved not to snap the children's heads off Mary taught them with that long-suffering, martyrish gentleness and patience which are so maddening to those who are being suffered and endured. The children only vaguely understood the situation but they did feel that they were being treated as though they were naughty, when they were not, and that by their beloved Miss O'Hara, and with that unerring sense of suitability which children possess they made the crime fit the punishment and became naughty, and the morning ended in tears. At dinner time they were still damp, and there was underdone cod and overcooked rice pudding, and the rain had come on again worse than ever.

"Ought you to go out, now it's turned like this?" asked Miss Giles after dinner.

"I must walk it off," said Mary. "Of all the tempers I've ever been in this is the worst. I tell you, Giles, I've never been quite so hateful as I am today."

Upstairs in her bedroom she could not find anything. She had finished her face powder and though she had a new box somewhere it had disappeared. She dropped her lipstick and it rolled into a dark corner and vanished. She could not remember where she had put her beret, and dragging out a heavy drawer to look for it she pulled the drawer too far and fell over backwards with it. "Why? Why?" she demanded furiously of fate. "Yesterday

218

was such a lovely day. I was so well and looked so pretty and I felt a saint." The contrast between yesterday and today was so ludicrous that she began to laugh. She had noticed before that health and the consciousness of beauty caused what felt like a holy serenity to spread through one's whole being and one's pride mistook the source of it. In a chastened mood she drew the hood of a very shabby old brown raincoat over her head, hiding her bright hair. Her face she left as it was, red-nosed and shiny; on a day like this no one would be out and no one would see her. She stuffed her handbag full of handkerchiefs and ran downstairs. Just as she was opening the front door to escape from the hated house Annie came out into the hall and waylaid her.

"Miss O'Hara, I'm that worried about Mrs. Belling. She's sleeping so heavy."

"Well, do her good, Annie," said Mary impatiently. "You told us she was having a day in bed because she was tired. Though what she does to make her tired only she and heaven know."

"But she didn't eat her lunch, Miss O'Hara."

"Mary O'Hara, I hate you," said Mary to herself. "That last remark of yours was quite vile. Now if Annie says Aunt Rose had dover sole and strawberry mousse you are *not* to remark that the school had cod and rice pudding."

"Such a nice little bit of sole and a peach to follow," said Annie sadly. "Very dainty it was."

"Really?" said Mary with sarcasm. "Nicely cooked I expect, neither underdone nor overdone, not like—" She bit her lip. "Don't worry, Annie," she said gently. "People don't feel hungry when they're in bed. But she'll wake up ready for her tea. You'll see."

She slipped through the front door and turned to shut it, but Annie had hold of it. "I wish you'd just step up, Miss, and take a look at your aunt."

"It's my half-day," said Mary desperately. "And anyway I'm

no good at illness. If you're anxious ask Miss Giles to look at her."

She turned and ran, and did not stop running until she was some way down the road. Even then she walked quickly, with a queer feeling in her spine, as though she expected a long hairy arm, with a clammy hand with clutching fingers at the end of it, to reach out of the gate of Oaklands, take hold of her about the waist and pull her back again. The sensation is well known by those who have only one half-day a week.

She walked a little further and saw the old granite bridge spanning the river. A faint gleam of sun shone through the rain and lit the wet stone to silver. The tops of the tall elms were faintly flushed with color and a hint of a rainbow in the sky echoed the arc of the bridge. The fugitive moment of beauty came down like a bright sword between Mary and Oaklands. When it passed she was set free. She stopped hurrying and turned quietly to the right across the bridge and stood there leaning on the parapet looking at the slipping water, pearl grey and dimpled with the rain.

But though she was free from the oppression of Oaklands she had not forgotten about it and she felt ashamed that she had not gone upstairs to look at her aunt. After all, she *was* her aunt, and it would have been kinder to Annie; also to poor old Giles. The fact was that she had funked it. She had dreaded going back to that room after the interview of the morning. It had been an utterly horrid interview, and yet she did not quite know why. Nothing had happened exactly, except that she had been rude to Aunt Rose. She was ashamed of that and yet somehow not ashamed of the interview as a whole, for she had fought as well as she could. It had been an odd sensation, that feeling that a fight was on and that she and her aunt had in their private quarrel been like the two spearheads of opposing forces. Those forces must have had great strength, for she had felt as though she leaned back against immense power. "Is it ludicrous?" she wondered. "Would such power make use of a rude, undisciplined, self-righteous gawk like me?" She supposed it would. She supposed that any human spirit was at every moment a spearhead for one side or the other. The battle faced all ways and it was always a hand to hand tussle, and yet always with the power of all behind each. "We won that," she thought. "I had a queer feeling in the middle of it as though ... I remember ... as though far off the tide turned. . . Did I really think that or is it the river making me think I did?"

She blinked, for the water was now liquid silver. The sun was out again. She turned, conscious suddenly of someone with her, not just passing by but with her as no one had been with her yet. A tall scarecrow figure, in a disreputable muddy mackintosh and an obliterating dripping hat, was standing near her. He raised the hat, revealing a countenance startlingly other than Mary had expected, and immediately replaced it again.

"Please forgive me, but could you tell me where the vet lives?"

"Which vet?" asked Mary. "There are two."

"Fool that I am!" lamented the man. "I never asked which vet."

"Is it cows and pigs or dogs and cats?" asked Mary. "They both do both, but they are specialists."

"Cows and pigs," said the man. "One pig, to be correct, Josephine."

"That'll be Mr. Viner," said Mary. "I hope it's not serious?"

"Not quite the thing. Just to call at his leisure. Our telephone is out of order, but I wanted the walk. It's my half-day."

"Mine too," said Mary, and found that she had crossed the bridge and was walking towards the little town in the scarecrow's company. "I appear to be showing you the way," she said, in surprise.

"It's very necessary that you should," he replied, "for I don't know it."

She suited her stride to his, contentedly and easily, walking not as people walk in the town, going a short distance in a hurry,

221

but as they walk in the country, going a long way for pleasure. Standing beside her he had been with her as no one had ever been with her, asking for guidance he had said something that she knew was of profound importance to both of them, walking together she could scarcely believe that five minutes ago she had been alone. What was happening? She did not feel anything about him particularly, except an overmastering curiosity to see his face again. Accustomed to go straight for what she wanted she said, "That hat is a wonderful combination of hat and umbrella in one, but it *has* stopped raining."

He laughed and took it off. She looked at him, as she was accustomed to look at every stranger, with frank interest. Then not knowing what she did she pushed her hood back, for it was getting in the way of her vision, and looked at him with slowly growing recognition. So when it happened suddenly this was how it happened. She had often wondered. But the magazine stories had got it all wrong. It was not an affair of sudden heartbeats, and hot and cold flushes, as though one were going to have influenza, it was just this quiet recognition. But in the approach of love there must be a sharpness, for that moment of beauty that had come down like a sword had cut her life in two. When she crossed the bridge she had crossed from her girlhood to womanhood.

The moment of understanding passed and she was aware of the dark eyes of an extremely attractive man looking at her with that sparkle of lively appreciation with which she was familiar in attracted males. She responded with her accustomed reciprocal sparkle, delightfully conscious as she smiled and dimpled of her own prettiness. Then she sneezed, and remembered. No lipstick, no powder, a cold in the head, hair anyhow. A slut like Aunt Rose. Like Annie. She was betrayed now by her own indiscipline. She looked away from him. It had not been appreciation she had seen in his face, only a puckish mockery. She would not look at him again but as she walked on, sadly blowing her nose, she could still see his vivid mocking face. It had only been a short

222

journey together after all. She stopped, turning her head away to sneeze once more. "It's that house there," she said in muffled tones. "The one with the green door. Good-bye."

"You've a rotten cold," he said. "Bad luck." She resented the amusement in his tone with a sudden flash of the demon, but her quick movement away from him was rendered a little uncertain by her inability to remember where she was going. "Wouldn't a cup of tea do you good?"

"It's not tea-time," she said. "And I've shopping to do." Then she remembered her manners and turned towards him. "But thank you. Good-bye."

Yet she remained where she was. Yes, he was amused, but not unkindly so; from the way he looked at her she might have been Winkle. He was a much older man than she had thought. He had taken off the ridiculous mud-caked mackintosh, much too big for him and obviously not his, and she saw that he wore shabby but well-made clothes. He had an air of assurance and distinction that made her suddenly feel like a little girl, like Winkle, and yet he had an exhausted look that made her feel intensely motherly. She hesitated, for once in her life at a loss as to what to do, and she was glad when he abruptly took charge.

"Look," he said, "you go and do your shopping and I'll go to the vet, and then we'll meet at the teashop over there. It won't be so early by that time. I know you're not the kind of girl who lets herself be picked up in this casual fashion, but then I'm not the kind of man who does casual picking up, but this once, why not? I'm staying at Belmaray as temporary pig-man and gardener to Miss Wentworth at the manor. I think her nephew the vicar would vouch for me; though I'm bound to say he doesn't know me very well. Is that all right?"

"Quite all right," said Mary, smiling. "I teach Mr. Wentworth's little girls."

"Do you? Then we can talk about them. I like Margary. Good-bye for the moment then." He smiled at her and went quickly across the road without looking back. She watched him, thinking how well he moved, and then suddenly realized that she was watching him and turned away, feeling suddenly desolate. This sense of recognition, was it possible for one person to have it and not the other?

She got the concert tickets and then went to Boots, where she bought a tonic for herself and Giles, and lipstick and powder. Then going upstairs to the library she sat on the window seat and did her face. She was humiliated to the depths to see the fright she was looking. The scarecrow he had seemed at first could have felt kinship with such an object, but not the man who had emerged from the chrysalis. Pig-man and gardener? He must be keeping pigs for a joke. Or as a cure. Country people said being with sheep cured whooping cough. What did pigs cure? Now she came to think of it he had had in his face that something indefinable that makes the beholder sorry even when he is only a passer-by in the street. Something contrary to well-being is there, some strain or conflict or sickness of mind or body, and one hates to pass on and to have done nothing to help. Was it true, as Giles had said, that human nature was fundamentally cruel? Fundamentally compassionate too, surely. She had snapped the children's heads off this morning and yet she would give her life for any of them. One was very ready to give one's life for those one loved, even though one was not very nice to them always. Whatever it was or wasn't, she thought, human nature was fundamentally odd. And having reached this profound philosophic conclusion, and being distinctly pleased with it, she went downstairs and out into the street.

She walked to the teashop slowly and with a queer mixture of eagerness and reluctance. She wanted to be there and yet she had a sense of inadequacy, of shrinking from something that might be too much for her. With her usual self-confidence at a low ebb she arrived at the teashop shy and hesitant and found the pig-man already waiting for her; with on his side no lack of self-confidence as he got up and welcomed her, helped her off with her coat, settled her in her chair and ordered their tea. She had never dined at a fashionable restaurant or had supper at a night-club, but that was where he made her feel that she was. She realized that his actions and manner had the ease of long custom. His talk was the gay automatic patter of a man who takes pretty girls out to meals so often that he can entertain them in his sleep. His eyes were distant and troubled and she thought he had not noticed the change for the better in her looks. She was suddenly piqued and her shyness left her. She waited for a pause in his easy talk about nothing at all and then asked abruptly, "Shall I call you the pig-man, or have you a name?"

There was a sudden odd, sharp pause. Had she been rude, she wondered? She knew that she was, sometimes, in her abruptness. She looked at him anxiously and saw that he was looking at her with such profound awareness of her that she realized he had never been unaware, only his awareness had gone deeper than what she had done to her face. She was ashamed. "I'm sorry," she said.

"What about?" he asked sharply.

"I was—trivial."

"So was I. Such a waste of time. My name is Michael Stone."

The name seemed familiar but she could not remember why. Both Michael and Stone were, after all, very usual names. Perhaps she had met a Michael Stone before. She smiled and said, "My name is Mary O'Hara. I'm afraid it sounds rather like a musical comedy but I can't help that. I'm Irish." He laughed in sudden delight and she wondered why. "Is that so funny?" she asked.

"Funny that you should think it necessary to tell me you're Irish. Apart from the name your looks give you away even before you open your mouth, and when you speak you're damned entirely."

"Damned?" she asked, affronted.

"In the eyes of these stiff English. They're so damned superior. We Celts are the blood in their veins but they don't know it. Their loss, of course."

"You don't look Irish," said Mary.

"Heaven forbid! I'm Welsh."

"But Stone isn't a Welsh name."

His face tightened and Mary thought she had been abrupt again. "I'm Welsh," he repeated.

"From the mountains?" she asked.

"I was born in the mountains," he said.

"I live in a valley running down to the sea," said Mary. "Miles from anywhere. The gales roar over your head but it's warm and sheltered in the valley."

"You must like it here," he said gently. "With the greenness and the soft air and the wind from the sea. Do you know Belmaray?"

"Not yet. I've not been here long. I teach at Oaklands, my aunt's little private school. But Mr. Wentworth asked me to go and see them at Belmaray. "

"You must go," he said. "And when you come you must see the manor and its garden. Ruined, but so lovely. They've very little to do with this world at all. And neither has Miss Wentworth."

"Is she so extraordinary?" asked Mary.

"Very extraordinary. She gave me the job, though I had no reference, and when I told her I'd been in prison she never asked why."

It seemed to Mary that the room was tipping over. The table in front of her seemed to be on a slant and she braced her shoulders. But the earthquake was in her own mind, where recent thoughts and phrases were falling headlong one over the other... Human nature is fundamentally odd. Ruined but so lovely. One is loath to pass on. I always wanted to marry a hero but I would give my life for one of the children... The room steadied about her again and she found that he was helping her on with her coat. She had not looked at him. Why all this melodrama in her mind? No one was asking her to give her life. Nothing was required of her at present but common politeness and not to pass on. She turned round and smiled at him. "Are you in a hurry to get back to Josephine or shall we walk as far as Farthing Reach, where the swans are? It's up-river a little way. Not far."

"Yes, I'd like that," he said.

Outside they found fitful sunshine, pools of clear blue above them in the sky and reflected below in the shining tarmac of the road. It was cool and fresh with now and then a scent of flowers drifting across their faces, for Silverbridge was one of those towns that have old walled gardens hidden away behind the house fronts, gardens where the violets have been multiplying for generations. When they reached the path by the river they had these gardens upon their right and every now and then, through an open door in an old stone wall, they could see drifts of daffodils and the crimson and gold of polyanthus. Beside one of these garden doors Mary noticed a board up, "For Sale," and through the door she could see a particularly attractive little house. "What lunatics, to sell a little house like that," she thought briefly, and then forgot it, intent upon talking to Michael. It was she, now, who kept their talk going for Michael's mood had become one of exhaustion and discouragement. He had taken a very sudden decision, she guessed, in telling her what he had, and now he wished he had not done it.

"I wonder where you got that hat?" she asked him, laughing.

"Borrowed it from Bob Hewett, who's laid up at present. He's senior gardener and pig-man. I haven't had time yet to collect any suitable pig-garments of my own. He's a grand old chap. Doesn't resent me."

"He's glad to have you, I expect."

"Possibly."

"And you like Margary best of the Wentworth children."

"She's like her father."

"It's Winkle who's my pet," she said, and kept him going with stories of her children, racily told, until they came to Farthing Reach, where the river widened almost to a lake, with

227

small streams winding through the sedges and the water-meadows carpeted with kingcups. Year after year the swans nested deep within the sedges and a few of them were always to be found here. There were three now, floating serenely on the blue water. A small wooden bridge crossed a stream here and they stopped and leaned their arms upon the parapet while stillness and silence held them. The sun was low and the streaming gold from the west burnished the kingcups to an unbelievable brilliance. Michael shut his eyes against the bright blue and green and gold, and the intolerable whiteness of the swans. The gentleness and softness of the west-country, that just now so suited his mood, was absent from this scene, and there was something piercing about its brilliant beauty.

"Gorgeous birds," murmured Mary beside him.

"Yes," he answered.

"You're not looking at them."

He abruptly opened his eyes. "I'm sorry. And you've brought me all this way to look at them. Their plumage is sheer light. Beautiful but rather alarming."

"They're made of alarming stuff," Mary agreed. "Light and power. Don't you think a swan is one of the birds of power? They focus something, as a stormcock does."

"Something I've never liked the thought of," said Michael.

"They heard you. They're moving away," said Mary. To her there was no sharpness in the bright beauty, though it woke almost unbearable longing in her. All about her she was conscious only of a pure distillation of good will, but she could not reach it. It was odd, she thought. With her aunt this morning, that regular churchgoer and indefatigable knitter for charities, she had been conscious of such evil. With this man, of whom she knew nothing except that he had lately been in prison, of such good, his good a part of the good will that she could not reach. She thought of her own longing for goodness, her deep intent of love, and of her abysmal failure today. There was a missing link. Until the death of self had come to pass the deep intent could not make contact with the good will that waited, longing as the heart longed to bring the seed to flower.

"Another man would not have told me," she said suddenly, her own truth delighting in this absence of the guile she hated.

"I told you because it struck me that when you came to Belmaray I should like to be the one to show you the manor. If I had done that without telling you what I have told you we should have advanced very quickly to friendship." He smiled at her. "Two Celts in a foreign land. It wouldn't have been fair to you."

He was still looking at her and the sadness in him seemed to dim the brightness. She realized now, with awe and fear, that the recognition had not been on her side only.

"Now it will be quite fair," she said. "And I couldn't let anyone but you introduce me to Josephine."

They were walking back towards the town now. He was looking away and did not immediately answer. Then he looked round and smiled again, a smile of such delight that it took her by surprise. "You're as extraordinary as Miss Wentworth," he said. "I believe you would do as she has done, let it go on to friendship and never try to find out, from myself or another, what crime I've committed."

"It wouldn't go on to friendship if I did," said Mary. "I believe asking questions is fatal to—to—any sort of happy relationship. I try not to ask them even in my mind. I don't mean that I don't wonder about people and try to understand them, I do, but never—" She paused, blushing hotly. She was sounding conceited and trite.

"We have a right to our own experience," said Michael. "It's a part of our house of life. You don't go into other people's houses unless they invite you in."

"No," said Mary in a small voice. It struck her suddenly that that was an invitation that had never come her way. In the large turbulent family to which she belonged intimacy had been only of the physical sort. Their bodies had tumbled over each other in a constricted space but the harassed parents had shown little of themselves to the children and invited no confidence in return. To have that sort of door opened to you by someone you loved, to go in, and thereafter for the same house of life to shelter two souls. Did that ever happen? Or was it like the contact she longed for, a happiness achieved so rarely that she could scarcely hope for it? If it could happen, as the fruit of much patience and selflessness, then it might be one of the best things life had to offer.

"But no one can be expected to build a friendship in a vacuum," said Michael, smiling. "There must be a few facts to make some sort of scaffolding." He paused and she could feel by the unease in her own body how difficult it was for him to go on. Then he plunged jerkily and curtly into it. "I had two professions. I was a writer, and a solicitor as well. A mistake, I think, for me at any rate. Rather like having two wives, you're bound to love one more than the other and sacrifice one to the other. And that's what I did. Of course during the war I had to abandon both of them and fight, but after the war I took up with them again. I wrote a play that I thought pretty good. Other people didn't agree with me and they wouldn't back it. I was a conceited oaf and didn't think that anything that had my name to it could possibly fail. So I backed it myself, with trust funds. You know what that means? I was sure I'd be able to pay back what I'd borrowed but the play failed and my client's money was lost. I was what is known as a fraudulent solicitor. In other words, a common thief. I got a stiff sentence and I deserved it. That's the bare outline of a nasty story."

"I remember now," said Mary. "I read about your trial. And I've read two of your books, and I saw one of your plays acted by a repertory company once."

"Did you like my books?" he asked.

"No."

"Do you still want me to show you Josephine?"

"Of course. All that has nothing to do with Josephine and me."

"Did you ever read the poems of Thomas Sturge Moore?" he asked.

"No, I don't think so," said Mary, bewildered. "I'm afraid I don't read as much poetry as I ought."

"He wrote a poem about a swan that might appeal to you," said Michael. "And one about kindness that appeals to me. Here we are, back at the bridge. You go across it, don't you? I stay this side."

He'd had enough. He was abrupt about it but she did not mind. "Good-bye," she said, "until I come to Belmaray."

She turned once, at the top of the bridge, and waved to him, and then went lightly away down the other side. He stood and watched her, and the words of an Irish poet came into his mind. "My thoughts are going after her, and it is that way my soul would follow her, lightly, and airily, and happily, and I would be rid of all my great troubles."

12

WINKLE had inherited not only her father's love of the creatures but also his knight-errantry. At a tender age she had been fishing spiders out of the bath, putting moths out of the window and placing creatures that had got upside down right way up again. She was ever on the watch for those unfortunates who had fallen into, or been placed in, an environment unsuited to them, and no considerations of personal safety or convenience were ever allowed to stand in the way of their immediate rescue. And neither were the conventional prohibitions of society. She would have been the first to pull an ox or an ass from a ditch on the sabbath day, and the fact that Baba belonged to Mrs. Belling was not to her way of thinking sufficient reason why Baba should remain at Oaklands when it would be better for him to be at the vicarage. Pat might think so but she did not. Her sense of property had as yet been a merely one-sided development. She yelled blue murder if any beloved object was removed from her, but she had not yet realized that what she desired to lay her hands upon was not necessarily hers to dispose of by divine right. The sense of divine right died hard in her, and the fact that it was coupled more often than not with the crusading spirit did not make her occasional pilfering any less embarrassing for her family. She had not relinquished Baba on Friday afternoon because her conscience had been persuaded, but because even in the midst of tears and temper her good sense had realized that the moment for abduction was not yet. But upon this wet Monday the golden opportunity was hers, and she seized it with a promptitude and skill remarkable in one so young.

"Please may I be excused?" she asked Miss Giles in the middle of the afternoon's handicraft lesson, which was irritating her extremely. She was not good with her hands and her woven raffia basket was looking less like a basket and more like a bird's nest with every moment that passed. The more she pulled at it the worse it got. The palms of her hands were sticky and she felt hot and bothered and as wicked as could be. Miss Giles looked down at Winkle's crimson, exasperated face, and the tangled mess of her basket, and thought peacefully that a brief period of separation between the two of them would be good for both. "Yes, Henrietta," she said. "But you must be back in this room again in five minutes' time."

"Ten minutes," said Winkle, who had in mind a short trip to her country for the refreshment of her jaded spirit.

Miss Giles, who beneath the new serenity was still Miss Giles, quelled the giggling of the class with a sharp look and said firmly, "Five minutes."

Winkle glowered and slid to the floor. She had every intention of being fifteen. She had started the day as good as gold, and while Miss Giles had been reading the story about the little girl who had gone through a door and found the secret garden, just as she went through her door and found the country, her spiritual state had been that of a cherub. But her adored Miss O'Hara's bad temper had upset her completely. Her idol had fallen and now she was so miserable that naughtiness was her only hope. She was rarely miserable, but she had discovered that when she was disobedience gave her a feeling of revenge which was very soothing. She walked to the door with clumping feet and a truculent lower lip, and shut it behind her more forcibly than was necessary.

But out in the hall Winkle knew suddenly with dismay that it was no good going to the broom cupboard because she could not go to the country. She knew it intuitively, as a horse knows he cannot take a fence too high for him and balks and turns aside. In her disillusionment and naughtiness she was much older than she had been. She was the Winkle she would be in a few years' time, longing for the country but not able to go there any more. Where should she go? Standing miserably at the foot of the staircase she remembered that the day girls were forbidden to go upstairs, so she thought she would go there. If it was not going up the stairs to the door of the country it was a least going upstairs and that was something. She mounted slowly and stealthily, feeling rather small although she was also feeling so old, towards the forbidden territory of the upstairs landing.

When she got there she did not like it. The only light came from the hall below, and through a closed dirty little window curtained with ivy outside and cobwebs inside. It was murky and stuffy and chilly. The landing was carpeted with a mud-colored oilcloth and the draughts that came from under the tall brown doors ran over it and coiled themselves about Winkle's ankles like slimy eels. At the end of the landing the back stairs fell away into blackness, and up them came a dirty sort of smell compounded of faulty drains, stale food and the kitchen cat. Outside the closed bathroom door a pool of water lay on the floor, where Annie had spilt it when she had been emptying Mrs. Belling's slop pail. To Winkle, standing at a distance, it looked thick and horrible, like a frightening picture of Darnley's murder that she had seen once in a history book; and what was the form lying there with arms flung out and head tipped back, groaning and gasping? And whimpering too. Or was it someone else who was whimpering? Some little boy who was slowly being put to death like the other horrible picture of the princes in the Tower.

For the first time in her life Winkle was in the grip of intolerable fear. She felt sick and dreadfully cold, and a little rivulet of sweat was running down her back. She wanted to cry out, but her throat had closed up and she could not. She wanted to run away but her feet would not move. She was lost and cast away in this evil place and there was no help for her either in heaven or earth for she had lost them both. Her country was gone and home was gone and she was alone. "Mummy! Mummy!" That was the little boy crying out, the little boy who was being murdered. "Mummy!" No, it wasn't, it was herself. Her throat had opened again and she was crying aloud for her mother in this dreadful place. But her mother couldn't hear her, for she was miles away in the different darkness of home, the different chilliness, that clean darkness of the house and that coolness of the fresh spring. But the thought of her mother saved her. Mummy was alive and at home waiting for her. She must get to Mummy.

She began to edge forward towards the top of the stairs. She must get down backwards she thought, keeping her eyes on the groaning thing on the floor, for otherwise it might come alive and jump on her from behind. She began to feel sick again but she went on edging forward, keeping her eyes on the thing and the pool of blood under its head. And then suddenly, in the stronger light at the top of the stairs, she saw what it was; just a pile of dirty clothes lying on the floor waiting to be counted for the laundry. And the pool of blood was only a pool of water. "Mummy!" she breathed in relief, not crying out this time, just remembering the talisman of the name that had saved her. She knew where she was now, not lost but just on the upstairs landing at school. And that wasn't someone groaning, but someone fast asleep and snoring behind that half-open door. And it wasn't a little boy whimpering but a dog. It was Baba! She stood still and listened, courage returning as crusading zeal burned in her once again. She turned and made her way back down the landing to another half-open door from which the sound seemed to be coming. To reach it she had to pass that other door, and it took all her courage to pass it, but she could get at her courage now, and scuttling past that horrid snore she pulled open the door of the cupboard and dimly saw Baba in a shivering heap on the floor. She snatched him up, scuttled past the snore again, and pelted down the stairs to the broom cupboard. She ran in and sat down with Baba in her arms. One of his eyes had been cut at the corner and one paw seemed to be hurt. She rocked him in her arms and crooned to him, and soon he stopped whimpering and was comforted.

Now what should she do? She had surely been gone a long time. At any moment now the handicraft class would come to an end and an angry Miss Giles would be coming to find her. What should she do with Baba? She pulled forward the front of her tunic and wondered if he could be bestowed between her tunic and her blouse. Though he was so tiny he was very fat. But then so was she, and perhaps an added corpulence about the region of her chest would not be noticed. She was wondering about it when she heard the sound of slamming desk lids and the ring of voices. The class was over and the door had been opened. Then followed the sound of the familiar stampede to the cloakroom, and then she heard Miss Giles coming down the passage.

"Keep still and don't make a sound," she whispered to Baba, and she fastened her belt more tightly round her waist and put him inside her tunic. Then she opened the door and came boldly out into the passage straight into Miss Giles, so close to her that they stood with their bodies almost touching each other. Winkle stood with her head tipped back, her hands clasped at her chest to keep Baba in position, and her blue eyes gazed up into the face above her.

"I've been all this time," she said.

"So I observe," said Miss Giles drily, and cast about in her mind for some suitably castigating remarks. Biting words usually flocked to her unbidden, but today none came. Her whole mind was captured by the attitude and face of the child. Standing so close to her, looking down on her from above, she saw nothing unusual in the shape of the stout little figure; what to her was unusual were the hands clasped so beseechingly beneath the child's white face. For Winkle's usually rosy cheeks had lost their color. She had passed through moments of intense horror and fear and she had not recovered yet. There were dark circles round her eyes and her mouth had lost its baby curve of entire happiness. Miss Giles saw in the white face and imploring hands the fear of all the nervous little girls flayed by her bitter tongue over a period of years. Misery had driven her to unreasoning revenge and Margary had been the last of many, but until today she had deliberately not known it. That was where her sin lay. She had not willed cruelty but she had willed self-deception. She had thought she had enough to bear on the surface of her life without research into the murky depths; and there again, in the attempt to evade suffering, there was sin. Why should one evade suffering? Evasion was denial of truth. "Brother Fire, God made you beautiful and strong and useful; I pray you be courteous with me," Saint Francis had said when the man came to cauterize his eyes. One could ask a brother to be courteous but one could not deny his brotherhood. To turn aside from one brother was to turn aside from all the brethren, from birds and beasts and flowers and children, from verse and music. One could not pick and choose. It had to be all or nothing. No wonder she was a lonely woman. It was herself whom she was flaying now with her thoughts, and upon the surface of them there floated the white face of the child.

"Don't you feel well, Henrietta?" she asked gently.

"I feel sick," said Winkle with truth.

"Would you like to lie down?"

"I'd like to go home," whispered Winkle.

"Run along then," said Miss Giles. "I've just seen your mother come with the car."

Winkle scuttled down the passage to the cloakroom, her hands still at her breast, and plunged into the welter of hurtling wellingtons and flapping mackintoshes and flailing arms that was the school dressing to go home. No one noticed her and she was able to button herself into her mackintosh without comment, and she was the first to be out of the house and trundling down the drive to her mother and the car. It was all she could do not to throw herself into Daphne's arms, so great had been her longing for her, but without even looking at her mother she bundled herself and Baba into the back seat.

"Aren't you coming to sit by me, precious?" asked Daphne, hurt, for Winkle's place was always beside her. She was the more hurt because her thoughts had been obsessed by her youngest all the afternoon, and she had got the car out and started for Oaklands ten minutes before time.

"No thank you," said Winkle politely.

"I will then," said Pat, who had come out after Winkle, and all the way home the unobservant Margary sat beside Winkle and never noticed the heaving of her breast.

2

At the vicarage Winkle immediately scrambled out of the car and ran upstairs to take off her things. Margary went to find John and Daphne turned to Pat. "What's the matter with my Winkle?" she demanded. "She didn't look herself."

"I expect she had a dust-up with old Giles," said Pat. "She asked to be excused from class and went and played games in the broom cupboard. She does, you know, when she's bored."

"How very naughty of her," murmured Daphne.

"They must go somewhere," said Pat. "Margary goes behind the woodshed. I'm leaving, so I don't care."

"About what?" asked Daphne sharply.

"I've told you before, Mother," said Pat, "that Oaklands is a foul stinking hole." She went indoors before her mother had time to expostulate, and Daphne put the car away and followed her in that low state of mind familiar to parents whose children are beginning to get out of hand. Bringing up children, she thought, was like pouring ginger beer into a tumbler. All went well up to a certain point, and then it all frothed over the top.

It was only Pat, so far. Margary was not the frothy type and she still had her Winkle down at the bottom of the tumbler.

"I'm going to get tea in the kitchen, Winkle," she called up the stairs, for Winkle loved to help her get the tea.

"In a minute," came Winkle's voice.

The tea was nearly ready before she reappeared, and then she came so quietly that her footsteps were lost in the sound of the kettle coming to the boil.

"Look, Mummy," said Winkle behind her mother's back. "For you."

Daphne swung round and beheld Winkle nursing the smallest, fattest and most unattractive Pekinese she had ever seen. It was old, with a grey muzzle, and in very poor condition. One eye was closed up and mattering at the corner while the other bulged at Daphne in such a startling manner that she stepped back a pace. She had never seen such a horrid little dog and she hated to see such an unhealthy creature held against Winkle's breast. "Winkle, put it down!" she commanded.

Winkle obeyed and Baba gave a little whimper of pain, staggered and then righted himself, holding up his injured paw out of harm's way and wagging his bedraggled scrap of a tail. That gallantry of a hurt animal, that instinctive determination to make the best of things, was Daphne's undoing. Revulsion was lost in pity and she sat down on the floor, lifted Baba to her lap and examined the paw and the eye. She did truly love animals. The touch of Baba's pink tongue upon her hand as she acknowledged with gratitude her desire to help him, moved her. It was years since she had owned a dog, for they had felt they could not afford one.

"Who gave him to you, Winkle?" she asked.

"No one did," said Winkle. "I just found him. He's for you."

Daphne fondled Baba's ears. He was one of the royal dogs of Peking, who in the days of their glory had paced in a double line behind the Son of Heaven, holding up the Imperial robe in their

239

mouths. A dog of heavenly lineage, descendent of Buddha's lion, who for love of his master had changed himself into a little dog that he might nestle in his arms. And now come to this.

"Did you find him in the road, Winkle?" asked Daphne. "And how naughty of you to go in the road."

"He was lost," said Winkle.

"Then we ought to take him to the police station," said Daphne uncertainly. "He must have been a valuable little dog once." He was a sleeve dog. His ancestors had been bred as small as possible so they might be carried in the wide sleeves of the ladies of the Imperial family, and lie there in silken comfort.

"But he's for you, Mummy," said Winkle in hurt tones. "I brought him home for you."

"He must have been the sweetest little thing at one time," Daphne thought. Even now his white chest was soft to the touch and in spite of the grey muzzle she doubted if he was as old as he looked. Bathed and brushed and cared for, he might be a dear little dog. "I must see to this eye, Winkle," she murmured absently. "How could it have got like this? And I think the paw is sprained."

"I knew you would like him, Mummy," said Winkle. "Shall I give him some milk?"

"In that saucer on the dresser," said Daphne. "Carefully now, Winkle."

Baba was set gently on the floor before the saucer of milk and lapped hungrily. Daphne and Winkle sat back on their heels and watched him.

"What on earth?" asked John. He and Margary had come hand in hand into the kitchen, and hand in hand gazed with startled eyes at the object on the floor. Margary, even more astonished than her father, opened her mouth and then shut it again. Like Brer Rabbit it was her habit to lie low and say nothing. She had found that amidst the many complications of life silence was best.

"He's a stray dog Winkle found in the road," said Daphne.

"He has no collar. Winkle brought him for me, but I suppose we ought to tell the police?"

Kneeling on the floor, looking appealingly up at him, she seemed to have lost ten years of her age, and John found it difficult to harden his heart. "Certainly we must notify the police," he said. "And what was Winkle doing out in the road?"

"I was excused from class," said Winkle.

"Not to go out in the road, I'm sure," said John.

"No," said Winkle briefly to this side issue. "It was in a very frightening place that I found him."

"Where?" asked Daphne sharply.

"Dark and frightening," said Winkle, her face blanching at the memory. "And he was crying. I had to bring him away."

"Where was this place, Winkle?" demanded Daphne in a panic.

"A horrible place," said Winkle, "I won't go there again. There was something lying on the floor and I thought it was a dead man, only it wasn't."

"Where was it, Winkle?" asked her anguished mother.

"I think we had better have tea without waiting for Pat," said John. He was a great believer in tea as a solvent for intellectual problems. It soothed the nerves and cleared the mind and was often of assistance to a lapsed memory.

Baba was settled on a cushion before the stove and John handed the children bread and honey. A distracted Daphne had just poured strong tea into Winkle's mug and milk and water into John's cup when Pat burst into the room. She had nothing in common with Brer Rabbit. Her method amidst the complications of life was that of direct challenge.

"Good lord!" she ejaculated. "How did Baba get here?"

"You know the dog?" asked John mildly.

"Good lord, yes, he's Mrs. Belling's. Poor little brute. But if you pinched him, Winkle, there'll be the stink of a row when the old girl finds out."

Winkle, absorbed in the delight of strong sweet tea in her

241

mug, raised her face from it to say briefly, "He's Mummy's now," and returned to her mug again.

John drank a little milk and water to give him strength and then said with as much sternness as he could compass, "Winkle." His youngest bit deep into a slice of bread and honey and smiled at him sweetly over the top of it. "Winkle, you must tell Mummy where exactly you found that dog."

Winkle masticated a large mouthful at her leisure and then replied, "Upstairs at school. It was dark and horrid there and I was frightened. There was someone snoring but the dead person was only lots of dirty things."

"But Winkle, Baba is Mrs. Belling's little dog," said Daphne.

"Not now," said Winkle. "I tried to bring him to you before but Pat wouldn't let me."

"I wouldn't have let you today if I'd seen you," said Pat. "You are just a common thief, Winkle."

Winkle drained her mug of delicious strong tea, set it down and prepared to roar. But just as she got her mouth wide open and her eyes screwed up, and started to take the first deep breath, John interrupted with, "Now stop that, Winkle. Tell me why you wanted Mummy to have Baba."

Winkle, endeavoring to shut off the roar, got entangled in her deep breath, choked and hiccuped, frightened herself and began to cry. Between the sobs of her genuine distress her anxious parents caught the broken phrases. "Baba was hurt in the dark cupboard. She doesn't love Baba. I wanted Mummy to have Baba. I hate school and I was frightened. I won't go back to school ever again. I'm *not* a common thief!" And picking up a handy currant bun she threw it at Pat, felt better, took another deep breath and was able to put it to its intended use. There was nothing to be done now but to remove her, which John did, shutting her in the study; the only known way of terminating Winkle's roars being solitary confinement. Tender-hearted parent though he was he had little compunction about it. There was no grief in these seizures of Winkle's, only self-

242

defense and determination to get her own way. When he came back it was to find only Pat enjoying her tea. Daphne and Margary seemed to have lost their appetites.

"As soon as we have finished one of us must telephone to Mrs. Belling and set her mind at rest about her dog," he said to Daphne. "And then I'll take him back. Winkle had better not see him again."

"I wish I could have kept him," said Daphne in a low voice. "He's such a sick little dog."

"Mrs. Belling feeds him on chocolate creams," said Pat. "How can you expect a dog to keep in condition on chocolate creams?"

Baba, asleep on his cushion, whimpered in his sleep.

"If we took him for walks, and fed him right, he'd become a nice little dog, wouldn't he, Mummy?" said Margary.

"He's well bred," said Daphne. "A little sleeve dog. I've always wanted a sleeve dog."

"We've always said we couldn't afford a dog," said John.

"He'd eat so little," pleaded Margary.

"Mummy, when we get his fat down, he'll just go in the sleeve of your Chinese coat that Daddy gave you," said Pat.

John tried to take a grip of the situation. "Daphne," he said, "if you've finished tea, leave Pat and Margary to clear away and ring up Mrs. Belling while I get the car out."

Daphne got up slowly. "No need to be in such a hurry, John," she said. "Don't get the car out till I've telephoned."

Crossing the room she stooped to caress Baba's head. He woke up and kissed her hand again.

"He'd look smashing in the sleeve of your coat," repeated Pat.

"Yes," said Daphne, and left the room closely followed by her husband. Out in the hall she lifted the receiver and dialled the Oaklands number. "Yes, I'm going to do it," she said to John. "You needn't stand over me... Oh, is that Annie? This is Mrs. Wentworth speaking. Could I speak to Mrs. Belling?

Isn't she well? I'm sorry. Did she? Well, sleep is always the best thing. Has she an extension in her room? Well, if she's awake now I'd like to speak to her... John, don't look at me as though you thought it was from me Winkle got her acquisitive habits. I never stole a dog in my life... Is that you Mrs. Belling? Daphne Wentworth speaking. I'm so sorry to hear you are not very well today. I'm afraid you've missed your little dog and I'm sorry to say Winkle is the culprit. She was very naughty. She buttoned him up inside her coat and brought him home and I never noticed. My husband will bring Baba back at once... What did you say? ... What... do you mean? What?"

"What's the matter?" asked John, for Daphne had replaced the receiver, the color draining away from her face. "What's the matter, Daphne?"

"She cut me off," said Daphne.

"Righteous indignation," suggested John.

"No. She said, 'Keep the little brute, I don't want him.' John, she sounded horrid. Her voice was thick as though she'd been drinking."

"Nonsense," said John.

"Horrid," repeated Daphne, and even her lips were white.

"Well, we've got the little dog," said John.

"John, I always thought she was such a sweet old lady."

"Did you?"

"Didn't you?"

"I wasn't sure," said John.

Daphne turned round and looked at him. "John, I'm not at all sure that's a good school."

"What makes you say that?" asked John cautiously.

"The way the children were talking. Winkle so frightened. Pat's language. That poor neglected little dog. The sound of that old woman just now. Do you think it's a good school?"

"Without any evidence to support my doubts I've had them," said John.

"Why didn't you tell me?" asked Daphne irritably.

"Would you have listened?" asked John.

She looked at him and saw that he was unsmiling. "No," she said, and suddenly collapsed in his arms in a storm of tears.

"Whatever's the matter, darling?" he demanded. "Is it the kids? If you feel like that about Oaklands we'll take them away at the end of term."

"It's you," she sobbed.

"Me?" ejaculated John.

"You're quite right, I wouldn't have listened to you. I didn't listen when you said you didn't want Margary to go to school today. Why do I always think I know best about everything? It isn't as though I'd ever brought off a single thing successfully."

"Surely, many things," said John gently.

"No," said Daphne. "Even our marriage is not what you'd hoped it would be."

She was still sobbing. The roaring behind the study door was now intermittent, but still going on. John felt distracted by so much distress, and puzzled too. Daphne, like Margary, never cried.

"Darling," he said helplessly, "our marriage is everything I hoped it would be. What *is* the matter with you?"

"Thinking back over things," she said breathlessly.

"Then don't," he said. "Now stop crying and let's go and tell the kids you've got a sleeve dog for your Chinese coat."

13

"I T'S Michael who's made me think back over things," said
Daphne to herself as she bathed Winkle that evening. "Why
has he got to turn up like this? Why? Why?"

It did not seem possible that it had only been two days ago
that he had opened the drawing-room door and walked in; it
seemed more like two weeks. "Keep still, Winkle!" she said a
little impatiently, for it was Winkle's fault that he was staying.
Winkle had made a mother of her and it was the mother in her
who had seen Michael as a child. What nonsense. He was two
years younger than herself, and she was forty, and should be
ashamed that after ten years of marriage the reappearance of an
old lover should have thrown her completely off her balance.
It was both infuriating and humiliating. Why could she not
have been let alone to jog along as before?

For she had gone on fairly steadily since she had married
John; not very happy, but steady. She had achieved a certain
pattern in her life and thoughts, forced it down upon her inner
discontent and restlessness, and subconsciously she knew that
a changing pattern might mean a changing outlook; and her
outlook had not until tonight allowed for the possibility of error
in her own judgment. It had been a sustaining outlook, that
had kept her well afloat upon the surface of things, and she
did not want to lose it.

There is a certain kind of weather which can come in spring
with the east wind; blue sky and sunshine, bird song and blossom

on the trees, but day after day the same, beautiful but parched, beautiful but going nowhere. Then the wind shifts into the southwest, and a tremor passes over the hard bright world as it waits for the wind and the rain that will break up the old pattern and make a new one holding within it the power of growth.

Daphne felt this same tremor in herself. There was to be change. Michael's return, the mistake she had made over Oaklands, even the coming of the little dog, had all shaken her. Against her will her outlook was veering like a weathercock. The wind and the rain were coming and she did not know what they would do to her.

"*Look* at your feet, Winkle!" she cried in exasperation. "Why is it that you look like a coalheaver at the end of every day? What do you *do?*"

"I just live," said Winkle serenely. "Living is dirty work, but I like it."

Her mother paused and looked at her. Winkle was a pleasant sight at any time but at bedtime she was particularly attractive. Bunchy and creased up in the bath she looked like a gloire de dijon rose. Where the sun had not touched her skin it was the pinkish cream color of the inner petals, but her face and neck and fat arms and legs had the golden tinge of the outer ones. The pink of her cheeks, over the gold, was a color so freshly lovely that Daphne's heart suddenly sang for joy. She laughed and kissed her and forgot her fear.

Winkle in bed and asleep it was time to help Harriet to bed, to get the supper, to shepherd Pat and Margary to bed, to put Baba to bed in her big old work basket beside the stove and then to do the washing up alone because John had been sent for to a dying old man at the far end of the parish. "It would be tonight with all these saucepans," he had lamented in departing. It was always he who got backache over the saucepans, while Daphne, sitting in the kitchen chair, took the weight off her feet and dried; except when, like yesterday, he forgot to come home to supper.

"What a brute I was about it," she thought. "Most men, expected to wash up every evening, would forget to come back to supper more nights than they remembered. Would Michael have washed up for his wife?"

Winkle's robin mug dropped to the floor with a crash and she found herself in tears again; she who never broke anything and never cried. She had always prided herself upon control of thought and attention; John's woolgathering had always annoyed her. She snatched up the robin remnants and carried them out to the dustbin, and taking the lid off was confronted with the bits of the sugar-bowl that had been missing over the weekend. They were placed as conspicuously as possible upon a pile of tins... John... Her tears turned to laughter and slightly hysterical she laid her own fragments with his. Then changing her mind she picked all the broken bits out of the bin, carried them to the drawing room and put them away in the sandalwood box in the Chinese cabinet. "They're not past mending," she thought. "I'll see what I can do."

She went back to the kitchen, finished the washing up and prepared Harriet's hot milk. It was supposed that if Harriet had a soothing nightcap the last thing it helped her to go to sleep. Harriet disliked hot milk and longed for a cup of tea instead, but she liked to foster illusions about her sleeping. Also it was part of her code in illness to accept whatever was done to her, given to her and said to her in the way of treatments, medicines, food and advice, with equal gratitude, dislike it or not. Illness was admirable training in the creative art of grateful acceptance. Pain accepted was just pain, and heavy, but Harriet believed that pain gladly accepted took wings, went somewhere and did something. She based this belief on her experience of hot milk, which just drunk down lay heavy on the stomach but gratefully accepted settled well. Harriet was not a naturally pious woman, and she was not sentimental. She merely went by results.

248

"Thank you, dearie," she said to Daphne, as the cup was put in her hands. "That'll do me a power of good. Sit down, love. It's early yet."

It was generally John who took Harriet her milk and Daphne had a sense of unfamiliarity as she sat down in the little armchair by Harriet's bed. She lived her life in such a rut of routine that the unusualness of what she was doing was yet another thing to make her feel jolted out of herself. Living as she did in a state of perpetual nervous exhaustion, always driving herself beyond her strength lest the tasks of home and parish accumulate beyond her ability to cope with them, afraid to relax lest she collapse altogether, she had largely lost the power of wonder, and with it the power of looking at familiar things with fresh appreciation. She had not really looked at Harriet's room, or at Harriet herself, for a long time, but now her shaken thoughts were captured by them.

The furniture was Harriet's own and had come from her father's Cornish farm. There was a bow-fronted mahogany chest of drawers with brass handles, and a little swinging mirror with a surface spotted by age on top of it. On one side of the mirror hung a blue crochet hair tidy and on the other a pink heart-shaped pincushion with a frill round it. There was a mahogany wardrobe and a small three-cornered washstand that fitted in the corner of the room. Harriet did not like painted walls and her wallpaper was cream with a satin stripe, and had a frieze of rosebuds and forget-me-nots to match the hair tidy and the pincushion. She was much attached to her old-fashioned bedstead and mattress. She did not hold with modern divan beds with no rail at the foot to keep you in; they made her feel she was floating downstream and might at any moment slither over the edge of a waterfall. Nor did she like mattresses that could not be persuaded to sink in the middle; you might roll out either side any minute, if you hadn't already slid over at the bottom. But though Harriet was decided in her preference she was not arbitrary. If John had wanted her to endanger her life in a divan bed she would have done it. If Daphne had wanted her to sleep in a room with plain white walls like a greenhouse or a lavatory she would have done that, but as they gave her her choice in these matters her choice, like her personality, was her own.

Daphne looked at her, dainty and fresh in her snowy shawl and frilled white nightcap, charming and serene. "She's got something," she thought. "I wouldn't know what it was, but something—some sort of wisdom."

It struck her suddenly that, in the possession of Harriet, so had she. She leaned back and relaxed and through the uncurtained window saw the first stars above the trees.

"You're wise, Harriet," she said, and there was appeal in her voice as well as the statement of a fact.

"No," said Harriet. "I never had no education. If you was to ask me where Buenos Aires was I'd have no idea. Though I feel I don't care for the place."

"South America," said Daphne, smiling. "There's a big meat-canning factory there."

"Fancy that," said Harriet. "I never did hold with tinned things. Nice for that young fellow to be staying with Miss Wentworth."

Harriet's abrupt changes of subject could be disconcerting and Daphne was disconcerted. Harriet noticed it. Why was Daphne the way she was, sitting there so quietly, yet unstrung, not like herself? She finished her milk, put her cup down on the bedside table and adjusted her shawl. But she was not feeling as serene as she looked. She felt as though she and Daphne were in a boat together, heading for that waterfall. She fixed her eyes for comfort on the rail at the foot of her bed.

"Did Mrs. Wilmot tell you about him?" asked Daphne.

"Trust Alice Wilmot," said Harriet. "Got it all out of Jane Prescott. He's paid his bill at the Wheatsheaf now. Must have borrowed it off Miss Wentworth for he hadn't paid it when he left. It's sad so young a chap should have tuberculosis."

250

Daphne turned suddenly in her chair. "Harriet, how can Jane Prescott possibly know he has tuberculosis?"

"She's observant, is Jane. He coughs a bit and keeps his window open. Rain all over the floor on Saturday morning. Miss Wentworth calls him by his Christian name so Jane says he's likely to be the son of an old friend. Miss Wentworth set him to work in the garden on Saturday but he gave her the slip and went into the library. Jane said the way he handled those dirty old books she was sure he'd kept a secondhand book shop. Now that was a silly thing to do in a place like Manchester. Poring over dirty old books in a town full of dirt and smoke. No wonder it went to his lungs."

"Manchester?" asked Daphne weakly.

"Jane, she heard him mention Manchester in conversation with Miss Wentworth. He had an old book open in his hands and was talking about the Knight of Manchester. His father, Jane thought. Mayor, perhaps, and knighted at a royal visit. You'll let him stay, dearie? Summer's coming on and out in the open he won't infect the children. Do him a power of good to stay at Belmaray."

Daphne's head reeled. The knight of La Mancha. So he still loved Don Quixote. And why was Harriet's voice so pleading? "What do you mean, Harriet?" she asked.

It was Harriet's turn to be disconcerted. "I have queer fancies," she said. "Seeing you out in the garden with him I felt you had it in your heart to send him away. As well as fear for the children you're a proud woman."

"What's my pride got to do with sending him away?" asked Daphne sharply.

Harriet's hands trembled a little as she fumbled with her shawl. Never in all these years had she spoken a word of criticism of Daphne, either to Daphne herself or to anyone else. What had come over her? "Proud folk separate themselves from others, judging them," she said at last. "You can't help it, love, but you're too critical of John, too critical of the children.

To criticize others we must hold them from us, at arm's length so to speak. And then before you know where you are you've pushed them away and you're the poorer."

"This time, Harriet, you're wrong," said Daphne. "I'm not pushing Michael away. The fool that I am told him to stay."

"I don't think you'll regret it," said Harriet. "Why should you?"

"I was engaged to him when we were young, Harriet," said Daphne, and then stopped, aghast at herself. She had not meant to say that to Harriet. She seemed to be passing beyond her own control.

There was a deepening of the kindly lines in Harriet's face. "Does John know he was not your first fancy?" she asked lightly.

"Yes," said Daphne, smiling. "But what he does not know is that my first fancy was Michael Stone. And he's taken a liking to Michael and thinks he can help him—you know what he is—and so I can't tell him."

"Why not?" asked Harriet, a twinkle in her eye. "Knowing the poor young chap had been jilted by you, dearie, would surely make John more pitiful-like than ever."

There was a silence. Daphne's lips were folded in a hard line and Harriet's eyes became extremely penetrating.

"I told Michael I wouldn't," said Daphne. "He likes John."

"Ah," said Harriet, so much in the tone of one who has at last found out the riddle of the universe that Daphne looked up, startled. "Now why, dearie, should you still dislike a young chap who jilted you so many years ago that it's a wonder you even recognized him?"

"He hasn't changed," said Daphne. "And I can't think one kind thought about him."

"Fancy that now," said Harriet. "What are you letting him stay for then?"

"He suddenly seemed such a child. I lost my head."

"Well, there you are then," said Harriet. "If you lost your head, you lost it, and no good crying over spilt milk. And you don't feel emptied of kindness when you're with children, surely?"

"It was only for the moment that he seemed a child," said Daphne. "His calculating cruelty, once, was not that of a child."

The tone of her voice shocked Harriet, but she gave no sign. "Children can be cruel," she said. "Though not our children. But ours can calculate. Pat wasn't more than three when she had it all worked out as to when was the best time to go after the sugar. I'd be making the beds and you'd hear the postman and have to go to the door. She knew."

Daphne smiled. "Harriet, you've lived with children all your life. Except for John, who does not count, you don't know men."

"Don't I?" said Harriet. "I've dealt with a few in my day. With some, it always helped me to concentrate on their perambulators or their deathbeds. And why should John not count?"

The question shot out with such sharpness that Daphne was taken aback. "You know what I mean, Harriet," she said weakly.

"I do not," said Harriet. "Is a man less of a man because he's learned to hold his tongue? Though mind you, dearie, I think he's wrong. If John had given as good as he got it might have done you a power of good."

"I have no idea what you mean, Harriet," said Daphne coldly, but with two angry spots showing on her cheekbones.

"There are some people," said Harriet, "who don't realize what it is they are doing to others until they are paid back in their own coin. But those are not the worst. The worst are those whose unkindness is calculated; as you said, my dear."

Daphne thought to herself that Harriet's forthrightness really passed all bounds. But one could not be angry with her, and she mastered her anger and tried to listen.

"I know it says, 'Do as you would be done by,'" said Harriet, "but I've known times when 'Do as you are being done to' has had such good results you'd be surprised. Of course, love, John would be shocked to hear me but I've never been as good a woman as he thinks I am."

"Nor have I, Harriet," said Daphne.

"You've been sharp-tongued," said Harriet, "but you've been faithful, you've stuck at it. There now, love, you must forgive me! I've never been accustomed to speak right out to you this way."

"That's all right, Harriet," said Daphne. "It's my fault for bothering you with my past."

"Bothering me!" ejaculated Harriet. "If you think, dearie, that arthritis cripples a woman's curiosity as well as her body that's where you make your mistake."

Daphne leaned back in her chair and thought about Harriet. The old woman's plain speaking had been very plain but behind it she was aware of Harriet's love, not only for John and the children but for herself too. Surely that was odd. Harriet idolized John and one would have expected her to be jealous of John's wife. But she was not. She seemed incapable of jealousy, self-pity, or self-assertion. It struck Daphne suddenly that she was one of those rare people who have ceased to revolve around themselves. That was her special wisdom, the "something" that she had. She had been a children's nanny and in the children's world selfish women are soon broken on the wheel... Yet how safe had been those nurseries of the big houses when Harriet had been young, how gloriously secure and safe. Perhaps Harriet had never known what it was to be hideously afraid.

"Fear can make you very selfish," she said slowly.

"It has a lot to answer for," agreed Harriet. "What you call calculated cruelty has its roots in fear as often as not."

Daphne smiled. It was obvious that Harriet had been attracted to Michael and would be lynx-eyed for extenuating circumstances. "For my generation all our days have been uneasy when they haven't been downright terrifying," she said. "But I don't think fear that you share with the whole world warps you. It's personal fears that do that. Michael could not have known those for he was always healthy and successful. I was neither, and I was afraid of failure, and so he was not only the man I wanted but the success I wanted too."

Now she had started she was not finding it hard to talk to Harriet. She felt rather like a little girl running into one of those safe Edwardian nurseries where Nanny sat darning before the fire.

"Did he act in plays with you, love?" asked Harriet shyly. She had never been to the theatre in her life and was ignorant of the phraseology.

"No, he is a writer, not an actor. He writes vile but exciting plays and hateful but very gripping thrillers that are read all over the world. You know what thrillers are, Harriet?"

"The body in the first chapter and the hanging in the last. I've tried to read a few but I've not the intellect for it," said Harriet humbly. "I couldn't seem to make sense of how it was they got from one to the other, and what I could understand took away my appetite."

"Michael's first play would have taken away your appetite," said Daphne. "It was horrible."

"Were you acting in it, love?"

"Yes, I was the parlormaid."

"Parlormaid!" ejaculated Harriet. That a Wentworth (and Daphne's mother had been a Wentworth) should even in a play demean herself by waiting at table shocked her profoundly. "A parlormaid! You should have been the heroine, my dear."

"That's what I thought," said Daphne, smiling. "And I was determined that Michael should think so too. It was too late for me to be the heroine of his first play but I made up my mind I'd get a good part in his second. I'd had to fight hard before Uncle Pete and Aunt Mary would let me go on the stage; they said I'd neither health nor talent for it and I was wild to prove them wrong; but when I met Michael I was already twenty-five and had got no further than playing small parts at a theatre in the suburbs. His first play was tried out there. He was only twenty-three and already famous. His first thriller was published when

255

he was nineteen, and made into a movie, and there had been two successful books after that. He was the *enfant terrible* of literature. Think of it, Harriet, twenty-three and famous! And a junior partner in a flourishing firm of solicitors as well. And I'd got nowhere." She paused. "It was the Christmas of 1938."

"The last Christmas before the war," said Harriet. "Was the play a success?"

"Of course," said Daphne. "Everything Michael did was a success. It was transferred to the West End and I went with it. I only had four words to say but at least I was saying them in a West End theatre, in a play that was assured of a long run, so that I was assured of time in which to captivate Michael. I had my work cut out for he was as popular as his play. I think people were intrigued that so young a man should have such a horrible imagination. Contrast was always part of his charm. He'd be full of vitality one day, and great fun, and the next day he'd be drifting about like a lost spirit, looking into your face as though he wanted to ask the way but expected you would strike him if he did. And his good looks had the same sort of contrast; he was so wiry and energetic and yet he had the sort of grace that makes people appear fragile when they've really got a rhinoceros toughness."

"Physical toughness," said Harriet, "not nervous toughness. Folks don't fall from laughter to fear in that way when they're nervously strong, and nerves take their toll of the body in the end."

"I never noticed a thing wrong with his nerves," said Daphne.

"But you noticed his fear, though you did not recognize it," said Harriet. "When I was a nanny I always gave a scared child phosphates. I hadn't been a week with John before I started him on phosphates, so scared as he was of those other wretched boys, that Judith's children, and he never developed anything worse than catarrh and headaches. What sort of childhood did he have?"

"Michael? I really don't know," said Daphne. "He never

spoke about it. Really, Harriet, you can't trace every mortal thing back to childhood."

"Every mortal thing," said Harriet. "It's only the immortal thing that a man can be judged on, that bit of himself that he makes as he does the best he can with what fate handed out to him. Well, I'm listening. What day was it that you stopped wanting his money and fame and went mad all in a moment for the steel of his body and the fire of his blood?"

Daphne was profoundly startled by the sudden energy with which Harriet spoke, and looked in astonishment at the serene old face in the frilled nightcap. The bright eyes, so deeply set in their wise puckers, were regarding her with twinkling but penetrating amusement.

"I wasn't born in a wheel chair," continued Harriet placidly. "And I've not lost the use of my memory. It's surprising how hot a man's lips can be when he desires you, and there are times you think his arms will crack your ribs, and yet you glory in it. There was a man once; he was married. My old dad locked me in my room, and I lived to thank him for it, though at the time I all but kicked the door down. Proper little vixen I was. But I could never seem to take to another man and so I became a nanny. At least I'll have children, I thought, even if they're not my own. Go on, love. You won't shock me."

"Yes, I will, Harriet, because I never did."

"Never did what?" asked Harriet.

"Never stopped wanting his money and fame."

Daphne looked again at Harriet and saw that she had indeed shocked her. Passion Harriet could understand, calculating passion she could not. Seeing the bewilderment that had taken the place of amusement in Harriet's eyes Daphne found she was ashamed. The word calculating echoed in her mind, for she had used it long before. She had said that Michael's cruelty had been calculating, and Harriet had tried to qualify her statement. She did not want to go on with this conversation. She drank from Harriet's implicit judgments.

257

"I'm making you tired, Harriet," she said.

"You can't stop now, love," said Harriet firmly. "And me with the ears sticking out of the side of my head."

"No," said Daphne, and knew she couldn't. The commonplace humiliating little story had been her secret but now, shaken as she was, it seemed running out of her like liberated poison. "But I wanted Michael himself too, for it was just as you say, Harriet. He kissed me casually one day and the carelessness of his kiss suddenly drove me wild. I wanted the other sort."

"Did you get them?" asked Harriet.

"Not at once, and the scheming for them made me more in love than ever, for I've never been patient. I was clever, I think. I found out a little weakness of Michael's—he was a snob. I played on that. He hadn't been to a public school or university, he'd gone straight from a grammar school to the solicitor's office, and he was sensitive about it. He had a ridiculous longing to be intimate with a class to which he didn't naturally belong. He had thought his fame would help him there but it hadn't altogether. But I could help. I took him to the right places and introduced him to the right people and he was so adaptable that very soon no one would have known, outwardly, that he had not been born among them. He had always admired me and now he was intensely grateful to me, and also in need of me. Because you know, Harriet, however brilliant their veneer people are never wholly at ease among people who are not their own people. They're lonely. The acting of a part exhausts them. But I showed Michael that he need not act with me. I worked it so that we were in a delightful conspiracy together. I was the princess smuggling him into the palace in his fancy dress. I showed him that I loved him and he was flattered. It wasn't long before he was as much in love with me as I was with him. We got engaged and we had great fun; and yet it wasn't a comfortable love, Harriet. It was like a fever."

258

"Then you got quarrelsome," stated Harriet. "I remember you in a fever as a child. Regular little spitfire, you were."

"He said we must wait to get married," said Daphne. "He said his career was not firmly established yet, which was nonsense. He kept putting it off and our nerves got frayed to ribbons."

"It's the responsibility frightens a young man," said Harriet.

"Then the war broke out and he said he would not fight. He had not told me before that he was a pacifist and I was furious, Harriet. The lovers and husbands of my friends were all going into the services and I was ashamed. But though I argued with him I tried to keep my temper for his second play was going into rehearsal and there was a good part in it that exactly suited me. You see at that time it was only the phoney war and parts in plays still seemed important. But when I asked Michael to get me the part he said casting was not the author's business. He wouldn't even try. I forced him to say why and he said I wasn't a good enough actress. If the play was not perfectly cast he was afraid it might fail. I lost my temper and he lost his. He said I was a careerist. I said he was a coward. His cruelty made me so furious that I lost my head and said I wouldn't marry him."

"Why was he cruel?" asked Harriet. "Why should he have put you in his play to harm it?"

"I wouldn't have harmed it," said Daphne shortly. "I was a good actress, and if he'd got me the part I'd have been able to prove it."

"Well, there now!" said Harriet soothingly. "But he wouldn't and so you returned his ring. Was it diamonds?"

"No, an emerald. Then the war broke out properly, the real war, and France fell, and not long after I heard that Michael was in the army. I'd been wretched, wanting him back again, and now I wondered if he'd given up his pacifism to get me back. I waited for a letter from him but it didn't come. Then I heard he was on leave in London and I asked a friend of ours to ask us both to her house but not to tell Michael I'd be there. She did that, and he was detestably courteous and polite, but after dinner

I took him into the little garden and asked him why he had given up his pacifism. He said he hadn't, that when the war was over he'd be a pacifist again, but that with England in such danger he couldn't keep out of it. I felt humiliated that it was nothing to do with me, but I said I was sorry I had called him a coward. He smiled but he didn't say anything, and so I told him I was leaving the stage and joining the A. T. S. Then he said, 'Daphne, I'm sorry I called you a careerist. Forget it.' But he didn't say anything else and I believe he would have let us part again, only the sirens went, and he had to take me back to my flat. I made him come in and then of course it was all on again."

"Had he kept the ring?" asked Harriet. She had Scottish blood in her and was of a saving turn of mind.

"No, he'd sold it," said Daphne harshly, for it still hurt her that he had not kept that first ring in the hope of putting it on again. "He gave me another, one that had been his mother's, a funny little pearl flower with a ruby in the center. I believe I've got it still, though I can't imagine why I kept it."

"It may come in useful," said Harriet economically. "Were you happy when you were engaged again?"

"Sometimes, but not always," said Daphne. "We could not be together often and when we were Michael was in such a moody state. I was patient. I did not press marriage on him. I agreed with him it should be sometime soon, perhaps his last leave before he was sent overseas. And then it was his last leave, and I had the weekend off. I was working in London then and still had my flat. He turned up on Friday evening and said he was leaving England on Monday. He did not know where he was going. I waited for him to tell me he'd got the licence and we'd get married before he went, but he didn't, and I realized that he hadn't even thought about getting it. His mind was obsessed with something else, not with me at all. His eyes had a queer look in them, as though he did not see anything that was happening about him but was looking at some vile picture inside his mind. I had seen him look like that when he was writing one of his hateful stories."

"Only this time it was going to happen to himself," said Harriet.

"We had a meal out and went to a show," said Daphne, "and he pulled himself together and was full of a wild sort of fun that was not in the least amusing. Then we went back to my flat for a drink and all at once he was in love with me again, as much in love as in the old days. And then suddenly, as though he hadn't realized at all how appallingly he had just hurt me, he asked me if I'd spend the weekend with him in the country. He said he knew of a place where we'd be at peace, and be able to love each other and forget the damn war. That was what he said. 'Have some peace and forget the damn war.' He begged me to go. He was like a child begging for a drink of water."

"You went?" Harriet asked.

"No," said Daphne. "I said, 'I'm sorry, Michael, but I can't do it.' "

There was an odd silence. The words of commendation for which Daphne was waiting from the Harriet who had brought up all her nurselings to such correctitude of behavior were not forthcoming. She looked up and saw Harriet looking at her with a puzzled look.

"But, Harriet—" she murmured, and was herself puzzled.

Harriet said, "Yes, love? Go on."

But Daphne could not go on. "Surely, Harriet, you don't think that I—Harriet, what *are* you thinking?"

"That you behaved as a well-brought-up young lady should have done," said Harriet evenly. "Your uncle and aunt brought you up very well, I will say that for them. Yet you didn't love them."

"I disliked them intensely," said Daphne. "Harriet, I don't understand you."

"I was wondering what held you back," said Harriet. "Not love for them. Not love of God, for you always told me you had no religion before you married John. And you loved Michael; so you say. What held you back?"

Daphne ignored the question and said sharply, "Harriet, don't you think I did right?"

"Yes," said Harriet dryly. "Above ground. But it's a poor sort of virtue that has no roots in love. It's why you do or don't do a thing that matters most to my mind. If love of God comes first with you then you deny yourself to keep His commandments, you give away your whole life to Him and glory in what the world calls loss. But there wasn't any obedience in your life at that time, Daphne, and no love at all except your love of Michael. Was it for love of him that you said no?"

Daphne was an honest woman when not self-deceived. "No," she said. "And I was not trying to do right either. I was just—reacting."

"That's what we mostly do," said Harriet. "But what were you reacting to? To the fact that he'd forgotten about the license? Punishing him?"

Daphne hurried on. "He came to see me on the Saturday and Sunday and was very gentle and courteous. We agreed that we'd be married as soon as he got back to England. I was in a queer state, in love with him, wretched because he was going away yet full of resentment too."

"We do feel resentment against those we've hurt," said Harriet. "It restores the balance."

Daphne flushed scarlet. This was an arraignment. It was as though with every quietly spoken sentence Harriet was writing an indictment against her that later she would have to read through and understand before she could plead guilty or not guilty before the tribunal of her own mind. Now honesty demanded that she tell Harriet the rest of the paltry little story as truthfully as she could.

"Michael fought in Crete," she said. "One is forgetting the horrors of the war now—at least," she added, seeing Harriet's eye on her, "those of us who did not endure them are forgetting them. Crete was awful. You remember, Harriet? But Michael was lucky. He had a head wound, not very serious, and was evacuated on one of the last ships that managed to get away. He soon got well again. But he was very changed."

"What was he like?" asked Harriet.

"Tired and secretive. He wouldn't say how he'd been wounded. I thought it would do him good to tell me, but when I asked him questions he wouldn't answer. He had a long leave and I could plan a really lovely wedding. He seemed rather apathetic about it all but he agreed to all my ideas and was so sweet to me that I was more in love than ever. Harriet, I really *was* in love."

"Wouldn't a quiet wedding have been better for him, if he was tired, and war time and all?" asked Harriet.

"I thought he needed taking out of himself," said Daphne. "And our engagement had lasted so long, Harriet. I was sure all our friends were talking about it, and perhaps thinking he'd got tired of me. Now it was happening at last I did not want it to be a hole and corner affair. Uncle Pete and Aunt Mary were pleased I was marrying a well-known man. They were glad, for the sake of family pride, that I should have the sort of wedding I wanted. We asked everyone, my friends and Michael's and all the family."

"Did you ask John?" asked Harriet.

"No, he was still in hospital. And at that time I think I'd almost forgotten John. I hadn't seen him for years."

"Years wouldn't have made him forget you," said Harriet. "But go on, dearie."

"I was in my room the night before the wedding," said Daphne. "Aunt Mary was with me and we'd just finished packing my suitcases for the honeymoon. While we packed I had one ear open for the bell, for Michael had promised to come round and say good-night to me. For the first time in my life I felt happy and triumphant. Things were going right with me at last. The bell rang and I went to the door. But it wasn't

263

Michael, it was a messenger boy with a note. It was carelessly scrawled and it just said, 'I'm sorry, Daphne, but I can't do it. Michael.' "

Harriet was silent. Such a blow breaks a weak woman, twists a strong one. From the angle of her intolerable humiliation Daphne would have looked askance at everything that had happened to her ever since.

"Poor girl, poor Daphne," she said at last.

"Like a scene in a second-rate film, wasn't it?" said Daphne, her voice expressionless.

"To be taking it to heart like this after all these years," thought Harriet. "Never to have forgiven it. And I don't believe she's ever told a soul." She felt a little nauseated as she thought of Daphne pushing the memory of her humiliation further and further down yet never able to get rid of it. The measure of her bitterness was the measure of her failure.

"Or like a scene in one of Michael's own horrid books," went on Daphne. "Cheap melodrama. The timing was perfect, of course, as in his plays, and the revenge nicely calculated. He'd ceased to love me, come to hate me instead I believe, and he repudiated me in the exact words in which I had refused him. Clever, wasn't it?"

"Unintentional," said Harriet.

"Nothing Michael did was ever unintentional," said Daphne. "He has the kind of mind that thinks everything out down to the last detail."

"And thinks out every disaster that might happen long before it happens, up to years ahead," said Harriet. "The worrying mind. Well I know it. My dad was that way. And then some sudden shock would hit him unexpected like and the pent-up worry would come rushing out like a spate of water when the dam's gone, and he'd be whirled into doing this, that and the other, and each thing sillier than the last. Yet in the usual way my dad was a sensible man. What did you all do come the morning?"

Her question was not mere idle curiosity. She wanted to lead Daphne on to the happy ending whose happiness she had never allowed herself either to admit or accept.

"Aunt Mary sent me straight down to my godmother, old Lady Wainwright, in Cornwall, while she and Uncle Pete cleared up the mess. I believe they said Michael had discovered that he was in worse health than he'd realized—something like that. He'd disappeared so they could say what they liked. I didn't care what they said so long as no one knew what had really happened."

"What did you do in Cornwall?" asked Harriet. "Did you take long walks?"

"I took too many. I got drenched to the skin one day and had pneumonia. That meant a long sick leave and I couldn't go back to work. Shut up with my old godmother and nothing to do. Think of it, Harriet!"

"Poor Lady Wainwright too!" murmured Harriet sympathetically. "The old, they can't help feeling for each other. Cornwall. That's where John went after he'd been discharged from hospital. He's always had a fancy for Cornwall. He was in rooms down there."

"In the next village," said Daphne. "I did not know he was there, and he did not know I was with Lady Wainwright, until we met by accident on the cliffs one day."

"Had he heard about it?"

"No, Harriet."

"Did you tell him?"

"Lady Wainwright told him Michael had broken our engagement. Nothing more. John was kind. He never asked me a single question—he never has—just set himself to deal with the state I was in."

"What sort of state were you in?"

"A despairing sort of state, Harriet."

"Well, really," said Harriet. "If you'll excuse me saying so, love, weren't you taking it to heart a bit too much? Jilted, that's

265

all you'd been. Didn't you call to mind that the worst war in history was on at the time?"

"Harriet, I'm selfish," said Daphne. "I've never thought much about other people's troubles. I've only wanted to take from the external world the things that make me happy."

"What were you taking just then?" asked Harriet drily.

"Nothing. What was there to take? For me, I mean. John at the time was probably going about in company with all the poor wretches in concentration camps, and finding a sort of para-doxical consolation in piling everyone else's miseries on top of his own." She spoke bitterly but, Harriet noted, with understand-ing of John.

"How did John deal with you?" asked Harriet with curiosity. "I didn't know he had it in him to deal with anyone. A rare old blunderer, I've always thought him."

For the first time a gleam of humor broke through Daphne's self-engrossment and she laughed. "Well, no, I don't think I used the right phrase. He took me out in a rowing boat and lost an oar, and he took me to see a rare orchid he'd found on the cliffs and it wasn't an orchid after all. He gave me a Siamese kitten and a pot of freesias, going all the way to Truro by bus to get them because he remembered how I'd loved kittens and flowers when I was a child staying in Belmaray. He'd remem-bered everything about me from those days; that I'd liked chocolates with hard centers and the poems of Walter de la Mare, and verbena soap and honey. He got me all those things and we laughed over them, and his care of me was balm to my shame. When I was a child, you know, he'd been in love with me in the idyllic way in which a boy can be in love with a little girl, and it was touching and sweet to find him still loving me in exactly the same way. When he asked me to marry him I thought about it and then I said yes. I didn't love him but when I was a child he'd seemed a rock of strength and I thought I might recapture some of that feeling. And I thought that after we were married, when he discovered the little girl had grown

266

into a woman, that his love for me might grow up too. Harriet, it never did."

"No," said Harriet. "For he's never grown up. Not in the sense that most folk use the word. But when there's a moment that matters, he knows things. Well, my dear, if he's never loved you in the way you wanted, marrying him made you able to hold up your head again. As Mrs. Wentworth of Belmaray you were somebody. And marrying John so soon after Michael left you, well, you showed the world how little you cared. I see now why, apart from loving you all his life, he was able to summon up enough self-confidence to ask you. He knows things."

The two women looked at each other and Daphne flushed again, not with indignation but as Winkle would have done, caught in the act of telling only half the truth.

"You know me better than I know myself, Harriet," she said.

"I know human nature," said Harriet, "and I know proud women for I was proud myself once; and if I'm not now humility is no virtue in me, for it was the arthritis taught me different. It took away my independence."

"Is independence so bad for one?" asked Daphne.

"Nothing worse," said Harriet. "It gives you a wonderful conceit of yourself."

"Well, that's all, Harriet," said Daphne lamely. The tale of her humiliation, never spoken of, had seemed a thing of nightmare proportion in the place where she had buried it, but brought out into the light it looked both paltry and ridiculous. She looked back with contempt to the girl who had stood upon the cliffs in Cornwall and found a sort of self-indulgent pleasure in thinking how easy it would be to throw herself over. And then she had heard a thud behind her and turning round had seen a prostrate man who had caught his foot in a rabbit hole and fallen headlong. She had run to help him get up again, and it was John. "Has this made you dislike me very much, Harriet?" she asked.

"You know I've always loved you," said Harriet. "You and Pat, I've loved you the best after John."

"Not Margary? Not Winkle?" asked Daphne, surprised.

"I'm sorriest for you and Pat," said Harriet. "Pride takes a lot of breaking."

"I love Pat least of the children," said Daphne. "In fact, sometimes I wonder if I love her at all. In some queer way she's like Michael."

"Bound to be, and you not able to rid yourself of the thought of him all the time she was on the way, and never telling John a thing about it all. Well, talk to him about it now. Do you good."

"Harriet, I couldn't! Not after all this time. And I promised Michael to hold my tongue."

"That's a promise that's only binding on you while he still wants to hold his. He won't for long."

"Harriet, he will. He values John's good opinion."

"That's why," said Harriet. "If John's taken a liking to him he won't find himself able to live with John's liking under false pretences. He's a decent young chap, from the look of him."

"Harriet, how can you say that after what I've told you!"

"I don't believe a word of it, dearie."

"Harriet!"

"I mean I don't believe a word of the interpretation you put upon it. There's John coming up the drive."

Her indomitable little figure relaxed against the pillows. They had fallen over the edge of the waterfall and passed through the whirlpool below. With the sound of John's step in the drive it was as though they had reached calm water again. But she could not ever remember having felt more tired.

"Harriet, you look as though you were going to faint!" ejaculated Daphne, half in and half out of her chair.

"What would that matter, and me safe in my bed?" asked Harriet tartly. "But there's nothing to prevent us all having a cup of tea."

Her eyes were twinkling and Daphne went downstairs reassured, and strangely light of heart, in spite of her premonition
that the worst humiliation of her life was still before her... But
the lightness of heart was also a premonition.

She was making the tea when John came in, saddened after a
death that had not been easy.

"Some celebration, darling?" he asked.

"A lightness of heart," she said. "Mine. But it was Harriet's
idea about the tea. Very bad for her so late in the evening but
it's a weakness with her. Make up the drawing-room fire while I
take hers up."

When she came back he had mended the dying fire and flung
a handful of fir cones on it, so that it was blazing merrily. "To
match your lightness of heart, dearest," he said. "And thank
you for lighting the study fire the other morning. I had meant to
thank you earlier than this but I forgot what the knot in my
handkerchief was for."

He did not ask her why she was light of heart because he
never asked questions, but as they sat in front of the fire together
his depression vanished in a happiness as infectious as a child's.
She was reproached that she could make him happy so easily,
thankful to him that he could let such moments come to them
without questioning. It is when children start to question their
happiness, she thought, that they lose it and grow up. In spite
of the distresses she caused him, in spite of his morbid self-
distrust, she believed that John was essentially a happy man.
Would she like it if he grew up?

14

JOHN shut the front door behind him and came down the steps of the house into amazement. He had expected the vicarage garden at six o'clock on an April morning but this was no place that he knew, and no time. It was true that through the silver music of the pipes and flutes, the rise and fall of crystal cadences, he heard six times the golden note of a bell, but it had nothing to do with time. The notching off of weariness into slow inches was as far removed from this rhythmic gleaming of light through light as was the vicarage front lawn and herbaceous border from this garden of immortal freshness in the dawn of the world.

He walked on and knew himself to be in Eden before the Fall. Why had he thought it unfamiliar? He recognized it now. Through the whiteness of the light he saw the river and the arc of blossoming boughs. He walked lightly, a song in his soul, and knew that he had within him now that which his boyhood had seemed to be without. Within him now the Seraph song, the birds' voices in the garden the echo of its song. The flowers about him, many-colored beneath the sparkle of dew, the branches misted with green and swaying in the morning wind, the rose-tinted sky of this April morning, were the faint reflection of a glory he had known and possessed still as seed in the darkness of the soul. He would know it again when the seed had come to flower. The child's country of escape, his playground, had become the man's cell and wrestling place, but in clear-sighted moments he knew them one.

The amazement passed, but he still walked lightly, his whole being light with the lightness of the day. On a morning like this the whole world seemed spun out of a rainbow. The clouds were mere breaths of rosy smoke away in the immensity of light where a single invisible lark was singing. The trees, the flowers and the very earth were so etherealized by the quality of the light that they looked as though they might at any moment vanish, like mist drawn up by the sun, and John, soaked in the same light, lost all sense of heaviness in body, mind or soul. While they lasted such moments could make the whole drab stretch of painful years seem well worth while, leading to such freedom.

When he shut the church door behind him again he could still hear the lark singing. How golden was praise. When he looked towards the altar he could see the gold flooding through the east window over the daffodils. He was quite unaware that as he walked to his stall he was croaking out words to some sort of a tuneless tune. "The glory of the Lord is spread over the heavens and His praise is in the earth." He fell to his knees in a state that was close to rapture. Prayer today would be no dry wilderness. He would be able today to pour himself out in wordless adoration, without distractions, without encroachment of evil, in perfect abandonment of will and libation of love. Today, just for once in a way, his prayer would not be quite so desperately unworthy of the God whose wealth of giving seemed washing through him now in wave after wave of warm life. He too would be able to give today. Ultimately it was the only thing he ever wanted to do. He laid his head on his crossed arms and sighed deeply, like a child falling to sleep. Within him the Seraph sang in profound stillness. Then the Seraph too was silent, and in the body of the man all his senses died.

A sudden violent jab of pain in a back tooth jerked John's head up and made the perspiration stand out on his forehead.

He leaned back against the seat of his stall and explored the painful area with his forefinger. It was that molar. He ought to have had it seen to months ago but his besetting sin of procrastination was always most pronounced where the dentist was concerned. The dentist's drill upset his raw nerves for days, and since the war distressed nerves brought with them a wretchedness and darkness of the mind that he dreaded more than pain; and heaven knew he dreaded pain more than enough. He was the most arrant coward who ever lived. He prodded cautiously. Yes, that was the one. Perhaps it would just be an extraction. The trouble was you could not know until you got there, and had the uncertainty with you night and day until the date of execution . . . and in these days an appointment two weeks ahead was the most you could hope for. But he'd ring up Woodcote as soon as he got in. He might be able to fit him in somewhere.

The clear note of a bell floated down and seemed to fall like a stone upon his head. Half past. For how long had he prayed? Five minutes? Ten minutes? What sort of priest was he that the least disturbance could shatter his prayer immediately? Well, why ask that question? " . . . children, tossed to and fro, and carried about with every wind." He knew what sort of man he was too; afraid of toothache. Contemptible! Not a man at all; not adult. The dust of his failure rose as a murky cloud and darkened the light. It seemed to grit in his teeth and drift into his soul. The Seraph was stifled there, choked and blinded. He was back again in the desert of aridity, with the grinning faces behind the rocks, the voices that taunted the useless hulk that he was. When the spirit of praise had been poured into a man he forgot what he was; he was like a cheap ugly glass made beautiful by the golden wine which filled it. Empty, he knew his ugliness. In prayer, for those as undisciplined and inexperienced as himself, there were times when one scarcely seemed the same person for five minutes together. He took a grip on himself and knelt upright, clinging to his belief that one was not the same being; one was the self that one was now in all the disturbance

272

and agitation of weakness, and the self that one would be when the compass needle had once and for all steadied to the north. His hands gripping the sides of the stall, he pronounced in words his belief that even for such as he, if he could endure to the end, eventual perfection was not only possible but certain through the grace of God, his conviction that despair was sin. The prayer of words was all he had now. The discipline of words must hold him up until the desert was crossed and the Seraph could sing again.

His toothache was raging now. Well, what of it? He opened the book in front of him and began steadily to say matins, offering each prayer and psalm as he came to it for one of the many for whose peace he prayed daily. Daphne and the children. Harriet and Michael. Great-aunt Maria. That woman who bullied Margary. Troubled folk in the parish. On his good mornings it was a delight to hold the thought of each in his mind while he repeated with attention the words that were as old or far older than the church in which he prayed, prayers and praises whose content of beauty had deepened through the centuries as the number of saints and martyrs who had used them as the vehicle of love and adoration had soul by soul enlarged the bounds of heaven. He liked to think how the luster of each verse, each sentence, had increased through the ages with every loving repetition of it, and tried hard to make his own repetitions worthy of those others. The brightness of the ancient words about the souls for whom he prayed seemed to unite them with all who had ever prayed, to make them part of the company of the saints.

That was on his good mornings, but on his disastrous mornings, such as this had so suddenly become, the whole business of intercessory prayer became no more than an arid discipline. Words. Words. Words. Why had he ever thought that they had any beauty? Each was as dry as dust as he forced himself on through them. Blast this toothache. That woman who had bullied Margary, and for whom he and Mary O'Hara had been praying together since the day of their meeting. The words of the Twentieth Psalm enfolded her without brightness, for she seemed toiling along beside him in the dust. "The Lord hear thee in the day of trouble." He had not been to see her yet. He was wanting to but he was shirking it. "Send thee help from the sanctuary." He was afraid of doing more harm than good, fool that he was. "Strengthen thee out of Zion." He'd not know what to say. "Grant thee thy heart's desire, and fulfill all thy mind." What was her heart's desire? How could he know unless he went to see her? "The Lord perform all thy petitions." Yes, but the Lord had a habit of granting the petitions of sinners through the agency of other sinners. He must go and see the woman. "Some put their trust in chariots, and some in horses." Dear old Rozinante, her brakes needed seeing to. He could take her to the garage, go on to Woodcote, if he had a free five minutes to look at this darned tooth, and then go and see Miss Giles. If she was in. She was sure to be out just when he had nerved himself to it, but he did not want to make an appointment with her. It must seem a casual affair. "Save, Lord; and hear us, O King of heaven." She'd be in if it was the will of God she should be. How appallingly his thoughts were wandering. This darned tooth! Psalm Twenty-one and Bob Hewitt. "Thou hast given him his heart's desire." What had the old boy ever wanted except to live and die at Belmaray?

He toiled on until the end of matins, and then once again the bell rang out over his head. Old Baker was ringing it for the eight o'clock celebration. Eight o'clock and he must celebrate, he, this sinner, half demented with the toothache, thoughts all over the place, and dry as dust. How could he exalt the Lord in this state? "Be Thou exalted, Lord, in Thine own strength: so we will sing, and praise Thy power."

He stumbled up from his knees, gripping his jaw, and loped off towards the vestry to put on his surplice. As he went he was vaguely aware of the singing of the birds.

274

"Are you in love, Michael?" asked Miss Wentworth.

Michael started and looked up from his plate of bacon and egg at Miss Wentworth all but obliterated behind the enormous old silver coffee pot.

> " 'Thou, silent form, dost tease us out of thought
>   As doth eternity,' "

he murmured, half blinded by the coffee pot with the sun upon it.

"No doubt of it," said Miss Wentworth. "I have asked you twice to pass the toast, and only the lovesick or the mentally deficient quote poetry at breakfast."

"That depends upon the breakfast," said Michael, passing the toast. "A Belmaray breakfast is a far greater inspiration to poetic expression than either love or frenzy. How do you get the bacon crisp at the edges like this? And never in all my life have I seen such spreads at this hour of the day."

"I don't believe in economizing on food," said Miss Wentworth. "You only end in a nursing home, which costs more a week than decent food. Nor do I hold with these modern breakfasts. A bit of hay in a soup plate, cereal they call it, and weak tea. No wonder they have religious doubts."

"Who?" asked Michael, passing his cup for more coffee.

"Your generation. Insufficient nourishment in the early morning leads to pessimism and doubts."

"I doubt it," said Michael. "I mean I doubt if we have doubts. Our trouble is that we haven't anything to have doubts about."

"I'm glad you recognize the condition as being a trouble," said Miss Wentworth drily.

"Yes I do," said Michael. "Without faith your mind gets fouled. Look at Cervantes. He was a man of faith and nothing fouled Cervantes, not even war and slavery. He wrote the first part of *Don Quixote* in prison."

Miss Wentworth, who had known what he was telling her before he was born, laid down her toast and listened with great courtesy.

"And look at me," he went on. "In the shadow of the galleys I only wrote deliberate trash and in prison I wrote nothing at all."

"Did you write successful trash?" asked Miss Wentworth.

He smiled at her bleakly. "Yes. Very smart and clever. Gilded dust. I was one of the most successful writers of thrillers of this generation, and it just shows how much behind the times you are that you have never heard of me. Have you heard of existentialism, or the Folland Midge jet fighter? Or the Carter-Davis case?"

"I have not," said Miss Wentworth. "And don't expound them unless you think they'd appeal to me. Good thrillers do. I like nothing better than a first-rate healthy thriller."

"Then don't read mine," said Michael.

"You should be able to write again here," said Miss Wentworth. "It's quiet."

"It is, and I am," said Michael.

"A good thriller?"

"Rotten poetry. It's trash but at least it's not deliberate trash. What would you like me to do today? If old Bob feels well enough he's going to help me plant out the geraniums, but that won't take all the morning."

"You might clear away those nettles that are choking the rosemary tree by the gazebo," suggested Miss Wentworth. "Of course I know weeding the front garden is a task one cannot even attempt but I am fond of the rosemary tree. It's considered unlucky, you know, not to have rosemary in your garden. Only you must never buy rosemary. It must be a gift from a friend."

"Who gave the rosemary to Belmaray?" asked Michael.

"The legend in the family is that Queen Henrietta Maria was wearing a sprig of rosemary when she came here to take refuge towards the end of the Civil War. She gave it to Rupert

276

Wentworth, who was in love with her, and he planted it in the garden. It sounds unlikely."

"Why?" asked Michael. "Only some three hundred years ago and rosemary trees can live to a great age. And he painted her with a sprig of rosemary in the bodice of her dress."

"That's merely sentimental evidence," said Miss Wentworth. "But all the same, that rosemary tree has potency. It's odd, isn't it, that some trees and shrubs have a power that others haven't?"

"Why odd?" asked Michael. "Look at those legends of nymphs and goddesses taking root and turning into plants. Who's to know who a shrub is? For all we know that rosemary bush is inhabited by the ghost of Queen Henrietta Maria. Shall I clear away? Mrs. Prescott washes up today, doesn't she?"

Miss Wentworth got up, smiling a little as she watched him deftly piling china on the tray. In so short a while he had made himself utterly at home in the manor. Nevertheless he did not belong here. "Saturday again," she said. "Time passes so quickly when you are old."

"You like Saturdays?" asked Michael.

"Yes. Sometimes one or other of the children comes to see me. Today my lawyer is coming. Thomas Entwistle. That's not so pleasing."

It was not his business to ask her why, but he was sorry for the shadow on her face. She left the room quietly, a figure of immense dignity in her old tweed clothes and heavy boots. He cleared away the breakfast things and went down the flagged passage, pausing to look at Rupert and Henrietta Maria as he passed them. "You couldn't marry her, poor devil," he said to Rupert. "Commoners don't marry queens, and ex-convicts don't marry respectable young schoolteachers with red hair. There are gulfs which cannot be crossed. I must not see that girl again; not fair to her. I hope she's forgotten what I said about showing her the manor. Rupert, I won't just weed round the bush, I'll clear the whole flower garden for your sake, so that your ghost can walk there with the little queen."

He went out into the sunshine and found old Bob, somewhat recovered now from his recent attack of the screws, glowering at the pots of geraniums. Walsingham was there too, lying on his side on the sun-warmed stones of the terrace with his back against the warm wall of the house, the sun pouring down on his exposed flank. He thumped his tail on the stones when Michael approached but did not move. Warmth was what he liked most at his time of life; oven-like warmth that warmed the whole body to a temperature of extreme heat. Michael bent to pat him before he turned to gloat over his geraniums. He had now made contact with his bank manager and the geraniums were his gift to Belmaray. He had bought every kind of geranium and already the terrace was a blaze of color in his mind's eye.

"Nothing ain't never come to naught in them urns," growled Bob.

"I filled them with fresh earth," said Michael. "Pass the spade, Bob. I'll dig and you can hand me the plants and tell me what a ruddy fool I am."

Bob growled. He liked Michael. The young chap was a hard worker, and teachable, which somewhat mitigated the exasperation of his ignorance. Nor had he put himself forward at all, except in this one matter of geraniums in the urns and the moon-shaped beds, and in that Bob had decided to let him have his own way. The fact was that Bob himself had always had a hankering for geraniums on the terrace, but his hints had made no impression on Miss Wentworth. "Geraniums and calceolaria, now, with lobelias for a border," he suggested. "They make a pretty bit of color."

"Very pretty," agreed Michael. "No, Bob, I'm sorry, but I can't have blue and yellow together. Too like Crete."

"Never been in foreign parts," said Bob. "Never been out of Devon."

"Don't go out of Devon," said Michael. "Once in Devon only a fool would leave it."

"What's Crete like?" asked Bob conversationally.

"In spring, full of brilliant yellow marigolds against a deep blue sky. Enough to blind you. Later, heat and flies." He dug furiously in silence for a few minutes. "Ghastly place to fight in. No cover."

"What's the good of cover in wars like we has now?" asked Bob. "You and your cover, blasted to bits together, so they tell me."

Michael stopped digging and looked at Bob. It was curious to hear a man say "so they tell me" about the horrors of modern war. What would Bob have made of the sickening wreckage that he had looked at so often? What would Bob have done when the devilish fear came upon him? What he had done? No. He exonerated Bob. The old man would have weathered it with the dogged courage of his type. John Wentworth? He would have stuck it out though it cost him his reason. He turned back to his digging, with that familiar sickening shame wrenching his vitals again. Shame could wrench just as fear did. Thinking how other men would have behaved in his place was the most searching form of humiliation that he knew; and he knew a good many. "You're right, Bob," he said. "But cowards like to fool themselves with a bit of cover. I was no credit to the army, Bob."

"Nasty bit of fighting in Crete," said Bob. He spoke gently, for the look on Michael's face had not been wasted on him. "But it's a long time ago and best to forget it now."

Michael stopped and looked down over the tangled garden to the river lying in pools and curves of silver below the glory of the woods. In the stillness the birds' song rose to them with incredible beauty. There were things one could never entirely forget however hard one tried. No matter how fair the blossoming hedges on either side of you the hooded figures ran along on the other side of the trees. What had induced him to speak of

Crete to old Bob? If he could not manage to forget what was below the surface need he dig for the worms in the way he was doing? It was none of his doing that he had found Daphne here, but he had deliberately told Mary the nature of his offense against the law, he had tried to jog Miss Wentworth's memory about the Carter-Davis case, and now he must needs tell old Bob that he had not acquitted himself well in Crete. What was the place doing to him that he must spill the beans like this? Perhaps solitary places encouraged worm-digging. There were men, he remembered, who had withdrawn to hermitages in the desert, to caves in the mountains, in order that they might know themselves. That meant a deliberate confronting of one's past. If unknowingly he had walked into his own heritage when he had walked into Belmaray, then he must become a beadsman. But how could he, who had never been a knight?

> Where does one go from a world of insanity?
> Somewhere on the other side of despair.
> To the worship in the desert, the thirst and deprivation,
> A stony sanctuary and a primitive altar,
> The heat of the sun and the icy vigil.
>   T. S. ELIOT

That was the man's equivalent to the child's country of escape. There was always the hidden life. For the child the journeys to the little land, the land of the memory and foretaste of paradise, for the man who was truly a man, the secret discipline. There were those like himself whose hidden life was merely a ceaseless exhausting attempt to evade that discipline, but they were not men.

"Bob," he said suddenly out of a long silence, "ought a man to forget his own vile actions?"

Bob's blue eyes were puzzled as those of a child, and he made no answer. He knew nothing about vile actions. Michael thought he had never been in the presence of a man who possessed such a depth of innocence. One could almost bathe oneself in it, as one bathed oneself in the soft air of the west-country. And why not? The worth of one man was surely as much at the service of another as the warmth of the sun, if that other had a sufficient realization of his need for it. "And I have, God knows," thought Michael, as he planted the last geranium.

"That's the lot, Bob," he said. "If you don't want me for anything I'll tackle the weeds down below."

"You can't do no harm among them weeds," encouraged Bob. "Nor yet you won't do much good either, not under a twelve-month. But 'tis good exercise... Sir," he added suddenly, and went off round the corner of the house trundling the barrow. He did occasionally let fall tokens of respect, and always when Michael was feeling most disintegrated by a sense of his worth-lessness. They seemed to be bestowed to join him together again, for Bob seemed always moved by that strong creative impulse which only the best men have. In most men, Michael thought, even decent men, the destructive impulse is strongest in the presence of weakness.

Knighted, Michael attacked the nettles and bindweed round the rosemary tree with exhilaration. Bob had touched his cap to him before, he had opened gates for him, but he had never yet said Sir. Upon this day of silver sunshine the accolade had fallen.

3

An hour later, exhausted but triumphant, he sat down on the wall of the paved court, sleepily relaxed in the sun, and contemplated the result of his labors. He thought it good, for like all amateur gardeners he did not worry about roots he could not see. The whole bed below the wall was (above ground) clear, the lemon verbena could breathe and the sun could reach the white violets under the wall, and the small deep purple ones that grew about the roots of the rosemary tree. The bush itself astonished him, for freed from the mass of weeds which had dwarfed its height it seemed to have grown in power and dignity. It was so old that its trunk and branches were twisted and looped like those of a wistaria. Yet the small leaves grew thickly and the shape of it was that of a silver shield. It shone against the blue sky with strength and brilliance. Nothing feminine about it; not the ghost of a dead queen but a virile and entirely masculine presence. How immensely strong must be the spirit of the man who held it that he could so invest the shield with his own power; and the great cross-handled sword which he held in his other hand. "I wish I could see him," thought Michael, "but that blue is so bright it dazzles the eyes." Between sleeping and waking he blinked, yawned like a cat, leaned back against the stone urn behind him and shut his eyes.

Suddenly it seemed he was awake again, his heart beating hard, his eyes more than ever dazzled, not this time by the brilliant blue of the man's cloak but by the nearness of the sword and shield. They were being held out to him. They were his. Had he slept on vigil? That was unpardonable. Yet he was still on his knees, his eyes fixed on the cross-handled sword and the shield, one more of the many who had kept vigil in this place. He was Michael, one of the knights of Belmaray, each in himself a weak and sinful man yet as a member of the brotherhood strong with the power of the man who held the sword and shield. Who was he? Strange images chased through Michael's mind. He thought of the Holy Grail and of a white dove, of fire in the rock and immense wings filling the sky. Then he thought of the doors that had opened in his childhood to that immensity, and the darkness beyond the walls of his man's experience. "Ye know not when the master of the house cometh, at midnight, at even, or at cockcrowing or in the morning." The God who had thrust him through in the darkness with probings of dread and shame was the same God who now held out the sword and shield.

"Yes, I will," said Michael, and he held out his hands and took them.

He half woke up to see a woman's grave blue eyes looking at him out of the rosemary bush. Queen Henrietta Maria after all. His first fancy had been the right one. The man cloaked with the sky who had offered the sword and shield had been just another of his absurdly vivid dreams, woven out of the blue day and the silvery bush, and memories of stories read in his childhood. This was reality, this queen become a bush. Or was this only another dream? Was he awake, or wasn't he?

"Henrietta," he said gently.

"She's with Aunt Maria," said the bush shyly and sweetly. "It's me."

Michael sat up straight and saw bits of a lilac frock showing through the rosemary tree, below the parted branches through which a child's face was smiling at him. The fingers holding back the branches were thin and brown and he dimly saw slim bare brown legs below the dress. This child, of the three of them, was the most intimately a child of Belmaray. That was why he liked her best.

"Come out of it Margary," he said. "It's enough to startle a fellow out of his wits."

Margary came out from behind the tree and sat down shyly beside him on the wall. It was April now and the day was so warm that she wore a cotton frock and sandals, and there was a rosy glow of sunburn in her cheeks. She was always happy in this garden but just now she was almost always happy because something very odd had happened at school. When Miss Giles snapped at her she no longer minded; the one who minded was Miss Giles.

"Please, what is?" she asked.

"Having the rosemary tree turn into you. Though I might have known it. Mistress Margary Wentworth was a very flowery lady. Do you know the poem about her?"

"Yes," said Margary. "Father called me after her."

Michael repeated the second verse, bending over to pick a sprig of rosemary.

> "Plainly I cannot glose,
> Ye be, as I divine,
> The pretty primerose,
> The goodly columbine."

He looked at her and saw that her whole face was rosy, and her eyes were wide in wonder as she looked at him. She was, he realized, being treated as a woman by a man for the first time in her life, but she was neither mischievous nor coy, merely full of wonder as to what this new thing could be. Though she was what most people would have called a plain child he saw beauty in her smallness and delicacy, in the hollowed flushed cheeks and the slim fingers laced together on the pointed knees. A breath of warm wind stirred in the garden, bringing the scent of the violets under the wall, and lifting the child's hair back from her face so that he saw the blue veins on her temples and the small ears close against her head. A wave of happiness broke over him with the wind. He seemed to be making up for lost time, falling in love practically at first sight for the second time in a few days. And with no loss of devotion to his first love in capitulating to the second. Could a man be in love with a little girl? He smiled at Margary and was met with a smile of such delight that it startled him. Her shoulders straightened and her fingers relaxed, so that he could slip the sprig of rosemary into the hollow of her hands. He did not know yet how instantly she responded to delight in others but his sense of her sudden well-being increased his own.

" 'There's rosemary, that's for remembrance; pray you, love, remember,' " he said, and wondered as he spoke how many times those words had been spoken in this place, and if he was saying them now because they echoed here.

"Yes, I will," said Margary matter-of-factly, and her fingers closed on the sprig of rosemary. "Did you know we have a dog?" she added.

He laughed. Certainly a man could fall in love with a little girl if such was the bent of his mood, gently and idyllically in April sunshine, but he must not expect any sentimental response to his nostalgic utterances. "What sort?" he asked.

"Pekinese," said Margary. "He is too fat just now but he won't be when we have walked him a bit. He loves being our dog. Winkle is showing him to Aunt Maria and Walsingham. Are you going to stay with us for a long time?"

"Until I wake up," said Michael. He was astonished at his answer, but he realized it was the right one. The dream of the silver shield had been a dream within a dream. The world of Belmaray was no more the world of reality as he knew it than that had been; or perhaps one might put it another way and say that the dream of the shield had been just as real as this dream of Belmaray. But reality as one knew it was what claimed one's allegiance. Deepening experience might change one's conception of it but until that happened the life one knew was the life one had to live. "When I wake from this dream I shall have to go back."

"But you have woken up," said Margary. "You were asleep when I looked at you from behind the bush but you aren't now. Do you want to go on weeding? If you do I'll help you."

"I want to weed the whole garden," he said.

"I'll help," she repeated, and slid off the wall.

Five minutes later they were struggling with the weeds side by side and talking irrelevant nonsense in the way that two friends do who are happy and at ease together, drifting from one subject to another without knowing how they got there. They talked of books and brown sugar, the relative merits of toffee and fudge, gilt on gingerbread, and then with the remembrance of dust that is a little gilt, and the gilt o'erdusted, he suddenly found he was declaiming Shakespeare to her, and she was sitting back on her heels and drinking in the music of the words. It was the great speech from *Troilus and Cressida* which he had once learned by heart but had not dared to think of for years. "For honor travels in a strait so narrow . . . keep then the path." The words no longer had power to stab him because he had committed himself.

15

ONLY his great age, which made him reluctant to exert himself, and his sense of duty as a host, kept Walsingham from seizing the thing as though it were a rat and shaking it until it died. He had never seen such a creature and scorned to give it the name of dog. He sat back on his haunches, outraged, and looked down the delicate pencilled line of white fur that travelled the length of his nose, from his wise forehead to his quivering nostrils, to the thing beyond. Not far enough beyond. He could smell it overwhelmingly. He could see it more than enough. With every quivering hair he knew it had come to stay.

He would say for it that it implored permission. Cringing there on the stones before him not only the whiskers but the whole obese body quivered, and the bulging terrified eyes seemed about to pop out of the head at any moment. It was the size of a rat but not the color. Its color was actually a pleasing golden-brown. He growled slightly and in a paroxysm of alarm the object rolled over on its back on the stones, its ridiculous forepaws clutched at its chest and its hind legs stretched out in a manner expressive of the depth of abject humility. Its chest, like his own, was white. He had a soft spot for white-chested dogs. Shirt fronts always gave an added air of distinction to a gentleman, though they increased the vulgarity of the mixed breeds. Was this a gentleman? He advanced his nose half an inch and definitely smelled good breeding. There was grey on the muzzle, for like himself the creature was no longer a callow youth. It was possible they might have something in common. He relaxed and his jaws parted in so tolerant a manner that the creature's parody of a tail trembled slightly on the flagged stones; he relaxed further and the tail fluttered, still more and the tail thudded. He lay right down and Baba rolled over and crawled a little nearer, he closed one eye and Baba slobbered with relief. He closed the other and Baba crept as near as he dared and lay down also. They communed together. "Sir," said Baba, "I had a bad home and now I have a good one. I have, now, a mistress who will keep faith. I adore my mistress. Sir, I have found a refuge for my old age." Walsingham replied, "Sir, you may remain." He slept and Baba did the same.

"Is it all right?" breathed Winkle.

"Deep has called to deep," said Miss Wentworth. "It's a question of the mutual recognition of gentlemanly birth."

"Orlando likes him too," said Winkle.

"There's no accounting for the taste of cats," said Miss Wentworth.

"Do you like him, Aunt Maria?" asked Winkle anxiously.

"I am delighted that there should once more be a dog at the vicarage," said Miss Wentworth guardedly. "What is a vicarage without a dog? A well-trained dog is like religion, it sets the deserving at their ease and is a terror to evildoers."

"Yes," said Winkle, swinging her fat legs. She did not always understand what Aunt Maria was talking about but this worried neither of them. They were sitting together on the wooden bench on the terrace regarding the geraniums, Winkle with pleasure and Miss Wentworth with patience. The dogs slept now at their feet. Winkle's small fat hand was within her great-aunt's and she was sitting as close to her as she could. Winkle was independent and did not generally want to be close to people, but Aunt Maria was different for they were very much one person. Their names, Henrietta and Maria, linked together made up the name of a queen whom they regarded as one of the family. When they were with each other they both unconsciously had an added air of regality.

Mr. Entwistle, approaching along the terrace, noted it, and noted for the first time that Miss Wentworth, with her hat perched well forward over her forehead and her bun of hair sticking out behind, was in silhouette not unlike the Red Queen. Winkle, of course, with her smooth gold hair tucked back under its snood, was the image of Queen Alice, but that he had always known.

"Your Majesties, your humble servant," said Mr. Entwistle, bowing hat in hand, portly and pink, his beautiful white moustache gleaming in the sun. "You get younger every day, Miss Wentworth. Little Henrietta, how she grows!"

"My good sir, children do," said Miss Wentworth with a touch of asperity. "Sit down. Winkle, shake hands with Mr. Entwistle and take Baba in to see Mrs. Prescott. I want to talk to Mr. Entwistle."

Winkle went away with Baba cradled in her arms like Alice's pig-baby, and Miss Wentworth turned to Mr. Entwistle. "How's your gout?" she asked, her asperity infused with sudden kindliness. Mr. Entwistle's compliments had always annoyed her but he had been her faithful friend for fifty years and he was now her guest. She waited with genuine anxiety for his answer.

"So-so," sighed Mr. Entwistle, his fat hands on his knees. "I'm not so young as I was."

"A mere seventy," said Miss Wentworth. "I remember you in your perambulator. Will you take anything? A glass of wine?"

"No, dear lady, not on any account," said Mr. Entwistle in horror.

"But you like a glass of wine," said Miss Wentworth.

"My own taste and that of my gout are not identical," said Mr. Entwistle.

"I don't hold with pandering to the body," said Miss Wentworth. "A body is like a dog. Once let it have its own way and you will never have yours. A cup of tea? No? Then smoke, old friend, for goodness sake. You like your pipe I know, and I'll have a cigarette." She took one from her gold case and lit it from the lighter he held. "Food and tobacco do so soften difficult situations. What are we to do this time?"

Mr. Entwistle lit his cherry wood pipe, that harmonized so perfectly with his large white moustache, his bald head, his round rosy cheeks and his gold spectacles, and puffed in silence for a few moments. He was the very picture of kindly benevolence but the eyes behind the glasses were very shrewd. Miss Wentworth had discovered through many troublous years that if she disregarded his advice she was sorry afterwards.

"Miss Wentworth," he said, "there's nothing we can do this time."

"Are you quite sure?" she asked quietly.

"Quite sure," said Mr. Entwistle.

Miss Wentworth smoked on serenely for a few moments and gazed upon the garden with untroubled eyes, but Mr. Entwistle, observing her acutely without appearing to look in her direction, was well aware that this was a bad moment. It was the same for him and he could not, himself, put the situation into words. It was she who did that.

"Belmaray must go on the market," she said.

"Unless your nephew can enormously increase his contribution to its upkeep," said Mr. Entwistle.

"You know he can't do that," said Miss Wentworth. "He gives more than he can afford already."

"Will you explain the situation to him or shall I?" asked Mr. Entwistle.

"Neither of us will at present," said Miss Wentworth. "For my sake he would be most painfully distressed and plunge into some quixotic action that might ruin himself but do no good to me. You know what he is, one of those half-way cases; neither sufficiently a saint nor sufficiently a sinner to have much sense. Oh yes, saints have sense; when they really *are* saints. It's surprising how sanctity clears the mind. Mr. Entwistle, I am talking for the sake of talking." She paused and for the first time the misery of her mind was evident. Her hand shook and some ash fell from her cigarette and lay unheeded on her lap. "The publicity," she said. "The advertisements in the papers. Prospective buyers always coming over. These old places are hard to sell. Perhaps in the end Belmaray will have to be auctioned; or bought by the county council for lunatics or moral delinquents."

"Sometimes congenial sales can be privately arranged," said Mr. Entwistle gently.

"Have you anything in mind?" asked Miss Wentworth.

"Have I your permission to continue private enquiries?" he asked.

"What have you been up to?" asked Miss Wentworth sharply. "Telling half the county the Wentworths must leave Belmaray before you tell the Wentworths?"

"No, no," protested Mr. Entwistle. "But I've a client, in point of fact an old friend of my own, in need of just such a property as Belmaray."

"You're up to something," said Miss Wentworth resignedly. "Underground, like a mole, and I suppose I should be thankful for it. I have, in the past, been thankful for your private burrowings."

"And never found your confidence misplaced?" asked Mr. Entwistle gently.

"No," said Miss Wentworth. "Not once in fifty years. You can put that on your tombstone if you like. Go on with it, then, and we won't speak of it to my nephew until we must. How's your son in Kenya doing?"

The talk turned to Mr. Entwistle's affairs, upon which he expatiated at some length, and he did not say good-bye until he had asked for and received her sympathy and advice in full measure, and could leave her feeling she was still of use. Mr. Entwistle was a very clever man.

2

Driving back to Silverbridge in his shining little car Mr. Entwistle thought chiefly of Miss Wentworth. He understood her very well. It would not be the loss of what she possessed that might break her so much as the loss of the sphere of her usefulness, that had grown to fit her as her own body. Belmaray and her own heart alike received their guests, alike gave the shelter of their courtesy and warmth. He feared for her, leaving Belmaray. Could a woman so old achieve again that delicate adjustment of character and environment that can give the maximum of usefulness to both? At Belmaray it had grown with her growth. In a new home it would have to be something willed and wrought. Those who loved her, and he counted himself among them, would have to make considerable and well considered demands upon her.

He was thinking of the nature of these demands as he drove past Oaklands, and his thoughts were deflected, for Mrs. Belling had also been one of his clients for many years. It was he who had succeeded her husband as solicitor at Silverbridge. He had heard that she was not well, though not sufficiently indisposed to have sent for the doctor. So far as he knew she had made no will. Why was that? In his experience those who made no wills either had nothing to leave, feared death too much to face up to its preliminaries, or had so little imagination that unless some sudden shock brought it home to them they could not visualize it in connection with themselves. Leaving Oaklands behind him he tried to put Mrs. Belling out of his mind, for in spite of her unalloyed sweetness he did not like her and did not at all want to be summoned to her bedroom to help her make her will.

Now he came to think of it he remembered that he had not

292

added a necessary codicil to his own will. A poor thing if a solicitor had to have a shock before he... "Hi, you darned idiot!" he
yelled. "What the blazes do you think you're doing? What
the... phew! My God!"

It was the mercy of heaven that his sudden swerve had
brought him crashing into nothing more solid than a wooden
garden fence, that had gone down before him like matchwood.
The fool who had shot out of a side road on the wrong side
had skidded and collided with a stationary greengrocer's van.
Out of the corner of his eye he could see oranges and cabbages all
over the road. Whether the fool was hurt or not was a matter of
indifference to him, kindly man though he was by nature. He
had had a nasty shock and at his age it was impossible to sur-
mount the experience with charitable feelings towards the
shocker. "Damn fool!" he growled. "He'll have a piece of my
mind when I get my breath." He puffed and blew, stroking his
beautiful white moustache with his white handkerchief. "A piece
of my mind. And I'll report it." He paused, his handkerchief
suspended in mid air as a tall figure reared itself up beside him
and an agitated well-known voice smote upon his ear.

"Sir! The fault was entirely mine. Are you hurt at all? Entwistle!"

Mr. Entwistle put away his handkerchief and beamed all
over his face, for he was very fond of John Wentworth of Belmaray. "Not so much as a bruise," he said heartily.

"My fault," said John. "I don't know how it happened. I
must have been thinking of something else." He caught himself up, aware of insincerity. "I do know how it happened. My
brakes need attending to and I *was* thinking of something else,
and I didn't sound my horn."

"You were on the wrong side of the road, Sir," said a policeman who had apparently risen out of the ground, and was now
producing notebook and pencil. A small crowd had collected;
the irate owner of the smashed fence, the driver of the greengrocer's van, women with prams, several small boys, several

293

dogs and a tall badly-dressed woman with a shopping basket. The policeman licked his pencil. "The Reverend Wentworth, isn't it? The Reverend Wentworth, Belmaray Vicarage."

An anguished expression crossed John's face. He would have to appear in court. He was a bad enough example for the youth of the parish as it was, what with one thing and another, without this. "And my only excuse, I was thinking of something else!" he mourned, unaware that he spoke aloud.

"So was I," said Mr. Entwistle. "I was thinking of wills. Officer, I am bringing no summons. The fault was as much mine as Mr. Wentworth's. I did not sound my horn either. Yes, sir, your fence will be repaired at my expense and that of Mr. Wentworth. The officer has our names and addresses. No, my man, you will get into no trouble over those cabbages. Get along, boys, get along."

The affair promising no further excitement the crowd, with the exception of the tall woman, melted away. Mr. Entwistle, who had an engagement, talked a little to John and then wrung him warmly by the hand and drove off... The dear fellow was a fool, but engaging, and he had never liked him so much... John remained helping the driver of the van to pick up the oranges and cabbages, with such a touching humility, and such abject apologies, that the man was led to revise his hitherto unfavorable opinion of the clergy; especially after a handsome tip.

"Thank you, Sir," he said. "Good-day, Sir. Oh, thank you, Ma'am."

It was the tall woman, who had retrieved some oranges that had rolled down the gutter. She handed them over and the greengrocery van drove away.

"How very kind of you," said John. All through the disturbing affair he had been vaguely aware of her, hovering medusa-like on the outskirts of the fray. Her sallow face, her straight grey hair arranged in a snaky coil beneath her hard felt hat, her dark grey-clad figure, had sent a further chill through his already shivering body. Shock always made him icy cold. He had been deep in serious cogitation as to what on earth he could say to Miss Giles and the sudden jar of finding that he was driving a car that had collided with a greengrocery van had been a severe shock. Fumbling to lift his hat he found to his shame that his hand was shaking, then seeing the look of sick weariness on the woman's face and the number of things she had in her shopping basket he forgot about himself. "As you see, I'm not fit to be trusted with a car," he said, "but could I drive you anywhere with that heavy basket?"

"I live quite close, Mr. Wentworth," she said. "At Oaklands. I teach your daughters. Won't you come in and rest?"

"Can you possibly be Miss Giles?" asked John joyously.

"Yes," she said, astonished to see him as warm and confident as he had hitherto been nervous and distracted. His smile flashed over his face. The woman was delivered into his hands! With what bounty and withal with what humor did heaven answer prayer. He had been praying for the right approach to Miss Giles all the time Woodcote had been pulling out his tooth. He still had no idea what he would say, or in what further ways he might be called upon to make an ass of himself, but somehow or other all these things would work together for good for this poor woman.

Beneath his joyousness he was painfully moved by her face. Looking away from her as he took her basket and opened the car door for her he saw it as he had seen Michael's, with that strange visual gift of his which seemed to stamp a face upon the very air and sunlight, so that the light made the truth of it plain to him. The mouth was not actually cruel but it had that thin-lipped bitterness of unhappiness that has found no help anywhere, no outlet but the distillation of itself acid drop by acid drop in word and thought and act. The eyes had looked into his straightly. He thought that the mind behind the eyes would not flinch from convicting truth however unpalatable. He wanted to hear the voice again. He believed it had had beauty.

"It's not so much rest I am in need of as a cup of tea," he

confided to her as he took his place beside her. "Should you say it was round about eleven?"

Miss Giles consulted her watch. "Six and a half minutes past," she said.

He observed she was an accurate woman of a mathematical turn of mind; only mathematicians bothered with half minutes. Yes, the voice was musical. Mathematics and music were closely allied.

"I thought you might like a cup of tea," she said. "That was why I waited. I recognized you, for I saw you once waiting outside Oaklands for the children. And also, Mr. Wentworth, it seems a chance for me to consult one of the parents about the difficulty we are in just now."

"Here we are," said John, scraping the paint off the gate post as he turned into the Oaklands drive. "And I'm entirely at your service."

The sudden precision of his tone surprised Miss Giles. Her amused liking for the amiable muddler was infused with sudden respect; which was not lost when he stopped the car with such a jerk that her head nearly went through the windshield. He was out of the car in a moment, apologizing and helping her out in a manner that could not have been more courteous had she been a duchess. Four shallow steps led up to the front door of Oaklands and such is the power of suggestion that she walked up them as though she were a duchess, and led the way to the drawing room with an air of elegance and grace that smote John's heart with profound compassion. Another man might have thought it merely laughable, contrasted with her shabby clothes and ravaged face, and the dusty stuffy room to which she brought him, but to John it was as though he saw a fine and delicate flower struggling for life in some airless slum... And an airless slum was exactly what the room was, for Annie had not touched it since Mrs. Belling had taken to her bed. Ashes of a dead fire were still in the grate and chocolate papers lay on the floor.

"Please sit down," said Miss Giles, "and I'll ring for Annie to bring some tea."

He sat down, struggling with a hideous depression. It had been a delight to find Miss Giles but, as usual, his joy had been short-lived. Never had he felt so utterly inadequate, such an abysmal failure as he felt in this room. He had been in it once before, upon some gala occasion when there had been fresh flowers in the vases and a bright fire in the grate, and such a concourse of clean children and proud parents that the room itself could not emerge. Now he saw it and felt it; sluggish, unclean and deceitful.

"This is a horrible room," he said in a quick whisper to Miss Giles.

"It's a vile room," she agreed, also in a whisper, and then they both started guiltily as Annie came in.

John looked at Annie pitifully as Miss Giles ordered the tea. He had seldom seen a more slovenly maidservant, and she obeyed Miss Giles insolently, on the verge of rebellion. Yet she did not disgust him as the room did. However much the weakness of one human spirit may be dominated by the strength of another it retains somewhere its own wavering individuality, but a room takes the stamp of its owner as helplessly and surely as soft wax. He hated the room but not Annie.

"Poor woman," he murmured to Miss Giles when she had gone.

"She can be managed," said Miss Giles, aloud this time and in a grating voice that had lost its beauty. John started and looked at her. Since their meeting until this moment she had been relaxed and softened, now she was taut with anguished control. He felt her strength, but it was less than the strength that had so long inhabited this vile deceitful room and it was now very nearly exhausted.

"What a time you must have had," he said, "holding things together here. Trying to give the children some sort of an education, impose some sort of discipline. Well, you've an ally now in Miss O'Hara."

"I don't suppose she'll stay," said Miss Giles bleakly. "They never do."

"Why do you stay?" he asked.

"Partly because at my age I'm afraid of not getting another job," said Miss Giles, "but chiefly because I'm accustomed to it here. You must think that very odd."

"No," said John. "You're a sick woman. In a state of physical weakness it's so much easier to function in the groove you know. It seems to hold you together. I know. I'd be terrified now if I had to cease to be vicar of Belmaray."

"Yet surely that's work you love," said Miss Giles.

"Yes," said John. "You're right. Our conditions don't really bear comparison. And I make such a mess of my job and you do yours so well."

"No," said Miss Giles. "I've become embittered. One can admit no worse failure than that, can one?"

"I think so," said John. "Embitterment shows a failure of humor, of humility, but not necessarily of tenacity. If you still know how to hold on you can still redeem what's lost."

"Even love?" said Miss Giles. "I detest the children now."

"Children are frequently detestable," agreed John equably.

"I have been cruel to your daughter Margary," said Miss Giles, two red spots showing unbecomingly on her cheek bones.

"Yes, I know," said John, and then said no more because Annie came in with the tea, and he sprang up and took the heavy tray from her, putting it down on a table beside Miss Giles; crooked, so that the milk slopped over. By the time Annie had fetched a cloth and mopped it up, and accepted his embarrassed apologies, she was his friend for life.

"It was not Margary who told me," he went on when Annie had gone. "She would never have told me. She has her own kind of strength."

"Yes, she has, and if I had not lost the power of love I think I should now be finding Margary the most lovable child in the school," said Miss Giles. She spoke in a tone of flat despair and then said, "Mr. Wentworth, you must dislike me very much."

"No," said John. "And yet, Margary being my child, I'm astonished that I don't." He suddenly smiled at her. "You know, Miss Giles, you're all wrong about yourself. People who have lost the power of love don't grieve over its apparent loss. They don't grieve over anything. If you've lost the power of love you've lost the power of grief. Hold on and the tide will turn."

"Hold on to what?" asked Miss Giles.

"To grief," said John.

Miss Giles was silent. "I've never done that," she said at last. "I mean, I've never welcomed anything difficult or painful. I've always resented it and hit back. I can see now that to have welcomed the slings and arrows might have been to welcome love."

"There's never any 'might have been' with those who retain the power of grief and the power of tenacity," said John.

Miss Giles got up, walked to the window and opened it, so that the spring air flooded into the stuffy room. "Why didn't I do that before?" she wondered. "Because Mrs. Belling always keeps this window shut I forgot it could open. It's a lovely day."

She stood by the window, looking at the day with astonished recognition, as though she had not seen an English spring for twenty years. John thought that possibly she hadn't. Beauty awakened such intolerable longing that people often shut their eyes to it, unaware that the longing was the greatest treasure that they had, their very lifeline, uniting the country of their lost innocence with the heavenly country for which their sails were set. He dared not move or speak while she took hold of her lifeline again. When she turned round and came back it was with an air of bewilderment, as though the familiar groove had for the moment eluded her.

"What was it you wanted to ask me about?" he said gently.

299

She looked at him gratefully, glad to be steered back to her groove again. As Daphne had done she had felt within her that tremor of anticipation with which the human spirit acknowledges the shadow of coming change. Things seem the same and yet one is aware that they will not be the same for very much longer. There may seem no reason for change, one may not even wish for it, yet the shadow is there, and in it familiar objects seem for a moment or two to be floating away, as though in a dream that will soon vanish. Ahead there is nothingness, behind a dream. The moment has its fear and one can be glad when the dream hardens into reality again, however ugly the reality may be.

"It's Mrs. Belling," she said. "It's difficult to know what to do about her and what to do about the school."

"Is she ill?" asked John.

"Not exactly ill. We think she may have had a slight stroke, though we don't know for certain because she won't see a doctor. Physically she seems to have recovered, but mentally she is very odd. She is in bed and won't get up. She won't exert herself in any way at all."

"In what way did she previously exert herself?" asked John.

Miss Giles wondered if he intended sarcasm, but when she looked at him he was only wanting to know.

"She sat in this room as headmistress of Oaklands," said Miss Giles. "She had a queer strength. Oaklands is Mrs. Belling."

"Yes," said John.

"This term is nearly finished," said Miss Giles, "But the Easter holidays are short and what are we to do next term? Miss O'Hara and I can hardly take her authority from her and run the school as our own."

"It's a little difficult for me to give advice about next term," said John, "because my wife and I are not sending the children back next term."

Miss Giles looked at him. "You're quite right," she said.

"Oaklands is not the best place for them. Nor am I the best teacher for them."

"If you were headmistress of Oaklands I would not take them away," said John. "In your own school I believe you would be an excellent headmistress."

"You cannot believe that," said Miss Giles. "Not after what I've told you."

"I would not have believed it if you had not told me what you did," said John. "But I can believe every possible good of anyone possessed of the power of self-knowledge."

"And so of grief?" she asked.

"It's always a grief," he acknowledged. "It's the very grief that makes you turn your eyes to where perfection is, and thankfully love that because you cannot love the other. But we're getting away from your groove. What are you to do about next term? I've no idea. Couldn't you wait until next term to see what to do about it?"

"Mr. Wentworth, you don't understand. Mrs. Belling won't do anything. She won't answer letters. She won't even sign a cheque. How can we engage the new matron we need so badly? How can we pay the tradesmen or even get our own salaries paid?"

"It's certainly very awkward," agreed John. "Is Entwistle her lawyer?"

"I don't know," said Miss Giles. "She has always been secretive about such things."

"He's sure to be," said John. "He's the only solicitor in Silverbridge. I'll talk to him. Can the vicar make anything of her?"

"She won't let him try," said Miss Giles. "He called but she would not see him."

"He should just have opened the door and walked in," said John.

"Would you like to do that?" suggested Miss Giles.

John was on his feet in a panic. "Miss Giles, I couldn't. Besides, she's the vicar's preserve."

"If it comes to that I suppose I am too," said Miss Giles, "but you didn't think it poaching to help me."

"That's a different thing," said John. "And I didn't come here to preach to you, but to tell you that you were tormenting my child. And then you told me you had been unkind to her and so I saw you no longer were. I had to say something and so I preached, because that's my groove."

"Were you coming to see me?" asked Miss Giles.

"I was," said John. "I was coming to see you when I ran into Entwistle. I must go now, Miss Giles, I really must. I must go and see Entwistle. He's your man. But I'm your man if you ever want to start a school of your own. I'll back you in every way I can. Good-bye, Miss Giles. Thanks for the tea."

Before Miss Giles knew it he had fled. She heard his efforts to get his car started, and then the bumping and creaking as it jerked itself down the drive and out into the road. She leaned back in her chair and laughed, and then suddenly cried; tears of quite unexplainable relief and joy. The approaching change had ceased to be a shadow and became a beam of light. The future was just as obscure but it had no darkness in it.

3

The day that had dawned for John with a music and a beauty that would never be forgotten was closing for Michael in much the same manner. "Remember it," he said to himself. "Remember this room, the mist upon the field and the evening star, the thrush singing and the voice of the river below the hill. Remember the flames of the candles, the books and the white page under your hand. When you go back you can take this with you. Remember it. Nothing is lost that is stamped upon memory. You may lose it for the time being, you may go mad and curse and rave, but what has once entered into memory is never effaced. Madness passes, memory does not. It is one of the things which is given back to be your heaven or hell. Take this and be thankful, for there will be plenty of hell for you in the place of judgment. That's what judgment is; memory. You remember every shameful thing you ever did, every cruel word you ever spoke. The hooded figures behind the hedge will keep up with you right to the end, and then crowd in upon you and you'll see their foul faces at last. You'll be the victim then, for your own words will wound you and your own actions choke you. That's hell, and you'll not endure it and live if there's not a sweetness in the air from another's forgiveness and your own remorse, and hills in the distance touched with this light of beauty recognized, accepted and adored."

He laid down his pen and took his hand from the page where he had just written the last word of a shockingly bad poem. He leaned back in his chair and let what he looked at do with him what it would. It chose to take from him all consciousness of himself, reducing him to the apparent nothingness of vision only. He was in the small book-lined study that he had seen from the field on the day of his arrival, but he did not know it. He only knew the room, dusky, and smelling of the old volumes on the shelves, of the wallflowers under the window and the wax of the candles that had nearly burned away in the candlesticks on the table. The table was old oak, black like dark water, and the light of the candles swam in it. The blue and yellow flames were so small, vanishing in wisps of smoke, yet they lit the gold lettering on the backs of the old brown books and showed a ruby glow from floor to ceiling where the curtains hung on either side of the two windows; torn and stained old velvet curtains by daylight, by candlelight sculptured pillars of red stone. The light of the candles guttered and died, the room with them. Michael, looking from the shadows, knew now not the room but the loveliness of the world beyond the windows.

Looking west he faced the afterglow of the sunset. The mist was rising upon the field in smoke-grey swathes but above it the sky was barred with rose and amethyst, melting into the deep cool blue of late evening. There was a tall old thorn tree growing on a hillock in the field and its trunk and branches were black against the strangeness of the muted color, and just above its highest branch shone the evening star. The tree looked strange too, like the fantastic figure of some bent old man, but the thrush was singing in it without fear. Michael moved further and further out from his lost self. He was the mist upon the field, the old black thorn tree, the bird singing, the evening star, and the light of the rising moon. He was the man walking towards him, the old bent man leaning on a stick. . . He seemed to be moving out of the room and walking to meet himself.

Then quietly and slowly he came back to consciousness of the room about him and knew the old man to be not himself but another, a monk of some sort, wearing a dark habit. He got up from the table and came up to the open casement window, leaning his hand upon the sill.

"Is it the river one hears?" asked the old man. He had a voice like a frog's, croaking yet attractive. Standing beneath the window, where Michael had stood upon the day of his coming, he looked less old. His eyes were dark and bright in his brown wrinkled face, his hair iron grey. He seemed vaguely familiar.

"Yes," said Michael. "The tide's coming in."

"The sea's not far?"

"Only a few miles," said Michael.

"Then there will be gulls at times," said the old man.

"Plenty," said Michael. "And the smell of the sea when the wind's in the west."

"I'm not on private property?" asked the old man anxiously.

"No," said Michael, smiling. He had never set eyes on such a rum old bird but he liked him immensely. "Would you like to come in?" he asked. "If you follow down the hedge and go through the gate between the yew trees and up through the garden I can let you in."

"No, no," said the monk with a touch of shyness. "Thank you, but it's late and I don't want to intrude. I just want to get the feel of the place."

Why, wondered Michael. Aloud he said, "I wish you would come in and sit down."

"I'm not quite as old as I look," said the monk, smiling. "And I am used to standing. The recitation of the divine office, you know." Michael did not know and remained silent. "But you're not used to standing, perhaps, and I mustn't detain you here at the window. I have friends with a car waiting for me at the field gate. I am on holiday. Good-night, Sir." And he turned away.

Though his Sir was the natural expression of the courtesy of his generation it touched Michael as old Bob's had done. He wished the stranger would not go. He did not speak but the old man stopped and half-turned round again, looking out towards the valley and the river.

"A wonderful evening," he said.

"The light is amazingly lovely," murmured Michael.

"The light of afterglow, and the moon rising," said the monk. "And such sweetness in the air. I don't know why but this particular light of a spring evening always puts me in mind of forgiveness. Good-night."

He turned away once more and did not pause again or look back. In spite of his lame leg, his stick, his age and his bent figure he seemed to move quickly and the mist soon took him. Had he ever been there? Michael fitted fresh candles in the candlesticks, lit them and sat down again.

Such sweetness in the air. The light of a spring evening. Would Daphne forgive him if he asked her? He had shamed her, but Miss Wentworth had said shame could be offered for shame. If he told her the whole shameful story would she forgive him? He'd tell her on Monday. If she did not forgive him at least he'd have offered his shame.

He put the pages of his poem together and settled down to reread and correct it. It was a depressing experience. He had tried to avoid the gilded dust of everything he had written up to now, but if this had a sound kernel of sincerity that was all it had. The fruit and the rind seemed to him the most sloppy and sentimental stuff he had ever read. And yet what he had written had been the best expression he could encompass of deeply felt experience. Now why? There hadn't been a trace of sentimentality in the poisonous stuff he had written with the one purpose of feathering a safe nest for himself. And yet, as an example of poison, it had been well written poison, while this, as an example of sincerity, was so completely amateurish that it shocked him. It was not that the medium of verse was unfamiliar to him, for though he had never published it he had written a good deal of verse for his own delight; what was unfamiliar was the new outlook that had come to him at Belmaray and the sincerity with which he had tried to express it, and because in the realms both of vision and morality he was in the kindergarten, his effort at self-expression was comparable to a child's scribblings with colored chalk on brown paper.

"The children of this world are in their generation wiser than the children of light." That was the artist's problem as well as the man's. Progress in evil was quick and easy; Apollyon was not a chap who hid himself and he gave every assistance in his power. The growth in goodness was so slow, at times so flat, so dull, and like the White Queen one had to run so fast to stay where one was, let alone progress; and there were few men who dared to say they had found God. It was easy to be a clever sinner, for the race to an earthly visible goal was short to run, so impossibly hard to be a wise saint, with the goal set at so vast a distance from this world and clouded with such uncertainty. Patience with the apparent hopelessness of spiritual growth was the man's task, patience with the breaking chalks and the smudgy drawing the artist's. And for both the grim struggle of faith. It was hard to believe that the pothooks before him were of greater value than his gilded dust. Did men such as John, and the old man who had come from the mist and vanished into it again, at times lose their faith that an hour spent in mental prayer was not a shocking waste of time? Probably, as he would lose faith in the discipline of pothooks. But he was going on struggling with them. He had taken his vow by the rosemary tree and this fight would be part of the greater one in the stony sanctuary.

The vow had been taken only in a dream, of course, but this morning's dream had been as much a part of the everlastingness of memory as that other dream of the knights riding out of the fortress of the church that was the subject of his poem. He had not understood that dream at the time but he did now. The squires of Belmaray, riding out on their fantastic quests, from Elizabethan Francis who had built the manor to John Wentworth, were not forgotten by Belmaray. No man who loves it and serves it ever leaves a countryside. He cannot. That bit of earth had him and that bit of earth keeps him as he was when he loved it for as long as the earth itself endures, and it only needs some slight shifting of the focus for a newcomer in love with a place to see its former lovers riding by. It was the Lord of Life to whom he had made his vow and the man in the blue cloak had carried a shield in token that the knights of Belmaray did not live within the memory of Belmaray only. One might just as well call eternity the memory of God.

"I've missed something out though," thought Michael, gloomily reading the last verse of his poem. "How did that end? Not with the knights. There was another chap who came out after them and shut the door. An old monk."

He stopped, laying down the paper. It was the same old monk who had just disappeared into the mist. He sat without movement for a full five minutes and then gave it up. This was a rum place and only time would show. Meanwhile there was his poem. For another half-hour he struggled with it, then tore the whole thing up. It was no good to anyone. The kernel had been all right but useless to anyone except himself and his God, to whom he now addressed his first prayer in years. "I've doubts about you but at least you are now something to have doubts about."

16

IT WAS Monday morning and Daphne was gardening in the company of a contented robin. John was at Silverbridge attending a meeting and was to have lunch there, and the children were at school. She and Harriet were going to have a lunch that needed no cooking and all the things she ought to have been doing she had decided not to do. These warm spring days could not last. In a little while it might be snowing, the English climate being what it was, and she was not going to miss the chance of a morning's gardening in the sunshine in peaceful loneliness. She made no excuses for herself. She did not want to be indoors doing the usual Monday morning washing, she wanted to be in the back garden getting up weeds, and so she was. "And I'm content as the robin," she said to herself in amazement as she bent to her work. "It's the spring, when I'm usually mad with restlessness, and yet I'm content."

There was not a cloud in the sky and all about her was the strong growth of yet another triumphant spring. The smell of the earth was pungent and fresh as she worked, and the scent of violets came to her from John's frame, open to the sun. The old apple tree outside the kitchen window had become a mass of pink and white blossom. She was kneeling almost under its branches and now and again she could smell the flowers. The birds were singing in every bush and tree in the garden, in every spinney and wood and hedgerow in the countryside beyond, and in the clear still air she could hear depth beyond depth of music. "Have the birds always sung like this?" she wondered, "or is it that I have not noticed it before? The purity is piercing, especially that one song."

She sat back on her heels, listening. The singer was quite close to her and as she listened his individual song seemed to detach itself from the chorus of praise ringing out for the world and to give itself to her heart only, sharply, like a stiletto. Yet it was a gay, sweet song. "What singer are you?" she wondered. "I don't know you." She had been brought up in London and she did not know much about birds. Flowers, because of her love for them, she had studied, but not birds. It was John who knew about birds. Careful to make no sound she moved a little so that she was sitting on the grass patch under the apple tree and could look up into its branches. Above her head in the apple blossom she saw what she thought was a bluebird singing to his unseen lady. Yet when she looked again he was not blue but brown, with white tips to his tail feathers and wing quills, a carmine patch on the crown of his head and carmine upon his breast. For a moment she had been dazzled by the sheen of blue that was in his feathers, as it was on every flower and tree, not dulling the underlying color but burnishing it. It was strange, this heavenly burnishing blue. One did not see it in summer but only on these first cloudless days of spring. Even one's own dull sight seemed burnished by it. Daphne could see the small bird with astonishing clearness now, and caught her breath at his bright beauty. Yet in spite of the cap and breastplate of carmine that he wore for the wooing of his lady he was an austere little bird and his austerity suited the purity of his song. They both pierced her. "I am a detestable woman," she thought. "I have no place in this fair blue day."

She became conscious that she was not alone in the garden. She had heard no sound but she was aware that she was sharing her shame with another. She turned her head and saw Michael sitting on the edge of the violet frame, looking not at her but at the austere little bird. He had come uninvited into her garden, invading her lovely loneliness, yet the anger which had blazed in her when he had come before did not spring up again. She was conscious only of the sharing of this shame. He was so intent on the bird in the apple tree that she could look at him unobserved, quietly and calmly, as she had not been able to do a week ago. Then she had seen Mike Davis, the man who had treated her so badly and whom she had never even wanted to forgive, but now she saw a man whom she hardly recognized. She had not realized that he had changed so much. He had looked a young man then, and superficially, with his spare alert figure, he looked a young man now, but looking at him intently she noticed how sharpened and brittle-looking his face had become. He still had his puckish look but he was a Puck who was afraid of the shadows behind the trees.

The bird finished his song and flew up to the top of the tree, and she said, "Michael."

He looked at her and smiled and said, "I'm trespassing."

"Did you want to talk to John?" she asked, "because I'm afraid he's in Silverbridge."

"I wanted to talk to you."

"Then come over here," she said. He looked at her in astonishment, for her voice was gentle and almost welcoming, then got up and came to her. "Sit on the grass with your back against the apple tree," she went on. "It's comfortable like that. Do you mind if I go on weeding? I'm close enough to hear what you say. Michael, what was that bird?"

"A linnet."

"Was that all? I thought he was something rare and wonderful."

"So he was, so close to us," said Michael. "They don't usually come into gardens. We are favored. Do you remember Robert Bridges on the linnet?

"The phrases of his pleading
Were full of young delight;
And she that gave him heeding
Interpreted aright
His gay, sweet notes—"

"Yes, it was a gay song," said Daphne. "And yet it made me ashamed of myself."

"I bracket a linnet with a stormcock for making me ashamed of myself," said Michael. "With the thrush it's his courage, with the linnet his—I was going to say the integrity of his song, but that sounds far-fetched."

"I know what you mean," said Daphne. "This clear blue day just suited that linnet. When I was a child I was frightened of a cloudless sky. There didn't seem a thing between me and God. He could look right down and see me, and the wicked things I did. I was so frightened of God that I decided not to believe in Him. And I didn't until I married John. My Nanny was a Seventh Day Adventist. What was yours?"

Michael laughed. "Daphne, you haven't changed. You always knew how to talk nonsense while a man got himself to the point. I always admired your social sense."

"What's the point, Michael?" she asked.

"Truth," said Michael. "The linnet's song was appropriate. I behaved abominably to you once. I want to tell you why. I also want to tell you why I'm at Belmaray."

"Do you want to tell me for my sake or for yours?" asked Daphne.

"I think for both our sakes. For your sake, I'd like you to know that I'm even more despicable than you thought I was, and be thankful to your merciful stars that you married John. For my sake, because if that is possible I'd like your forgiveness."

"You have it already," she said.

"Daphne, what's come to you?" he asked. "You were loathing me like poison last time I came."

"I'll tell you later what's come to me," said Daphne. "Now get it off your chest while I go on with my gardening."

To his relief she turned away from him to the flower border she was weeding. "I'm a coward, Daphne," he said. "I have been all my life. I've been afraid of most things, including poverty and responsibility, but after the war broke out I was chiefly terrified of injury, pain and death. I was chiefly a pacifist from fear."

"You conquered that fear," said Daphne quickly.

"To no purpose," said Michael. "In Crete, towards the end, do you remember that I was shot in the head? I shot myself rather than go on any longer. I've always been a rotten shot and I couldn't even shoot straight into my own head."

"Did you mean to kill yourself?" she asked quietly.

"Yes. And it was not a sudden temptation. It was deliberate."

"But you've just said you were afraid of death."

"And injury. Daphne, some injuries are frightful. And you don't die. Sometimes one fear can entirely conquer another and that was how it was with me. In the confusion of everything it was not realized how I'd come by that wound. I got away with it. And the man who took over my platoon, Bill Harris, a friend of mine, is still alive, blind and mad. Because of what I did he got the injury I'd been trying to escape."

"Michael, that's awful," murmured Daphne. "What a ghastly thing to have to carry with you all your days."

"Pretty ghastly, but worse for him," said Michael.

They were silent, and then she said, "But what has it to do with the way you treated me the night before our wedding?"

"I'd always been afraid of marriage, Daphne. Afraid of the responsibility. And then, after Crete, there was the shame of what I'd done. I was too much of a coward to tell you, or anyone, about it. So it ate into me. Then, on the day before our wedding, I heard for the first time what had happened to Bill Harris. The shock sent me crackers I think. Or else completely

313

sane. I saw myself as some sort of a filthy reptile. Marriage with a decent woman was out of the question."

"I doubt if I'm a decent woman," said Daphne. And then, after a pause, "Do you remember the wording of the note you sent me?"

"No. I just scribbled something or other."

"Michael, did you hate me for refusing to go away with you that weekend?"

"Hate you? Good heavens, no!"

"How did you feel about it?"

"Ashamed. You weren't that sort. I was, but you weren't. It was because you weren't that sort that I'd wanted to marry you. And then, it seemed to me, I'd tried to pull you down to my level. I was too ashamed, afterwards, to look you in the face."

"I see," said Daphne slowly. " 'I see men as trees walking.' I wish I had not been born blind. Any more, Michael?"

"Not much more," he said. "Just why I'm here. I'm just out of prison." Daphne steadied herself and went on gardening. "For embezzlement. I backed a play I'd written with a client's money and the play failed. It was a cause célèbre, for we were both well-known men."

"John and I never read the paper thoroughly," said Daphne. "John is too conscientious to be headline-minded. He reads the *Times* leading article slowly and repeatedly until he has understood every word, but that's all he has time for. I read headlines only, and if the children are ill I don't read even those. Perhaps your trial coincided with Pat's appendix."

"Perhaps it did," said Michael wearily.

Daphne abandoned her gardening, turned round and looked at him. She realized she had been right to think he was a Puck who was afraid of the shadows behind the trees. What could one do or say that healthy breezes might blow again through the Athenian forest? John would know.

"Michael, may I tell John?" she asked.

"I'd like you to tell him," he said.

"Before, you know, you did not want me to tell him who you were."

"That's past. I can't have him thinking me a decent chap when I'm not. I'd like you to tell him all I've told you."

"I'll tell him," said Daphne. "I've a certain amount to tell him about myself too. As I said before, I doubt if I'm a decent woman. It's only because I had the good fortune to marry John that there's even room for doubt."

"If a good husband was necessary for your salvation you were lucky," Michael agreed. "There'd have been little hope for our marriage with me a partner to it."

"With *me* a partner to it," she corrected him. "For I didn't love you."

He was silent. In moments of bitterest shame he had been accustomed to tell himself that he had at least won the love of a beautiful and well-born woman. Now it appeared he hadn't.

"I was in love," she went on quickly, "but not with you, only with what you stood for, success and so on. And, oh yes, I was in love with you in the obvious way."

"But you—" He stopped and paused.

"Wouldn't do that weekend," she finished for him. "That wasn't because I was a decent woman, as you thought it was, and as I thought it was. When I refused I was simply reacting. You'd hurt me by forgetting that we were to have been married during that leave of yours, and I hit back. My reactions have always been entirely reflex. That's all."

Michael looked bewildered.

"You don't understand," said Daphne. "It was my pride that was hurt and you're a humble sort of child and don't understand the vindictiveness of proud women. If I could have loved the humble child we'd have come together earlier than we did. We might even have been happily married long before the war and I expect you would never have had to say, 'I've been in prison.' So don't you think it's I who should ask for forgiveness, not you?"

He stared at her. "Daphne, what *has* come to you?"

"I've heard a few home truths," said Daphne. "Harriet, our old nurse, after ten years of behaving so nicely to me that I quite thought she shared my own opinion of myself suddenly showed me that she didn't. Not that she behaved other than nicely. She couldn't. But she made me look at myself, and I've been trying to get to know myself through all the days and nights since. The nights have been the worst."

"They are," said Michael. "I've been doing the same thing."

"And can you laugh at yourself now?"

"No."

"You must, you know," said Daphne. "And so must I. If I can't laugh at the fool I am I'll despair at the beast I am. You must laugh at yourself, Michael."

"I expect you're right," he said. "One must come out on the other side of despair before one can find that stony sanctuary."

"And laughing at yourself gives you freedom."

"From what?" asked Michael grimly.

"From hating yourself. One can be just as self-engrossed in self-hatred as self-love, and either way be as blind to the quality of those about you as I was when I wanted you for what you could give me and married John for the same reason."

"But you love him now, don't you?" asked Michael quickly.

"Yes," said Daphne. "He'll be surprised when I tell him. He has a lot to forgive me. And so have you. When I said that laughter brought freedom I wasn't forgetting about forgiveness. One can't begin to laugh until one's forgiven. Do you forgive me?"

"That goes without saying," said Michael. "Daphne, this has been an astonishing ten minutes."

"Not all one's minutes are presided over by a linnet," said Daphne lightly and gaily. "I'm glad you came to Belmaray, though you've caused a lot of upheaval. Do you know what you've done? Opened the eyes of a woman born blind, introduced geraniums at the manor and made Harriet fall in love again. She saw you out of her window. Would you like to go upstairs and talk to Harriet?"

Michael got up. She was right to send him away now, for they had no more to say, but not right to send him to Harriet. Not yet. He wanted to get away by himself into the cool spaces of the valley, where the birds were singing so riotously. He shook his head at Daphne, smiled at her, and went away through the garden with a quick stride like a boy's.

When he had gone Daphne went and sat where he had sat, her back against the apple tree, and looked up into the blossom above her head. She could no longer see the linnet but the robin was singing up there now. His song was not quite the linnet's clear exposition of the truth but he came very near it with a merry ditty expressing his contentment with the situation in which he found himself. He was himself the picture of contentment, bright-eyed and humorous, and somewhere his lady, equally contented, was listening to him and interpreting aright "his gay, sweet notes."

"Was I interpreting aright when I told Michael to laugh at himself?" Daphne wondered. "The words seemed to fall into my mind. I hadn't thought before that we must laugh at ourselves. But it's true. I've never had a sense of humor. I'd better take lessons from the robin before it's too late."

She was tired after her bad nights. Her eyes closed and she fell asleep. She dreamed that all the birds in the world, singing gloriously, flew up through the blue air and spread themselves across the sky, becoming one bird, a Seraph whose wings covered the world. And the world was darkened. But for Daphne there was no fear in the dark, as there had been in the clear skies of her childhood. In her dream she turned and put her cheek against it and knew herself beloved.

John's meeting had been followed by lunch at the Silver-bridge hotel, at the invitation of Mr. Entwistle, but even the roast chicken and apple tart, chosen by Mr. Entwistle as likely to elevate the spirits but not upset the stomach of a nervous and sensitive man, had done nothing to make him feel less wretched. There was a private mental home on the outskirts of Silverbridge and he and Mr. Entwistle were both members of its committee of management. Once a month they debated its affairs and talked to its inmates, and once a month John was plunged into such misery that Mr. Entwistle did not know what to do with him.

"Why did you go on the committee?" he asked now in slight irritation, as John pushed away his plate of apple tart almost untouched. "Not your sort of job at all."

" 'But for the grace of God, there go I,' " said John. "I very nearly went out of my mind in the war, Entwistle."

"All the more reason for giving lunatics a wide berth now," said Mr. Entwistle. "Wentworth, this is very good apple tart. Try some cream with it."

John pulled his plate back and tried again. "No," he said. "All the more reason for serving the mentally sick in every way open to me."

"They're not as unhappy as you think they are," said Mr. Entwistle comfortably.

"How do we know?" said John miserably. "We don't know, Entwistle."

"Very well then, we don't know," said Mr. Entwistle. "And I refuse to spoil good food worrying because I don't know something which would probably give me no pleasure if I did know it."

"I am being a most discourteous guest," said John apologetically. "As you said, Entwistle, it is very good apple tart."

"Have some coffee?" suggested Mr. Entwistle.

"No, thanks."

"I will," said Mr. Entwistle. "I need support. I'm not looking forward to my afternoon."

"Selfish beast that I am," said John. "Here I am, absorbed in my own depression, and you no doubt with a funeral before you. You must see a lot of sadness in your profession, Entwistle."

"I should feel no sadness at Mrs. Belling's funeral," said Mr. Entwistle with rosy, smiling honesty. "But I do not at all look forward to interviewing her this afternoon and persuading her to sign that power of attorney."

"I've let you in for this, I'm afraid," said John.

"You have," said Mr. Entwistle. "And had better accompany me."

"No, Entwistle, no!" implored John. "I'm no business man. You know that."

"I do," said Mr. Entwistle, "and I'm not requiring you in that capacity. But you have excellent persuasive powers. If I cannot persuade the old lady to put pen to paper you may have better success. Now will you join me in some black coffee? Yes? Waiter, two black coffees, please. I told Miss Giles and Miss O'Hara, Wentworth, that they must send for the doctor with or without Mrs. Bellings' permission. Were she to die without having seen a doctor they would be severely censured. I wonder how they got on."

The question was answered when the door was opened to them by a tired-looking Mary. "It was hateful when the doctor came," she said. "Aunt Rose shouted at him. It was horrid."

"She should be in a nursing home," said Mr. Entwistle.

"That's what the doctor says," said Mary. "He thinks she's very ill. But how can we persuade her to go? Do you think you could, Mr. Wentworth?"

"All in good time," said Mr. Entwistle. "First I'll have a little talk with her on the subject of this document. There's Miss

Giles. Good afternoon, Miss Giles. Is your patient ready to see me?"

"As ready as she'll ever be," said Miss Giles with gloom. "I'll take you up now."

"I'll ask for your assistance if I need it, Wentworth," said Mr. Entwistle. "I may be able to manage alone." And he mounted the stairs with a buoyancy which filled John with profound admiration. Entwistle was a very brave man.

"Come into my schoolroom to wait," said Mary impulsively to John. "It's the only decent room in the house. Though of course it looks nicer in term-time, when it has the children in it. We've sent the boarders away to various friends. We thought it was better for them."

"Much better," said John, looking round the fresh, clean little room. "But I like the room even without children. Has Miss Giles been sitting here with you?"

"You're observant," said Mary, laughing and removing some dun-colored knitting and Boswell's *Life of Samuel Johnson* from a chair. "I don't fly to the classics for comfort, as Giles does. I'm too frivolous. Worthy people always read the classics when things are difficult. I was wrong about Giles, Mr. Wentworth. She's good."

"I'm glad you've made friends with her," said John. "I'm glad I have. I like and respect her. But none of us are good."

"However hard we try to do a job of work well it's always smirched somewhere by what we are, isn't it?" said Mary sadly.

"Every darn thing," said John. "But don't let that depress you. I think it's even harder to accept the faults and limitations of one's work than of oneself, but what else can we do? Our work will be perfect when we are, and not before. So you're too frivolous to turn to the classics for comfort. Is poetry frivolous?" He picked up the open volume that lay on the jade-green sweater she was knitting. " 'The Dying Swan' and 'Kindness.' Were you reading 'Kindness'?" He read the last four verses aloud, reading as he always did musically and with delight, forgetting himself.

"Oh! well may the lark sing of this,
　　As through rents of huge cloud,
　　He broacheth blue gulfs that are bliss,
　　For they make his heart proud

"With the power of wings deployed
　　In delightfullest air.
　　Yea, thus among things enjoyed
　　Is kindness rare.

"For even the weak with surprise
　　Spread wings, utter song,
　　They can launch ... in this blue they can rise,
　　In this kindness are strong, ...

"They can launch like a ship into calm,
　　Which was penned up by storm,
　　Which sails for the islands of balm
　　Luxuriant and warm."

"That chap liked birds. Nothing about birds is frivolous reading, Mary. Birds are an extremely serious subject. Do I call you Mary?"

"I should hope so," she said. "But I was reading 'Kindness' for a frivolous reason. A man I know told me he liked it. He thought I'd been kind to him and it was his way of paying me a compliment." The pink in her cheeks deepened. "I like compliments."

"So do I," said John, putting the open book back on her knitting again. "I seldom get one but when I do it does me more good than a bottle of tonic."

Mary took a deep breath and put her finger on the second verse,

　　　　Of the soul that absorbeth itself
　　　　In discovering good ...

but before she could pay him the compliment of saying it aloud the door opened and Mr. Entwistle came in.

"Wentworth, I think you'd better come upstairs," he said, and such was the urgency of his tone that John went with him at once, with hardly any sensation of dread. He was generally all right once the trumpet had sounded.

"Yes?" he asked.

"Neither Miss Giles nor I can do a thing with her. She must be entirely crazy. We'll wait outside on the landing while you have a try. She's merely to sign her name either to a deed of attorney or, if she doesn't like that, to a few cheques. See what you can do."

Miss Giles on the landing opened the door and John went in and shut it behind him. "Good afternoon, Mrs. Belling," he said, and sat on the chair beside the bed. The hot, stuffy, luxurious room did not affect him as the drawing room had done because his whole mind was focused in dismay upon Mrs. Belling herself. He did not know her, for the mask had gone. The sweetness, the placidity, had vanished, and this was Mrs. Belling. She was speechless with rage, shaking with it, her face purple, her hands plucking at the soiled eiderdown, but what he saw in her eyes was fear. He had sat by the dying so many times, and seldom seen fear, and when he had it had been the fear of a child shrinking from the dark, not this dreadful animal fear. Worse than that, for animals die submissively. Demoniacal fear. Yet was she dying? No one had told him so.

"You'll take a turn for the better now this bright weather has come, Mrs. Belling," he said, and heard his banal words coming as from a great distance. He himself was at a great distance from this woman. Nothing he could do or say would bridge the gulf because there was nothing here to appeal to. There was nothing here but anger and fear, things in themselves entirely sterile. Divorced from the love of righteousness, the fear of God, they were nothing. There was nothing here. He had not realized before the ghastly evil of negation. He had seldom felt such evil. Nothingness was a bottomless pit and it was that she feared. He began to understand her a little. She was not crazy, as Entwistle

322

thought. To sign that paper giving the power of attorney to Mary was to part with the one possession that she still had in this world. Power. While she refused to sign she had power to paralyze the life of the house, to keep Miss Giles and Mary in entire dependence upon her. She had been a woman of power all her life, not least when she had used her power for the procuring of her own comfort only. For a sick woman there was no comfort any more, but there could be power while she refused to sign that paper. Once she had signed it she had nothing, and would be consigned to nothing. The words to which Mary had pointed rung hopelessly in his mind. "The soul that absorbeth itself in discovering good." There was no good to discover here. There was nothing. He had never felt more helpless.

Yet he must try, and he heard himself making the usual appeal, the one that any man or woman turned to instinctively when persuasion was needed, so much is a modicum of kindness a normal part of humanity. "Mrs. Belling, it would be doing a kindness to Miss Giles and to your niece if you would sign this paper. And to Annie too, who is in need of her wages. If you would prefer it you could sign some cheques but you have said yourself that you do not wish to be bothered with that. This just enables your niece to transact your business for you until you are better again. It's just a matter of kindness, Mrs. Belling. Look, here is your fountain pen, and the paper. I'll hold it steady."

She took the paper from the blotting pad he held for her and with all the strength she had tore it across and across. Then with an effort ghastly to see, but so savagely powerful that he was incapable of stopping her, she reared herself up and attempted to fling it, as she had flung Baba's ointment, into the fire. The scraps of paper fell on the eiderdown and she fell back, sagging heavily to one side. He tried to call out for Miss Giles, but the words would not come. He felt as though he were in a nightmare. Gritting his teeth he bent over her and lifted her gently back onto her pillows. He looked in her eyes, still full of that terror, and saw that she was dead. Again he tried to call for help but his throat felt parched and dry. He fell on his knees but the familiar prayers would not come to him. When the other two came into the room he was still on his knees, but trembling as though the hot stuffy room had suddenly turned cold.

3

For the next few days Michael did not leave the manor house garden. This halcyon weather would break soon in storms from the sea and while it lasted he must clear the brambles and the weeds from the beds and paths of the garden, so that the children might play there in the sunlight and a queen and her lover walk there under the moon. And Miss Wentworth too, he kept reminding himself. But he had to keep reminding himself, for Miss Wentworth seemed strangely detached these days. She was as delightful a hostess as ever, she busied herself as usual with her house, pigs and poultry, but he felt a change in her. She was not in any way losing her grip on things, for he felt a new resolution in her, but it was a resolution towards detachment. Vaguely uneasy, he gardened madly and thought of the old man who had appeared out of the dusk and talked to him through the library window. He kept picturing him in the garden. Once or twice he could have fancied that he heard his footfall on the flagged path behind him. He had very soon discovered that one can have very odd sensations while gardening. A close union with the earth seemed to involve one in union with a good deal more than the earth.

In spite of his unease about Miss Wentworth, of his anxiety as to what John was thinking of him at the moment, these days were happy for him. Daphne's strange, sudden softening, the completeness of her forgiveness, had come upon him like rain upon parched earth. He felt unspeakably eased and was ready to receive the spring as he had never before been ready. "Let no

324

flower of the spring go by me." Last year, he remembered, he had hated it. The whole thing had seemed a lie. This year, as he listened to the larks, he could believe it. Resurrection happened. The thought of death as irretrievable destruction had always obsessed his mind. Now he wondered if there was any conceivable situation in which one could say, it is the end. Was the word hopeless one that ever had any truth in it?

"I'd like to ask John," he said to himself one evening. He was tired after a hard day's work and a pang went through him. He stopped digging, leaning on his spade. Would he ever ask John anything again? Could even John forgive his treatment of Daphne, his cowardice and fraud? The garden was darkening about him and the song of the birds seemed receding. He put his tools away in the gazebo, went indoors and found Miss Wentworth getting supper ready. It was a rather special supper, he noticed. She delighted in preparing meals that were a little different, or served in a different room, or in dishes that were not the usual ones. She hated unalterable routine and life with her was full of the little varieties that give spice to living.

"John rang up with a message for you," she said.

Michael's heart leaped. "Yes?" he asked.

"'The Knight of the Wood. Chapter Ten, paragraph One.' Now wash your hands quickly. I'm making an omelette. John's mad. Does a message like that make sense to you?"

"Yes, it makes sense," said Michael, and ran upstairs whistling.

He was gay through supper, and through the washing up, but it was hard to wait until Miss Wentworth had gone to bed and he could escape to the library and take down Don Quixote. He lit the candles, sat in the chair where he always sat now in the evenings, and turned the yellowed pages. As he did so he had a picture in his mind of John as a boy sitting here as he was doing and reading the same Don Quixote, and the Malory that was beside it. His head must have been full of knights in armor. He found the passage and read it.

"Sir," answered Don Quixote, "I have so hearty a desire to serve you . . . that I might know from you whether the discontents that have urged you to make choice of this unusual course of life, might not admit of a remedy; for, if they do, assure yourself I will leave no means untried, till I have purchased you that ease which I heartily wish you. . . . If then good intentions may plead merit, or a grateful requital, let me intreat you, Sir, by that generous nature that shoots through the gloom with which adversity has clouded your graceful outside; nay, let me conjure you by the darling object of your wishes, to let me know who you are, and what strange misfortunes have urged you to withdraw from the converse of your fellow creatures, to bury yourself alive in this horrid solitude. . . . And I solemnly swear," added Don Quixote, "by the order of knighthood, of which I am an unworthy professor, that if you so far gratify my desires, I will assist you to the utmost of my capacity, either by remedying your disaster, if it is not past redress; or at least, I will become your partner in sorrow, and strive to ease it by a society in sadness."

The Knight of the Wood, hearing the Knight of the Woeful Figure talk at that rate, looked upon him steadfastly for a long time, and viewed and reviewed him from head to foot. . . .

Michael put the book down and laughed. The message of friendship and encouragement was unmistakable, and relieved him enormously, but he did not quite understand. If Daphne had told John what he had told her John knew the facts. What more was there to tell? But he'd go down to the vicarage in the morning.

But in the morning there were an unusual number of odd jobs to do for Miss Wentworth and it was half-past three before he set out. As he approached the vicarage gate he beheld the extraordinary sight of John poised dangerously on top of a stepladder, struggling to fasten a walking stick to a branch of the tree beside it. Tied to the walking stick by its sleeves was a red smock. The three children were assisting John. Pat and Winkle were holding the stepladder steady and Margary was anxiously clutching her father's leg. Michael approached with caution, lest any sudden sound cause John to fall headlong, but Pat saw him and let go of the ladder and called out a greeting.

"It's Mr. Stone. Hullo, Mr. Stone. Be careful, Father! Father, what *are* you doing?"

John rocked wildly backwards and forwards on the ladder, missed his footing and jumped to safety, the red flag remaining hopelessly askew in the tree. The stepladder overbalanced on top of Winkle and her roars rent the air. Extricated, she was found to be unhurt, but just as she was being soothed back into her normal state of placidity the red flag fell out of the tree and hit her on the nose, and her roars became more horrific than ever.

"Stop it, Winkle!" shouted Pat angrily. "The bus will be here any minute and the flag not up. You're not hurt. Stop it, you little beast!"

"How dare you call her a beast!" flamed Margary, who though sweet-tempered could upon great provocation become inflamed with righteous indignation. "Beast yourself. It was you let go of the ladder."

"Children! Children!" mourned John distractedly. "Your language is deplorable!"

Michael righted the stepladder and mounted nimbly to its summit, flag in hand. "Is it a birthday?" he enquired above the uproar.

"No," said Pat. "Stop it, Winkle! Miss O'Hara's coming to tea on the three-forty-five bus. It's to turn her thoughts."

"Winkle's form mistress," explained John. "She's had a shock lately in the death of her aunt and, as Pat says, we want to turn her thoughts. She has leanings towards the left, and though we're all good conservatives here we thought we'd like to make her feel at home."

"It was my idea to put it in the tree," said Pat.

"It's my smock," said Margary.

"*My* Miss O'Hara," hiccuped Winkle.

"The disaster alone is mine," said John humbly.

"I'm rectifying it," said Michael gaily. But within he panicked. "I must fix this darn flag and get out of it," he thought. He went hot and then cold. "I can't see that girl again. Not fair on her. Damn!" The stick had slipped again just as he'd got it fixed. He rocked on the stepladder.

"Not as easy as it looks," said John, cheered by his lack of success. "Now if it had occurred to me to bring a piece of string we'd have got on better. Why do I always think of these things too late? Ah, that's the style!"

Michael had remembered his dark red silk handkerchief and was binding the stick in place with that. He was listening anxiously for the sound of the bus but the children, restored to good humor, were chattering loudly and John was saying something or other about a walk after tea. Down by the river. "I'll show you the white rhododendron," he said.

"Is he talking to me?" wondered Michael irritably, and then was ashamed. This magnanimous man was inviting him for a walk as naturally and charmingly as though his opinion of him was still what it had been a week ago, and he, Michael, was feeling no appreciation of his magnanimity. He must get down off this ladder. But John had his foot on it. "The tide will be in," he said.

"Get off the ladder," said Michael hoarsely.

"That's a lovely flag, Comrade," said Mary, and the children fell upon her with shouts of joy.

Michael sat down on top of the ladder. No hope of escape now. His legs felt as weak as his will. He had not known it could come upon a man with quite such overwhelming suddenness. At his age too. Was he nineteen, to be such a fool? He was thirty-eight. Getting on for middle-age. But she couldn't be much more than twenty. She had that lightness of movement of the very young. Not fair on her. "It is that way my soul would follow her, lightly, and airily, and happily, and I would be rid of all my great troubles."

John was introducing them and Mary was saying they had met before. He got off the ladder and shook hands with her speechlessly. Her eyes were alight with fun as she asked, "How's Josephine?" But he could not return her smile. Nor could he find the words in which to excuse himself and go away. And then it seemed as though the children and John and Mary closed about him and bore him with them up the drive. The power of their good will seemed immensely strong. There was some purpose here and he abandoned himself to it in sudden content.

Daphne met them at the front door, serene, elegant and cool. She was an excellent if slightly aloof hostess. She greeted Michael as an old family friend with whom she had been in daily contact for the last twenty years, and Mary with a charming motherliness. She made them both for a moment or two aware of their age; the one feeling tarnished and old, the other raw and young. But seated round the dining room table, with Winkle clamoring for honey and John upsetting the sugar basin, their unease vanished. It was difficult to feel unease in the presence of either John or Winkle, and when they were both present the stage was set entirely for comedy. And in a moment or two Daphne's mask of cool elegance had slipped a little and she became shy and uncertain, almost a little awkward. Michael felt a pang of warm feeling for her. He knew what it was like to have lost belief in one's own excellence. One could not move through life without a measure of outward assurance any more than one could go about without a suit of clothes, but it needed a lot of practice before one could hold the thing steady outwardly while remaining inwardly aware that there was nothing to be assured about. To help her he adjusted his own mask firmly and took charge of the conversation. John marvelled at him. Yes, he'd be able to go back into life. A man who could maintain such ease of manner with the woman he had loved once sitting on one side of him, and the woman he loved now sitting on the other, would be able to keep an even keel while he wore down the contempt of a whispering world. Mary was just the woman to help him; provided she could keep her temper with the whisperers.

Did they know yet, John wondered? They had betrayed themselves utterly to him at the gate but he did not know if they had betrayed themselves to each other. They went into the drawing room for cigarettes and John said suddenly, "Children, go and pick a big bunch of flowers for Miss O'Hara."

"But we want to show her the toad," said Pat.

"The bus does not go till five-thirty," said John firmly. He was not often firm but when he was the children obeyed him.

"That was too obvious, John," said Daphne. "Pat will be listening outside the window."

John had a moment's astonishment at Daphne's lack of knowledge of her own children. Did she not know Pat had a sense of honor? Probably not. She knew little about herself and consequently little about others. All that she had told him these last few days had made him love her more than ever but had given him a new light on her character. He had thought of her poise as being that of a woman of experience, and been a little afraid of it, he saw it now as the self-confidence of a girl whose adolescent pride had never been shattered. And now it had been shattered, by humble old Harriet of all people, and they could start again together in equal immaturity. Glancing round the room he decided that Mary was the most sensible of the four of them and it was to her he addressed himself.

"Mary, I think that the school should go on, and that Miss Giles should be its headmistress. What do you think?"

"I'll work under her," said Mary loyally. "But not in that house."

"It can't be in that house," said John. "Entwistle tells me that Mrs. Belling left no will and so her property passes to her eldest nephew."

"My father's eldest brother's son," said Mary. "I've never seen him for Father quarrelled with his eldest brother... The O'Hara temper... Do you know, I took Giles to a concert the other night. She hadn't heard good music for years and so of course she went to pieces in the middle and told me her heart's desire. That's what the thwarted always do in the middle of good music."

"What is it?" asked John eagerly. "I was wondering what it was in Church the other morning."

"A cottage in the country," said Mary. "And to make her tea the way she likes it. Annie never makes it with boiling water. But Annie could be taught. Now I come to think of it, she must come too. We need to begin again together, Giles and Annie and I. At Oaklands the pattern was all snarled up. We need to take ourselves, the school and the children, and get things clean and straight again."

"In a cottage?" asked Daphne.

"A small house," amended Mary. "There's one for sale on the way to Farthing Reach. A lovely little old house with a walled garden. The front door must be in Farthing Square but from the upstairs windows on the other side you'd see open country and the swans on the river. Giles could call it Farthing Cottage."

"I believe I remember the little house," said Michael. "We saw it the day you took me to Farthing Reach."

"Now when did they pick each other up?" wondered Daphne, disturbed. It was no good, a woman could not see a man she had once wanted passing to the keeping of another woman without profound annoyance. She failed to keep sarcasm out of her voice as she enquired, "Who's the financier behind this wonderful scheme of regeneration?"

John's eager face, and Mary's, fell, and she reproached herself. Michael, she noted, had thought of this before. Michael also was disturbed. Mary was beyond his reach but it was distressing all the same to have her making plans for her future that left him out. Before he knew what he did his eyes met hers, reproaching her. She smiled at him, bringing him in. "How odd," thought Daphne. "When he was young he took so long to fall in love with me but now he's not so young I believe he's fallen in love as suddenly as a boy. Thank heaven, here are the children back again."

Pat dumped an armful of daffodils in Mary's lap and demanded, "*Now* can we show her the toad?"

Michael took a grip on himself and got up. He must separate himself from Mary once and for all. "Good-bye, Miss O'Hara," he said. "When you return from the toad I'll have gone back to my work."

"Good-bye," she said sweetly and gravely, and went away with the children to the kitchen garden.

"What about that walk, Michael?" asked John when she had gone.

"Let's go now," said Michael. "Before I go back to work. I'll wait for you outside," and he went out through the French window without saying good-bye to Daphne.

"He's forgotten my existence," said Daphne. "Well, that's right and very good for me. Go along, John. I'll make your apologies to Mary."

4

"The birds are singing wonderfully this evening," said John as they tramped along.

"You've a 'thing' about birds," said Michael.

"They're the greatest wonder in nature," said John. "Look at their instincts, their flight, their song. And to me they're entirely symbolic. Look at the nightingale. He keeps the same mate all his life. Each spring, when he comes back to us after the winter migration, he meets her in the same tree or bush where he sang to her first. In the darkness. 'There is in God, some say, a deep, but dazzling darkness.' I've yet to hear any music that expresses love more satisfactorily than the nightingale's song."

They were striking down through the fields to the river. The tide was in and the river brimming with light. A mist of gold lay upon the blue distances and faintly veiled the fresh green of the trees beyond the river. There was not a breath of wind. The chorus of bird song rose to them with a touch of solemnity and the shadows lay long upon the grass. They came down through a great thicket of rhododendrons already in bud and turned along the river road. John was in an anguish of shyness and Michael took the plunge himself.

"I looked up the 'Knight of the Wood'," he said, smiling at John, "and I should like to 'comply with your desires, which your great civilities and undeserved offers oblige me to satisfy.' But I was puzzled. What more can I tell you? Daphne gave you the facts."

"Only the facts," said John. "Not the reasons for the facts. Why you do a thing is what matters. It is there one looks for the springs of character. Facts mean little."

"I doubt if the fact of a good man blinded meant little either to him or his wife and children," said Michael harshly. "That was one of the facts that were the result of my cowardice."

"I think what you call your cowardice is also a fact," said John. The reason, the root of it all, is further back still. I know I'm probing, Michael, but you wouldn't have come along this afternoon if you hadn't been prepared for that."

"I don't mind being probed by the lance of the Knight of the Woeful Figure," said Michael. "Though I wouldn't stand it from any other man's lance. But aren't we being a bit introspective?"

"Certainly," said John. "Once and for all. Rather than live with a bad smell all your life isn't it better to find the corpse?"

"It was my mother's," said Michael suddenly and violently. John was shocked into silence and they walked on and said nothing, until Michael added, "I'd not thought of that before. It

333

was the fear of poverty that obsessed me when I was a boy. The other fear, of sickening injury, blood and pain, death, did not take hold until the war."

"How did your mother die?" asked John.

"In a street accident. I was out for a walk with our maid and I saw my mother on the other side of a narrow street and called out to her. She was not expecting to see me and turned quickly and eagerly to come across to me. A drunken brute coming along in a car accelerated instead of putting the brakes on. But it was really her fault I suppose... Or rather my fault for calling to her... I really can't tell you what happened. In the confusion of it all no one thought of removing me. I hear my mother's screams in nightmares even now, and see the ghastly mess her face was in. She was a pretty woman."

"How old were you?" asked John.

"I was eight," said Michael.

"It was as well the fear of poverty could obsess your conscious mind in boyhood," said John. "It was some sort of anaesthetic. Were you poor?"

Michael told him about Mr. Davidson and the inkstains on the table, about his schooldays and his early struggles to write. He realized as he talked that he had never told anyone these things. He had never told Daphne. She had never shown any wish to enter into his house of life, to share his experience. He had wished sometimes, in the days when he had loved her, that she would ask him into hers, but she never had. He doubted if any couple in love could have known less about each other. He and John walked more and more slowly, taking no notice now of the beauty about them but unconsciously eased by it.

"Once your terror of wounds and death emerged you were probably one of the bravest men in the war," said John. "For you had no serious failure of nerve, did you, until the final one?"

"What do you mean by failure of nerve?" asked Michael. "Good lord, my nerves were in ribbons the whole way through."

334

"So were mine," said John. "But you still fought and were considered an efficient officer?"

"Yes. I was considered efficient."

"Which is more than I was," said John, smiling. "After one naval engagement, and getting torpedoed once only, I kept seeing mutilated bodies where there were none, and that sort of thing, and any efficiency I might have had vanished. But complete failure of nerve didn't happen to me until I spent all night on a makeshift raft roped to two men who became corpses overnight. Then they put me in a nerve hospital. I've never been so ashamed in my life. Had the means of self-destruction been at hand, as it was in your case, I might have done what you did."

"I've only managed to make two great friends in my life," said Michael. "One was Bill Harris and the other was a chap called Simon Matthews. He was killed beside me. It was that evening I couldn't aim straight into my own head. I've never been much good at friendship."

"I don't think I have," said John. "Too self-absorbed and introspective. We're much alike. My childhood was not unlike yours, though far easier. My mother died young and my father was a drunkard. My God! How hard it was to fight the drink after I came out of hospital. I've often wondered how I dared to marry my wife. Yet one must dare these things. Even men like you and me who have no trust in ourselves. Without these desperate plunges we'd do nothing but gibber in a ditch." He turned to Michael and smiled at him with extraordinary sweetness. "Yet I'm glad you funked Daphne. It meant I got her. But I think you treated her badly. If you felt yourself too much of a worm to marry her why didn't you tell her what you'd done and leave the decision to her?"

"We'd never told each other things. And there was something else. I was afraid I couldn't support her. After I got back from Crete I tried to take my mind off what had happened by writing. I couldn't. I was in a panic then. No more best sellers might mean a lean time for my wife and kids as well as myself."

"But surely, after all your success, you'd got some capital behind you?"

"No," said Michael.

"What had you done with it all?" Michael hesitated. "Out with it. I want to know."

"Given it to Bill Harris's wife, for Bill and the kids. There are four kids."

"Yes," said John. "I hope I'd have done the same in your place. You fought well in Africa, later?"

"Yes, I think so. I felt less fear there. I was too wretched to care."

"And after the war?"

"The solicitor I had been with before the war took me back into partnership. Then he died and I was in a panic I'd not make a success of things without him. The old fear of poverty started to play me up and I tried to write again. This time I found I could do it and I wrote a play that I thought was the best thing I'd ever done. But the powers that be were doubtful and no one would back it financially. I had in my hands at that time a sum of money that I was reinvesting for a client. I was so absolutely certain of the play's success that I backed it with that. It was odd, but at the time I hardly realized what I was doing. I'd more or less lost all self-respect by that time, and that's a sure way of blunting one's integrity. The play failed. Mercifully my client was an exceedingly rich man and the loss to him was negligible. But he wanted his pound of flesh."

"Surely, with your reputation, there must have been those who would have advanced the money to save you from prison even if they wouldn't advance it to back your play?" asked John.

"Possibly," said Michael. "I'd a host of acquaintances, if few friends. There might have been a few who'd have helped me."

"Didn't you ask them?"

"No."

"Why not?"

336

"I was not court-martialled for attempted suicide," said Michael. "I thought it was time I paid the price."

"I see," said John. "Do you mind if we sit down? It's amazingly warm, and I can never just walk through this bit here. I'm obliged to stop and take a look at it."

A grass-covered bank sloped from the road to the river and here the rhododendrons grew thickly. John led the way to one that had wide spreading branches and sat down with it at his back, Michael beside him. Behind them was the hill upon which the manor house was built, wooded upon this side with mountain ash, silver birches and hawthorns, and a stream ran down through the wood, crossed the road under a bridge and ran out into the river quite close to them. Behind them in the wood there was a waterfall and they could hear its music clearly above the singing of the birds. In front of them the river widened out and a little further down it turned a corner before the last straight reach to the sea. The air was fresh here, with a tang of salt in it, but the sun was warm and there was still no wind. A rowing boat was anchored close to them and the small ripples slapped its sides. There were a few gold-colored clouds in the clear sky and the water mirrored them. Moorhens were scurrying about close to the banks, some ducks were standing on their heads, and a few gulls sailed slowly and gracefully overhead, but the great swan was motionless on the water. John gazed at it and Michael thought he was forgotten. He was thankful. He was also thankful that John had made no comment whatever upon his story. The relief of having told it was so great that he wanted no other. He did not want to be whitewashed or excused. Whitewash brought no comfort. The real comfort was to have one's sins and weaknesses not explained away but understood and shared. John's identification of himself with Michael in so much was what he needed. He found strength in it, as he had found strength in the shame that he had offered to Daphne and shared with her in the garden. It struck him that it can be as much by our weakness as by our virtue that we can serve each other.

337

He lay back on the grass and looked up into the great cavern of cool green that he did not doubt was the white rhododendron, and he believed it was the yunnanense. He tried to imagine what it must be like covered with great white scented blossoms, the only white rhododendron among the flaming masses of crimson and orange and gold, each petal of each flower most delicately curved, like the feathers of the peerless white swan over there. As much at ease with John as though he were alone he began to speak the words of the poem he had commended to Mary.

"O silver-throated Swan
Struck, struck! a golden dart
Clear through thy breast has gone
Home to thy heart.
Thrill, thrill, O silver throat!
O silver trumpet, pour
Love for defiance back
On him who smote!
And brim, brim o'er
With love; and ruby-dye thy track
Down thy last living reach
Of river, sail the golden light...
Enter the sun's heart... even teach,
O wondrous-gifted Pain, teach thou
The god to love, let him learn how."

"Is the swan the symbol of death, John?" he asked.
"Of course," said John.
"In these verses, surely of love?"
"Same thing," said John. "A killing thing, love. The symbols are interchangeable. So far as I know a swan is the only bird, except the nightingale, who keeps the same mate for life. When I was a boy, sitting here with the whiteness of this bush in bloom blinding my eyes, I heard a swan singing. I did not see him for he was round the corner. But they found his dead body later. You can laugh if you like but I maintain that I heard him singing."

"Why should I laugh?" asked Michael. "When I was a boy I could get inside a foxglove bell. Children do these things. What was the swan's song like?"

"Can you imagine a Seraph singing?"

"No."

"It was like that. Something you can't imagine."

"Imagination is much overrated," said Michael. "It takes you nowhere really. 'Enter the sun's heart.' I agree. I have ceased to think of death as irretrievable destruction. That is, invariably so. Is it conceivable that it could be?"

"The other day," said John, "I was at the deathbed of a well-to-do, well-thought-of and respectable old lady. I thought her death the end. It was easy as deaths go but it was to me more horrible than any I witnessed in the war."

"Why?"

"I don't think anything existed for her but herself and her own comfort. She loved no one. 'Charity... without which whosoever liveth is counted dead before Thee.' It struck me she had died in that sense some while before dissolution came to her body. But how can I know? We know nothing."

"How can one know if one lives?" asked Michael. "There are times when one feels made of ice."

"A capacity to offer something," said John. "If it's only your shame. A willingness to pay the price. If you can do either of these things you're very much alive, and very much in love."

"In love?" asked Michael quickly.

"With whoever receives your offering and the payment of your debt. And when it is God to Whom they are willingly paid the debt becomes a free gift. That's one of the particular mercies."

Clear in the still air came the sound of the church clock striking seven and John leapt to his feet. "Good lord! And I've a meeting at half-past six!"

They hurried distressfully towards home, but presently John slackened speed.

339

"Why hurry?" he asked gloomily. "The meeting will be over long before I get there."

"And why be distressed about it?" asked Michael. "Surely your parishioners know you by this time?"

"God help them, they surely do!" said John, and became more cheerful, telling Michael of the comic situations which had arisen through forgotten funerals and weddings. "And talking of weddings," he said, "I think what I said about them just now was true."

"Did you say anything about them?" asked Michael.

"I think I said a couple of things about marriage and women in general. I said, apropos of my marriage to Daphne, that utterly unworthy though I was, one must dare these things. If the woman loves you, or needs you, or both (for if she loves you she does need you) I think that's true. Also it's not your business to decide if a woman you love should, or should not, marry you. It's her business. Tell her all about yourself and leave the decision to her. God knows it's trouble enough having to make one's own decisions in life without having to make other people's too."

"It's much easier to make other people's decisions," said Michael, smiling. "Also isn't it sometimes necessary to protect the young from making irreparable mistakes?"

"Certainly I should protect Winkle from deciding to see if the river would bear her weight," said John. "But once men and women reach physical maturity it's difficult to say who's old and who's young. Common sense and good judgment can develop early, in a man or girl of twenty for instance, or not at all, as with myself. Good lord, there's old Arbourfield! He's as late as I am. If I can catch him I'll be in time to say the final prayer. Good-bye, Michael, see you tomorrow!"

His voice faded away as he raced down the river path. Beyond the field that sloped up to the vicarage Pizzle bridge spanned the river, and an ancient farmer in an ancient car could be seen surmounting it. John's wild shout brought him to a standstill on the farther side of the bridge. Michael followed slowly, delighting in the spectacle of John hurling his loose-limbed body into the car. At such moments he seemed to have a greater number of arms and legs than most men.

"And in the end how easy it was," thought Michael. "How easy he made it, even as Daphne did."

He walked slowly back to the manor, walked into the drawing room, where Miss Wentworth was patching sheets, and said, "Miss Wentworth, would you mind if we asked Winkle's form mistress to tea one day?"

"Certainly," said Miss Wentworth calmly. "I've always heard good accounts of the young woman. She might like to see the pigs."

"Yes," said Michael. "That's what I thought. Thank you."

17

MRS. BELLING'S nephew, a London business man whom she had not seen since his boyhood, hurried down for the funeral, arranged that the house and furniture should be auctioned and hurried off again. He had however been kindly. Hearing that Miss Giles was thinking of starting a school of her own he presented her with the children's desks and other school furniture as a gift, shook her warmly by the hand and wished her well.

"He looked such a dried-up sort of stick you wouldn't have thought he'd be so generous, would you?" said Mary.

They were engaged in the detested task of sorting and packing Mrs. Belling's clothes, which were to be sent to a charity. The room had been thoroughly cleaned, and they had the windows open, but even so they hated it and did the job the two of them together, never one alone. For though the evil that had gathered about the focal point of Mrs. Belling was dispersed now it seemed to Mary that something of it still clung to her possessions. There was no question of a fight now, the fight was over, but there was still a taint in the air. She'd be thankful when she and Giles were out of Oaklands, staying at the farmhouse up in the hills where they had taken rooms, with Annie at her cousin's not far away.

"People *are* generous," said Miss Giles. "Look at yourself, Mary, selling your little pearl necklace to give us this holiday. And you can't really like me at all."

"Yes, I do," said Mary. "I didn't, but now I do."

"Why?" asked Miss Giles.

"One doesn't know why one suddenly, or perhaps gradually, likes people," said Mary. "It's all part of it, I suppose."

"Part of what?"

"The interweaving."

"I've never been able to see much pattern in life myself," said Miss Giles.

"Nor have I," said Mary. "But I do sometimes feel myself being pushed through the eye of a needle. I can't describe the feeling, but I feel it. What about the blackboards? Did my cousin throw those in?"

"Anything to do with the school, he said."

"The boarders' beds had better go in the sale," said Mary. "Thank heaven, there'll be no room for boarders in a small house. We'll have our evenings to ourselves. Think of the peace of it. Books, and good music on the radio. A small garden to look after, and a cat. You don't mind if I have a cat, do you?"

"No. But I can't expect to keep you long, Mary. You'll get married."

"Certainly I shall," said Mary. "I've intended marriage for myself ever since I was old enough to intend anything. But until my wedding day I stay with you. And at the moment, Giles, Dickon has not proposed to me."

"Do you think I take *The Secret Garden,* and the rest of the children's storybooks?" asked Miss Giles. "They're hardly school books."

"You take them," said Mary firmly. "There's *Undine* among them, and Hans Andersen. They're literature and you're going to teach English literature."

Miss Giles suddenly sat down on the floor in a panic. "O'Hara, how has it happened that I am to restart this school? Who's idea was it?"

"No one seems to remember now," said Mary. "But someone must have had the idea. I think it's a very good idea."

343

"But should a woman who is brutal to children have a school?"

"Certainly not," said Mary. "I can think of nothing more frightful."

Miss Giles smiled. "But O'Hara, it's not very easy for a leopard to change his spots."

"Your spots aren't a part of the pelt," said Mary. "They're only accretions." And then she blushed furiously. She could have kicked herself. There she went again. Poor old Giles would think she was referring to her acne. She stole a cautious glance at old Giles and found she was laughing; she also noticed that her acne was much better.

"How's your indigestion?" she asked.

"Better since Annie has been taking more trouble over the cooking," said Miss Giles. "And since I've been able to order what I like for lunch."

Mary made a mental note that one of the chief causes of indigestion is frustration, and said aloud, "You shall always order what you like at Farthing Cottage."

Miss Giles once more panicked. "O'Hara, we've not even seen Farthing Cottage yet."

"Mr. Wentworth has got the order to view," said Mary. "He'll be here at three o'clock. It's two-forty now."

"But O'Hara, I've no capital," lamented Miss Giles. "And nor have you. We can only buy the cottage on borrowed money, or on a mortgage. It's most dangerous. The debt we'd have round our necks would be appalling. And how do we know we'd make a success of this school?"

"Don't panic, Giles," said Mary soothingly. "You're not committed to anything. You can back out of the whole thing to-morrow if you want to, and go and serve in a tea shop, if you think your feet are equal to the strain. Now wash everything out of your mind except that we're going for an agreeable outing with an agreeable man on a beautiful spring day. Let's get ready."

344

"But there's another twenty minutes," said Miss Giles.

"If it doesn't take you twenty minutes to get ready to go out with a man then it ought to," said Mary.

"Leaving Mr. Wentworth out of it, I don't know that I think a great deal of men," said Miss Giles. "In fact, I think nothing of them."

"Oh, nor do I," said Mary. "It's women I think a great deal of. I think we're wonderful, Giles, and I think it's very important for the salvation of mankind that we should keep the ascendancy. There'll never be peace in the world till we do. And if you can keep the ascendant with your skirt dropping at the back and your nose shining I can't."

"What nonsense you talk," said Miss Giles, but she went laughing down the passage to her room. It struck Mary, as she shut her door, that today was the first time she had heard old Giles laugh. She had a pretty laugh.

Behind her own shut door Miss Giles had a look at her skirt in the long glass and pulled it up to hang evenly. Then she sat down before her dressing table and looked with terror at the rows of bottles upon it. She had had a birthday two days ago, and Mary had given her a complete set of all that was necessary for presenting to the world the sort of face that Mary thought should be presented to it. Miss Giles had not dared to use any of the bottles yet but she had read all the little booklets enclosed with them, had mastered their contents and now had a clear working hypothesis for future procedure. Yet she remained terrified. "I must, to please O'Hara," she said to herself, took a deep breath and shook the first bottle.

Yet as she applied the contents with her fingertips apprehension was lost in a wave of sheer delight as she realized that there was more than liking, there was love, between herself and Mary. Until this moment she had not fully known it. She looked at her bed and remembered the day she had had migraine and Mary had brought her tea. It had begun that day. Half blind

345

with pain as she had been then she had thought Mary's curly hair looked like the feathers of a bird, and remembered the poem about patience.

And where is he who more and more distils
Delicious kindness?—He is patient. Patience fills
His crisp combs, and that comes those ways we know.

"If we wait for it, in such simple ways," she thought, "through a bird's song, a cup of tea, a child with a bunch of flowers, through men and women of good will. Why did I despair? Could I not have emulated, just for a moment or two, the eternal patience?"

2

"The cottage is in Farthing Square," said Mary. "The front door is in the square, not on the river walk."

"I've always thought I'd give my ears to live in Farthing Square," said John. "No, not my ears, for I couldn't hear the birds, my tongue. The tongue is an unruly member." He began to whistle under his breath as he spurred Rozinante from side to side of High Street. He was in high spirits. It was halcyon weather and everything seemed going right. He was aware, of course, that sooner or later things would go wrong once more, that was life, but meanwhile he could pray again, he and Daphne had achieved a new happiness together, Harriet's arthritis was better, the children were delivered from Oaklands, and Michael, Mary and Miss Giles had all three a springlike air about them. Especially Miss Giles. He had not liked to stare too much as she got into the car but her face had had almost a look of youth about it; smoother and less sallow.

"I've never been in Farthing Square," said Miss Giles a trifle breathlessly, for this was only her second outing in Rozinante and she was not yet adjusted to John's driving and Rozinante's springs.

"Giles!" cried Mary, who was sitting behind her. "It's the

346

loveliest thing in Silverbridge. You've been here all these years and you've never been to Farthing Square!"

"It's right on the edge of the town," said Miss Giles apologetically. "A long walk."

Mary was silent. Poor old Giles. Farthing Square a long walk. How tired she must always have been.

Rozinante swerved madly to the right to avoid a cat, to the left again to avoid the old lady who had nearly been murdered through avoidance of the cat, leaped into the air and arrived in Farthing Square. John jammed on the brakes and she came to rest against the pillar-box.

"Just to have a look at the square before we find the house," explained John.

"Why, it's like a village green!" whispered Miss Giles.

Delightful little Regency houses, all of miniature size, were built about a square of bright green grass. They were not identical though they conformed to the same pattern and all were built of mellow red brick. Some had dormer windows in their tiled roofs, some had not. Some of the little front doors had fanlights over them, others had fluted columns upon either side, some had both, and just a few had lantern holders in their front railings. Each house had a narrow strip of garden between itself and the railings and the scent of hyacinths and wallflowers filled the square. There was not a sound to be heard except the singing of the birds in the gardens behind the houses and no one was about except one tortoise-shell cat.

"I suppose people *do* live here?" asked Miss Giles. She was still unable to raise her voice above a whisper. She had a feeling that if she spoke out loud she would wake them up out of their dream.

"They must all be lying down," said Mary. "We must remember Giles, that an afternoon siesta is *de rigeur* in Farthing Square. We must keep the children quiet then."

"It's no place for a school," whispered Miss Giles in anguish. "People come here who need peace."

"And who needs peace more than the modern child?" enquired John. "I'm sorry Pat is going to boarding school. She might have quieted down in Farthing Square."

"It's all right, Giles," said Mary soothingly. "It's only at break that the children are really noisy and the old ladies can arrange to do their shopping then. It's a Dames' School we're going to open, Giles. What could be more in keeping?"

Miss Giles glanced sideways out of the corner of her eye at the little house outside which the pillar-box stood. It had everything, the fluted pillars, the fanlight and the lantern holders. The door was painted green and had a brass knocker on it. There was a syringa bush in the garden and the paved stone path led to the front door through a tangle of deep-red wallflowers. She was afraid to look at it too much because of them all it was the one she liked best.

"Now we must find Number Ten," said John, and pressed the self-starter. They crawled slowly round the square, examining the numbers on the gates. There seemed no plan in the numbering, it was all anyhow, but that was in keeping with the charm of the place. What disturbed them was that they could not find Number Ten. "There's no such place," thought Miss Giles. "I was right. This is a dream."

"Well, now we're back where we started from," said John, bumping into the pillar-box again.

"And this is Number Ten," said Mary.

"There's no number," said John.

Miss Giles could not bring herself to look at the little house.

"Yes, look," said Mary. "Hidden under the syringa bush. But the house looks lived in."

"The old man died but his housekeeper is still here," said John. "The agent told me. Can you manage to get out, Miss Giles?"

Miss Giles abruptly came to life and led the way. "It's not true that I'm walking up this path," she thought. "It's not true that I'm knocking at the door."

348

A voluble old woman opened the door and was pleased to see them. She was anxious to see the house sold, she said, for she wanted to get away and live with her married daughter. But she'd promised the old man's son to stay till the house was sold. "An empty place gets cold and damp and gives a bad impression," she explained. "This way, Madam, please."

Miss Giles had never been called Madam before. She would be, if she became headmistress of her own school. The tradespeople would call her Madam. She would be respected.

There were only two sitting rooms, but they were a good size and looked south into the walled garden behind the house. The kitchen was roomy and comfortable and Annie would like it, Mary thought. There were three bedrooms upstairs and the windows of two of them looked over the garden wall to the river, the swans, the meadows and the woods and hills beyond. The garden had a camellia tree in it, roses and lilacs and a small green lawn.

"A bit small for a school," said John doubtfully.

"Two good classrooms," said Mary. "And plenty of room in the hall for the children's coats and hats. For the little children we'll have, that's all we'll want."

"But where are you and Miss Giles to sit in the evenings?" asked John.

"The desks can be folded up and stand at each end of the two rooms when the children have gone," said Mary. We'll make ourselves comfortable enough, won't we, Giles? And we'll have these enchanting little bedrooms. Will you have this one, Giles?"

Miss Giles turned bemusedly from the window. She had always longed for a bedroom like this, with a wide view and a south window. Hers? Nothing was ever hers. Quite suddenly she suffered from violent reaction. This was madness. As a general rule, she told herself, she was a practical woman, not addicted to dreaming, but she had been living in a dream ever since the day Mr. Wentworth had run into the greengrocery van, come back to Oaklands with her and made her feel herself a duchess. She was not a duchess and he was much to blame that he had made her feel that she was. These wild quixotic day-dreamers were nothing but a danger to the community.

"Mr. Wentworth," she said coldly, "it's not possible, either financially or psychologically. I've no capital. I'm too old to incur debt when I'm also too old to change the sort of woman that I am, a woman who can win neither the love of children nor the respect of their parents. How can I hope to make a success of this school?"

"You *must* make a success of it," said John, "both financially and psychologically. As I see it, you've got to." She looked at him. He had spoken as coldly as she had and there was nothing quixotic about the sternness of his face. "Financially, it should not be difficult. I have been talking to other parents of the Oak-lands children and I am not the only one who wants the school to continue. If you like this house it will be bought for you and you will pay rent as its tenant. As regards what you said about respect and love, it's not true. You have my respect and Mar-gary's love. Can't you, psychologically, make a start with that? What do you want, Miss Giles? Do you want to write yourself off a failure, or do you want to take up again this job of teaching that you have in some respects done badly and do it again well? The element of the miraculous has come into your life. You are being offered a second chance."

Miss Giles sat down on the nearest chair. "I must think about it," she said weakly.

"Of course," said John. "Meanwhile we haven't seen the garden."

3

Driving back to Belmaray John knew she would take her second chance. In the garden, as she picked a bunch of white violets under the garden wall, Mary had said, "I wonder if Aunt Rose ever refused a second chance?" No one had answered her but he had seen a look of panic on Miss Giles's face.

There was at the moment a look of panic on his own. Where was he to find the three thousand pounds for the little house? It was true that other parents to whom he had spoken were glad for the school to continue. It was the only one of its kind in Silverbridge and they were prepared to take John's word for it that Miss Giles humanized by Mary O'Hara would be a good working team. But John did not suppose that a single one of them was prepared to contribute much, if anything, towards the buying of the house. He had done it again. He was always getting himself into these terrible fixes. A course of action likely to benefit some man or woman would leap to his mind's eye and he would go baldheaded for it, and remember too late that the means to encompass their good was not within his power. Yet how often, some way or other, the means had been found. They must be found again. He could not fail Miss Giles. He must see the other parents. He must see his bank manager. How much were his beloved stamps worth? He believed a great deal, but Margary loved them too. There were still treasures left at the manor that might be sold, but Aunt Maria had had to part with so much over the years and was so attached to her china and silver. And so was Daphne attached to Queen Henrietta Maria's day bed and the French mirror. The thought of asking her to part with them made him shake in his shoes. That was the worst of it; his wild actions always involved others rather than himself in the annoyance of material loss. Sacrifice for others, though it may be painful, is not annoying when it is your own idea, but when somebody else thinks of it for you it is annoying as well as painful. To his astonishment he found he was at home. He put Rozinante away in the garage and went in to tea.

He drank his tea in silent anguish and then asked Margary to come into the study with him. He must make a beginning somewhere and the only possible point at which to begin was with something that was really his own. Margary came with him, as Isaac must have gone with Abraham, not knowing what was to be asked of her.

351

"Sweetheart, I'm in such a mess," he said, dropping into his armchair. He had no need to act distress of mind. Never before had he so sympathized with Abraham. "A dreadful mess."

Margary went pink with pleasure. All her life her first reaction to another's plight was to be one of pleasure, followed instantly by one of compunction; now one could do something, but how awful to be pleased even if you could do something. Her flush faded and she stood before her father in a state of grave and sorrowful anxiety.

"Whatever have you done?" she asked. She had several times overheard Daphne ask the same question and it came spontaneously.

"Promised to buy a house for Miss Giles and Miss O'Hara without having the money to buy it with," said John. "Sit here and I'll tell you about it." She sat down on the arm of his chair, wide-eyed. "They want to start a school together and they can't have Oaklands any more now that Mrs. Belling is dead. There is a nice little house in Farthing Square they would like to have. They would be my tenants if I bought it. I'll explain what that means later. It has a garden with white violets in it and on the other side of the garden wall there is the river with swans on it. Would you like to go there to school?"

"Who would be headmistress?" asked Margary.

"Miss Giles. I don't think she would scold you in that house, because it would be her own and she would be happy in it. Also it's to be called Farthing Cottage and how could anyone scold anyone else in a house called Farthing Cottage? But you needn't go to school there if you don't want to."

"I'll go," said Margary. "Only you haven't bought it yet. Will it cost much?"

"Not a great deal as houses go," said John. "Only we'll have to sell things to get the money."

Their eyes roved anxiously round the room. One of the stamp albums was lying on John's desk, for he and Margary had been putting some stamps in last night.

352

"You could sell the other chair," said Margary. "Only then what would the parish sit on? Is the clock worth much?"

"Nothing in this room is worth much except our stamps," said John heavily. "And they're worth a great deal."

"But you like the stamps," said Margary.

"So do you," said John.

There was a silence, and then Margary said, "Do Miss Giles and Miss O'Hara want the little house very badly?"

"Yes," said John. "Very badly."

"All right," said Margary. "I don't mind about selling the stamps if you don't."

"Actually, I do mind," said John. "Only I haven't anything else to sell."

"Will there be enough when you've sold the stamps?" she asked.

"Not quite enough," said John truthfully.

"Then you'd better have my pearl brooch my godmother gave me," said Margary. "There'd be heaps then, for there are real pearls in it."

"But you like your pearl brooch," said John.

"Yes, but I'd like Miss Giles and Miss O'Hara to have the little house."

"All right," said John. "We'll sell your brooch as well as the stamps. Thank you. Margary, this is our secret. No one must know that we sold our stamps and your brooch to buy Farthing Cottage. Except, of course, Mummy. Later we'll both tell Mummy."

"I won't tell anybody but Mummy, ever," promised Margary.

He had faith in her word. With no other child could he have entered into this conspiracy, but with Margary he could. "I know a man who'll buy the stamps," he said. "He'll come here to look at them, but we must know what we've got. We must make a list. It will be hard work. Shall we start now?"

She jumped up in delight. To have work to do with Father

was almost worth the pain of parting with the stamps and the brooch. Five minutes later they were happily engrossed.

4

For the Wentworths it was a day for buying and selling. Up at the manor Miss Wentworth was sitting in her drawing room with Mr. Entwistle. She had her best boots on and her battered felt hat was skewered on with unusual firmness. There were fresh flowers in the vases and she wore her mother's diamond ring. The boots, the flowers and the ring were not to make a good impression, for Miss Wentworth never cared two pins what impression she made, good or otherwise; she believed she had assembled them with some vague remembrance of the finery Rupert Wentworth had donned for the painting of his portrait, with the cause lost and his queen not for him.

Yet though outwardly bedecked and serene she was inwardly troubled. "I can't get used to the idea," she said to Mr. Entwistle. "I can't get used to it at all. It's some comfort that you know the man."

"At school together," said Mr. Entwistle. "Up at Cambridge together, and kept in touch ever since. Not bad, eh?"

"You're the last man in the world I can imagine being friends with an Abbot," said Miss Wentworth.

"Bob wasn't an Abbot at school," said Mr. Entwistle.

"For one thing, you never go to church," said Miss Wentworth.

"At Cambridge, nor did Bob," said Mr. Entwistle, and grinned reminiscently.

"I don't hold with it," said Miss Wentworth.

"Going to church?" asked Mr. Entwistle.

"Don't try to keep my spirits up by being flippant," said Miss Wentworth. "And anyway, they're not down. What must be done, must be done, and what's the good of moping. I mean I don't hold with men and women shutting themselves up in monasteries and convents. I don't at all like the idea of Belmaray becoming a monastery."

"Nothing is settled," said Mr. Entwistle. "You're just going to have a talk with Bob, that's all, and let him have a look at the house. He may not think it suitable. And if he does, and his order makes an offer, you may refuse the offer. It's all as unsettled as the weather."

"Which is very settled at present," said Miss Wentworth.

"Have it your own way, dear lady," said Mr. Entwistle. "It's settled, then. Here's Bob."

An ancient car had driven up to the front door, a young monk at the wheel and an old monk beside him. Mr. Entwistle went out to welcome them and Miss Wentworth stayed where she was. She looked round her drawing room and knew a moment of sudden and absolute misery. Until this moment she had not fully realized what it was she was doing. Her mind had known that she must leave Belmaray, her will had been resolved to it, but while she made her decision, and while she set the necessary machinery at work to carry it out, her home had been holding her close as it had always done. In every sorrow of her life Belmaray had held her, and until now she had not fully realized that in this sorrow Belmaray would hold her no longer. Now full realization smote at her heart. She got to her feet as the door opened and came forward but for the first time in her life she was a tongue-tied hostess.

Only one man had come in and she heard him say that Tom Entwistle was showing Brother Martin the garden. She supposed they had shaken hands. She found they were sitting down.

"Old Tom was always a steady sort of chap," she heard a harsh voice croaking out beside her. "Kept me out of any amount of trouble when we were younger. Always gave me good advice. Always knew where I'd find what I wanted, boots or brandy or a top hat. 'Try so-and-so in the West End,' he'd say. Never surprised at what I wanted. Never turned a hair when I said I wanted God but said, 'Try the East End.' He was right. It was

355

in Limehouse that I found God. So when I wanted an abbey I asked old Tom."

"You too," said Miss Wentworth, "are trying to raise my spirits by flippancy."

"I think I was trying to raise my own," said the Abbot. "I understand you have lived here all your life."

For the first time Miss Wentworth looked at him. He was bent like some old tree and his habit was the color of the bark of an old tree. His hands were swollen with rheumatism. She had not known a face could be at once so ugly, so attractive, so humorous and so relentlessly austere. He had a bright dark fierce eye, but she was aware of great kindness in him.

"The climate should suit your rheumatism," she said. "It's mild, and the house is high enough above the river to avoid the damp."

"What I have to discover," he said with a touch of sharpness, "is not the suitability of the climate to rheumatism, but to the life of prayer. Does one fall asleep here?"

"Certainly not," said Miss Wentworth indignantly. "The liars who tell you that you fall asleep in the west country are only equalled by the liars who tell you it never stops raining. Both those statements are contrary to fact. I do not at all know that I want this house to become an abbey."

"I understand," said the Abbot mildly, "that in the last resort the decision does not rest with you?"

"It rests with my great-nephew," acknowledged Miss Wentworth. "But it was for my sake only that we have struggled along here for so long. Had it not been for me he would have sold Belmaray long ago. To save him distress I am conducting these preliminaries without his knowledge."

"When you have conducted them is there any likelihood that he may refuse his consent?" asked the Abbot. "I am not very happy, Ma'am, at going so far in this matter without your great-nephew's knowledge."

"John is accustomed to having practical matters arranged behind his back by his womenfolk," said Miss Wentworth. "He is also accustomed to doing what they tell him. He is that type of man and his wife and I are that type of womenfolk. His daughters are still children."

"No sons?" asked the Abbot sympathetically.

"He has no son," said Miss Wentworth. "The line dies with him."

"I had imagined the young man a son of the house," said the Abbot. "He seemed so entirely happy here."

"What young man?" asked Miss Wentworth.

"I must confess to you that I have been here before," said the Abbot. "I came here prospecting after Entwistle had told me about it. I strolled about one evening in that field with the thorn tree in it. There was a young man writing in the small library and I spoke a few words to him through the window."

"That was Michael," said Miss Wentworth. "He is staying with me. But though he is not related to us he has become, as you say, very much at home here."

"I liked the man and I am sorry to disinherit him," said the Abbot.

"You seem very certain Belmaray is to become your property," said Miss Wentworth with a touch of tartness.

"Not mine, Ma'am," said the Abbot with almost an air of panic. "Monks have no property. The property of my order. The property of God. But I am aware, of course, that your great-nephew may share your dislike of placing this property in the hands of God."

"I don't think so," said Miss Wentworth slowly. "He has placed much in the hands of God. And so, I think, have I."

"This one thing more," said the Abbot.

"If I could see it in that light," said Miss Wentworth.

"You will," he said.

She got up. "I'll show you the house. From what you have seen you think it suitable?"

"The peace seems unassailable," he said. "We are obliged to

move from our old home for they have built an aerodrome at our front gate. Jet planes scream up over the chapel roof all day long. It had been a matter of shame to us all, especially to myself who am the eldest of us, to find ourselves so little possessed of the grace of detachment for which we have striven so long."

"There is no aerodrome within miles of Belmaray," said Miss Wentworth. "The hills protect us." They had passed into the dining room, the Abbot's dark fierce eyes appraising it as they talked. "I have seen many aeroplanes, of course, but I do not think I have experienced a jet."

"The noise, Ma'am, when you have the thing more or less scraping a tonsured head, is quite diabolical."

She liked the archaic manner of his address and the special quality of his courtesy. He did not belong to this century any more than she did. She warmed to the thought of him established in the peace of Belmaray.

"I do not know how to address you," she said as they walked down the flagged passage. "I have never talked to a monk before. I don't approve of them. Do I say Father Abbot?"

He did not at once answer her. He had stopped abruptly in front of the portrait of Rupert Wentworth in his bright armor. "Who is this young knight?" he asked.

"My ancestor, Rupert," said Miss Wentworth. "He fought for King Charles."

"I like that face," said the Abbot. "I like it as I liked the face of the man you call Michael. A most vulnerable face. If they can survive they go furthest. You asked me how you should address me. Would beadsman do?"

She smiled at him in quick delight. "It will do very well," she said. "I see you know the old poem. One verse of it is inscribed round the sundial in the garden in honor of the first Queen Elizabeth. Francis Wentworth, who built Belmaray in his old age, was much attached to her."

"You must be much attached to the poem," said the Abbot, as they went up the wide beautiful staircase.

"I am," said Miss Wentworth.

"And yet you don't approve of a man who serves on his knees?"

"At your age, yes," said Miss Wentworth. "But not at the age of that young man whom I saw beside you in the car. I like activity in young men."

"Ma'am, prayer is the greatest activity there is," said the Abbot. "It is directed not only to the praise of God but to the redemption of the soul of man. But I won't talk of that just now, though I should like to another day. Now I'll just tell you for your comfort that we are not inactive in your sense of the word. We take retreats and missions. We do much manual labor to support ourselves. The young lay-brother whom you saw in the car just now is an expert gardener and bee-man. When I was a lay-brother I was the swineherd. Ma'am, those pigs were the pride of my life."

Miss Wentworth stopped on the stairs and turned round. "Pigs?" she said. "You appreciate pigs? No wonder I liked you on sight. What breed did you keep?"

"Tamworths," said the Abbot. "Not the most beautiful breed but I think it was their ugliness that endeared them to me. I've never been a good-looking man. I had a fellow feeling."

"We'll look at the upstairs rooms later," said Miss Wentworth. "Now we'll go straight down to the orchard and look at my Welsh Whites. What to do with my pigs has been one of my problems. You'll keep pigs again, of course?"

"Not personally," said the Abbot, following her down the stairs. "But I will seriously consider the advisability of Brother Martin combining pigs with bees, if that would set your mind at rest."

"You could take over old Bob Hewitt, my pig-man. There's not a better man with pigs in the whole of the west country. You'll do that?"

She hurried him out of the garden door. She had shed ten years of her age.

"It will all need consideration," said the Abbot. "But I will meet your wishes in every way possible." He smiled at her. "Pigs, and bees in the helmet. I think you will come to feel at last that this is ordained... This garden, with the old mulberry trees, will be a great temptation to me. I shall want to spend far too many hours in this garden."

They walked slowly through the kitchen garden and reached the orchard, where four absorbed backs were presented to their view. Four men were standing in front of the pigsties, wrapped in admiration of the ladies within. "I hope Brother Martin and Mr. Entwistle are being discreet," said Miss Wentworth. "Michael and Bob know nothing of all this."

"I can vouch for their discretion," said the Abbot. "Ma'am, what beauties! Ma'am, what wonders of Welsh Whites! Not even my Tamworths in my swineherding days were equal to these." And with two strides he had reached the pigsties and propped himself on the half-door beside Bob and Michael.

Miss Wentworth sat down on a fallen apple tree near them and listened for a few minutes, with a half-smile on her face, to the scraps of conversation that drifted to her. She liked to hear men talk of the technicalities of a craft. It was astonishing how much Michael had learned about pigs in a short while, and Tom Entwistle could always keep his end up. She kept aloof from them. A woman, however knowledgeable, was always a slight intrusion upon masculine talk. It was warm in the sun but her sudden pleasure in the Abbot's admiration for pigs was draining away, leaving her cold. What had he said? "This one thing more." She remembered the night of Michael's coming and how she had lain in bed through the storm thinking how things fell away from you in old age, but that she still had Belmaray. Now she had lost it. The misery she had felt in the drawing room overwhelmed her again. In the pride of life you stood with your hands full of roses, but in old age the petals turned to dust; and then even the dust fell away through your fingers, leaving you with nothing but your empty hands, stained with dirt... Just your sin, that was all you seemed to have at the end... She should have loved Charles. That not loving Charles had been one of those deliberate sins of which Michael had spoken, because she had meant to keep Charles outside. What harm that had done... And now she had nothing but her empty dirty hands... She sat bemusedly looking at them and slowly her misery turned to a faint glow of inward joy as she began to wonder if perhaps they had more value than all she had possessed. Empty, they could be cleansed. She was humble now, she had nothing and could be cleansed. It might be true that the loss of Belmaray was the one thing needful.

She looked up and saw the Abbot standing beside her. It seemed to her a very long time since he had last been beside her, but again she could not speak to him. Her powers had deserted her. The Abbot waited beside her for a few moments and then helped her to get up. His bony rheumatic hand under her elbow, his fierce old face when she looked at him, had a strength that startled her, and she wondered what connection the thoughts of the last few moments had had with the power that was in him. Probably none, for he had seemed absorbed in the pigs.

They walked slowly back through the garden. A stormcock was singing at the top of one of the mulberry trees and there was a lark high up in the golden evening sky. It was as though two spirits sang. The eagle beside her was silent but a verse from the book of Wisdom came suddenly into her mind. "The praise of courage is in his actions." Perhaps she had not understood the heights to which prayer must rise before it becomes pure praise, the fortitude that is demanded before it can share in the redemption of man's soul. The man of prayer beside her had said it was action, the greatest activity there is. She began to believe him. She began to be content that Belmaray itself, that aged knightly man, should now turn beadsman.

5

Michael weeded the garden and kept one eye on the front door. He understood it now; the withdrawal that he had felt lately in Miss Wentworth, the old man's visit late in the evening to "get the feel of the place," his own dream of him as the last of the knights of Belmaray. Well, it had to happen. The maintenance of this place was obviously getting beyond Miss Wentworth. And if it had to happen, this that was happening seemed to him fitting. Yet he felt an almost savage anger and resentment. Someone should have left Miss Wentworth a fortune so that she could have finished her life here in peace. Someone should have done something. Though she had known about it some while he doubted if realization had come to her until this evening. When he had half-turned round from the pigs and seen her sitting on the fallen tree he had known that realization had come to her. He had longed to go to her but he had been afraid to blunder. It had been a relief to him to see the Abbot go.

And now he was hanging about in the hope of speaking to the old man. They were all four inside now, Miss Wentworth, the two monks and Mr. Entwistle, but they couldn't be much longer. He didn't know what he wanted to say to the Abbot. It was presumptuous of him to want to say anything at all. But he might never see him again and he wanted to say—something. You could not see someone in a dream, and then see them in the flesh, and not feel you were in some way vitally connected with them.

The door opened and the three men came out. Mr. Entwistle had come by bus today, but was being taken back to Silverbridge in the Abbot's car. There was some difficulty in starting it. The self-starter was not functioning and girding up his habit Brother Martin was settling down happily to a long spell of mighty cranking. Michael stepped out of the flowered bed into the court by the sundial and the Abbot strolled down to join him.

"I am glad to meet you again, Sir," said the Abbot. "Is this the sundial of which Miss Wentworth was telling me?"

Michael nodded. Now that the chance of speech had been given to him he stood beside the monk quite speechless. The Abbot bent down to look at the worn lettering.

"Beauty, strength, youth, are flowers but fading seen;
  Duty, faith, love, are roots, and ever green,"

he murmured, and walked round to the other side.

"Goddess, allow this aged man his right,
  To be your beadsman now, that was your knight."

He came back to Michael. "I understand that the sundial was put up in honor of Queen Elizabeth the First," he said.

Michael swallowed and managed to articulate. "And the rosemary bush was planted in honor of Queen Henrietta Maria." He looked at the Abbot bleakly for a moment and then looked away again.

"It seems that queens have always been honored here," said the Abbot. "The tradition will be maintained. Monks are kings' men but in our chapel we have a statue of Mary, whom some men call the Queen of Heaven, and we honor her. And there is another lady whom we honor, and for whom we pray ceaselessly; the soul. We pray for bodies too, the bodies of the sick and poor, the exiles, the prisoners and the persecuted, but pre-eminently for the soul. The soul, you know, like a ship, is always 'she.' That fact turns any man of prayer who battles for her into a knight. You possibly think I am talking a lot of nonsense and your thoughts are with Miss Wentworth."

"Yes," said Michael.

"For her it is indeed grievous," said the Abbot. "But she is a great lady, no doubt trained as these great ladies are to a selfless sense of social duty. Wherever she is, as long as she is able to do it, she will find much to do. We will not forget her in this

363

place. And we will not forget you. I, especially, will remember you, my son."

He bent upon Michael a look of such extraordinary kindness that honesty blazed up in him.

"You wouldn't call me your son if you knew the sort of man I am," he said roughly and almost rudely. "More or less of a heathen too."

The Abbot laughed. "More or less, you say. Does that include a willingness that I should pray for you?"

"I would like you to," mumbled Michael.

"It won't do you any harm, you know," said the Abbot with twinkling eyes.

"You could do no one anything but good, Sir," said Michael.

"My good man, it has nothing to do with me!" ejaculated the Abbot in sudden exasperation. "It's not in my power to do anyone good. Prayer is the Word. He made the heavens and the earth without our aid. Spring comes again whether we live or die. Bringing men to rebirth He works differently, through the souls that are offered up to Him to be the channels of His will. Good-night."

Brother Martin had started the car, and the old man limped away towards it without looking back.

6

A few days later Daphne and John sat in the drawing room after supper. Daphne, sitting on the sofa with her feet up, had turned on a shaded lamp beside her but they had not drawn the curtains and could see the rising moon. She was wearing her Chinese coat and Baba her sleeve dog lay beside her. Baba had shed years of his age, was sleek and healthy and entirely happy. John sat in the big armchair, his long legs stretched out in front of him. A small log fire was burning in the grate and the murmur of the flames was the only sound in the silence. They were doing nothing.

"I ought to be doing the darning," said Daphne.

"There are piles of unanswered letters on my table," said John, "but I'm not saying I ought to be answering them because I know I ought not. There are times in life when sitting down and doing nothing can be a duty."

"Such a mercy when a husband and wife can think it a duty on the same evening," said Daphne. "It's so trying when one does and the other doesn't."

"You don't often think it a duty, Daphne," said John.

"My dear, you married a restless creature," she said. "One of those inwardly discontented creatures who wherever they are would like to be somewhere else, and whatever they do think they might have got what they wanted if they'd done the other thing. It's just sheer pride. They don't even know what they want, but such is their opinion of their own desserts that when they are given a life as near perfection as one can have in this world they are not satisfied even with that."

"Are you describing yourself, Daphne?" asked her astonished husband.

"Yes, John. I've been converted to the idea that I'm a lucky woman. It's not a sudden conversion so there's hope it may last. It started on the day you forgot the daffodils."

"How can I know which day that was?" asked John. "You know I forget everything every day. I've now forgotten I forgot the daffodils. What daffodils?"

"For the church vases. You forgot to pick them and I had to. In the end we both picked them. It doesn't matter if you remember or not. All that matters is that I sat in the church by myself and meditated. Don't look so astonished. I meditated. At least I think so."

"What method did you use?" asked John with twinkling eyes.

"I know nothing about methods," said Daphne. "I've never listened when you've told me about them. I've always thought Belmaray church was like a rock and I merely thought suddenly that the vicarage pew was my particular hole in that rock, and then somehow or other I arrived at knowing that I'm lodged like a seed in a cranny of some much greater rock; immovably great... What I'm saying has been said before of course."

"Something like it," said John smiling. " 'A man shall be as a hiding place from the wind, and a covert from the tempest... as the shadow of a great rock in a weary land.' "

"Who said that?" asked Daphne. "Saint Paul?"

"Isaiah. You don't listen when I read the lessons."

"Not always," confessed Daphne. "But I will in future, for it's disgraceful for a parson's wife not to know who said what. There's fire in the rock and it's quite inexorable. It means to burn me into some sort of shape, and I can only grow to what I will be from what I am, and where I am, so discontent is quite useless. Much more sensible to accept the one and love the other. Don't laugh, John. I know I'm being crude."

"I wasn't laughing," said John. "Everyone's meditations are crude. Human nature is crude and all our aspirations are as crude as our nature; but they're the stuff of growth so what does it matter if they are? Nothing could have been cruder than my meditation that morning."

"Tell me about it," said Daphne.

"It began with the apple tree outside the kitchen window," said John. "The sun came out while I was washing up the breakfast things and it was covered all over with drops of light. The light seemed to wash into the kitchen, making it clean. I went on thinking about it at intervals all day. I thought of each drop of light as an individual enclosed in his own experience as an anchorite in his cell, united by it to the tree of life, as your seed was united by its cranny to the rock, united by that experience and no other. I thought of all the obvious things; that the sun transforming each drop of moisture to a diamond was like the birth of God in the soul, transforming it, and that the tree of life is the tree of the cross, union with God's will, Christ Himself. Our apple tree looks like a madman praying but they thought the cross mad. 'To the Greeks foolishness, to the Jews a stum-

366

bling-block.' The light of transformed lives, held up on the cross, cleanses the world, and above the tree the Seraph sings. As you say, our pictures of things are very crude but most of us are never anything but children in this world and we must learn from our pictures, just as children do."

Daphne swung her feet off the sofa, went to her Chinese cabinet and opened it. Behind her head Queen Henrietta Maria's mirror reflected the moon and a great wave of thankfulness went over John that he had not had to ask her to sell it. Now that the manor and most of its contents were to be sold, it would be possible to make up the sum needed for Farthing Cottage without selling anything from the vicarage except his stamps and Margary's brooch. That decision was not to be altered. To him and to Margary the stamps and the brooch were the two foundation stones of Farthing Cottage. In the mingled sorrow and relief with which Aunt Maria's decision to sell the manor had plunged him the thankfulness that nothing Daphne loved need be sold was uppermost.

"What on earth?" he asked, as she came to him carrying some broken china in her hands.

"I broke Winkle's mug the other day," said Daphne. "And when I took it out to the dustbin there was the sugar bowl you'd smashed."

"How do you know Mrs. Wilmot didn't smash it?" asked John.

"If she had she'd have hidden it at the bottom. You put it at the top. That's the kind of man you are. I rescued them both for some reason. I didn't know why."

John got up and put his hands on her shoulders. "And now you do know why?"

She looked up at him. "It was that night I first began to realize my need of you."

"Did you?" he said. "Cracked vessels, both of us, but not to be parted. Was that it?"

"Something like that," she said. "But since that night I've

realized much more, John; that our marriage has been my salvation. If it's not been as happy as it ought to have been the fault has been mine."

He took the ridiculous bits of smashed china out of her hands and put them on the table and put his arms round her. For almost the first time in their long companionship he was neither awkward nor deprecating but entirely confident and happy in his handling of her. She gave herself to his arms with a sigh of relief, wanting from him now neither passion nor strength but only this blessed easy sense of equality that her humbling of herself had given to their relationship. In her heart she knew that there was not equality, that in all ways he surpassed her, but she knew too that to humble herself too much before him would be to distress him. When he said, "My fault, Daphne, not yours," and kissed her with an equal humility, she smiled and let it pass. She would have liked to ask him to forgive her but she knew that to bring himself to acknowledge her need of it was something he could not do. She must do without the relief of hearing the words spoken. After all, forgiveness was implicit in this fresh beginning. Without it, a fresh beginning would not have been possible.

"Winkle says she likes living," said Daphne. "With you, John, I do too. You'll be surprised to hear it, but I'm a happy woman." They laughed and clung together, and upstairs Margary, who had not been able to get to sleep, was suddenly happy, turned over and slept instantly.

18

MICHAEL was perched on a stepladder, painting the walls of Mary's bedroom at Farthing Cottage honeysuckle color. Miss Giles and Mary had gone to Otway to choose curtain material, and he was having a day of solitude in the cottage to get on with the painting. Unlike most people he liked the smell of paint. It was to him an invigorating smell, the smell of cleanliness and of a fresh start, and it went well with the scent of apple blossom that came in through the open window. Now and then he looked out and marvelled at the beauty of the earth and the row the birds were making. A month had gone by since he and Daphne had heard the linnet singing in the vicarage garden. The weather had broken in torrents of cold rain but now it had mended again and this was the second day of its mending. Everything had rushed into bloom. The apple blossom had passed its perfection but the gardens were full of hyacinths and wallflowers. Beyond the sparkling river he could see the brilliant green fields, the buttercups and lady's-smocks, and the hedges white with hawthorn blossom. The trees were in full fresh vivid leaf and high white clouds were sailing fast before a northwest wind. The birds could scarcely contain themselves in this world where sunshine and warmth had returned.

It had been an eventful month. In lives where there had been no change for so long there had suddenly been cataclysmic change, as startling as this change from cold grey rain to brilliant sunshine. Belmaray manor house had been bought by a religious order. Oaklands had been bought by a retired, wealthy, jolly brewer with a family of rollicking sons and daughters, the volume and power of whose high spirits it seemed that not even Oaklands could depress. Farthing Cottage, so far as the knowledge of everyone except John, Daphne, Margary and Miss Wentworth went, had been bought by the parents of the former Oaklands children and leased to Miss Giles. Miss Wentworth had bought a little house in Silverbridge. Michael had been up to London, reopened his flat, stayed in it, met and faced the careful smiles or the equally careful cuts of the men and women he had known in the days before his imprisonment, met one friend whose smile was what it had always been, the brother of his friend Simon Matthews who had been killed beside him in Crete, and through him got a job as an assistant at a bookshop. He had also, during the lonely and rather desperate evenings in his flat, tried to rough out the plot of a new kind of thriller, the type Miss Wentworth liked. But he had found it as difficult as the writing of the poem he had destroyed, and realized with depression how hard it would be to acquire new habits of thought and work. Well, there would be the bookshop while he struggled. Setting his plotting aside he had written a long letter to Mary, which he had not posted until two days ago. He had not seen her since and there had been no answer by this morning's post.

He thought of her with aching compassion. With just a few more meetings love had come quickly and warmly between them, to her cloudless joy and his secret wretchedness. He had made a clean breast of it to Daphne and John, he had now told Miss Wentworth, but he had not been able to tell Mary the whole story to her face. He had had to write it. But he had not been able to write it until he had gone back to London and faced alone what they would have to face together if and when she married him. When he had found that he could do that he had written his letter.

Which she had not answered. Well, how could she so quickly? She was overwhelmed by it all, his treatment of Daphne, his cowardice, the full details of his dishonesty, the hard struggle for reinstatement which as his wife she would have to share. It had been Miss Giles, not Mary, who had rung up last night and asked if he could get on with the painting alone today, because they were taking Annie with them and going to buy curtain material. Would she ask for time, would she refuse him, what would she do? He steeled himself against a rising hopelessness and went on grimly with his work. Whatever happened now he was glad he loved her. The mere fact of loving her had restored to him a certain measure of self-respect. When he was not despairing his manhood rejoiced in her and in rejoicing made him more aware of itself. His hopelessness lessened as he worked. Empty, quiet and clean, the house was as fresh as the spring, as full of delight as the birds in the garden. He could imagine he was splashing sunshine onto Mary's walls.

Mary herself had painted Miss Giles's room next door pale pink, after an argument with Miss Giles who had wanted it grey. But Miss Giles was coming round now it was finished and she would surely be happy in the warmth and glow. Annie needed no persuasion where Mary's color schemes were concerned. To everyone's astonishment she had in this new beginning showed that she possessed astonishing recuperative powers. Once she had recovered from the shock of her mistress's death she had transferred to Mary the devotion she had given long ago to the young Mrs. Belling. It was a blind unquestioning devotion that awed even while it amused Mary. It was amazing that any human being should be such a chameleon. Annie, who had become a slut because her mistress had become one, was now rapidly becoming as devoted to bright colors, fresh air and cleanliness as Mary herself. Miss Giles, though she did occasionally put up some resistance to Mary's despotism, was now equally her devoted slave. Yet she kept somewhere, though in abeyance now while she was still so tired, her own independence and power of authority, her strong sense of discipline. When she was rested, and if and when Mary left her, she would be able to continue successfully alone. But it was Mary who was laying the foundations of the new school. There was not a single person connected with its establishment who did not turn to Mary for orders.

"She has power," thought Michael. "The kind of power that takes women captive as well as men. 'My thoughts are going after her.' And with that power the kernel of her is sound as a nut. Why didn't she write to me? Something, anything, to keep me going. She knew I would not see her today. Perhaps she's writing letter after letter and tearing them up, trying her best to express herself with truth without wounding my feelings. That's hard to do when you're honest. What's the time? Five o'clock. The room's done."

He got stiffly off the ladder and found that he was uncommonly tired as well as thirsty and hungry. He'd go home and see if there was a letter by the second post. Whatever was in it he would at least be clear of these alternations of hope and hopelessness.

"Are you still there, Michael?" called a voice.

He strode to the window and looked out. Mary, hatless, was down below him in the garden. A full basket was at her feet and she had a new frying pan in one hand and a coal scuttle in the other. "Timothy White's," she said. "We've had a grand day. How have you got on? Have you finished?"

"I've finished," said Michael.

She looked up at him, laughing. There was no change in her easy happy manner. She might have received no letter. Perhaps she hadn't. Perhaps it had gone astray. His face looked drawn and grey as he looked down at her, and she realized that he was not only a great deal older than she was, but also weaker both in character and body. Also that he loved her far more than she had realized. Also that he had been in doubt as to her answer, and she had kept him waiting two days, not knowing that he doubted her response; clear to her on the day she had first met him, unwavering even after the blow he had dealt her then. Also, and this last with a flash of vision, that she had it in her power through the kindness of love to make of this weakling a very fine man.

> For even the weak with surprise
> Spread wings, utter song,
> They can launch ... in this blue they can rise,
> In this kindness are strong ...

All the motherhood in her surged up in such a flood of tenderness that she dropped the frying pan and coal scuttle and held out her arms.

"Michael!" she cried, her cry sharp with the distress of her love and compunction. "Michael, come down at once and have some tea!" And dropping her arms she bolted in through the French windows of the sitting room.

He raced downstairs and met her there and they kissed each other passionately, yet more as two passionately loving children would have done than as man and woman. Every vestige of his heavy weariness fell from him and he felt himself light and buoyant within the strength of her arms. And she, feeling the unexpected strength of his, knew strength to be an entirely relative thing. A weak man, struggling with circumstances too hard for him, might put up a stronger fight in failure than the strong man in success. He might even be more worthy of respect and love. Anyway she respected Michael and would show him so by every means in her power until she died.

"I'll be proud to be your wife," she told him vehemently. "And if you ever thought I wouldn't be, that just shows what a fool you are."

Her vehemence made him burst out laughing and rubbing the tears out of her eyes she laughed too. The empty room with its freshly painted walls echoed their laughter.

"I'll love the smell of paint until I die," said Mary. "And I'll love you too so you needn't be jealous. Now come out into the garden. I've a thermos and sandwiches in the basket."

2

A hilarious and delightful supper party, arranged for very early in the evening so that the children could be present, was drawing to its conclusion with Winkle refusing to be hurried over her peach. Nor did anyone except Pat wish to hurry her. She was right to be as long as possible over every mouthful, to pursue every escaping drop of juice with her exceedingly long hummingbird tongue, and every now and again to heave a heavy sigh of repletion and satisfaction, for she was not likely to taste a peach again in a hurry. She was only tasting it now because this party was in celebration both of her birthday and Mary's and Michael's engagement, and Michael had provided the peaches. Miss Wentworth had provided the cherry brandy, the very last bottle left in the Belmaray cellars, and Daphne and Mary together had made the iced birthday and engagement cake, the host of little cakes and the tipsy trifle.

"Hurry up, Winkle," cried Pat in exasperation, for she knew there were to be games with prizes in the drawing room afterwards.

Winkle squinted sideways at what was left of the trifle. "I didn't have any of that," she said.

"Mother!" ejaculated Pat. "If she has that on top she'll be sick."

"Queen Alice will not be six years old again," said Mr. Entwistle.

"Nor will Mary and Michael get engaged again," said Miss Wentworth. "Let the child alone, Pat."

"Could I have a bit more trifle, Mother?" asked Margary shyly. She did not really want it but she wanted to keep Winkle company. It must be rather hard to go on eating by yourself

374

with everyone looking at you. One of the things that Margary had not yet discovered, intuitive though she might be, was that other people did not always feel as she felt. Winkle had no objection at all to people watching her while she ate.

"May I have a little more trifle too?" asked Miss Giles, for with Margary in a minority of two, and the party numbering twelve counting Baba and Orlando, plenty of glances would come her way and a faint flush was already coming into her face. In judging Margary by herself Miss Giles was not in error. She had been just such a child, and during the last few weeks of spring memories of her childhood and youth that had been firmly sealed in under the ice had come flooding back on her. She was becoming unfrozen. It was a painful process but she knew that if she could abide it she would be glad.

"Trifle! Giles!" thought Mary. "She'll have the most awful indigestion. How she must love that child!" She caught Michael's eyes and smiled at him. They were both enjoying this party. Sharing the honors with Winkle, and Winkle's lack of inhibition being what it was, they were saved the embarrassment of too much limelight.

"Let's all begin again," said John. "Mary didn't make those wafer biscuits just to be looked at. Daphne, did Harriet have a glass of cherry brandy?"

"I put one on her tray," said Daphne.

"Isn't alcohol bad for arthritis?" asked Miss Giles, relishing the sherry in her trifle. It was years since she had dared to eat trifle and she had forgotten how delicious it could be.

"Miss Giles, anything is good for you if you enjoy it," said Miss Wentworth, and then lowering her voice, "My dear, I've a pretty little Queen Anne escritoire that I don't want to put in the sale. I think it would be just the thing for your bedroom."

Miss Wentworth and Miss Giles, lately introduced, liked each other. They both deplored the lack of discipline in the present generation. They both thought Daphne unworthy of John. Miss Wentworth, sharing with John the knowledge that the sale of

375

Belmaray had made possible the purchase of Farthing Cottage, found herself in the position of benefactress to Miss Giles and accordingly had a feeling of tenderness for her. Miss Giles, immensely touched by the motherliness that softened the asperity of the old lady's manner when she talked to her, felt the years slip off her in Miss Wentworth's presence. When there is no one left in the world to whom you seem young you feel old indeed, and that had been her condition for a long time.

Michael accepted the cigarette John offered him and sat back happily behind its smoke. He looked round the table counting heads. Mary, Daphne and John and their children. Miss Wentworth. Miss Giles. Entwistle. The dog and the cat. Of the group of people who had drawn so close to each other these last weeks only Annie, old Bob and the Abbot were not in this room. But Annie and old Bob were in the kitchen, taking high tea with Mrs. Wilmot and Mrs. Prescott, and whenever there was a pause in the dining room conversation, sounds of mirth could be heard coming from that direction. And the Abbot was very much present with Michael. Looking out of the uncurtained window he could imagine he saw his tall figure in the shadows of the trees.

And there was the old nanny upstairs. She had not been well and neither he nor Mary had seen her yet and so he kept forgetting her. She probably belonged too.

It was odd how they had been drawn together like this, their lives intertwined to their immense happiness and advantage, all in a few weeks of this unusually lovely spring. Did rhythmic times of fresh growth come in the lives of men and women, as in the world of nature? And did one growth help another, as birds build their nests where the new leaves will hide them? What was the motive power behind it all? "The Word." When he saw the Abbot again he must ask him what he had been talking about that day.

Winkle was satisfied at last and the others went into the drawing room while Michael and Mary went upstairs and knocked at Harriet's door. Michael had a bunch of pink carnations that he had bought for Harriet in Silverbridge. Mary in her heart thought he had been highly extravagant. He had not even seen Harriet before and the garden was full of flowers. She wished they had not got to visit this sick old woman on their engagement day. She was feeling her usual dread of illness. She was ashamed of herself but she couldn't help it. It was no good; when people were ill and suffering they scared her stiff. Unconsciously she slipped her hand into Michael's and he smiled down at her reassuringly. He supposed she was feeling shy and was oddly touched, as he always was when she showed him by word or look that she was not as old as she looked. Only twenty. It was she, not he, who would set the tone and direction of their lives, he knew that and rejoiced in it, but it was he who had the age and experience and every now and then she showed him by a gentle deference that she knew it.

"Come in," said Harriet's clear decided voice, and they went into her fresh room hand in hand like a couple of children. "Come in. I'm pleased to see you. I've had a good look at you both out of my window and you are no strangers to me. What, Sir? These carnations for me? Why, I've not been given such flowers since I was the age of your young lady. And carnations, my favorite flower of them all! There now, anyone would think it was my engagement day. You'll make your young lady jealous. And she's pretty as a picture; though she shouldn't wear pink with that hair."

Mary laughed and sat down, her shrinking gone. Harriet, bright-eyed and inquisitive as a cock robin, was not at all her idea of a suffering invalid. Except for her wheel chair and the rug over her knees there was no sign of invalidism about her. The vivacious humorous old face held Mary's eyes and she did not look down at the twisted hands lying in Harriet's lap. Michael did and pity wrenched at him as he remembered that Harriet's legs were almost useless to her. Awful to be imprisoned like that, your freedom gone, entirely dependent. He sat down on the window sill and began to laugh and joke with Harriet, his thin charming face alight with fun and tenderness. As they talked he noticed that Harriet's tray had not been fetched and was in her way, and he moved it. Her rug slipped and he tucked it skilfully round her again. He fetched a vase and filled it with water and arranged the flowers better than Mary could have done. This to Mary was a new Michael. He would be far better at looking after her when she was ill than she would be at looking after him when he was. They had fallen in love knowing so little of each other, but as the days passed she was increasingly loving in Michael all that they revealed.

Mary defended with spirit her choice of a pink frock. To say that pink was not to be worn with red hair was merely superstition, like saying you mustn't be married in green. Didn't she look nice in her pink frock? And she would be married in green just to flout superstition again. Irish green, with shamrock in her buttonhole. Michael could have a leek in his. They thanked heaven they were not English. They were Celts.

"And when will you be married, love?" asked Harriet.

"Not until after Christmas," said Mary. "I promised Miss Giles to help her with her school before Michael asked me to marry him and I can't let her down. I must get her well started before I leave her."

Harriet nodded approval. "And Mr. Davis, he'll get himself well started in business and a bit laid by before the two of you set up house."

"You know a lot about us, Harriet," said Michael. He was smiling but he did not speak lightly and Harriet answered with a grave sweet seriousness.

"Yes, Sir, I know a good deal about you but you mustn't mind that. Mrs. Wentworth and I, we're the only two women in the house and whom should we talk to if not to each other? And I've known Mr. Wentworth since he was a child. I can't rightly say that of you but it's hard for me to believe that I can't. Some people you can see every day for years and never do more than

378

pass the time of day as with a stranger, and others you can see just a few times from your window and it seems as though you were old friends."

Mary got up and picked up Harriet's tray. "I can hear them washing up downstairs," she said. "You stay here, Michael. Please may I come and see you another day, Harriet?"

Harriet, bright-eyed, nodded to the girl. She was a good girl. A girl as young as that who knew the right moment to efface herself was a very good girl indeed. Mary went out and closed the door gently behind her.

"She's a good girl," Harriet repeated to Michael.

"Too good for me," said Michael. It was not the usual conventional remark, and Harriet was quick to sense the panic that had come over him. "You should have no fear," said Harriet. "There's no sense in fear."

"I've been afraid all my life, Harriet," said Michael.

"Nonsensical all your life, you mean," said Harriet. "But a person being nonsensical through the first half of his life is no reason to my way of thinking why he should be nonsensical through the second half too. It's nice to have a bit of change."

Michael laughed. "You don't get much change, Harriet."

"I get more than you'd think," she said. "The weather, now, that's always changing. Yesterday it was as gay as a knight in armor, and today it's a grey day like it was the day you came to Belmaray."

"Harriet, how wonderful of you to remember what the weather was like then."

"Not at all," said Harriet tartly. "When Mrs. Wentworth told me about you, just the other day it was, I remembered that the day you'd come I'd been praying for prisoners because it was a grey day."

"You think prisoners lead a grey life?" he asked. "Well they do, of course."

"To be sure," said Harriet. "But it wasn't for that reason. I'd been thinking that not only colors are imprisoned on grey days

379

but the sun too. For when there's a grey wall between one and the other who's to say which is prisoner and which is free? When the heart aches one for the other there's little to choose between them. That's a cruel thing men do to God, making a prisoner of Him."

"I don't think I know what you mean," said Michael.

"The grey clouds, they are like men's unbelief," said Harriet. "And men live frozen and afraid when a touch of the sun would change all that. But they imprison the sun."

"Many who would like to believe, can't, Harriet," said Michael.

"That's a lie," said Harriet calmly. "If you want a good thing badly enough you get it. Not overnight, maybe. But you get it."

Michael looked at the old woman keenly. Like Mary, she had power, and far more power than Mary. He began to understand what immense concentration of power there can be in a life withdrawn if discipline can keep pace with withdrawal. Without discipline withdrawal was a disintegration, but with it what he felt in Harriet. This spring day was a festival day, a day for rejoicing in new warmth and new life for several people. How much that had to do with Harriet's refusal to imprison the sun, with one soul's power to dispel the clouds for another, he'd no idea.

"Perhaps faith is hard to come by when you're alone, Harriet," he said. "Until now I've been alone."

"We're never alone," said Harriet. "That's the mistake so many make. There'd be less fear if folk knew how little alone they are."

She moved her left hand, that had been lying on her lap, and opened it with difficulty. A small old-fashioned pearl ring lay in the palm of her hand. Michael looked at it in bewilderment for he was sure he had seen it before.

"Your mother's," said Harriet. "You gave it to Daphne. I asked her to give it to me to give back to you. You can't give one woman's engagement ring to another, that would never do, but

380

in a couple of years' time you could give it to Mary as a Christmas gift. You've forgotten your mother, maybe?"

"No, I never forget her," said Michael.

"Then it's an odd thing you thought yourself alone," said Harriet.